THIS CH

She stood, straightening her spine. "I'm Danielle Sharpe. Welcome to Moosby's in Kismet, Mr. Hamilton. You're late. Really late. We were starting to wonder if you'd ever arrive."

Her blunt approach had its desired effect. He forgot about shaking her hand—something Danielle wanted to avoid, given its mind-scrambling effects on Betty—and apologized instead.

"Yeah. I know. I'm sorry about that." He ducked his head, treating her to an intimate view of his rumpled dark hair.

It looked soft. She wanted to run her fingers through it.

Wait. *What?* No, she didn't. That was crazy. Super crazy.

He'd been wearing a Santa hat a while ago. Where was it? If he'd still had on that hat, he might have seemed less appealing.

Ha, her inner sense of flutteriness mocked. *As if.*

"I'm not used to driving in the snow." He offered her a bashful smile, then raised his hands. "My hands are L.A. hands. Good for surfing, going to parties, and putting on sunglasses. Not so much for steering through snow flurries, I'm afraid."

Of course she looked at his hands. How could she not?

He'd invited her to. Even as Jason frowned at them with faux chagrin, Danielle studied them herself. She couldn't help drawing an altogether different conclusion than he had.

His hands were big but graceful. His fingers were long but elegant. His palms were slightly callused. They looked manly.

How did a posh, spoiled-to-the-max CEO get calluses?

"I dunno," Danielle mused aloud. "Your hands look plenty capable of doing interesting things to me."

Praise for the Lisa Plumley's Kismet Christmas romances!

TOGETHER FOR CHRISTMAS

"Plumley makes her third trip to Kismet, Mich. (after *Home for the Holidays*) in this laugh-out-loud Christmas romp. This sweet romance tugs at the heartstrings from the beginning and doesn't let up until the final page."

—*Publishers Weekly*

"This is a genuinely fun story, with complex, engaging characters and a thoroughly charming holiday atmosphere. No matter what, Lisa Plumley knows how to craft a terrific, heartwarming story with deliciously happy endings."

—*The Romance Reviews*

"The chemistry between these two characters was intense. And waiting to see if Casey would overcome his bah-humbug ways left me feeling hopeful and starry-eyed."

—Melissa D'Agnese, *First for Women* magazine

HOLIDAY AFFAIR

"Secrets and subterfuge add complexity and zing to this well-crafted, heartwarming story that features a wealth of engaging characters, including five remarkable, memorable children, and great sexual tension. A deliciously satisfying, cocoa-worthy holiday read."

—*Library Journal*

"Lisa Plumley's latest holiday novel delivers. It has warm, gooey holiday moments complete with happy children, Christmas traditions such as caroling and decorating Christmas cookies, and, oh yeah, hot-and-steamy romance. Loaded with fun pop-culture references and witty dialogue, *Holiday Affair* delivers on entertainment!"

—*The Romance Reader* (5 hearts)

"A delightful story with utterly charming characters. It brings to life the sounds, smells, and tastes of Christmas as it brings together more than just the two main characters for a joyous holiday season."

—*Romantic Times Book Reviews* (4½ stars)

HOME FOR THE HOLIDAYS

"Lisa Plumley once again gifts readers with a Yuletide story sure to put you in a holiday mood. This is vintage Plumley. She's created a cast of characters that are a bit eccentric, quirky, and likeable and spun a story that will make you smile."

—Lezlie Patterson, *McClatchy-Tribune News Service*

"A delightful secondary romance adds to the fun in this upbeat romp that is touching, hilarious, and lightly dusted with seasonal charm."

—*Library Journal*

Other Books by Lisa Plumley

MAKING OVER MIKE

FALLING FOR APRIL

RECONSIDERING RILEY

PERFECT TOGETHER

PERFECT SWITCH

JOSIE DAY IS COMING HOME

ONCE UPON A CHRISTMAS

MAD ABOUT MAX

SANTA BABY
(anthology with Lisa Jackson,
Elaine Coffman, and Kylie Adams)

LET'S MISBEHAVE

HOME FOR THE HOLIDAYS

MY FAVORITE WITCH

HOLIDAY AFFAIR

MELT INTO YOU

TOGETHER FOR CHRISTMAS

SO IRRESISTIBLE

Published by Kensington Publishing Corporation

All He Wants for Christmas

LISA PLUMLEY

ZEBRA BOOKS
KENSINGTON PUBLISHING CORP.
http://www.kensingtonbooks.com

ZEBRA BOOKS are published by

Kensington Publishing Corp.
119 West 40th Street
New York, NY 10018

All Kensington titles, imprints, and distributed lines are available at special quantity discounts for bulk purchases for sales promotion, premiums, fund-raising, educational, or institutional use.

Special book excerpts or customized printings can also be created to fit specific needs. For details, write or phone the office of the Kensington Special Sales Manager: Attn. Special Sales Department. Kensington Publishing Corp., 119 West 40th Street, New York, NY 10018. Phone: 1-800-221-2647.

First Printing: October 2014
ISBN-13: 978-1-4201-3155-0
ISBN-10: 1-4201-3155-9

First Electronic Edition: October 2014
ISBN-13: 978-1-4201-3156-7
ISBN-10: 1-4201-3156-7

10 9 8 7 6 5 4 3 2 1

Printed in the United States of America

To John Plumley,
with all my love.

Chapter One

Los Angeles, California

Three minutes into the board meeting Jason Hamilton had been shanghaied into attending, he realized he was being set up.

Not two minutes. Or one minute. But three minutes.

Three whole minutes went by before he understood that his persnickety squad of planners, investors, and overgrown babysitters had an agenda that went beyond figuring out how to move even more Barbie dolls and Tonka trucks at the Moosby's Toy Stores that (nearly) covered the globe.

Hell. He must be losing his edge. Ordinarily, his bullshit detector would have gone off the minute he'd gotten the first phone call summoning him back from his pre-crunch-time vacation.

Instead, he'd blithely agreed to this meeting without giving it much thought. Or preparation. It was four days after Thanksgiving. Everyone should have been knocking back turkey sandwiches and pumpkin pie, not sitting around a boardroom table sharpening their knives for a good absentee CEO slice-and-dice.

Because that's what this was. Jason could tell, now that

he was paying attention. He hadn't gotten to the top of his field by being oblivious. The rarefied boardroom air held a definite hint of "this is all your fault," tinged with a "so fix it" chaser. He was there to be called on the carpet. For . . . something.

Well. This took the buzz off the freedom he'd been enjoying while out of the office. It wasn't nearly as much fun as being named *People* magazine's first-ever CEO "Sexiest Man Alive," either. He'd kind of enjoyed that. Disgruntled to know he'd been suckered by the board, even temporarily, Jason leaned back in his executive chair. He'd have to handle this situation differently than he'd planned to.

But that was all right. He could roll with the punches.

Proving as much to himself, he caught the eye of the nearest board member, Mary Sue Marbury, who was fifty-six and steely, with a dignified demeanor. He gave her an easygoing nod. Mary Sue blushed in response. She grinned. Jason grinned back, then pulled a funny face. Mary Sue touched her hair. She glanced away, seeming simultaneously amused and pleased.

Ah. That was better. The first step in defusing a disaster was lightening the mood. The second step was collecting allies. Those were things Jason was good at. Those skills had taken him—a kid who'd loved cracking wise in the back of the class (when he showed up)—and turned him into one of the youngest and most successful CEOs ever. At thirty-two, he'd been the subject of innumerable media profiles, a fair amount of Wall Street speculation, and more than one *Man of the Year* designation.

Fun was officially Jason's business. He excelled at it.

The chairman of the board droned on, describing the day's agenda. On the table, Jason's cell phone vibrated. Offhandedly, he glanced at it. He blinked, then squinted at the suggestive text message on his screen. *Whoa.* Apparently, Mary Sue Marbury was a *lot* more freewheeling than he'd given her credit for.

Another board member cleared her throat. Everyone sat up straighter. They turned their attention to the agenda again.

Suppressing a sigh, Jason did too. Board meetings made him antsy. Even dressing up Moosby's luxurious top-floor boardroom with a towering Oregon Christmas tree and swags of garland at the floor-to-ceiling windows didn't make up for all the tedium involved. If he'd known that success meant nothing but memos, meetings, and PowerPoint presentations, he might have thought twice about becoming a world leader in targeted niche retailing.

Whatever the board had gotten worked up about this time, though, Jason knew he could handle it. He was ready, capable, and relaxed. He'd cut short his tropical Thanksgiving vacation just that morning to fly into L.A. He probably still had beach sand between his toes. That showed dedication. None of the women and men who comprised his board of directors could say that.

Besides, he was the CEO. He was the heart and soul of Moosby's. He'd brought the company into the big leagues and into public trading . . . with all its attendant profits and demands.

Sure, technically Jason served at the board's behest. They'd hired him. They could fire him. He could, theoretically, lose everything he'd worked so hard for. But business was booming. Expansion into overseas markets was burgeoning. Days after Black Friday, the official kickoff to the holiday shopping season, Moosby's had never sold more toys to more kids in less time than they had this year. There was no reason anyone in their right mind would want to oust their fearless leader.

". . . and so we've decided to take meaningful action," intoned Chip Larsen, Moosby's elected chairman. He pointed at the screen that was the meeting's focus. "In response to *this* image."

Jason transferred his attention to the image being shown.

It was a photograph. A grainy, crookedly framed, utterly

incriminating photograph. *Of him.* At a party. With several other people. In it, five scantily clad women clustered suggestively around Jason. All of them were laughing. Most of them held cocktails. The woman nearest Jason was lifting her mojito with one hand and hoisting her sequined tank top with the other, gleefully showing her (now digitally pixelated) breasts.

The photo must have been taken a few days ago. Jason couldn't remember posing for it. Probably because he hadn't.

He was no stranger to seeing surprise photos of himself. These days, who was? But that unplanned photo jarred him.

Examining it gave Jason time to realize a few things. First, that *this* was undoubtedly what had prompted his board-instigated ambush here in L.A. Second, that nothing made an ordinary man look like a knuckle-dragging mouth breather faster than the sudden appearance of bare breasts. To Jason's credit, though, he knew he'd tactfully looked away an instant later.

He'd also held the woman's mojito for her while she put on her top again, having accomplished her mission for the night: being a part of a new Internet meme involving posting topless "selfies" taken with "hot" strangers.

Unfortunately, those gentlemanly impulses of Jason's had *not* been caught on camera. Instead, in the photo, Jason was grinning while holding up his Guinness stout . . . giving the unmistakable appearance of not just ogling Miss Best Breasts' nudity but also *saluting* her breasts for good measure.

At that moment, Jason recalled, he'd been surprised to find himself looking at a topless woman. His board members were not similarly caught off guard now, though. In response to the photo, a dry buzz of disapproval made its way around the room.

For another man, smoothing over this issue would have been impossible. For Jason . . . well, he *was* famously charismatic, wasn't he? That word turned up so often in articles about him that he occasionally joked about having it tattooed on his forehead to spare journalists the trouble. Sure, it was flattering—the first two dozen times or so. After that, the novelty wore off.

Jason knew he was just a regular guy. A guy who'd gotten lucky. A guy who wanted to *stay* lucky, if he could.

Fortunately, he knew he could. He always had. In this situation, all he had to do was explain himself. His board members knew him. They knew who he was. Plus, he'd been on the straight and narrow for so long that his character was unimpeachable. He'd simply explain what had happened, and then—

"Public disapproval of this image is *overwhelming*," Chip went on in a censorious tone. "Our customer hotlines have been going crazy. Our website actually crashed. Two days ago, our Twitter account single-handedly pushed the service over capacity."

"Well, all publicity is good publicity, right?" Jason said, looking for a segue into his explanation. Maybe now would be a good time to mention his charity work. "Speaking of which—"

"Not when it comes to the face of our company—our *family-focused* chain of *toy stores*—looking like a giant perv." Tony Estes, another board member, shook his head. He did not, Jason noted, swerve his gaze a single millimeter from the photo while he spoke. He just kept right on gawking. "We sell toys! To children! You plus booze plus nude coeds *isn't* good publicity."

"Okay. Come on, now," Jason cajoled with a grin, not bothered by their corporate-mandated outrage. His board members were required to be dicks about misunderstandings like this. They were doing their jobs. He knew he could make them see reason. In fact, he was happy to have things out in the open, where he could deal with them. "Yes, I had a few drinks," Jason told them genially. "I was on vacation.

Yes, they were coeds—grad students in anthropology, to be precise. I know that because I had conversations with them during the party. And yes, one of them is topless in that photo." He took a moment to make eye contact with each board member, making sure they understood his explanation. "But that was a big step forward for Bethany. She's very shy. She's been coping with some body-image issues—"

The men around the board table scoffed. But the women looked interested. Also, sympathetic. For whatever reason, Jason usually had greater success building alliances with women.

Maybe that was because he liked women. He liked most people. He had two younger sisters and a younger brother. He couldn't have survived his rocky childhood without them.

"—and posting her picture online was going to be a big deal for her," Jason finished, knowing that, if nothing else, the woman who'd made him look most guilty of wrongdoing would not have minded that image becoming public. That was the whole point of the meme. There weren't any secrets online. But Bethany probably hadn't bargained on *this*. He needed to contact her and apologize for the media mêlée. He'd been unplugged while on vacation. He hadn't known. "She was proud to be part of the—"

Meme, he'd been about to say, winding up his (technically unnecessary) explanation and earning his (almost) inevitable absolution. All he needed was a chance to tell his side of the story. But Tony Estes cut him off with an impatient hand wave.

"Save it for the Oprah show, Hamilton," he said. "We're not here to listen to you wheel and deal. This is an epic disaster."

"'Wheel and deal'?" Jason tightened his jaw. For the first time, he felt irked. Also, unfairly dissed. What had he ever done to Tony except earn him scads of cash? "I'm telling you what happened, straight up. I went to a party. I met those five women. I met lots of other people, too. I got caught on camera—"

"I'll say you did." Chip made that snarky comment without so much as glancing up from his PowerPoint presentation. "It was bound to happen sooner or later. We all knew it. This is the downside of your popularity, Hamilton. We never should have—"

Kept you on as CEO, he was about to say. Jason knew it. That's what Chip always said whenever there was a problem.

Rather than be sidetracked, Jason kept his focus.

He was a patient man, he reminded himself. He could be patient with his board members. He had to be.

He'd survived worse circumstances than this.

"Look, this photo is misleading." Jason gestured at it. He shrugged. "It's one moment, frozen in time. It's not indicative of anything except that Bethany has a very nice smile *and* nice breasts, and I have an appreciation of a good Dublin stout."

"Looks to me like your 'appreciation' has more to do with her boobies than it does with your beer," Tony chortled.

All but offering up his palm for a high five, Estes looked around the table with a grin. *Am I right?* his face asked. *Am I?*

"Mr. Estes, that kind of talk is inappropriate. Frankly, it borders on actionable." Mary Sue pinned him with a stern look. "I'd suggest you keep your puerile observations to yourself."

"We were all thinking it!" Tony nudged his tablemates.

They sat stonily, rightly not agreeing with him.

"I'm just glad someone had the good sense to pixelate Bethany's image." Jason angled his head toward the digitally blurred portions of her anatomy. The pixelation, while leaving the scandalous situation clear, managed to preserve about as much modesty as a bikini would have. "She would have appreciated that." Which made him wonder . . . "Where did you get this, anyway?"

"I did that! I did the pixelation," the admin, Amber, piped up before he could pursue his latest line of thinking. "That was me." She aimed a chastising glance at her boss, Chip. "Mr. Larsen said we should present the photo 'undoctored' at the meeting today, for the sake of 'veracity,' but I disagreed. I mean, at some point, it just crosses the line, doesn't it?"

"Good call, Amber." Jason flashed her a smile. "Nice job."

She flushed, looking pleased. "Thanks very much."

"No problem. Now let's get back to clarifying things." Confidently, Jason got up to pace the room. He wanted to engage everyone. "This image is out there now. It can't be taken back. It can't be changed. But I *can* assure you that this is a misunderstanding. In fact, an instant later, after this photo was taken, I looked *away* from Bethany. Politely. Considerately."

A few skeptical sounds wafted toward him from his board members. Undaunted, Jason veered toward the doubting Thomases.

"Not long after that, I held her drink so she could get dressed again. We talked for quite a while. It wasn't indecent—"

"If you expect us to believe that, you're dreaming," Chip interrupted hotly. "Whatever you want to *pretend* happened—"

"*It happened*," Jason said tightly, "*exactly* the way I said it did." He hated being doubted. His integrity was rock solid.

Maybe it hadn't always been rock solid, but it was now. He'd be damned if anyone would doubt his integrity and not get called on it. He'd earned the right to be taken at his word.

Especially with this group of reactionary corporate stiffs.

"—it *looks* like you're a drunk degenerate preying on young college students!" Chip argued. "Did Walt Disney scam on his nubile twenty-something animation artists back in the day?"

"'Nubile' is beside the point, Chip. And anyway, I doubt they were farsighted enough to hire very many female animators during the golden age of cartoons." Jason's own board of directors was reasonably assembled of five women and three men. Why shouldn't it be? They were all qualified—even if they were a pain in his ass most of the time. "It's too bad, really. Who knows what kinds of stories we might have gotten if they'd been more visionary?"

Chip fumed. "Does Barney the dinosaur peddle tricycles while—while—while *ogling* Miss Piggy next door on *Sesame Street*?"

There were so many things wrong with that idea.

Jason wasn't sure where to start.

"Miss Piggy is a Muppet, sir," Amber said.

"Right. Also, Barney isn't selling anything." Jason had viewed two lifetimes' worth of that big purple dinosaur while babysitting his younger siblings. "Except maybe friendship, cooperation, and learning to tie your shoes. Neither is *Sesame Street*. Or the Muppets. They're licensed characters, but they aren't damning examples of corporate leadership corrupting their innocent customers." With a deliberate frown of fake puzzlement, Jason added, "That *is* what you're trying to do, right, Chip? Draw a parallel between me and a misbehaving kiddie figure?"

Chip turned purple. "Fine. Does Ronald McDonald show up in a raincoat and flash kids on the playground?"

Jason shuddered at the very idea. So did several others.

Curly red hair . . . *all over*? Only one thing needed to be said.

"You're getting out of hand, Chip."

"Not at all! This is serious. Our social media tells the story." With anticipatory triumph, Chip wielded his mousing finger. Using it like a weapon, he clicked. "Just look at this!"

Squinting, Jason eyed the screenshot his chairman put up. It depicted a torrent of irate, mostly unintelligible messages.

"Well, you've all been telling me you're desperate for social media traffic," Jason observed, cracking a grin. "You keep saying you want more customer engagement on the Web. There it is! That looks like bona fide customer engagement to me."

"That is *not*," Chip huffed, "what we're after."

"Well, I'm not the king of good grammar," Jason admitted cheerfully. "Maybe 'fuk you and your scum toyz' is correct?"

Chip aimed a quelling look at him. "You're not taking this seriously enough." He gave a theatrical sigh. "As usual."

That was nothing new. Chip was always riding him. He never missed an opportunity to suggest "a change in leadership"—code for installing one of his old-school cronies at Moosby's. But to Jason's annoyance, this time a few board members nodded in agreement. He looked around for allies. Even Mary Sue glanced pointedly away. Evidently, they *were* all serious about this.

For a heartbeat, Jason actually felt . . . *betrayed*?

He recovered quickly, though. He had to. It didn't pay to show weakness. Not when it came to leading his company.

"You have all got to be kidding me. It's one photo. At a party." Jason shot an exasperated look at the screen as Chip clicked back to that condemning image. "What else can I do?"

Tony smirked. "You can try *not* partying with coeds."

"I wasn't partying with coeds."

Meaningfully, everyone stared at the photo.

"Fine. It *looks* as if I was partying with coeds." Briefly, Jason felt nostalgic for that simpler, happier time when he wasn't tussling with his pedantic board members. "But *I wasn't*. I already explained." He decided to leave out the Internet meme that had spawned the original photo series. It would be way too much for this crew to grapple with. "I can't help it if Bethany decided to take off her top. I'm innocent of any wrongdoing."

He waited for the inevitable apologies to roll in.

They did not.

"'Mothers on Responsible Toys' have already organized

an online petition. There was a protest yesterday." Chip's voice tightened, then lowered ominously. "There's talk of boycotts."

His hushed tone conveyed far more dread than the situation called for. Jason knew that. "No one will boycott. Not even MORT," he admonished. He knew the toy business. He'd built his company from the ground up, store by store. "You're all overreacting to the social media stuff. It's officially the Christmas shopping season! This will blow over by next week."

"And if it doesn't?" Mary Sue prodded.

"We can't take that chance," Barbara Ellington put in.

"I think we're going to have to take that chance," Jason argued, feeling increasingly tense. He couldn't believe his board members had so little faith in his good judgment. In his word. In *him*. "I don't see any other option."

"Said the original laissez-faire CEO," Chip sneered. He'd never approved of Jason's mostly hands-off approach, despite its proven success. Chip never missed a chance to inspire doubt. "We have to take action. A wait-and-see approach won't work here."

Fine. Jason eyed them. "How about an apology?"

Everyone perked up. Of course. The bastards.

Their eagerness only stoked his sense of injustice.

"Too bad. Because I don't have one. I didn't do anything wrong." Casting a reproachful glance at his board of directors, Jason shook his head. Their disloyalty bugged him. So did his own inability to win back their trust. That had never happened before. "If you'll excuse me, I'm going back on vacation."

He was out of the boardroom, down the hall, and on his way back to Antigua before any of them knew what had happened.

Screw them and their skepticism, Jason told himself as he strode toward the elevator bank. He didn't owe anyone a damn apology. He wasn't giving one. Period. Wild horses couldn't drag him into one of those corporate press conferences where sweaty, contrite CEOs tried to talk their way out of trouble. No way.

Behind him, the boardroom door opened. Someone shouted.

"Jason! Wait up." Jogging footsteps sounded.

Annoyed and unrepentant, Jason stabbed the elevator call button. That gesture didn't stop his friend and most frequent board member ally, Charley McIntosh, from following him.

"Save your breath, Charley. I'm not doing it." Impatiently, Jason waited for the elevator to reach the top floor. "Tell them you did all you could to change my mind. I'll back you up."

"It won't be that easy this time." His friend shook his head. "They're serious about this. Chip and Tony are gearing up to have you replaced. They're racking up support, too. Barbara Ellington's in, for one. It's a coup in the making in there." He hesitated, probably to allow that to sink in. "You can't go into self-destruct mode just because someone doubted your word."

"Oh yeah?" Jason stared straight ahead. "Watch me."

He'd lived without having his own company once. He could do it again. No harm, no foul. *It's been fun. That's all, folks.*

Charley heaved a frustrated sigh. "You're not exactly a saint, Jason. We both know that. You can't just leave."

The elevator arrived. The doors opened.

"Too late." Jason cast Charley a stubborn, pissed-off glance. He knew it wasn't rational, but . . . "I'm already gone."

"You can't screw around with this!" Charley grabbed his arm. "I know things usually have a way of working out for you—"

"Usually. When my friends back me up. In the room."

Charley looked embarrassed. He was right to. "But maybe

you won't get so lucky this time. There's . . . something else you should know."

"Chip Larsen is a petty tyrant? I knew that already."

"No. Well, yes. That's true. He's a complete power-hungry prick." Charley cracked a smile. But he sobered quickly. "But there's more to this. I think you'd better know about it."

Chapter Two

Kismet, Michigan

When the call came that was destined to change her work life forever, Danielle Sharpe dropped the phone.

It wasn't her fault. She was caught off guard. She had her hands full, too. Literally. The Christmas shopping season at the Moosby's toy store she'd managed for the past six months was the craziest time of the year. Most days, Danielle could barely think, much less juggle a box of Baby Wets-A-Lot dolls, an old-fashioned landline phone, and a whole lot of holiday-tinged buzz from the not-so-distant sales floor. Also, she was *technically* in the midst of perpetrating some against-the-rules inventory manipulation when the call came in. Danielle was new at subterfuge. She felt 90 percent convinced the bigwigs at Moosby's HQ had somehow caught her red-handed. Her comeuppance was nigh.

"Hello? Is anyone there?" From the toy store's tiled floor, the phone receiver issued that faint but irate query. Impatient silence. Then, "Get me the manager. Right away."

Oh crap. This was really happening?

She glanced at the caller ID again. Moosby's Corporate.

Well, if they were on to her, she certainly wasn't going

down without a fight. She had perfectly good reasons for what she'd been doing with her inventory and that of the other stores in her region. An itemized list of twelve reasons, to be exact.

Awkwardly juggling her box, she picked up the phone.

"Is this the store manager?" the caller demanded to know.

Danielle inhaled. "*Non*, I'm sorry," she said in a flagrantly over-the-top French accent that was inspired by Gigi, one of her best salesclerks. "*Un moment*. I will get her."

Feeling her heart race, Danielle put down the phone. Then she set aside the contraband box of plastic dolls—which belonged to another regional Michigan Moosby's inventory—and shook out her hair. She plastered on a smile, inhaled deeply, then picked up the phone again. She was ready. Ready to handle anything.

Wait. Not yet. She glanced at the framed photo of her three children—Karlie, Aiden, and Zach—that she kept on her office desk amid all the Moosby's promotional materials, the work schedules, and (ironically) the official Moosby's employee handbook. Seeing her kids' smiling faces helped. *Okay.* Now she was ready.

"This is the store manager," she said confidently into the phone, ignoring the customer hubbub outside. "How can I help you?"

Danielle was still reeling when she reentered the sales floor. A cacophony of conversation, squawking toys, and squealing children surrounded her. Christmas carols underlaid all the madness, spinning on constant jolly repeat from October to New Year's Day. The air smelled Christmassy in the store too, redolent of fresh evergreens, spicy gingerbread, and minty candy canes. Not that she was thinking too hard about the overall ambiance, given the game-changing news she'd just received.

As Danielle made her way between stacks of Lego sets

and piles of new video game consoles and homey displays of Moosby's own *More More Moosby's!* exclusive line of handcrafted toys, Gigi glanced up. Her freckled French face lost its grin immediately.

"*Oh là là*! Danielle! What is wrong?" Gigi hurried nearer, temporarily abandoning the job of tidying the store's hands-on play table. Its Crayola, Play-Doh, and glitter-filled surface attracted dozens of children every day, coaxing them into trying out a rotating assortment of toys—and into showing up for Moosby's daily demos. "Did something happen?" Gigi gave her one of her patented no-nonsense (yet somehow flirtatious) looks. "Is it Henry? Did he do something? Because I would be happy to speak to him about it. I know *exactly* how to set that man straight."

At the thought, Gigi's elfin face took on a certain . . . mischievousness that didn't bode well for Henry. He'd been in Gigi's romantic sights ever since she'd arrived in Kismet. So far, Henry had (inexplicably) eluded her.

Not that Gigi was dissuaded. Gigi was never dissuaded.

"No, it's not Henry." Danielle shook her head, automatically scanning the sales floor for things that needed to be done. She added a few essential items to her ongoing mental to-do list. It was her safety net. Without her to-do list and the security it provided, she would have been sunk. Her job was complicated. Her *life* was complicated . . . now that she had a demanding job, three elementary-school-age children, one (two-timing) ex-husband, and one ex-husband's new (much younger) wife to deal with. Deliberately, Danielle refocused on the *now*. "It's Moosby's HQ. I just got off the phone with them."

"With the company head office? In Los Angeles?" Gigi sighed. "I suppose they are asking us to play that corporate-mandated *boring* Christmas music instead of our custom mix?"

"No, that's not it." At Danielle's Moosby's, they sneaked

in a few holiday songs performed by local artists. They were big hits with their customers, many of whom knew the performers.

Adding a personal, down-home touch was one of Danielle's goals for her store. It was working brilliantly. Plus, she enjoyed coming to work when she felt she was helping people. The local artists really got a boost from having their music played.

"They want us to wear those hideous yellow aprons?" Gigi wrinkled her nose. "No one looks their best when they appear to be an enormous banana. I will go on strike first. I promise."

Danielle couldn't help grinning. "No, it's not the aprons, either." Those garish but practical garments might have to make a reappearance, she knew. Sadly. "Although we *might* have to toe the line a little bit more around here. Just for a few days."

"But why? Everything here is *très parfait*!" Indicating as much, Gigi expressively threw her arms to the sides. Around them, customers thronged the cozy toy store as they filled their red and green seasonal Moosby's reusable tote bags—customized by local artists—with merchandise. Several of them consulted with other members of Danielle's staff, getting toy recommendations and gift ideas. "This place is like a well-oiled machinery!"

Danielle nodded. Gigi's English grammar might not be perfect, but her assessment was accurate. Ever since taking over for Edna Gresham, the store's curmudgeonly (and by-the-book) previous manager, Danielle had tripled sales. She was proud of that.

"Well, corporate does agree that things are going well here." Danielle paused to relish her impending announcement, feeling ready to burst with pride and excitement. This was an accomplishment she'd engineered on her own—with the help of her loyal employees, of course. Danielle needed this recognition. Especially after her divorce and all the upheaval that had followed it. "That was a congratulations call. We are now the top-selling Moosby's in the whole chain. In the whole world!"

Gigi's eyes widened. She shook her head. "No effing way."

Gigi loved American profanity. With her Parisian accent and enthusiastic delivery, her abbreviated swearwords somehow seemed more charming than vulgar. But Danielle glanced around to make sure none of their customers had overheard, all the same.

The trick to business, she'd decided, was attention to detail. She'd put in lots of attention to detail during her tenure at Moosby's. Her meticulousness was about to pay off big-time . . . just the way Danielle had hoped it would someday.

"It's true. I heard it from Chip Larsen, the chairman of the board himself." He'd sounded like a smarmy nincompoop on the phone, to be honest. But Danielle could forgive him for that. The man obviously possessed *some* intelligence. He'd recognized *her*, hadn't he? "Because of our stellar sales record, we're officially being designated as a Moosby's model store—*and* we're getting a special congratulatory visit from Moosby's CEO. We're going to be the first stop on his holiday media tour. On TV! And in the news and in a series of Moosby's 'hometown' ads, too."

Chip had said they wanted *her* to appear in those ads, too, alongside the CEO. It was a real-time hometown advertising initiative they were trying out for the holiday sales season.

Danielle wasn't sure yet how she felt about being the "ordinary, down-home face" of the company she worked for, but she was willing to go along for the ride. Especially given the bonus HQ had offered to pay her for her additional work efforts.

She could use that bonus to buy gifts for her kids. It wasn't easy pulling off a memorable Christmas on her income. Last year—the first holiday since her divorce—had been a disaster. Her ex, Mark, had expected Danielle to handle everything for Zach, Karlie, and Aiden, just the way she'd done during their marriage. She'd thought they were splitting duties, now that they were living apart. After realizing they *weren't*—and Mark hadn't gotten *any* gifts on his own—Danielle had racked up a major last-minute credit card debt. She'd nearly bought out several parts of her own store to avoid disappointing her kids.

This year was going to be different, though. This year, they'd *love* Christmas. She had all kinds of special activities planned for them to share. But first . . . back to her big work news.

"Danielle! Wow! Congratulations!" Gigi hugged her, bringing with her a typically potent mixture of perfume, crayon wax, and espresso. Everyone knew that Gigi loved being girly, loved playing with the kids during toy demo time, and loved getting amped on strong black coffee . . . almost as much as she enjoyed flirting with Henry. "Lights, camera, action, right?" Gigi pantomimed aiming a camera at Danielle. "That is terrific!"

"The publicity isn't even the best part. Wait until you—"

"*Non*, the best part is the CEO who is coming here." Gigi nodded with assurance. "I saw his photo on the company intranet. He is hot! So he will be here, in our store, *oui*?" Eagerly, she eyed Danielle. "If you put in some effort, maybe straighten your hair, maybe put on a pretty bra for once in your life—"

"There's nothing wrong with my hair. Or my bra!" Danielle gawked at her friend, fighting an urge to cross her arms. "Which you've never seen, by the way. So how could you possibly know—"

"I know." Gigi waved. "Do not bother denying it. Americans wear *ridiculous* bras." She rolled her eyes with comical disdain. "Boring nude colors. No matching undies. No mystery. No fun! Not enough lace, either. And padding way out to *here*." She cupped both hands in the air at least eight exaggerated inches away from her breasts, pretending to fondle imaginary padded bra cups. "Foam and polyester belong in cheap upholstered furniture or weird cars from the future, *not* in a woman's lingerie."

"Can we just get back to my momentous news, please?"

"Mark my words, Danielle. A man wants to feel a *woman* when he touches her. Not a big round blob of foam and chemicals."

"Well, nobody's going to be—"

"Or you could always go braless. There is a good idea."

"—touching me anytime soon. So there's no problem."

Gigi gave a sympathetic moue. "Still no man for you?"

"Are you kidding?" Danielle knew better. Besides, she was busy. Too busy to risk upsetting her kids by dating. It was much too soon. "My last man ran off with a high-heeled Twinkie—"

"He likes the crème-filled snack cake?"

"—and then had the gall to *marry* her three months ago—"

"Ah. He does like the Twinkie. *Very* much."

"—so I'm not in the market for another man, believe me."

"All men are not disappointments. You have to choose well."

Danielle laughed. "That's just it. I *did* choose well." She'd chosen Mark Sharpe in college. They'd been inseparable all the way till graduation—after which they'd come to Kismet, gotten married, and gotten down to having children. One, two, three. "At least I thought I did. It turns out I was hideously wrong about Mark *and* his capacity for keeping a commitment." *To me and our kids*. "So until I can trust my own judgment again—"

"One bad choice is not your destiny. Trust yourself!"

As if she could do *that* anytime soon.

Danielle gave up on trying to explain. This wasn't the time. "That's easy for you to say. Men are *dying* to date you."

Solemnly, Gigi shook her head. "Francophiles? Yes. *Bien sûr!* But they do not count. They learn that I am from Paris and think that I am their own personal Amélie. I want a man who sees only *me*. I want a man like Henry. I am going to get him, too."

Looking at Gigi amid the toy store chaos, Danielle didn't doubt it. "Right. We're getting sidetracked. That phone call was *big*, Gigi. You'll never believe what Chip Larsen told me."

"Hmm. If it is good news, then I will guess . . ." Gigi's eyes brightened. "That the company is retiring those ugly hats we are supposed to wear?"

At the thought of those screaming yellow baseball caps, Danielle grimaced. In some ways, Moosby's management was stuck in the '90s, for sure. If they amped up the color of the aprons and turned the hats around backward, they'd all look like long-lost members of Marky Mark and the Funky Bunch. When properly outfitted according to the employee handbook, Moosby's team members looked like they'd stepped into a dorkiness amplifying machine and gotten stuck in there. It wasn't good.

"He didn't say anything about the hats."

"I will go on strike before I wear one of those hats."

"I know. Me too." In unified protest, Danielle and Gigi glanced toward the back room, where she'd stowed all three dozen pieces of plastic-enrobed headwear. Her employees had wanted a bonfire. A stash was a compromise. "Anyway, the big deal is—"

"They are allowing us to talk normally to customers?" Gigi speculated. "Instead of making us do the stupid patter?"

Danielle hesitated. According to the official Moosby's rule book and accompanying training video, they were supposed to begin each customer transaction with a hearty, "Welcome to Moosby's! Welcome to fun! How can I maximize your playtime today?" They were supposed to end each transaction by yodeling, "Thank you for shopping Moosby's! Have a fun-filled day!"

She made a face. "No, that's not it, either. But since we don't do that anyway, we're in the clear, right?"

Gigi gave a Gallic shrug, obviously never having planned on participating in the "stupid patter" in the first place. It wasn't surprising. Gigi had been hired after Edna Gresham had left—after Danielle had taken over and changed things a bit.

Belatedly, it occurred to her exactly how many rules she broke every day at work. She didn't consider herself a rebel. Far from it. Ordinarily, Danielle was organized, efficient, and reasonably fond of predictability. But when it came to Moosby's, a small dose of rebellion had definitely been called for.

When crunch time had come, Danielle had delivered that rebellion. She'd led the charge toward that rebellion, in fact.

How else could she have achieved such spectacular sales? She couldn't have succeeded by toeing the line.

"You do realize," Danielle mused to Gigi, "that you've already pointed out four things we *don't* do by the book here?"

That wasn't even counting the whopper—the inventory shuffling that Danielle had been engaged in when Chip called.

"*Oui*, I know. But you see why I did that, *non*?"

"Because you're planning to rat me out to the CEO when he gets here?" Danielle gave her a mock chastising look. "Blackmail won't work, you know. I've got all the dirt on you, too."

"Because if the big cheese is coming here for a visit, he will want to see us doing everything A-OK." Gigi rolled her eyes at Danielle. "He will want to see the aprons and the hats. He will want to experience the patter." She sighed, then cast her beleaguered gaze toward the store's Christmas light–bedecked ceiling. "He will want to hear the boring Christmas songs that make me want to poke out my ears with a Tinkertoy. He will!"

"No, he won't," Danielle assured her. "Because he'll be too busy deciding he has to promote *me* to a big-deal corporate job."

"We *have* to burn all those hats," Gigi announced, obviously still preoccupied with her doomsday scenario. "I'll get them."

"Didn't you hear me? I'm finally going to get promoted!"

"Oh." Gigi blinked. "That is what the HQ boss told you?"

Hmm. Gigi's nonchalance wasn't quite the ebullient reception Danielle had expected to receive for her big news.

"Well . . ." Danielle hedged. "Not *exactly*. Not in so many words, at least. What he said was, 'We're all *very* impressed with you. We just know you're going to come through for us with this.'" She paused. In retrospect, the things Chip Larsen had said to her on the phone had carried more *promise* than actual *promises*. She'd been so surprised; it was hard to remember all the details. "Then he said some things about 'corporate synergy' and 'moving the cheese' toward a 'more collaborative future.'"

Gigi looked suspicious. "Sounds like corporate doublespeak to me. What is he, some kind of d-bag?"

Well . . . sort of. "Sort of," Danielle admitted. "Yes. But he's also the chairman of the board at Moosby's. So when he tells me they're contemplating 'major changes in management' *very soon*, he's got to be hinting that I'm in the running for a top spot! You know, after I prove myself by acing this 'model store' visit. It must be a test or something." Giddily, she inhaled. "He probably can't commit yet. There are HR issues, liability details . . . Chip Larsen is a professional. He's doing things by the book, that's all. But I've made no secret about my aspirations. I've been applying for upper management positions for the past few months, remember? I'm totally getting promoted!"

"We should shred those foul aprons. Just to make sure."

"Don't you see what this means?" Danielle prodded. "I can finally get out of here, just the way I've always wanted to! I can take Aiden, Karlie, and Zach *out* of this Podunk town and give them the kinds of opportunities they really need." She glanced beyond the toy store's garland-draped and vividly decorated picture windows, seeing past Main Street . . . all the way to the future she'd dreamed of making happen for her children.

They couldn't count on their flaky, irresponsible dad. They needed *her* to come through for them. "They can have better schools, better extracurricular activities, opportunities to see the world! I was so naïve, growing up here. I had to wait until I went away to college to find out that, in most places, everyone *doesn't* know your name and your family and your whole history."

Now Gigi looked wistful. "That sounds . . . nice to me."

"Well . . ." *Sometimes it is, honestly*. "I want more. I'm going to get it, too. For all I know, the CEO is coming here to tell me about my promotion in person! Right? That *must* be it."

Merry Christmas to her! This was going to be *fantastic*.

"I hope you are right. If anyone deserves it, you do." Gigi hugged her again. She stepped back, waggling her eyebrows. "If you get a fat raise, you can afford sexy lingerie. So you can feel sexy when you are with the CEO. That is powerful stuff."

Danielle scoffed. "I'm not going to work my way to the top on the strength of a balconette bra and a matching thong."

"You are right. You will also need cute stilettos."

"Gigi!"

"And stockings. But I am encouraged that you know what to look for, at least. A balconette bra delivers much va-va-voom."

"I wasn't serious."

"*I* would be. If that CEO guy is half as hot as his photo looks, you will be serious, too. Right away. Mark my words."

Danielle dismissed that idea with a shrug. "Those pictures are all Photoshopped, I'm sure." Wasn't every glossy publicity image airbrushed and perfected? In the case of Moosby's movie-star-esque CEO, they had to be. "Besides, I already told you, I don't want a man. I don't *need* a man. I'm doing fine on my own."

"Mmm-hmm." Gigi seemed more preoccupied than convinced by that. "Do you know what? Maybe you should take off your glasses while he is here." Earnestly, she examined Danielle's owlish horn rims. "Unless he has a kink for the smarty-pants librarian type. If he does, you are *so* in there, g-friend."

"There's no talking seriously with you."

"I *am* being serious! I am helping you to get your man."

"I want a job, not a man," Danielle reminded her while eyeing the giftwrap center. "The CEO of Moosby's is not my man. He's a respected businessman with a reputation for innovation."

"*All* men are your men. If you want them to be."

"You're impossible."

"You are repressed!" Gigi nudged her. "Loosen up, okay?"

That wasn't going to happen. "I'm about to have the most critical onsite business visit of my entire life. The *last* thing I'm going to do is loosen up." Struck by the sobering reality of it all—and the short time she had to prepare—Danielle felt a knot of panic tighten in her middle. Oh, boy. This was *big*. "I have to get started. I have planning to do, lists to make—"

"Lingerie to buy . . ."

"—rule breaking to hide." *Whoa*. How was she going to conceal all the inventory shenanigans she engaged in . . . and everything else, too? How was she going to convince her staff to get on board with the Funky Bunch uniforms and the yodeling store greetings? Should she even try? Those *were* the rules . . .

With new purpose, Danielle examined the busy toy store and all the activity swirling around them. The Christmas carols filtered into her consciousness again, along with a clarifying realization: her store had succeeded *because* of her innovations. Not in spite of them. Sure, she might have to sidestep any pointed inquiries anyone made into her inventorying, but how likely was that? Moosby's CEO was coming to snap a few photos, appear at a small-town meet-and-greet, and probably be filmed while trying to look interested in board games and Transformers.

Oh, and to tell her about her promotion. Of course.

There was a good chance, Danielle reasoned, that an out-of-touch wunderkind type like Moosby's CEO wouldn't even *know* all the rules for his own stores' employees, much less expect them to be rigorously adhered to. After all, hadn't some US president or other been famously awestruck by run-of-the-mill supermarket scanners years ago? Sometimes rich, successful CEO types delegated so many things to their underlings that they didn't even known their own companies' operations anymore.

But *Danielle* knew how things had to operate at Moosby's. She knew how to satisfy customers and how to rack up big sales in the process. This December, she swore to herself as she surveyed her bustling toy store, *nothing* was getting between her and the most phenomenal sales season Moosby's had ever seen.

Not even the famous CEO of Moosby's himself . . . Jason Hamilton.

Chapter Three

Edna Gresham, the kind and grandmotherly manager of the newly designated Moosby's "model store" in Kismet, Michigan, was about to get the most attentive, in-depth, thoughtful, and upstanding corporate visit in the history of corporate visits.

That's what Jason swore to himself as he drove toward the small Midwestern lakeside resort town for the first time.

He'd been ready to bail on the "corporate apology" shtick the board had been panting for. Reasonably so. Even Charley's ominous warnings about there being something Jason "ought to know" about the board's plans hadn't made an impact—probably because the board's other issue with Jason had had to do with an unauthorized "tell-all" biography of him that was in the works.

"They're fired up about it," Charley had argued gravely. "It's supposed to contain some heavy-duty dirt about you. About your past, your tough upbringing, your ins and outs with—"

The law, he'd undoubtedly been about to say, but Jason had cut him short. All that stuff had happened a long time ago.

"That biography's been 'on the cusp of being published' for years now. It'll never happen." Charley hadn't been around the last time its publication had seemed imminent. Neither had a few of his newer board members—Chip Larsen included. "Someone is fishing. Nobody knows enough about me to fill a book."

Only his family came close. Because they'd been there. To some degree, Alfred Moosby knew a few things about him, too. But the real nitty-gritty? That was staying in the past where it belonged. Jason was a different man now. A better man.

"If I have to," he'd told Charley, "I'll bury that book."

His past was his own business. Nobody else's.

"It's got new traction now that that racy picture is out," Charley had insisted. "All the TV newsmagazine shows are covering the story of your wild weekend. They're saying it wasn't very family friendly. Especially for a toy store exec."

"It'll blow over."

"One of the twenty-four-hour news networks is running a constant crawl of the worst tweets about you. They're calling for Moosby's boycotts. *SNL* did a skit about you, dude!"

"Was it funny?"

"Jason!"

"Well?"

Charley hesitated. "Yeah. It was funny. But—"

"See? This is no big deal. I'm not worried."

"You're never worried. That's why you have *us*. We're here to worry for you. Professionally and at length."

"Aha." At that, Jason had grinned. "I see the disconnect here. Because I don't want anybody to worry about anything."

"Not even your board of directors? We're responsible for—"

"Responsible?" Jason had waved away the notion. "We run toy stores! It's supposed to be *fun*." He knew that above everything else. "Speaking of which . . . aren't you getting married soon? Why don't you go spend some time with your fiancée?"

"I . . ." Charley had seemed flummoxed. "I can't just leave."

"Sure you can." Jason had gestured toward the elevator. "We can both leave right now. The meeting's finished. You can blow off the traditional 'fuck Jason' postmortem, right?"

A grin. "That *is* what we usually say after you leave."

"I know. So come on!" Jason had urged.

Four minutes later, they'd both hit the street, said their good-byes like teenage miscreants skipping school, and left.

Jason had headed to the airport. While waiting for his plane to fuel, he'd fielded a call from the Guinness people about a potential "partnership opportunity." Then he'd called Bethany to apologize. She'd assured him everything was fine.

Things had been settled. Not long after that, though . . .

"Chip has done something you should know about," Charley had told him when he'd picked up another call. "It's not good."

"With Chip, it never is. What is it?"

Patiently, Jason had stood in a private airport lounge and listened in disbelief while Charley had relayed the news that Chip had retaliated for Jason's storming out of the meeting.

First, Chip had updated Alfred Moosby on the "dire situation." Then he'd threatened to have Jason ousted if he didn't cooperate fully with a public "apology tour" meant to atone for Jason's supposed photographic misdeeds.

"I already refused to do that. I'm not apologizing."

"Evidently, you are," Charley had told him. "Chip arranged the tour before you even got back from your vacation."

The bastard. But it was what Chip had done after Jason had gotten back—and subsequently left again—that was worse. He'd upped the ante (and the odds of Jason cooperating) by promising the manager of the Moosby's toy store in some flyover town called Kismet, Michigan that she'd be receiving a promotion, a featured spot in a "groundbreaking" series of social media ads, *and* a special congratulatory visit. From Jason. Tomorrow.

Now, *tomorrow* was *today*. But a single sundown and a single sunup hadn't made Jason any happier with the shake-down Chip had enacted. Jason was used to being threatened; he could handle that. He was used to dealing with the media; he could handle that, too. He could even handle the board. What he couldn't handle was the idea of his kindly retired mentor, Mr. Moosby, worrying about the survival of the business he'd founded.

That's undoubtedly what he was doing right now, too—despite the phone call Jason had made to Mr. Moosby to reassure him.

Even *needing* to make that encouraging phone call had rankled Jason. How dare Chip tattle to Moosby about this so-called scandal?

Alfred Moosby hadn't been involved in the day-to-day workings of the company for years. He did still have influence over Jason, though—because Jason cared about his mentor. If not for Mr. Moosby, his life would have played out much differently . . . with 100 percent more jail time and about a million times less success.

The bottom line was, Jason owed Mr. Moosby. He wasn't about to let one asshole on his board ruin Mr. Moosby's retirement.

"If this company winds up in someone else's hands," Jason had told Charley, "Mr. Moosby will be devastated."

"I don't think you're going to let that happen."

Damn right, I'm not. "Where is Kismet again?"

Charley had filled him in on the Kismet Moosby's. He'd given him all the necessary details about its misled manager, Edna Gresham, too. He'd even e-mailed a photo of Edna, which he'd downloaded from the "Meet Moosby's" area of the company's intranet. Now, duly armed with that information,

Jason was closing in on Kismet, having driven himself in a rented SUV from the airport in a larger neighboring city.

At least he *thought* he was closing in. So far it had been nothing but highways, blink-and-you-miss-it small towns, snow-covered pine trees, and a winding country road.

Everything looked the same out here. Rural and quaint.

Jason didn't mind that so much, though—not now that his head had cleared and he wasn't ready to go all "Hulk smash!" on his nitpicking board members. Visiting the Kismet Moosby's didn't have to be a big deal. It didn't have to involve an apology, either. What was Chip going to do—spy on him? Not likely.

He'd keep the media tour brief, Jason had decided in the end, with no entourage to slow him down and no handlers—just local papers and TV. Afterward, he'd still have time to continue with his vacation, then enjoy a beachy Christmas family reunion with his parents, sisters, and brother in Antigua.

They'd already arranged it, down to the Christmas Eve beach bonfire and AM gift exchange. He could be done with this bullshit media tour and back to his regular life in no time.

Jason didn't want to make an appearance at the Kismet Moosby's. Or any place else. But he was going to. Because when push came to shove, Jason refused to leave poor Edna Gresham, the Moosby's "model store" manager, stranded like a jilted bride when the CEO she'd been promised never materialized.

This time, Chip had successfully played him, Jason knew. Because the only thing Jason wouldn't do for the sake of his own integrity was disappoint someone who didn't deserve it.

Like Alfred Moosby. Or Edna Gresham.

Edna Gresham was probably thrilled about her store's supposed "model store" designation. But Jason suspected that moniker was nothing more than a ploy. It was a cheap shot designed to strong-arm Jason into making an appearance in the most wholesome store in the whole chain. Being there was supposed to convince Moosby's most traditional and conservative-minded customers that their CEO was just an average Joe . . . someone who could truly relate to them and their everyday lives.

The truth was, Jason could relate to them more than they knew. But he wasn't interested in making his business personal.

All he wanted to do was get in, make Edna Gresham happy with her store's "model success," then get out. Simple as that.

Because while it was officially true that Edna had somehow turned her store into Moosby's most unlikely top earner, that wasn't the reason Chip had designated the Kismet Moosby's a "model store." That wasn't the reason Chip had chosen it for Jason's initial appearance, either. He'd chosen it first because of its wholesomeness—and second because of its isolation.

While stuck in Podunk Kismet, Jason wouldn't be able to do much to prevent Chip's next move. Chip would have free rein to do all he could to convince the board to (finally) fire Jason—something Chip had spent years gunning for. Jason knew that as plainly as he knew, while driving down the snowy rural road leading to Kismet, that Californians like him weren't exactly at ease behind the wheel in the snow. But his hands were tied.

He couldn't let down Mr. Moosby. Or disillusion Edna Gresham. But he *could* go along with the board's plan . . . to a point.

After he'd taken a few requisite PR photos and shaken some hands, he'd be in a better position to bargain with his board members. He'd give a little. They'd give a little. Things would be fine. Moosby's would continue racking up profits while making kids happy, and Jason would probably . . . still feel dissatisfied.

Hell. Reminded of the sense of discontentment that had dogged him for the past year or so, Jason frowned at the rustic outskirts of town as he steered his SUV around the lakefront.

All around him, ramshackle houses hugged the snow-covered hills. They huddled closer together as he neared the town center, but all Jason saw was his own life skating on past him.

Meetings and presentations and endless strategizing didn't satisfy him. Neither did arguing with executives or dealing with his board members' ongoing obsession with increased profits.

He hadn't gotten into the toy business for this. He'd gotten into it . . . well, he'd gotten into it by accident, Jason admitted to himself as he drove past a kitschy gas-station-turned-diner. He'd gotten into it because Mr. Moosby had taken a chance on a scrawny kid with a bad attitude and an unrealized yen to do more than just screw around. These days, Jason wasn't scrawny anymore. But he wasn't idealistic anymore either.

The realization bugged him.

He switched on the SUV's stereo to forget about it.

A Christmas carol blasted from the speakers. Jason swore under his breath and turned off the stereo, shaking his head. He was already over Christmas and everything that came with it.

For him, the holidays had lost . . . something. When he was a kid, the Christmas season had meant family, treats, and hoping for a cool new toy under the droopy-needled family tree. It had meant something *special*. However corny it sounded, Jason had looked forward to it. He'd looked forward to surprising his mom and dad, pulling pranks on his brother and sisters, even seeing far-flung relatives. These days, though, Christmas was just another retail season—the most critical one. These days, Jason spent the run-up to

Christmas strategizing with his team and uncovering new ways to pull customers into the Moosby's stores that dotted towns and cities all over the globe. End of story.

Not that it was tough getting people to come into Moosby's and spend. His stores were unique in their ambiance—more like personalized boutiques than warehouse behemoths, with curated selections to match. They were also relentlessly ubiquitous. They had been ever since Jason had taken the company public.

One newspaper article had dubbed Moosby's "the Starbucks of the playground set." Jason figured that was an accurate take. Each Moosby's tried to be its neighborhood's Moosby's, a place to hang out and discover what was new in the world of fun.

At least that was the theory. Jason had quit going into his own stores a while ago now. Being there felt like *work* in a way that left him wanting to punch something. Or run away. Or sit in a corner and refuse to play nicely with the other kids on his Moosby's board. He was ordinarily an easygoing guy. So he didn't understand why his own retail empire had that effect on him.

He tried not to think about it. Mostly, he succeeded.

Except when Christmas carols jabbed into his brain space and forced him to remember. Then, Jason couldn't forget that, among other things, he spent every year turning Christmas into a retail battle. He morphed kids' letters to Santa into double-digit profits for his company. And he didn't blink while he did.

Not that there was anything wrong with that. His family, friends, and board members would have been the first to tell him that kids needed toys anyway. That the thousands of Moosby's team members he employed needed jobs. That it *wasn't* hideously cynical to start thinking about the holidays fourteen months in advance . . . and hearing cash registers *ka-ching!* with every carol.

All the same, these days, Christmastime made Jason feel

claustrophobic in a way that nothing else did. If he was lucky, Edna Gresham wouldn't have gone over the top with her store's holiday decorations. He'd be spending a few days there while shooting the first ad. He didn't want to be confronted with a bunch of jingle bell hoopla from the instant he arrived.

On the other hand . . . who was he kidding? He was about to meet a gray-haired, twinkly eyed, quilt-making, small-town toy store manager. The schmaltz levels were going to be sky-high. According to Charley—who'd looked into the situation after Chip had confessed that he "didn't even know the name" of the manager he'd promised to promote—Edna Gresham had sidestepped retirement more than once to continue managing her Moosby's store.

At least his managers were happy to keep working at Moosby's. Jason didn't know what was the matter with *him*. All he wanted was to have fun and make sure other people did too.

How had that plan gone so cockeyed on him?

Lost in thought while staring down a snow flurry, he almost drove straight past Kismet's Main Street. It was a good thing he hadn't sneezed. He'd have missed the town center altogether.

It was pretty small by international (or L.A.) standards. But it was decked out with storefronts and sidewalks and old-fashioned lampposts wrapped in holly and blinking Christmas lights. It was populated with bundled-up shoppers carrying bags of gifts. It was scenic and snow dusted and cozily charming.

It was, to Jason's disbelief, like something out of a Hollywood production of a Dickens story . . . except it was *real*. It smelled real (like gingerbread). It looked real (like sleigh bells and fire hydrants disguised as red-and-white candy canes). It sounded real (like Christmas carols being pumped into the streets via carefully disguised municipal speakers). It even *felt* real, as Jason waited at an intersection for a group of children—merrily costumed as Santa's elves—to cross the street.

He blinked, but they were still there. One of the kids gave Jason a wave. He lifted his gloved hand from the steering wheel and waved back, watching as the redheaded, pigtailed littlest elf scampered in her friends' wake. Behind her, an adult chaperone brought up the rear. She glanced at Jason. She did a double take. She smiled at him. He gave her a nod. Her smile broadened.

Uh-oh. He wasn't here to make friends. Especially female friends. He'd grudgingly promised the board—via Charley—that he would do whatever he could to rehabilitate his tarnished public image. While he was in Kismet, Jason had to be firmly on the straight and narrow. He couldn't risk another scandal.

Not if he wanted to keep his company, he couldn't.

For Mr. Moosby's sake, he had to do better.

Deliberately, Jason glanced down at his SUV's console, as if something there had caught his attention. The chaperone hesitated.

After a few seconds, she meandered disappointedly away.

Phew. Close one. He couldn't risk encouraging an encounter that might become problematic. For him—a born-again Mr. Rogers type from this moment forward—even the most innocent actions could be misconstrued. Jason had done what he could to make sure the chaperone didn't feel personally dissed—which was why he'd pretended to have been distracted—but he had to be more careful next time. He couldn't keep doling out nods willy-nilly.

From now on, Jason had to live like a monk. A toy-shilling, public-pleasing, squeaky-clean monk. Once he reached Moosby's, he knew he'd be home free. There wouldn't be any temptation on the horizon when he met Edna Gresham. She was older than his own mother and probably just as sharp. If Jason stuck by Edna Gresham's side for the duration of his visit to Kismet, it would be like having his own personal (improvised) chaperone.

He'd be smart to take advantage of that.

Vowing to do just that, Jason angled into a street-side parking space. He got out to feed the meter, only to realize it was already paid up. All the way to the top. Underneath its green *time remaining* indicator, someone had attached a hand-written note affixed with multiple rows of clear packing tape.

Parking paid for courtesy of Moosby's Toy Store. Happy Holidays!

Hmm. Squinting down the block—*way* down the block—to where the Kismet Moosby's toy store stood, Jason frowned. This was not company-sanctioned policy. As far as he knew, no single Moosby's store was authorized to dip into their petty cash this way.

Paying for one or two spaces directly in front of Moosby's would have been one thing. That encouraged customers to come in and browse freely. Paying for parking spaces all the way up and down Main Street, from the antique stores on one end to the colorful banner promoting the annual Kismet Christmas Parade and Holiday Light Show on the other, was something else again.

That's what Jason could see, too, now that he understood what those small, taped-on pieces of holly-bordered card stock were, stuck onto every parking meter in sight. If the Kismet Moosby's was spending its record profits on homegrown promotions like this, they might be posting a net loss in the end.

Well, it was a good thing he was here then, wasn't it?

He'd obviously spent too much time avoiding his own stores. Starting now, Jason Hamilton was going all in. He was going to rehab his image, save the stores that Mr. Moosby had entrusted him with, and post a record-breaking holiday sales season.

He was going to do it while behaving himself *perfectly*, too, he vowed as he sucked in an invigorating lungful of wintery air. If Chip Larsen and the board thought they could break him, they'd better think again. Because this time, Jason was . . .

. . . being followed?

Catching a hint of movement from the corner of his eye, he glanced backward. *Nada*. That was weird. He could have sworn he'd seen someone trailing him—parking a few cars back, getting out almost simultaneously, then staring intently up and down the street . . . exactly the way he'd done while examining the meters.

Now, though, all Jason saw was *Christmas*. The storefronts nearby were decked out with lights around their windows. The windows themselves depicted holiday scenes, too, painted with impressive artistry and/or childlike ebullience. The window nearest him had been done by "Miss Tate's class" at Kismet Elementary; the one he passed next credited a local artist.

As he crunched his way down the iced-over and recently salted sidewalk, encountering cheerful town residents as he went, Jason spied flyers for sleigh rides at The Christmas House B & B, for a gingerbread house construction gala, and for a neighborhood Christmas light show. He heard jingle bells and laughter, Christmas carols and cars driving past, and the unmistakable whine of a fire engine's siren . . . which turned out to be part of a "kids' fun ride" event for charity. Jason saw a telltale banner on the next slow-moving fire truck being driven by Santa himself. He smelled peppermint and chocolate fudge, and—growing stronger as he neared Moosby's—gingerbread, too.

If someone *was* following him, they were getting a hellaciously holiday-ed up experience while they were at it.

It was just as well that Jason considered himself immune

to Christmas and all its trappings by now. Because otherwise he might have been softened up by all the jolliness and bright-eyed people he encountered in Kismet. As it was, he could see all the holiday things for what they were. Manipulations. Efforts to instill positive feelings in shoppers—which they would then transfer to stores . . . along with their remaining cash and credit.

He reached his own little corner of the manipulative retail sales world and stood outside for a minute, studying the Kismet Moosby's toy store with a critical eye. *This* was what he'd worked for, sacrificed for, *changed* himself for. This was it.

It didn't look like a man's life's work. It looked like a small redbrick building, fronted by two picture windows that gave it a friendly appearance, frosted by snow and decorated with multiple strings of old-fashioned multicolored C9 lights. It looked popular, full of shoppers of all ages. Jason found that weirdly heartening. Most of all, it looked like a drawing of a toy store in a children's book come magically to life—as though it might, at any second, blink its windowpane eyes and use its awning-covered stoop to somehow crack a big smile.

At that fanciful thought, Jason scoffed to himself. What the hell was he thinking? Moosby's was enchanting because it had been designed that way. He'd employed teams of architects and designers, builders and decorators, all with the express intent of repurposing the old buildings they transformed into new sites and creating an ambiance that would feel welcoming and homey.

Of *course* Moosby's felt good. It was engineered to feel good. Even its location, on a corner fronted by a small, bench-filled open space, beckoned shoppers to come in and stay awhile.

He ought to feel proud, Jason knew.

Instead, he felt like a massive fraud.

Once upon a time, he used to love being at his toy stores.

He remembered being the first one to arrive in the morning and the last one to leave at night. He remembered being always ready to chat with customers and to show off the unique merchandise he'd featured as one-of-a-kind *More More Moosby's!* exclusives. Now, Jason delegated those responsibilities and took on others.

Now he took on responsibilities like getting his ass in there and being publicly impeccable, corporately unimpeachable, and 100 percent family friendly, Jason reminded himself.

If he didn't—and if Chip Larsen won—Jason stood a good chance of losing everything. So he drew in another breath, put on his game face, and opened the door.

Chapter Four

". . . and *go*!" Danielle instructed the people around her as the toy store's front door opened. Numbers one through eight on her to-do list had already been accomplished. Now all that remained was launching a proper welcome for the man who was here to reward her store and its employees for all their hard work.

Jason Hamilton. He'd been circling the lakefront for a while, Danielle had learned. He'd finally made his way downtown.

Her hometown spies had been reporting in all morning via cell phone as Moosby's meandering bigwig had progressed through the neighborhoods surrounding the iced-over lake, through the south side of town, and up to Main Street. She'd spotted him herself just moments ago. But she hadn't had time to do much more than stash her cache of meter-feeding quarters, clutch her leftover parking meter cards, and hurry back to the store.

She was surprised he'd driven himself. She'd expected a limousine. An entourage. A phalanx of roving reporters complete with popping flashbulbs and whirring cameras like something out of an old '80s movie. Instead, Jason Hamilton had made the trip from Gerald R. Ford International

Airport in Grand Rapids on his own. Just like a regular guy. That sort of . . . impressed her.

It worried her a little, too.

If Jason Hamilton *wasn't* a clueless Richie Rich type, it would be a lot trickier to hide her unorthodox store inventory methods from him. Not to mention her intentional nonadherence to the official apron, hat, ambient music, and yodeling policies. Because while Danielle had briefly considered reforming to bring her store in line with Moosby's official corporate guidelines, in the end, she'd decided it was better to be herself.

She was the one who'd excelled well enough to be named manager of Moosby's first-ever model toy store, wasn't she?

That meant she knew what she was doing. Even if what she was doing *was* technically against the rules.

The only thing Danielle intended to hide during Jason Hamilton's visit was her inventory wrangling. Because it involved other regional stores, and she didn't want to get her fellow Moosby's managers in trouble. Other than that . . .

Well, the way she saw it, if Jason Hamilton *was* a guy who cared about rules, he'd be so distracted with cracking down on the lack of Marky Mark uniforms and the proliferation of homegrown holiday music that he wouldn't have time to be on the lookout for any coinciding inventory shenanigans. It was all part of her newly created get-a-promotion strategy.

So was this welcome. Drawing in a deep breath, Danielle nodded to the conductor of the Kismet Klangers.

Right on cue, the town's adult hobbyist marching band launched into a raucous rendition of "Santa Claus Is Coming to Town." Ordinarily, the Klangers spent their December Saturdays at the Kismet town square, creating a festive atmosphere for downtown shoppers. As a special favor to Danielle, today they'd stopped in her store beforehand. Their music was unique. It was played with gusto, too, by musicians who all wore gaudy holiday sweaters embellished with rhinestones, appliqués, and more.

For an instant, the visiting CEO who'd caused all the hullabaloo stopped on the threshold. Framed by the wintery light behind him, Jason Hamilton looked tall, broad-shouldered, and handsome . . . and endearingly taken aback by all the hoopla, too.

For a heartbeat, he actually looked as though he wanted to bolt. But then he swept his dark-eyed gaze over the waiting customers, musicians, and Moosby's employees, stamped the snow from his shoes, and seemed to regroup. He smiled at them all.

A sigh actually rippled throughout the room. That was just how potent that smile of his was. It was one part confident retail genius, one part boyish surprise, and one part hubba-hubba manliness . . . and it was genuine, too. Danielle caught herself in midexhalation and couldn't believe her own gullibility.

She wasn't going to fall for the manufactured legend of Moosby's famously charismatic leader. She was smarter than that.

Like a rock star, Jason Hamilton raised his arm. "Hello, Kismet!" his deep, raspy voice rang out. "How are you?"

A chorus of squeals met his greeting. Danielle's employees and customers all surged, en masse, toward the doorway. They nearly trampled each other in their haste to reach him.

Once they had Jason Hamilton surrounded, they grew palpably expectant. Coquettish young mothers batted their eyelashes and played with their hair. Young fathers stood tall, inspired by Jason's example, and gave him macho man-to-man nods. Grandmothers held out tins of homemade spritz cookies and hand-crocheted scarves. Midlife female shoppers eyed Jason *and* his citified appearance with lusty-eyed approval. Two rushed forward to collect his coat as he shucked it. Several others exclaimed over everything from his gray flannel pants to his pristine white shirt and his casual black wool scarf.

Men didn't look like *that* in Kismet. In Kismet, the closest anyone had ever gotten to *GQ* coolness had been years ago, when trucker caps were in vogue. Down-home Kismet men had suddenly found themselves unintentionally (and unknowingly) on trend. Not surprisingly, that coincidence had never been repeated.

In the center of the mêlée, Jason Hamilton smiled again. He possessed both dimples *and* the kind of romantic, dark wavy hair that Danielle had glimpsed in Pre-Raphaelite paintings. His nose broke left, then right, ever so slightly. It was on the hawkish side, too. But that only made him appear even more *real*. He looked like a guy you'd want to approach—and everyone did.

His unexpected rock-star appeal might have begun with his smile, but it ended with his sincerity. Where other men might have simply stood there, arms wide, and soaked up the sudden burst of admiration coming their way, Jason Hamilton delved into the crowd instead. He met the first customer head-on, looked straight at her, and gave her a husky, "Hi. I'm Jason."

As if there was anyone within fifty miles who didn't already know that. Nonetheless, the woman turned cranberry red.

She wobbled. Her voice was a breathless squeak. "Hi!"

Her giddy giggles carried to Danielle. Danielle wanted to roll her eyes at the whole spectacle. Somehow, she couldn't.

Jason took her hand. "You have a wonderful laugh." He sounded absolutely sincere. Maybe he was. "What's your name?"

The woman gulped in a breath. "Jason!"

His smile became charmingly teasing. "Me too!"

"Oh! No! I mean—" Another titter. "I'm Amy. You're

Jason!" She clutched one of her friends. Both of them appeared on the verge of fainting. "He looks just like he did in *People*!"

Aha. Belatedly, Danielle realized that she'd seen the magazine cover the woman was talking about. Jason Hamilton had been named *People* magazine's first-ever CEO "Sexiest Man Alive."

"Ohmigod. He *does*!" The woman's friend swiveled her gaze up and down Jason's body. "I still have that magazine cover up in my locker at work," she told him, one hand excitedly covering her beating heart. "I'm a waitress at the Galaxy Diner. Maybe you've heard of it? Our specialty is pie-in-a-jar."

"Mmm." His contemplative rumble made several women nearby swoon. He seemed unaware of that fact. "Sounds delicious."

"You should come by sometime. Anytime! Anytime at all!"

"Thanks. I'll try to. I'll be sure to ask for . . . ?"

"Avery! Ask for Avery. That's my name. I'm Avery."

"All right, I will." Jason shook her hand warmly. He looked into her eyes, then smiled. "You're very kind, Avery."

Hearing him say her name made the waitress blush. Danielle *wanted* to be cynical about that fact. She wanted to believe that Jason Hamilton was shamelessly manipulating her customers. But she just . . . couldn't. Somehow, he seemed too authentic for that.

For the next several minutes, the store's meet-and-greet continued. One by one, each excited customer came face-to-face with Jason Hamilton. One by one, they each left their encounters with him appearing charmed and bedazzled and pleased. Pictures were taken. Autographs were scribbled. Gifts were piled on the table Danielle had set up. Even the men weren't immune. While meeting Moosby's CEO, they lowered their voices, straightened their shoulders, and offered crushing handshakes; when leaving him, they puffed out their chests and high-fived each other.

Overall, it was a remarkable scenario. Danielle knew she should come forward and take charge of the situation, but she didn't want to. Not yet. She was too fascinated by watching. She'd never experienced Jason's kind of effortless charisma before. Especially not up close and (almost) personal this way.

To her surprise, Jason Hamilton actually seemed *nice*. Not bland nice or boring nice, but *startlingly* nice. Nice in a way that made him seem trustworthy and kind—capable of being brought home to meet someone's mother without causing an aneurism.

Clearly, her company's CEO was going above and beyond. Since when did good-looking men need personalities, anyway?

Very quickly, the official Moosby's meet-and-greet devolved into an on-the-spot Christmas party. Jason found the homemade eggnog produced by a local Kismet dairy. He ladled out cups of it for everyone—but only after sampling it himself and then making the dairy owner beam by pronouncing it "perfect—just like grandma used to make." The Kismet Klangers quit playing long enough to individually meet the man of the hour, then kicked into an inspired, kooky rendition of "Jingle Bell Rock."

Customers started dancing. Employees started singing. Even the many, many children present got into the merry spirit by hopping around amid the toys, laughing, and becoming instant devotees of Jason. One little girl presented the picture she'd colored of him. Jason rewarded her with a bright smile and an on-the-spot joint Crayola session. One little boy demonstrated his skill at assembling Legos. He stood by, awestruck, as Jason did the same—only to pronounce the boy's creation "way cooler."

A toddler entourage formed in Jason's wake, sticky fingered and wobbly legged (and occasionally brandishing woobies) but nonetheless enthralled. By the time an hour had passed, Jason still stood chatting with a rapt Henry in the middle of the crowd, casually carrying one little boy on his shoulders while joking with another little girl about her favorite video games.

That was when Gigi arrived, having been given the task of tracking down the tardy local news crew. She raised herself on tiptoe to gain a better view. She grinned as she saw that Jason now wore a Santa hat as he took more photos with customers.

"Wow. It is just me, or is he super *miam-miam*?"

Her breathy French exhalation of that phrase—roughly, *yum, yum!*—made Danielle grin. "He's *miam-miam*, all right. But I think he's about to meet his match." She aimed her chin toward the doorway, where several people were approaching carrying signs. "Those look like protestors to me. I'd better do something."

With authority, Danielle made her way through the pack. Unfortunately, it was slow going. Her customers and employees had crammed themselves in so tightly to be near Jason that she might as well have been moshing her way through a concert crowd.

Frustrated, she craned her neck to see. Uh-oh. She was too late. The leader of the protest group had reached Jason.

Why would anyone want to protest here? Danielle wondered. Maybe that group had been picketing nearby and had been drawn, magnetically and inescapably, into Jason's orbit? But if not . . .

Worriedly, Danielle pushed onward. "Excuse me. Sorry," she said. "If I can just get through, please. Thanks. I'm just going to squeeze past you, Avery. Perfect. Now Amy, if you could—"

Suddenly, the crowd shifted. Danielle's momentum carried her into a newly created open space on the sales floor.

Unexpectedly, she stood directly in front of Jason Hamilton.

He didn't notice her, though. He was busy holding up one of the protestors' signs. He nodded at it in thought.

"This must have taken a *lot* of time," he was saying in an approving tone. "Creating a BOYCOTT MOOSBY'S sign out of nothing but old shopping bags and your own ingenuity? Incredible."

"Oh, not really," the protestor demurred. Danielle recognized her as one of the retirees who took Zumba classes at the local YMCA. "It's a simple braiding technique, that's all. Plus a whole lot of glue to keep it stuck to the cardboard."

"Really? I'm impressed," Jason insisted. "All that braiding would require a lot of dexterity. And so many bags, too! Your neighbors must have all donated their bags to your cause."

"Nope, they're all *my* bags. I've been shopping here at Moosby's for a long time. But it's not strictly *my* cause." The woman shrugged. "They said on the news that we ought to protest Moosby's. I'm retired. What else did I have to do today?"

"I bet a woman like you has a lot to do. You look like the leader here. You brought everyone down here. You inspired them."

"Maybe." She gave a meager grin. "I guess maybe I did."

"Have you always inspired people this way?"

"Maybe." Her grin broadened. "I guess maybe I have."

"Well, I'm honored by your effort." Earnestly, Jason held out his hand. "Thanks for letting me know how you feel, Betty."

Betty. Of course! Danielle had forgotten the woman's name. She and Jason clasped hands, then shook. Betty withdrew first. She gazed at her own wrinkled hand with bewildered pleasure.

Danielle began to believe Jason was some kind of corporate alchemist, able to turn enemies into allies with a simple touch.

Jason set down the child who'd been on his shoulders. He waited for the boy to scamper away. Then, conspiratorially, he leaned nearer. "Betty, do you think you could keep the protest outside, though? I don't want to scare all the kids."

Betty nibbled her lip. Then she waved her hand. "Nah. I don't think we need that protest. I think you were set up!"

Her fellow protestors milled around, nodding emphatically.

"Shoot, they can do all kinds of tomfoolery with computers nowadays." A man nearby lowered his sign. "For all we know, you weren't even in the same zip code as that hotsy totsy."

"Her name is Bethany," Jason told them all. "She's funny and bright, and she's studying to become an anthropologist."

"Good for her!" cried a woman to the left of Betty.

Before long, they'd all set aside their protest signs to claim cookies and delicious cups of nutmeg-dusted eggnog instead.

It was amazing. Watching things unfold, Danielle had the impression that if Jason Hamilton could have met one at a time with all the potential protesters across the country, he could have defused all their objections without breaking a sweat. He possessed a disarming directness that no one could resist.

Fortunately for her ability to think straight, none of that infectious charm had been aimed at her yet. It probably wouldn't be anytime soon, either. Because Danielle was still mulling over those comments about Jason Hamilton having been "set up." With Bethany. In a situation that was newsworthy *and* protest worthy.

What in the world was *that* all about, anyway?

For her, it had been a whirlwind twenty-four hours. Since receiving that phone call from Chip Larsen, Danielle had had to wrangle a gala welcome party, contact the *Kismet Comet*, organize a satellite link to the nearest northwestern

Michigan TV station, make sure her store was spic-and-span, and arrange for Karlie, Zach, and Aiden to spend a few days at their dad's house.

Even at the best of times, as a single mother, Danielle didn't have a lot of free time to keep up on current events. Now she had a feeling that her lack of news watching was about to bite her in the butt.

She hadn't known there might be another reason for Jason Hamilton's Moosby's media tour, aside from the usual corporate mania to "create a Christmas buzz." That's the way Chip Larsen had described the situation to her . . . not long after congratulating her on having a "model store" and strongly hinting about her upcoming promotion, of course. The fact that actual protestors had arrived concerned her—even if they *had* joined the Jason Hamilton fan club in lieu of creating havoc in her store.

She was seriously underprepared for this, Danielle realized. There was more to Chip Larsen's momentous phone call than she'd known. Why hadn't the chairman of the board simply confided in her? Why hadn't he told her there might be protestors? Didn't the upper management trust her? Hadn't she proven herself? According to the cherished handbook, they were all supposed to be "on the same team" at Moosby's.

This wasn't going to earn her the promotion she wanted.

Unless, as part of being tested for an upper management position, she was supposed to have intercepted the protesters herself? But how could she? The only thing she'd been prepared for was a celebrity CEO meet-and-greet . . . and maybe a few photo ops with the man of the hour, followed by an ad shoot. That's all.

That's all Chip Larsen had prepped her for, at least.

He must have known this might happen. He was the chairman of the board of Moosby's! He was plugged in. She wasn't.

Danielle couldn't believe she hadn't asked more questions during that phone call. She'd obviously been blinded by her own hopes for the future—distracted by her own pride at having her work recognized . . . just the way that unctuous jerk, Chip Larsen, had probably intended her to be, all along.

This was all so . . . *confusing*. Especially with happy-go-lucky Jason Hamilton partying down, ho-ho-ho style, in the middle of her store. With several dozen admirers. What had he been caught doing with Bethany, the future anthropologist, anyway?

Irked, Danielle spun around. She made her way past partying customers, neighbors, friends, and employees, feeling her unease rise with every jolly, eggnog-brandishing person she passed.

It looked as if Moosby's HQ had played her for a fool.

They hadn't clued her in at all. Instead, without her permission or her knowledge, they'd deliberately used her store to publicly put Jason Hamilton in the midst of all his fans . . . and his detractors, too. He was probably supposed to be there apologizing for . . . whatever outrageous thing he'd done.

Which was ironic, since he didn't seem at all contrite.

Maybe they hadn't told *him* that's why he was there, either?

Whether they had or not, Jason Hamilton seemed to have stepped into his own private Waterloo, complete with protestors to instigate trouble and cameras to catch his expected downfall. It was fortunate for him that he'd been able to sidestep it.

This time, at least.

Full of foreboding for the next time, Danielle strode away, headed for her office. Partway there, amid the crush of people, she glimpsed the satellite news crew and two reporters from the *Kismet Comet* newspaper—reporters she'd dutifully called in as the Moosby's chairman of the board had suggested—recording every moment of Jason Hamilton's Christmastime visit to Kismet.

Whatever Moosby's HQ wanted out of all this—redemption for Jason Hamilton's misstep with Bethany, a trial by fire for their newest corporate exec (aka her!), or something else—those reporters were hoping for another scandal. Because it was evident there'd been at least one scandal already.

Betty hadn't handcrafted a protest sign and brought her friends downtown just for giggles. She'd had a reason for doing that—a reason instilled by the gossip-hungry cable TV news channel that was ludicrously popular in Kismet, yes. But all the same . . .

Danielle had to know more. She had to inoculate herself and her store against whatever damage Jason Hamilton's visit might cause. She did *not* intend for her store and its staff to become patsies. They might be living in a small town, but they weren't hicks. How *dare* Chip Larsen even *try* to do this?

She wasn't a stranger to feeling like a fool, Danielle acknowledged to herself as she reached her office. She'd felt exactly this way when she'd learned that Mark had been cheating on her. She'd hated it then. She hated it now. Being the unwitting dupe in someone else's deception was the *worst*.

But just in case she'd misunderstood the situation . . .

A few minutes' Internet searching on her office PC revealed that she hadn't misunderstood anything. Jason Hamilton had been photographed in a fairly compromising situation with Bethany, the nearly naked anthropologist. As Danielle clicked her way through the search results she'd uncovered, her jaw dropped.

One or two media outlets were *really* out to crucify Jason Hamilton. The photo in question was incriminating, sure. But CEOs had done far worse things than offer a toast to a woman with a pair of bodacious ta-tas. It was almost, Danielle mused to herself as the holiday tunes and general party clamor grew louder outside her open office door, as if someone was out to amplify the potential offensiveness of Jason's behavior.

It was understandable for Moosby's HQ to want to project a family friendly corporate image. As a company figurehead, Jason Hamilton was money in the bank to Moosby's—as long as he didn't cause any trouble. Now that he had . . .

A knock on her office's doorframe startled her.

She looked up from her computer. Jason Hamilton stood there watching her, with the party in the background, looking every inch the gorgeous bad boy of toy retailing she now knew he was.

Or might be. Danielle wasn't certain. News could be manipulated, just the same way people could be. But not her.

Not anymore. From here on out, she intended to be smarter.

She never intended to feel as gullible as she had when Mark had divorced her and moved in with twenty-three-year-old Crystal. Not again. Not if she could help it. Not even at work.

Especially not at work.

"Hi." Her company's hotshot CEO smiled at her. "I'm Jason."

It was the same innocuous opener he'd used on 95 percent of the people currently boogying to the Klangers' version of "Last Christmas" on her toy-filled sales floor. She knew that. But for whatever reason, that didn't matter. Upon finding herself on the receiving end of Jason's dazzling smile, Danielle wound up feeling sort of . . . *fluttery* anyway.

Damn it. *She* wasn't going to be susceptible to this.

She stood, straightening her spine. "I'm Danielle Sharpe. Welcome to Moosby's in Kismet, Mr. Hamilton. You're late. Really late. We were starting to wonder if you'd ever arrive."

Her blunt approach had its desired effect. He forgot about shaking her hand—something Danielle wanted to avoid, given its mind-scrambling effects on Betty—and apologized instead.

"Yeah. I know. I'm sorry about that." He ducked his head, treating her to an intimate view of his rumpled dark hair.

It looked soft. She wanted to run her fingers through it.

Wait. *What?* No, she didn't. That was crazy. Super crazy.

He'd been wearing a Santa hat a while ago. Where was it? If he'd still had on that hat, he might have seemed less appealing.

Ha, her inner sense of flutteriness mocked. *As if.*

"I'm not used to driving in the snow." He offered her a bashful smile, then raised his hands. "My hands are L.A. hands. Good for surfing, going to parties, and putting on sunglasses. Not so much for steering through snow flurries, I'm afraid."

Of course she looked at his hands. How could she not?

He'd invited her to. Even as Jason frowned at them with faux chagrin, Danielle studied them herself. She couldn't help drawing an altogether different conclusion than he had.

His hands were big but graceful. His fingers were long but elegant. His palms were slightly callused. They looked manly.

How did a posh, spoiled-to-the-max CEO get calluses?

"I dunno," Danielle mused aloud. "Your hands look plenty capable of doing interesting things to me."

His expression changed. Surprise darkened his eyes.

Oh, his face said. We're going to play it that way?

Gigi would have been so proud of her.

"Saluting topless women, for one thing," she went on as she casually shut down her office PC. "Do you care to explain that?"

She punctuated her question with a deliberate look. Jason's formerly relaxed posture sharpened as he glanced over his shoulder. Good. She'd managed to put him off-balance. She didn't like being the only one who'd been caught unprepared.

Under different circumstances, Danielle might have felt bad about confronting him so candidly. But today she didn't.

Because, she reminded herself, today she didn't believe for one second that Jason Hamilton didn't know his own company was playing her for a patsy. They'd woefully underestimated her in the process, though. Danielle meant to prove it, too.

Chip Larsen had misled her during their phone call. He'd flattered her. He'd taken advantage of her eagerness. But he'd forgotten one crucial detail. Thanks to him, Danielle now had exclusive access to Moosby's star CEO. For as long as Jason was in town, she had a chance to impress him—to make him see that, whether they'd ever planned to give it to her or not, she deserved the promotion they'd dangled in front of her.

That's exactly what she intended to do, too.

After all, how many Apple underlings had ever gotten a direct line to Steve Jobs? How many Facebook programmers had ever had a chance to schmooze with Mark Zuckerberg? How many Amazon.com employees had ever stood within five feet of Jeff Bezos? Not many. Powerhouse CEOs weren't usually accessible to people like her. Now that Danielle had a chance to make an impression on her megaboss, she was going to run with it.

But first, she was going to get some answers. Because the only thing stronger than her yearning to get promoted and give her kids a better life was her need *not* to be deceived.

She wanted all the facts. She wanted them now.

Before she became even more susceptible to that smile of his. Fortunately for her, at the moment, Jason Hamilton's former boyish brilliance had dimmed considerably.

Just then, Moosby's vaunted CEO didn't look like a man who'd inspired a spontaneous holiday party on her toy store's sales floor. He looked like a kid who'd been caught taking not just one forbidden cookie, but the whole damn cookie jar.

He looked . . . crestfallen. Not necessarily because he'd been caught, but because now he wouldn't get any more cookies.

"Well?" Danielle prodded, arching her brow. "I'm waiting."

Chapter Five

Damn it. He *really* needed to find Edna Gresham.

Jason decided as much, as he met the don't-mess-with-me gaze of the bespectacled brunette who'd confronted him in Moosby's back office. Looking at her was like encountering the world's hottest starlet-turned-accountant . . . one who wanted his head on a stick.

Right about then, a nice, grandmotherly, milk-and-cookies type like Edna Gresham—the person he'd expected to find there—sounded pretty good to him. Instead, he'd come face-to-face with the small-town equivalent of The Inquisitor. Given the difficult past two days he'd had, Jason wasn't in the mood for this.

On the other hand . . .

"You're asking me to explain my side of things?"

"Of the scandal that brought protestors to my store? Yes."

That was interesting. "Nobody else wanted an explanation."

She crossed her arms. Jason experienced an unprecedented urge to wrap her arms around him instead. Which was weird. The last thing he was in the market for was a freaking cuddle.

"Maybe that's because they realized asking you for an

explanation was a lost cause," she speculated with another arched brow. "Since you're dissembling instead of explaining."

"'Dissembling'?" Her glasses weren't just for effect. She was brainy. She wasn't backing down, either. At least she'd given him credit for being able to comprehend her A-plus vocabulary. She wasn't talking down to him the way Chip tried to. That was nice. "That's kind of harsh, don't you think so, Ms. Sharpe?"

He lightened his objection with a genial grin.

She stared him down. She didn't even blush. Uh-oh.

Whatever mojo he possessed, it didn't work with Danielle Sharpe. He was on his own here. Naked. In a manner of speaking.

Not that he would have minded seeing *her* naked. Or both of them naked. Together. Someplace cozy and warm and private . . .

Hell. He had to focus. What was the matter with him?

It was as if he'd never met a cute brunette who filled out a red and green *More, More, Moosby's!* holiday T-shirt and a pair of well-fitted jeans before. Which he had. Definitely.

Jason just couldn't remember exactly when, at the moment.

All he could see was her. Her stubbornly raised chin. Her glossy red lips. Her tousled dark hair and her slender, athletic frame and her take-charge stance. Her posture told him *she* was in control here and didn't intend to let him forget it.

Danielle Sharpe might be the only person within five miles, it occurred to him, who hadn't tackled six people to reach him today. He'd thought he'd met everyone except Edna Gresham and maybe the person who mopped the floors. Obviously, he hadn't.

Perversely, it bugged him that Danielle hadn't joined the throng of eager Moosby's fans. But it also impressed him that she'd asked him for an explanation for Bethanygate, rather than jump to conclusions the way his entire board of directors had.

She wasn't similarly impressed with him. "Call me Danielle," she invited him. "While you're explaining yourself."

"Okay, Danielle. Thanks. Please call me Jason." Being on a first-name basis with her was a step in the right direction. He could work with that. With a nod, Jason indicated the office. It was tidy and organized. Just like her. "Mind if I come in?"

"Be my guest." She gave an elegant wave. "You're the boss."

"For the moment, I am. If I play my cards right," he joked, squeezing in between stacked-up inventory boxes, a mini fridge, and a marked-up whiteboard with monthly sales goals written on it. "If I don't, I won't be anybody's boss by New Year's Day."

"Wow. Sounds tough."

So did her unsympathetic, disbelieving tone. "It is."

"As if anybody would get rid of the star of the company."

"It's been known to happen."

"If you're trying to distract me by making me feel sorry for you, it won't work." Danielle tapped her temple, drawing his attention to her nerdy/sexy eyeglasses. "I keep an unbelievably long to-do list up here," she informed him. "Right now, *get an explanation from you* is hanging in the number one position."

Jason grinned. "I do like a tenacious woman."

"I like an honest man. Too bad they're so hard to find."

"Whoa." He swept his gaze over the office, belatedly taking in the details. A fuzzy size-*her* jacket that had been slung over the back of the desk chair. A takeout coffee cup bearing the imprint of her vivacious red lip gloss. A framed photograph of three children, neatly aligned next to the Moosby's corporate rule book. *There was a rule book?* Huh. "Plenty of men are honest."

She snorted. "So they say. I'll believe it when I see it." She propped her hip on the edge of her desk, then gave him another no-nonsense look. "Besides, I'm not debating with you."

"You started it."

"I did not."

"Did too."

"Di—" She broke off, catching herself just in time.

Wearing an abashed look, she smiled at him.

Jason felt as though he'd invented a jet pack or a flying car. Or done something equally improbable but totally cool.

"You have a beautiful smile, Danielle." He was rapidly losing interest in tracking down staid but safe Edna Gresham. Wherever she was. "It makes your whole face glow."

"Nice try. But that's just the Christmas lights I've strung up in here. They make everything look better."

Jason doubted it. It was her. But he frowned anyway.

Christmas. Bah-humbug.

"You don't like Christmas?" she prodded upon glimpsing his expression. "If so, you're in the wrong town."

He remembered being enveloped in holiday cheer when he'd driven in—recalled being ambushed in the toy store's doorway with cheerful crowds and flashing lights and freaking "Santa Claus Is Coming to Town" being played by an oompah band in cheesy sweaters and knew that she was right about that much.

Evidently, he'd been assigned to rehabilitate his dinged public image at the merriest toy store in Kismet. Possibly in the whole world. Around here, they appeared to eat, drink, and sleep Christmas. They probably pounded eggnog like whiskey shots, shit sparkly gold ornaments, and dedicated their neighborhood watch programs to sighting Santa's flying reindeer.

He regrouped. "So, you wanted an explanation from me?"

"About an hour ago now." Another grin. "Yes."

She was sarcastic, too. Great.

Seriously great. He liked a woman with verve.

"Okay. I was on vacation. In the tropics."

"Tropical vacation, huh? Sounds fancy. Must be nice."

"Usually, it is." *Except when you're deliberately running away from your own company.* "Anyway, I was at a party when some women came up to me," Jason went on. "We were all drinking—"

"As one does at a party."

"—and having a good time, when suddenly I look to the side and see one of the women whipping off her spangled top."

"Sequins *can* be awfully itchy," Danielle deadpanned.

"There was a lot of *woo-hoo*ing going on," he told her, "and some cell phones came out, but I didn't find out about that until later, when the pictures surfaced. At the time, I was busy holding Bethany's mojito so she could put her top back on."

"Back *on*? She was getting dressed? So quickly?" Danielle gave him a faux perplexed frown. "But how did you have time to autograph lefty?" She performed a game-show-hostess-worthy *ta-da!* wave at her own T-shirted left breast. "Or was it righty?"

She arched her eyebrows expectantly. Also, hilariously.

Jason couldn't believe she'd had the audacity to pantomime that gesture. She'd *seemed* like the supersexy librarian type.

"You *are* kind of a rock-star CEO," Danielle clarified. "Isn't signing unconventional autographs part of your oeuvre?"

With vigor, she made *rock on!* devil's horns with both hands. He figured he deserved a medal for not applauding her.

If he had to be banished to the heartland for a few days, he could do worse than spend his time around someone like her.

"All Bethany wanted was a photo with me," he explained.

Oddly, when he'd spoken with Bethany, she'd mentioned that the photo her friend had taken hadn't received nearly as many hits as the impromptu ambush photo, which was apparently still circulating nonstop on the news. Jason had been in the bizarre position of consoling Bethany because not enough people had viewed the "right" photo of her. "She wanted to be part of an online meme: topless selfies with strangers."

"Sounds kinky." Danielle crinkled her nose. She shook her head. "Nope. Can't say I'm familiar with that one."

"Yeah." Jason hadn't been either. "It was only supposed to be on Bethany's Facebook page. We talked awhile longer. I found out about her anthropology studies and her self-image issues. I told her about my upcoming trip to Antigua for Christmas—"

"You're going to *the beach* for Christmas?" Danielle gave an adorable *ugh* face. "What are you, some kind of communist?"

"—and that was that. I thought it was over with."

"It wasn't over with." Danielle examined him. It felt as though she could peer into his less-than-pristine soul. "Have you seen what the news media is saying about this?"

"I try not to look. There's no payoff in it."

She stared at him with disbelief. "You don't look?"

He shrugged. "What other people think of me is their business, not mine. It's not reality. It's opinion."

"The prevailing 'opinion' seems to be that you're a hard-partying degenerate with a penchant for racy situations and a complete disregard for the consequences of your actions."

"Hmm." Jason pretended to consider that. "In that case, maybe it's more like ninety percent opinion and ten percent fact."

Danielle looked him up and down. She appeared skeptical. She shook her head. "Sixty-forty."

"Eighty-twenty."

"Seventy-thirty," she relented. "But only if you *don't*

smile. If you smile, you look as though you're on your way to cause trouble."

He felt ludicrously encouraged. At least he'd made an impression on her. "You like my smile?"

Her answering grin said she did. Contrarily, she shrugged. "As one of the several million people in this hemisphere who seem to . . ." Her eyes sparkled at him, blue and forthright. "I guess your smile probably doesn't scare small children."

As flattery went, hers was . . . subtle. But Jason loved it anyway. Because *maybe* she liked him—at least enough to kid around with him. And he, he realized, *definitely* liked her.

Why wouldn't he? Alone among everyone he could think of, only Danielle Sharpe had given him a chance to explain himself before making any assumptions. She was smart. She was in charge. She was pretty and stubborn and much too untrusting for a woman who lived in the equivalent of *The Nutcracker* come to life.

Maybe he'd been staring at snow flurries for too long, but he felt . . . *drawn* to her in a way that didn't usually happen to him.

On the other hand, women typically drew *themselves* into his orbit. It was refreshing to meet someone who made him work for her attention. Even if she was smart-mouthed. Full of questions. And way too bossy for someone who was technically in his employ.

"Scare small children? Nope. Not since I got all the braces and headgear taken off, at least," he joked. "Before that . . . whew! All the screaming, the running away, the riots that occurred—"

"Aha. Orthodontia *would* explain your perfect smile. It's all just rubber bands and night guards and fervent hope at fourteen, right? Then wham! Overnight, you're a total babe."

"Maybe *you* are." *Perfect smile* sounded good. But he'd been ad-libbing the braces talk. Sentimental journeys about orthodontia were beyond his experience. His family had struggled and scraped to afford basic dental checkups. Perfection had been out of reach. "But me—"

He shrugged, indicating that he was far from perfect.

"Nope. Don't go all modest on me now. I'm counting on you." Danielle waved away his protest. With a suddenly energetic air, she sized him up. Blatantly. At length. Given her heels-to-head scrutiny, he began to feel sort of *objectified*. Not that he minded. Not as long as she kept on looking.

"You are going to bring *so* many people into my store! I didn't have time to prepare properly for this," she confessed, "or there would have been a lot better turnout today. Just wait till I get going."

Just when he was about to crack wise about feeling like a piece of beefcake, she lifted her gaze to meet his again. Her eyes gleamed with enthusiasm. Her posture crackled with energy.

She was serious, he realized. Serious about making the Kismet Moosby's store a raving success this Christmas. With him as the . . . featured attraction? Reward? Bait? Yeah. Bait. *Man bait.*

Jason wanted to help her. He didn't understand why. He'd theoretically been blackmailed into being there. He should have been hostile. Defiant. Grumpy and demanding and full of bad attitude. Except he didn't roll that way. He never had.

Besides, maybe her salvation could be his salvation, too.

Maybe they could be a team, he mused with a burst of hope as he watched Danielle pick up a clipboard and diligently study its contents. He could help her bring customers into Moosby's. She could help him . . . appear hot for one of his own employees.

Whoops. He couldn't risk that. Not right now.

What he needed was a diversion. A buffer zone.

A way to stop wondering if Danielle brought that unstoppable energy of hers to everything she did. Even the things she did in private. Or atop a desk. In broad daylight.

He liked the way she held a clipboard. Being cradled like that, so close against her chest, would have been . . . *ahem*.

He wished he'd closed the office door behind him.

"So," Danielle mused, "I guess the folks at Moosby's HQ weren't exactly thrilled with your racy vacation pics?"

Her return to the facts was like icicles dropping from the eaves and into his back. Edna Gresham couldn't have done any better at squashing his unbusinesslike interest in Danielle.

"No." Jason quirked his lips. "They weren't."

"So this appearance in Kismet—it's meant to be your chance to apologize for looking like a horndog? Is that it?"

Wow. She pulled no punches. "That's one way to put it."

"Because usually these things are done at a podium in a big city someplace in front of scads of reporters, aren't they?"

"At Moosby's, we like to do things differently."

Danielle pursed her lips in thought. She gave him a quizzical look. "Wasn't that the title of your TED talk?"

"'Do things differently'?" A nod. "Something like that."

"Hmm. Well, you're definitely doing apologizing 'differently.'" She went back to her clipboard. Checked off an item. Examined him again. "I have to say, you're not very good at appearing contrite. Maybe you can take lessons from my ex-husband. He was *really* good at seeming sorry. Not so good at actually being sorry. Or at doing anything about it."

Jason cleared his throat. "The last thing I intend to do while I'm here is apologize. I haven't done anything wrong."

"Not yet, maybe. But the way you look . . ." Catching his somber expression, Danielle stopped abruptly. "Oh. You're serious?"

He needed to change the subject. Lately, his talk about not apologizing didn't exactly go over big. "You're divorced?"

"Two years now." Her friendly gaze pierced him. "You?"

"Me?" *I'm just happy you're single*. It was wrong. But it

was true. "I'm a die-hard bachelor, always looking for love in all the worst places. Don't you read *People* magazine?"

She laughed. The husky, compelling sound of her laughter made him want to make it happen again. Often. Endlessly.

Uh-oh. He was getting carried away again. If a harmless crosswalk flirtation had sparked alarm in him earlier, this encounter with Danielle Sharpe should have kindled utter panic.

"Nope, I don't read *People*," she admitted, unconcerned with his newfound need to behave himself. "I don't have time to keep up with what's trending in gossip magazines. If I did, Betty and her protest crew wouldn't have caught me off guard today. I'm usually better prepared than this, believe me."

Her winsome smile assured him of it. So did her clipboard.

Jason still wanted to take away that clipboard of hers and take its place himself, cradled in her arms. It was dumb but inescapable. Something about Danielle got under his skin.

If he were smart, he'd find Edna Gresham. He'd get the hell out of there before he could get himself into any more trouble. Instead, he lingered. "I do believe you. You seem . . . efficient."

Also, smart. Intimidating. Sexy. Sweet.

All the things he couldn't indulge in right now.

She smiled as though he'd delivered her the world's most awesome compliment. Her enthusiasm for efficiency was endearing.

He was crazy for thinking so.

Must. Find. Willpower. And Edna Gresham.

"Which means," Jason forced himself to say before he could lose his resolve to be shrewd about this, "you probably know where I can find Edna Gresham. I thought she'd be here, but—"

"Edna?" Danielle looked perplexed. She crinkled her

nose. "My best guess would be the yarn shop across the street."

"The yarn shop?" Edna was blowing off work? Today?

A nod. "She's an avid knitter. Otherwise, you could try The Wright Stuff, Reno Wright's sports equipment store. It's not far from here. Edna also coaches a peewee ice hockey league."

"*Edna* does?" The grandmotherly woman he'd been imagining? Hmm. Maybe Charley had gotten confused about things. Also . . . "Reno Wright? As in Reno Wright, the former star NFL kicker?"

Another nod. "He's kind of a big deal around here."

"Because he's a local who made it big in the NFL?"

"Because he usually wins the Bronze Extension Cord every year in the Glenrosen neighborhood holiday lights competition."

"Seriously?" That was surprising. Also, Jason knew, he was getting sidetracked. As cool as it would be to meet a former NFL player, he was supposed to be looking for Edna Gresham.

"No, not seriously." Danielle grinned. "Reno's famous for football. But you might have heard of his wife, Rachel. She used to work in L.A. as a celebrity stylist. Now she has her own clothing line, Imagination-Squared. It's pretty cool."

It seemed to Jason that there'd been a scandal a few years ago involving "It" girl Alayna Panagakos, a nightmarish red-carpet gown, and the stylist responsible for it. He couldn't remember the details. He didn't follow fashion. Or gossip.

Not even his own gossip. Not if he could help it.

All he remembered was that his admins at Moosby's L.A. headquarters had been abuzz about the incident at the time.

Confused, he refocused. "Sure. Anyway, I need to find Edna Gresham," he clarified. "The manager who's in charge of the model store initiative. The one who's supposed to be promoted?"

"Promoted?" Danielle looked as though someone had

cranked her smile to the delirious setting, IMAX version. In stunning 3-D and all the rest. "Then it's *real*? The promotion is real?"

"My chairman of the board promised Edna Gresham a promotion," Jason hedged, baffled by Danielle's enthusiasm. "I'm here to make sure she understands . . . the situation."

"Then there's *really* an executive position available? Still? Is it at Moosby's in L.A. or someplace international?"

Why was she cross-examining him? "There's always room to promote qualified Moosby's team members. And yes, most of our executives work from the L.A. office." Jason said so by rote, only belatedly realizing that he shouldn't be discussing this with her. He wanted to give Edna Gresham an easy letdown himself. He didn't want to make her seem foolish for believing Chip's lies. The fewer people who knew about this, the better.

"I *knew* it!" Danielle crowed. She gave an air punch, then whirled around, still hugging her clipboard. "It's happening!"

"Nothing is happening yet," Jason cautioned. Maybe Danielle thought that, with Edna promoted, *she'd* take her place as manager of the Kismet Moosby's? "I can't give more details."

About Chip's imaginary, nonexistent promotion offer.

"Of course." Danielle's eyes shone. Her eagerness was palpable. "Of course you can't say anything *official* yet."

Gulping back what appeared to be a squeal of excitement, she strode across the office. Again, Jason's gaze was drawn to the personal items in that office—the jacket, the lip-glossed coffee cup, and the framed photo. The little girl looked—

"You do mean *me*, though, right?" Danielle burst into his thoughts with a frown. Her long hair whirled as she turned to face him. "I mean, Edna hasn't worked here for six months. She's not the one who made this place a Moosby's model store."

Model store. Ugh. That again. Given Danielle's proud,

shining face and expectant attitude, Jason didn't have the heart to disillusion her about that. Not yet. Maybe not ever.

Besides, parts of it were true. Technically.

"This store *does* have the best sales in the chain," he agreed, accidentally supporting Chip's lies in the process. *Damn it.* He just couldn't help himself. He didn't want to take the heat for Chip's asshattery. He also didn't want to see Danielle's proud expression fade. Not yet. "For the past six months, this store has posted record sales in all categories."

Danielle stopped in front of him. She beamed more broadly.

Her smile was, it occurred to him, exactly the same as the little girl in the photo. That's when the truth hit him, along with Danielle's words. Too bad they were on a ten-second delay.

"*You're* Edna Gresham," Jason told her.

Edna hasn't worked here for six months. She's not the one . . .

Six months. Record sales. "Some manager" whose name Chip hadn't remembered. Charley had gotten his reconnaissance wrong.

This wasn't Edna Gresham's office. It was Danielle's.

Danielle Sharpe was the one who'd spoken with Chip about her supposed Moosby's model store. That's why she was excited.

She thought she was getting a promotion. Because of Chip. Because Chip had gotten petty and vengeful. Because Jason had refused to do the apology tour. Because Jason had stormed out of the board meeting. Now Danielle was going to pay for it.

All because Jason had had an unguarded moment with a topless woman. It wasn't even his fault. This was so messed up.

"You could put it that way, yes," Danielle was saying. She grinned at him wholeheartedly. "I'm the new Edna Gresham at this store. Except I'm better at getting results. You'll see."

She went on to describe some recent sales initiatives she'd taken. Jason was too busy kicking himself to listen carefully.

". . . so when Chip Larsen said they were contemplating major changes in management," Danielle said next, "I knew what he meant. He meant there was a promotion in the offing. For me!"

Actually, Jason mused, Chip had meant that the board was considering replacing *him* as CEO. But he couldn't tell Danielle that. He couldn't tell anyone that. He refused to believe it.

He could stop it from happening, though. *If* he behaved himself. *If* he resisted the temptation involved in being paired with an adorably fast-talking, ridiculously dishy brainiac brunette instead of a harmless grandmotherly chaperone/manager for the duration of his image-rehab tour of duty. He could do it.

He could do it *and* he could make sure that Danielle got the promotion she wanted—the promotion she'd been promised.

Because it was the right thing to do.

Also, because it might make her smile at him again.

Right from that moment, that became his mission in Kismet.

One: Get Danielle Sharpe promoted. Two: Don't flirt with her.

The two didn't have to be mutually exclusive, did they?

Just as Jason made that noble (if potentially delusional) pledge, an uproar outside the office caught his attention.

He looked beyond the stacked-up inventory boxes and the mini-fridge, past the filing cabinet, into the heart of the ongoing holiday party . . . all the way to the four camera-wielding members of the media who were very determinedly headed his way.

They'd found him. In a situation that could (given the kinds of simultaneously sappy and X-rated thoughts he'd been having about Danielle) seem less than saintly. Again. Damn it.

He wasn't a bad guy! He just looked that way on camera.

He wasn't the kind of man who let down the people who were depending on him, though. Jason knew that. Even if those people didn't realize they were doing it. Like Danielle . . . who was now added to the list of his responsibilities, along with Mr. Moosby.

That said . . . sometimes when you found yourself too far on the wrong side of the field, it was better to punt than take chances.

"So." Brightly, Jason turned to Danielle. "I really need to get out of here. Is there someplace I could go?" He looked over his shoulder. Uh-oh. They were even closer now. "Out a back door would be a really good start."

Chapter Six

"Sure. I know just the place." Now that Danielle knew that being promoted to the executive level was a real possibility, she wasn't letting Jason Hamilton out of her sight. "Come on."

As the spur-of-the-moment holiday party continued on the toy store's sales floor, Danielle spun around. She pulled a knit beanie on her head, grabbed her fuzzy, bright orange "fun fur" jacket, then snatched Jason's far swankier outdoor gear, too.

She shoved his coat and gloves in his direction.

He gawked at them. "Where did these come from?"

Danielle angled her head. "I'm guessing . . . Brooks Brothers?"

A hasty grin. "I mean, I took them off out there."

He nodded toward the bustling sales floor.

"I brought them in here, where they belong."

"Wow. Stealthy *and* organized. Mostly stealthy. I didn't even see you do that." Jason glanced behind her, noticing for the first time where she'd retrieved his things from. He boggled. "No, mostly organized. I have a locker here already?"

"Everyone does." She didn't see what was so mind-bending about a simple employee locker with a neatly labeled name tag. "While you're here, you do, too. Come on. The door's this way."

Danielle led the charge toward it, expertly weaving between precariously tall stacks of boxed inventory. Officially, everything was supposed to fit neatly on the metal shelving that filled two-thirds of the toy store's back room and office area. Realistically, she had as much chance of making that happen as she did of making a candy cane fit up her nose. No go. At all.

"Whoa," Jason said. "There's a lot of stuff back here."

"Mmm-hmm." Danielle didn't want to talk about that. Many of the toys currently in the back room were in transition between stores as part of her self-devised inventory scheme. Instead, she leaned on the exit door. "Hurry up! They're gaining on us."

They weren't. Not really, she glimpsed as she nearly thrust her boss out the back door. The members of the local media who'd been headed toward the office area had been intercepted by Gigi.

Thanks, mon amie! Danielle pantomimed an *I'll call you* gesture toward her number-one salesclerk, then stepped outside.

There in the snowy alleyway, Jason paced, hastily pulling on his expensive-looking wool coat. He put on his gloves next, clenching his jaw as though frostbite might instantly set in.

California men. They didn't know what to do without sunshine. It was a perfectly acceptable December day, too, with bluish wintertime skies overhead and just enough brightness to make the snowdrifts glisten along the side of the building.

"Don't worry, Golden State," she assured him as she bit back a grin. "The back alley isn't our final destination."

"Good. A person could die out here."

"Sure. If they didn't have the sense to walk fifty feet."

"Those snow flurries are blinding."

"Not right now, they're not." Danielle drew in a refreshing gulp of icy air. Was she seriously about to play hooky from work? With her boss? Yes, she was. "Where are you parked?"

"Out front, along the street." Jason gestured. "At a free meter." His hard-jawed face darkened. "Speaking of which—"

"We'd better not risk it. I'm right around the block."

Determinedly, Danielle marched in the direction of her car, wiggling into her own jacket and gloves as she went, not wanting to give Jason any time to discuss the parking meter situation.

Judging by his expression, he wasn't a fan of her holiday initiative to bring customers downtown. It probably wouldn't be the first of her tactics with which the CEO disagreed, either.

"Here we are." Remotely, she unlocked the doors to her old but reliable sedan. She glanced at Jason as they neared its parking space. "I'll expect you to chip in for gas, you know."

Bringing up the rear, Jason stopped. He grinned at her.

"You think I'm kidding?" She stared at him over the top of her frosted-over car. "Times are tight, buster. Gas isn't cheap. I can't afford to gallivant all over town as your personal getaway driver. Not on what you pay me."

As bids for a raise went, it was a little weak.

But it was an opening salvo in her quest to get promoted, and that was all Danielle wanted. As soon as she'd heard Jason describing the executive opportunities at Moosby's in L.A., she'd been 100 percent in. Now her mission was twofold:

One: Get Jason Hamilton to promote me. Two: Don't flirt with him.

The first of those goals ought to be easy, she figured. She was qualified. He seemed reasonable. Success was inevitable.

The second . . . well, even now, Jason was making the second goal seem more difficult than it had to be. Why did he have to look so nice all the time? So handsome? So capable of using those hands of his to work a girl into a state of delirious bliss?

Just the fact that she was talking to herself in sappy terms like *delirious bliss* meant she was in trouble. Most of the time, Danielle knew, she was not the romantic pushover type.

Not anymore, she wasn't. Now she was jaded. Wary. And much too smart to get involved—especially with an easy-come, easy-go type like Jason, who was only in town for a few days at most.

He wasn't even being serious about repenting for the scandal he'd caused! That was incomprehensible. If *she'd* gotten in trouble with her board of directors, Danielle knew, she would have worked her tail off until she'd fixed the problem. Jason clearly favored a different approach to professional redemption.

A *stupid* approach, if you asked her. Which *ought* to have lessened his appeal. He wasn't at all her type. But she liked him anyway. Which was making it trickier than she'd expected to keep things professional. Not that she couldn't do it, of course. It would be easier, though, if he would, for instance, quit *smiling* at her! Even now, in midflight from the local media, Jason was grinning at her in a way that made Danielle wonder exactly what else could make him smile like that.

Puppies? Gingerbread men? *Her*, being penny-pinching in a way that he, Mr. Moneybags, had obviously never had cause to be?

Defensively, she added, "Look, I'm rescuing you here. The least you could do is not seem so entertained by my budget issues. *And* pony up a few bucks in advance, maybe, too." She held out her hand. "For all I know, you might stiff me later."

"Wow, you *are* untrusting."

"You're sidestepping the issue."

"Sorry." Jason sobered. "I'm not laughing at your budget."

Silently and (she hoped) dauntingly, she stared him down.

Gee. He had *really* nice eyes. Warm, brown, melty . . .

"I'm laughing at your jacket."

"What? Why?" Affronted, she looked down at herself—at her orange "fun fur" jacket. "What's wrong with my jacket?"

"Nothing." His grin widened. "It's a . . . surprising choice for a woman who brandishes a clipboard as effectively as you do."

"Huh?"

"A woman who, if I'm not mistaken, wielded a label-making machine just this morning to tag an employee locker for me."

"So?" Those label makers were wildly popular with kids.

"And who tidied up someone else's coat and gloves."

"I'm not sure what you're driving at."

"You act like a librarian CPA," Jason clarified, "all Dewey Decimal System and alphabetized clipboards." He grinned again. "But you look like Cookie Monster's glamorous kid sister."

"Hey!"

"After a drunken shopping spree."

He was hallucinating. "Just get in the car."

"You seem more like the classic peacoat type to me."

I love peacoats. She appreciated their traditionalism. They'd stood the test of time; she liked that about them. She couldn't imagine how Jason had guessed as much about her.

Her own mother hadn't been that astute. Instead, Blythe Benoit had given Danielle this fuzzy orange jacket as a part of her ongoing efforts to morph her staid offspring into the kind of artistic daughter she'd always wanted. Danielle hadn't had the heart (or the financial wherewithal) to refuse it. No matter what outerwear (peacoat) she'd have preferred (peacoat).

"You seem like the type who doesn't know when to stop talking." Danielle opened the driver's-side door. "I'm leaving. If you're coming with me, fork over your cash and get in."

She slid into the driver's seat and inserted the key.

Fifteen seconds later, the passenger-side door opened. A twenty-dollar bill fluttered inside. It landed on the console.

Jason came next, confidently settling his rangy frame beside her. "Remind me not to get started on your beanie."

Automatically, Danielle clapped her hand on her knit hat. "Hey! It's practical." She looked down. He was wearing glossy wing tips. "Which is more than I can say for those shoes. You need a pair of boots that can handle the snow. Stat."

He shrugged. "I didn't expect to be here."

"Me either." It was surreal having her boss in her car. Really surreal. Also, the fancy-pants CEO of Moosby's really *did* have fancy pants, it occurred to her. That gray flannel fabric looked especially luxurious when contrasted with the wadded-up homework papers, discarded granola bar wrappers, and single pink polka-dotted ponytail holder littering the front of her car.

Why hadn't she cleaned up yesterday?

Oh yeah. She'd been in a panic preparing for *him* to arrive.

Well, now she'd have to clean her car, text Gigi, get the Kismet Klangers a thank-you gift for playing today, call the—

"I think you said something about leaving?" Jason's husky, sardonic voice broke into her mental to-do list compilation.

Danielle glanced up, instantly snapped back to the present. Where she was sitting next to the man who could make her dreams come true with a single phone call. Ogling his pants. Whoops.

"Is there something wrong with my pants?" he asked.

Inevitably, she felt her gaze drawn straight back to them. To their fancy fabric. Their impeccable fit. Their tailored cut.

Their owner, who fit into them with enthralling ease.

He didn't even have the tiniest *suggestion* of a paunch, Danielle realized with disbelief. Most men she encountered locally, even those her own age and younger, were a little . . .

soft. But Jason seemed to be completely *hard*. Everywhere. Taut and toned and probably possessed of those six-pack abs she'd heard about but had never personally experienced for herself.

She may have missed out, Danielle realized, by getting married straight out of college to the third man she'd seriously dated in her whole life. She may have missed . . . a lot. Like Jason.

Who was still waiting for her to answer his question.

This kind of daydreaming wasn't going to impress him.

"No!" Purposely, Danielle gave a jovial chuckle. "There's nothing wrong with these pants of yours. Nothing at all!"

To prove it, she slapped her hand on his thigh. The gesture was supposed to be reassuring. Carefree. A man-to-man kind of thing. The trouble was, Danielle wasn't a man. But he was.

Beneath her palm, Jason's thigh felt like hot granite. Even through her cable-knit gloves, she could feel his body heat.

For an instant, their gazes met. Something . . . *sizzled* between them. She had the dizzying impression that he wanted her to touch him. There. On his thigh. Personally and directly. She had an equally dizzying impulse to slide her hand higher, higher . . .

Ahem. With effort, Danielle gave him a cordial pat.

"I should buy a pair of these for my ex-husband."

She removed her hand. Casually, she transferred it to the ignition key. Shakily, she started her car. It chugged to life.

Unfortunately, so did Danielle's libido. On hiatus for the two years since her divorce, it raged back in a single instant.

She wanted to touch someone. To *be* touched by someone. To kiss and caress and experience every intimate, erotic pleasure she'd denied herself during the breakup of her marriage. She wanted it. She wanted it all. She wanted it now. Somehow, touching Jason Hamilton had flipped a switch.

One moment, she'd been Danielle Sharpe: responsible mother, employee, and friend. The next, she'd morphed into Danielle Sharpe: lusty divorcée.

This wasn't going to help her get promoted.

Well, it *might*, Danielle knew. But she wasn't a woman who took things she hadn't earned. She never had been.

"You buy clothes for your ex-husband?" Jason asked.

Argh. Her common sense had deserted her today.

"We're very close," Danielle semi-fibbed. Because in the few months since Mark had married his ditzy bride, she *had* been closer to her ex than she wanted to be. She was constantly running into those two lovebirds, canoodling and cooing, around every Kismet corner. If she had to endure much more, she was going to lose her mind. "Almost *too* close, some would say."

"Good." Not catching her fib, Jason nodded. He was staring at her gloved hand on the steering wheel, probably wondering if her grope officially qualified as harassment. "Being able to maintain positive ongoing relationships with difficult people is an asset in any employee, for any position, in any company."

With that, Danielle felt even worse. Obviously, Jason was operating in employer/employee, all-business mode. Whereas *she . . .*

. . . was wondering if his voice got even huskier when he was aroused. She bet it did. She bet Jason sounded super sexy all the time, but especially when murmuring sensual suggestions to his partner in the bedroom. Or the toy store office. Or the car.

The car? Holy moly. She had to get a grip here.

And *not* on her boss's muscular, intriguing thigh.

"That's me. I have excellent people skills." Belatedly, Danielle realized that this meant that if Jason and Mark ever inhabited the same location at the same time, she would have to be especially communicative and kind to her ex-husband.

Not that she was bitter; she wasn't. She and Mark had worked out their issues. Her disappointment in their marriage was behind her. All that remained now was prudent wariness of future romances.

Which was why, her newly awakened libido pointed out eagerly, she needed a fling! Nothing more. Just a celebratory, *now I'm free*, casual kind of relationship. Something that would help her get back on the horse, so to speak. Something fun.

Jason Hamilton might be fun, Danielle considered. Even if her temporarily Midwesternized boss *was* bundling up in his coat as if they were enduring subzero temperatures inside her car.

"Cold?" she asked in her best solicitous employee voice. She was going to get promoted or go down swinging. No matter how challenging it was. "Here, boss. I'll crank the heat for you."

Congratulating herself on successfully stepping away from the libidinous brink, she did so. Then she pulled into traffic.

This, Danielle told herself with a fresh burst of confidence over her own self-control, *was going to be a piece of cake.*

Sitting beside Danielle in her boneshaker sedan, Jason stared out at the picturesque Kismet streets as they made their getaway from the journalists who'd pursued him at Moosby's.

They were only doing their jobs, he reminded himself. It wasn't their fault their jobs involved preying on every disaster, large or small. He was lucky he'd escaped when he had.

Not that he'd been doing anything wrong, per se. But, newly gun-shy after his recent PR debacle, Jason had *felt* as if he'd been doing something *very* wrong. He'd felt as if his thoughts had been written all over his face, ready for anyone to read.

Ready for anyone to discover that he liked Danielle Sharpe in more than a professional, *More More Moosby's!* kind of way.

Which was dumb. And unreasonable. And unlikely. After all, he had a kickass poker face. When given enough warning, he was capable of making sure his thoughts were his own. Maybe, after all he'd been through this week, he was getting paranoid.

That would explain a lot, Jason knew. Because he definitely wasn't himself today. For instance, Danielle had done nothing but sensibly question him, generously listen to him, and then (improbably) help him. And what had he done in return?

He'd gone from cold to hot, from intrigued to all-in, and from zero to half-mast, in twelve seconds flat. All Danielle had had to do was innocuously lay her hand on his thigh.

It was obvious, in retrospect, that she'd only been being friendly. In that aw-shucks, small-town, think-nothing-of-it way that probably came naturally to people here in Christmasville. He'd been the one who'd taken the whole encounter to Smutty Town. Only in his mind, sure. But in his mind . . .

. . . in his mind, Jason had imagined *so* much more. He'd envisioned Danielle smiling seductively at him as she scooted a little closer across the console, past the twenty bucks she'd extorted from him for gas. He'd seen her sliding her hand higher, then even *higher*, making his breath catch and his body go rigid with expectation and hope and surprise. He'd pictured her unbuckling his belt, unzipping his pants, freeing him . . .

Stop it. With an uncomfortable grunt, Jason shifted in his seat again. He pulled his coat closer for good measure (and for modesty coverage), trying to ignore the heat blasting him.

Cold? Here, boss. I'll crank the heat for you.

As if he needed to feel any hotter than he already did.

Ruefully, Jason thought back on their conversation. It seemed evident to him that Danielle was sincerely interested in earning a promotion to Moosby's executive level. He'd tried to play along with that. He'd tried to support her by praising her expertise at maintaining ongoing relationships with difficult people (like her ex-husband). But he'd been spit-balling, and Jason knew it. Not that that quality wasn't welcome in an employee. It was. Of course. But at that moment, the last thing he'd wanted to do was contemplate desirable employee skill sets.

Especially with a woman wearing an outrageous orange fur jacket. He still couldn't wrap his head around the dichotomy of that. Upon meeting Danielle, he'd pegged her as an organized, clipboard-wielding, superserious corporate climber—albeit a sexy, bespectacled one. Then she'd put on that ridiculous jacket—which he had already decided must belong to the little girl in the photograph on the desk but didn't—and all his assumptions had been blown out of the water. With that jacket and her vivid red lip gloss and her self-assured demeanor, Danielle was not the kind of woman he'd expected to find in Kismet. She was . . . not easy to pigeonhole. And he was fascinated.

Not that he intended to do anything about it. He couldn't. He'd already sworn to himself that he wouldn't even flirt with her. That meant that, say, putting his hand on *her* jeans-clad thigh, right then, was definitely off limits. Forever.

. . . *and* now he couldn't quit thinking about her thighs.

Brilliant. He was terrible at self-control. Not that he'd ever had to exercise much of it. Jason wasn't sure how it had happened, but he'd gotten in way over his head with this.

Maybe this was what came of actually going inside one of his own stores. At Christmastime. With more to come and no escape possible for days. He was right to have avoided it.

On the other hand, it wasn't as though he could just have his way with Danielle. She was clever. She was ambitious. She was willing to call him on his bullshit, too. He respected her for that. She'd recognized right away that there was more to his visit to Kismet than Chip Larsen had let on. She was no rube.

Inadvertently proving it, Danielle gave him an astute glance. "Now that your scandal has followed you here," she said, "you realize that you've put my store at risk, right? Along with my promotion? If we don't meet our sales targets, I'm toast."

He hadn't thought of it that way. Now that he had . . . it sucked. He wasn't sure how this problem kept getting bigger.

But he also wasn't willing to discuss it at length.

"That 'scandal' should have died down by now." At least talking about it obliterated the need to hide his lap with his coat. Jason opened it all the way, hoping to cool off from the tropical heat wave she'd induced on his behalf. "I don't know why it's keeping people's interest. It's just one photo."

"It's 'just one photo' that raises a few questions about you. About your character." Danielle braked to allow a group of workers carrying municipal holiday decorations to cross the road. Their huge, light-up jingle bells and neon ornaments bopped along in their arms, lending a quirky vintage Christmas vibe to the iced-over street they'd stopped on. "People trust you. They think of you as 'that nice guy who brings toys to my kids.' They don't want to feel they've mislaid their trust."

"They haven't mislaid their trust." This was veering dangerously close to doubting his integrity. Again. Jason frowned. Besides . . . "I never made any promises to anyone."

"Maybe not outright, you didn't." Danielle turned a corner, then cruised down a side street lined with small houses. Most of them boasted Christmas lights strung on their eaves and lawn ornaments propped in their snowy yards. One or two also had snowmen. "But after a while, people make assumptions. You've been in the public eye. You've built charities. You've been on TV. Familiarity builds trust. That's just the way it is."

"Maybe for some people." *Gullible people.*

"Trust leads to vulnerability," Danielle argued. "Vulnerability leads to hurt. *That's* why people are mad."

Huh? "You make that sound inevitable." He waited. Her silence told him she believed it was. "I didn't hurt anyone."

"How do you know that? Are you standing in their shoes?"

"Are we still talking about my public peccadilloes?" Jason aimed a speculative glance at her. "Or something else?"

Like, oh, I dunno . . . your busted-up marriage, maybe?

Her ex-husband must be a real piece of work, he decided.

"Peccadilloes? Nice vocab, boss."

Nice diversionary tactic on her part. His estimation of Danielle went up another notch. Affably, Jason said, "You can thank my board of directors for my diverse vocabulary. I think they were running out of new ways to describe how wrong I was."

"Aha. If the board had to go over things multiple ways with you, you must be the stubborn type. Hence, your non-apology."

"It's not stubbornness. It's standing my ground."

"Fine. All I'm saying is, nobody likes being duped."

"I didn't dupe anyone. All I did was go to a party while on vacation and get photographed in a compromising situation."

"Mmm-hmm. That sounds reasonable enough. I wouldn't suggest using that as your opening salvo in your public apology, though. You sound zero percent contrite." Sagely, she shook her head. "You think the facts are all you need here, but they're not."

"I already told you—I'm not making a public apology."

She briefly tightened her lips, which told him Danielle thought he ought to. But Jason didn't care. He'd already made up his mind.

"What you need to do is address the *real* problem," she told him, moving on without missing a beat. She was dogged. He'd admit that. "You need to change the way people feel about you."

"I don't remember asking for advice."

Coolly, Danielle adjusted her knit beanie. She squinted into the rearview mirror. "Maybe you should have."

"Maybe I'm getting it anyway."

"Maybe you are." She grinned, then turned a corner. A renovated gas station came into view, surrounded by a parking lot crammed full of cars. "Look, all I want is for you to make sure my store doesn't turn into a battleground. I can't afford to have the place full of noncustomers right now. This month, I need *shoppers* in Moosby's, not reporters and protesters."

"The reporters will go away now that the meet-and-greet is over." *Now that they can't catch me in another incriminating situation.* "I already took care of the protesters."

"Actually . . . I saw that. It was masterful."

"Masterful?" It was his turn to grin—and to feel a weird, warm glow spread in his chest, too. "I like the sound of that."

"Keep up the good work, then." Danielle pulled into the parking lot. She parked her car, then looked at him directly. "Do whatever you have to do to fix this problem. Okay?"

What he had to do was make himself look perfect, Jason knew. Probably, with her smarts, Danielle realized that, too.

"Feel free to use me to help out," she went on as she grabbed her purse. "I'm motivated, I'm capable, and I'm well connected around here. It benefits us both if your visit to Kismet is successful, right? If I were you, I'd be working overtime to do whatever makes the Moosby's board happy."

Jason blinked at her, once again surprised at her savvy. She'd sized up the situation and was meeting it head-on.

"I'll take care of it," he told her. "Don't worry."

Whatever else happened, it occurred to him, at least he

wouldn't have to tiptoe around Danielle's feelings. She wasn't just blunt; she was pragmatic, too. He liked that about her.

Now, if only she were *also* ridiculously well-liked, thoroughly respected in Kismet, and capable of single-handedly renovating his image for him. Then he would be set.

Because now he had carte blanche to use her to help him. Not that he planned to, Jason knew. But if push came to shove . . .

Well, Danielle *had* volunteered to be part of his Mr. Clean image rehab, hadn't she? That meant she knew exactly what he needed from her. She'd recognized that he wasn't A: apologizing, so she'd moved on to strategy B: making over Jason Hamilton into a new and improved, G-rated, triple-A-approved CEO.

"Telling me not to worry is like telling Christmas not to creep into stores the day after Halloween." Danielle gave him a wry smile. "The only antidote is to *do*. So whatever you need—"

What he needed, Jason realized in a single crazy moment, was to get closer to her. Closer, closer, *nakedly* closer . . .

No. He should not be thinking about getting closer to Danielle. He should be taking his cues from her instead. *She* was busy strategizing how best to rehab him. *He* was fantasizing an under-the-mistletoe tête-à-tête. Their two different approaches only underlined the truth. Danielle Sharpe was hardworking, wholesome, generous, and kind. Jason was . . . not. Maybe, he hoped, her positive aura would rub off on him while he was in town.

And that was as far as he wanted to go to "use" her.

"I won't need you to do anything special," Jason told her. "As far as I'm concerned, you've already done more than enough."

"What?" She laughed. "Of course I haven't already done enough! We've barely gotten started. You haven't even seen what I can do. Not firsthand." She shook her head at him. "At least let me have a chance to impress you before you turn into Mr. Munificent, okay? I'm looking for a win here, not a gimme."

"It's not going to be a gimme." If what Jason suspected was accurate, morphing himself into someone family friendly enough to satisfy the media mob and his board of directors would be hard work. "It's going to take effort, luck, and diligence."

It's going to take not exploring my interest in you.

"Effort, luck, and diligence? No problem." Clearly undaunted, Danielle shrugged. "I'm aces at all three."

"You can't be 'aces' at luck." Also, he wasn't 100 percent sure what "Mr. Munificent" meant. Her describing him that way puzzled him. Not for the first time, Jason wished he'd gotten a degree. Instead, he'd gone to work full-time for Mr. Moosby. Given his background, making a living had been more important than getting credentialed—not that he could have afforded college anyway. "It's luck. It either happens or it doesn't."

"Is that what you think?"

"That's what I know."

He also knew that Danielle looked *really* cute with her beanie and her glasses and even her dumbass fluffy coat. When those things were mixed with her take-charge demeanor and her extrasharp mind, the combination made for an intriguing package.

"I know that luck is what happens when preparation meets opportunity," Danielle informed him. "I make my own luck."

"I make my own popcorn and cranberry garland."

His deadpan delivery made her grin. "Ha. Nice try. Spend another hour in Kismet, and that'll be true."

Jason snorted with disbelief. "Never."

"You keep saying that. 'Never' apologize. 'Never' admit you're wrong. 'Never' pay twenty bucks for a short car ride." Her grin flashed again. "You'll see. In this town, cynicism doesn't stand a chance. Neither does disagreeing with me."

Uh-oh. This again? "If you think I'm going to back down—"

And apologize, he was about to say, but her telltale stubborn expression made clarifying himself unnecessary. She understood his position perfectly. She just didn't accept it.

Maybe he was wrong about Danielle being pragmatic.

"I think," she mused, "that by the time I'm through with you, you'll do whatever I want." Danielle nodded toward their destination. "I could have taken you anywhere. I'm taking you *here* to soften you up before making the rest of my moves."

Diligently trying *not* to hope that her "moves" involved performing some sort of naughty striptease for him, Jason peered through the windshield at the people coming and going from . . .

"The Galaxy Diner?" He examined the renovated gas-station-turned-diner. He appreciated its appeal. "Sorry to disappoint you, but I've experienced cheeseburgers and pie before."

"Not like this, you haven't."

He remembered the waitress, Avery, and her friend, Amy, from his meet-and-greet at Moosby's. "Aha. We're not here to eat. We're here to make sure everyone knows I'm in town."

"Bingo. Sooner or later, everyone comes to the Galaxy Diner." She gave him an approving look. "See? It's not so bad being reasonable and responsible. You'll get used to it."

Jason doubted it. Semimorosely, he eyed the place. It appeared even busier than Moosby's. "I'm going to get mobbed."

"If we're lucky. Yeah." Danielle tossed him another cheeky grin. "Half the town is in here. *You're* going to impress them."

"And *you're* going to reap the rewards when they all troop off to Moosby's afterward, or tomorrow, hoping to see me again."

Her nod reminded him of the facts: Danielle considered him man bait. Even under these bizarre circumstances, she was still trying to conduct booming business . . . whereas he was considering giving up everything just so he could be free to pursue her.

He never had been any good at impulse control.

Fortunately, at that instant, Jason caught a distracting glimpse of movement from the corner of his eye. It looked as though his unknown shadow from the street-side parking incident had followed him to the Galaxy Diner. But how? And why?

He couldn't be sure. But that flicker of movement reminded him that there was a lot at stake here. For Mr. Moosby's sake—and for Danielle's, even though she didn't realize it—he had to succeed. If Chip Larsen and the board *were* spying on him . . .

He had to be squeaky-clean. Unimpeachable.

"Well, I make it a point not to let people down." Jason meant her. And Mr. Moosby. And even Charley, who'd gone out of his way to try to prevent Chip's corporate coup—even if he *had* gotten the details wrong about Edna Gresham being the store manager in Kismet. "So let's get this ball rolling."

"Right. Let's." Danielle nodded. She inhaled. She gave him a final grin. "Last one inside pays for both of us!"

Then she opened her car door and sprinted through the snow.

Chapter Seven

With a strategic head start, Danielle reached the finish line—aka, the Galaxy Diner's packed entryway—in record time. As usual, the place was jammed with customers, all of them eager to taste Kristen Miller's famous pie-in-a-jar specialties . . . and to be wowed, however unexpectedly, by the "Sexiest CEO Alive."

Jason might not have come to town to apologize, Danielle reminded herself as she waited for him to catch up with her, and he might have refused to back down in his standoff with Moosby's board of directors. But he'd also delighted her customers today, *and* he'd offered to promote her on the spot, too.

She couldn't help feeling encouraged by that. After all, what else could Jason have meant when, earlier, he'd confided that as far as he was concerned, she'd already "done more than enough"? That sounded as though he'd already made a decision about her promotion. About *her*. About her future.

Who knew playing hooky with the boss could be so lucrative?

Not that Jason's enthusiasm was unjustified, Danielle

knew. She was an impressive, innovative toy store manager. She was extraordinary in other ways, too, she knew. For example, just moments ago, she'd managed to rein in her urge to grope him again (although she'd had to grip her steering wheel extra hard to keep her hands to herself). And, of course, she was notable in her determination to make Jason see reason and just *apologize* already, so she could get on with being awarded her promotion.

So she could get on with leaving Kismet. Sooner rather than later. For the sake of her kids and their future. And herself.

Despite everything, though, Danielle was savvy enough to realize that impressing Jason wouldn't be enough. Not if his own board of directors was mad at him. To be on the safe side, she needed to make sure Jason and the board were on friendly terms.

She needed to make sure he apologized, just the way Chip Larsen wanted him to. She'd already made inroads toward that goal, too. Jason had reacted with surprising cooperativeness when she'd demanded he keep the media and protestors out of her store. She'd been blunt, but her direct approach had paid off.

Obviously, so far, she'd chosen the right tactics to use with Jason. But that didn't explain the way he'd reacted when she'd offered to let him use her—and her store's exemplary sales performance—to his advantage. As far as Danielle could see, his being associated with a Moosby's model store would only impress the board *and* the public. So would his official apology, once she persuaded him to give it. She was sure she could do that.

She could do a lot, once she put her mind to it.

Today, for instance, she'd wanted to assure Jason that, even in his current predicament, she could be an asset to him. He'd responded as if she'd promised him he'd get everything he wanted under the Christmas tree this year . . . and more. She didn't understand his reaction. But that didn't mean she couldn't keep going forward with her plan to make the most of being with him.

She didn't need to understand Jason Hamilton to help him. Just as she didn't need to believe in the myth and celebrity of her company's CEO to benefit from that mythos. Because Jason had been right: Danielle *did* intend to drive traffic to her toy store by using his incredible magnetism to her advantage.

Why not? It wasn't as though Jason was oblivious to the effect he had on people. He knew people were drawn to him—including her. He didn't mind getting to know his company's customers. And she wanted him to get to know *her. Intimately.*

Except that wasn't part of her plan. It couldn't be.

Could it?

Breathless from her sprint inside, Danielle glanced toward the parking lot. She spotted Jason. He'd been waylaid outside the Galaxy Diner by a pair of excited Kismet tourists. Their multiple shopping bags—all from kitschy downtown antiques stores and expensive boutiques instead of discount stores—were dead giveaways. So were their knit stocking caps emblazoned with the words HAVE A VERY KISMET CHRISTMAS and the van that waited to ferry them back to one of the local B&Bs after their shopping spree.

Watching Jason amiably chat with the two tourists, Danielle couldn't help feeling even more attracted to him. He was just so *nice*. So generous. So ridiculously good-looking. Seeing him in the midst of her humdrum hometown surroundings was as bizarre as finding him in her car amid snack wrappers and homework papers.

Jason Hamilton didn't belong in her world. But he was all the more compelling because of it. What woman hadn't fantasized about meeting a gorgeous stranger . . . one who only wanted *her*?

What woman hadn't dreamed of a hot-hot-*hot* holiday fling? If that fling were with a rich, powerful, incredibly charismatic CEO, well . . . so much the better, right?

Too bad she was the only one who was stuck on that sizzling scenario, Danielle mused. As far as she could tell, Jason was focused solely on business. So far, he'd conducted himself like the perfect professional . . . whereas Danielle wanted to throw caution to the wind and treat herself to more than candy canes and fruitcake this year. She wanted to abandon her pursuit of a promotion and pursue Jason instead—with every intention of getting him naked.

Maybe she could, it occurred to her. After all, she'd already clarified her position with him. She'd already stressed that she didn't want Jason pulling some Mr. Munificent routine and handing her an undeserved promotion. He'd agreed to that.

They'd reached an understanding. She'd purposely taken the possibility of preferential treatment off the table. If she did get promoted, Danielle knew, it wouldn't be as a thank-you for sleeping with the boss. It would be earned on her merits.

There wouldn't be any confusion about their relationship, either. After all, Jason was a man. (He was *all* man.) Men could compartmentalize, couldn't they? Her ex-husband, Mark, certainly had. He'd compartmentalized his way into staying married to her while fooling around with Crystal. So if *that* was possible . . .

Ugh. Reminded of that disaster and all the unwanted fallout from it, Danielle shook herself. She was insane to even consider having a fling. She wasn't a fling kind of woman. She was . . .

. . . the kind of woman who gawked, hungrily and helplessly, at her unrepentant boss as he burst into the diner in her wake.

Yanked from her fantasies, she became newly aware of

the murmur of conversation surrounding her. Inside the diner, there was an appealing air of conviviality and an ongoing soundtrack of holiday music. There were tables full of customers and more Christmas decorations than existed in the whole seasonal section at Danielle's favorite local discount store—some of them collected by Kristen and her employees, others donated by her more famous sister, pop songstress Heather Miller.

But Jason had no awareness of any of those details. His hair was windswept. His expression was arresting. His eyes were that same melty shade of chocolate brown that she'd noticed earlier. Mmmm. *Chocolate.* Danielle liked chocolate almost as much as she liked unfastening a man's button-down shirt, peeling away its luxurious fabric, exposing the muscular chest beneath . . .

. . . staying employed and responsible. Damn.

If Jason wasn't into her, making a move on him would turn things awkward in a hurry. She'd better try to rein herself in.

"I hope your wallet's fat," Danielle said to distract herself, "because I *love* pie. And you're paying for both of us."

"Pie? Yeah, I guess pie's okay." Jason swept his gaze over the diner's unique décor, taking in its overall ambiance as well as its over-the-top Christmassiness. Holiday garlands wrapped around the chairs and along the vintage Formica countertops. Multicolored lights flashed overhead. Three Christmas trees of varying sizes had been wedged in between the dining tables, the kitchen area, and the painted windows. Each tree was decked out with more lights, garlands, and ornaments. Everyone in town knew that Kristen Miller was crazy about Christmas and everything that came with it. "I'm more of a cookie man, myself, to tell you the truth," Jason admitted. "I can take or leave pie."

"Not this pie, you can't."

Skeptically, he scrutinized the plates—each topped with

a tidy napkin, a mini-pie-filled wide-mouth Mason jar, and a garnish—coming and going in the hands of the busy servers. Those plates would not have been out of place in a glossy foodie magazine. Jason shrugged. "I think I'm immune to pie."

Several people waiting in the entryway gasped. Danielle grinned. "You probably think you're immune to Christmas, too."

"Aren't you?" he countered. "You work in retail. You know how the sausage is made. You're part of it all."

"My Christmas gullibility"—*or the lack of it, to be more precise*—"is not under discussion here."

"Aha. Gullibility, huh? That word choice says it all."

Whoops. "Well, I'm a townie," Danielle explained with a shrug. She didn't want Jason to think she was some kind of heartless Grinch. She wasn't. Years in, she'd simply grown weary of all the ho-ho-ho-ing. "I grew up with all this stuff. I'm not likely to get starry-eyed over tinsel and sleigh rides."

"There are sleigh rides? Awesome."

"I'll take you on one," she offered, "if you want."

"I want. Absolutely. How fast does the sleigh go?"

"You know." She gave a vague wave. "Horse speed."

Jason eyed her. "You've never taken a sleigh ride, have you?"

Guilty. "I didn't say that."

"You didn't have to." He shook his head with pretend dismay. "Surrounded by all this . . ." His gaze took in the over-the-top holiday brouhaha in the diner. Shifted outside to encompass the entirety of Kismet. Moved to her. "But immune to it all."

"I didn't say I was immune. Only a Grinch would be immune."

A Grinch might not be promotable. Not in the toy biz.

"So you don't like Christmas," Jason mused aloud, "yet now you manage the merriest toy store in Kismet?"

"Now I'm trying to get promoted *out* of Kismet. Remember?"

"But you want to stay in the toy business?"

"Of course. I love working at Moosby's!" She felt herself inadvertently jostled a few steps nearer to him as the entryway continued filling up. "When Edna hired me, it was a lifesaver."

His gaze turned compassionate. "Because of your divorce?"

"Partly. I needed the money. And the distraction."

"It must have been difficult. Were you married long?"

Long enough to have had three children and a lot of dashed hopes for the future. But Danielle didn't want to say any of that. She wanted to stick to a more businesslike approach.

"Long enough to know I'm better off divorced."

An astute look. "You can trust me with the truth."

"I'm a merry divorcée. That's the truth."

The skeptical way Jason pursed his lips unnerved her . . . and not just because it made her imagine kissing him. Repeatedly.

How did he know she was fibbing, anyway? Her own father hadn't known. Forrest Benoit was a sensitive, award-winning poet. He should have been able to discern her true feelings.

"Mark and I are getting divorced, Dad," she'd told him.

"Great! Now you'll have time to come to Burning Man with us! I always knew Mark was the reason you've stayed home."

Actually, the reason had been that Danielle was nothing like her artsy parents, who'd been pushing her for years to join them at festivals and workshops. But they'd chosen to blame her ex-husband for being a "stultifying influence" on her "essence."

"I liked it better when you were bossing me around," Jason said, breaking into her thoughts. "When you were commanding me to keep the press and the protestors out of your store—"

"Don't forget telling you to apologize."

"—*that* seemed authentic." His unabashed grin reminded her that she hadn't won that particular concession from him. Not yet, at least. "But this . . . well, let's just say you have a tell."

"A tell? Like in poker?"

A nod.

"I do not."

A wider grin.

"I do not!" Then, "Tell me what it is. I'll obliterate it."

"Then I wouldn't be able to use it."

"Why would you want to use it? And for what?" Danielle cast an exasperated glance at the crowded diner. "An itemized list would be nice. Don't be afraid to go into detail."

Jason gave her an offhanded shrug. Unfortunately, that blithe gesture only made her imagination run wild. Part of her wished he was hinting that he'd like to use her supposed tell as part of seducing her . . . exactly the way she'd imagined. The rest of her knew that giving in would be a colossal mistake.

She had to keep her head on straight, Danielle reminded herself. There was a lot at stake here. Time was tight. There was only one critically important Christmas shopping season every year, and it was happening now. She couldn't afford any screwups. Jason might be able to fool himself into believing he could finesse his situation without changing himself or apologizing. But she knew better. She knew he needed to do more.

Tricky situations didn't just improve with no effort.

As long as he allowed her to take the lead, she could make Jason look good. With her store's excellent sales performance. With her own personal expertise. With his association with that expertise. That's why she'd offered to let him "use" her.

Even if, just then, she wanted to "use" him to satisfy her

newly reawakened desire to spend an afternoon naked and sweaty.

"Never mind," Danielle bluffed. "I don't want to know."

"There it is again."

"My tell?" She gave a frustrated sound. "How in the—"

Before she could unleash the annoyed expletive she had in mind, his laughter cut her off. His dark eyes gleamed teasingly at her. "Gotcha. Again."

Again? Great. She'd been sure she hadn't been offering up any tells that time. Maybe he was making up the whole thing.

She'd been enjoying it, though. Bantering with him was fun. Danielle didn't want to admit it. But it was.

"So, *anyway*," she made herself say with new crispness, "as I was telling you, I needed a job after my divorce—"

Jason quirked his mouth. "Were you telling me that?"

"When Edna hired me," she went on, "I had a few years of on-and-off retail sales experience in college. That's all. But I was determined. I was smart. I knew everyone in town, and I knew toys. I was motivated, too. So I did well at Moosby's."

"You must have. I understand Edna resisted retirement."

Good. Steady ground. "She just wanted a worthy successor."

"And that was you?"

Danielle nodded. "Ask anyone. I'm *really* good."

"Oh?" His grin could have melted butter. "I'm intrigued."

And I'm an idiot. Why had she practically *purred* that boast about herself? She didn't sound capable; she sounded hot to trot. Double entendres weren't even her style.

What was wrong with her today?

It was almost as if being jostled against Jason amid the teeming crowd *accidentally* wasn't enough for her anymore. It was almost as if she wanted to feel his warm, solid chest and lean midsection and strong arms pushed against her *on purpose.*

It was almost as if, after years of being good, Danielle wanted to be bad instead. To live dangerously. Starting now.

Oh, wait. *She did.* She did want those things.

The crowd's next shift fulfilled her wish. Danielle stumbled. She put out her arms. An instant later, her outflung palms encountered deluxe, city-slicker fabrics and—even better—Jason's sturdy, masculine chest muscles underneath them.

Mmm. Nice. Those substantial muscles flexed as Jason effortlessly caught her. He squeezed her, briefly treating her to a personal demonstration of biceps strength. But that wasn't enough to completely stop her fall. Their legs collided, feet entangled as Danielle tried to steady herself and failed. Her nose bumped against Jason's broad, coat-covered shoulder.

He smelled like soap and spiciness. He felt like . . . *heaven.*

His warmth shocked her. It was as if he'd been superheated.

In her eagerness to please, maybe she'd turned up her car's heater too high. Or maybe they were both heating up. Uh-oh.

She looked up. Orange fun fur hovered precariously close to Jason's nose. Her jacket's collar wanted to be close to him too.

Would he mind if she enjoyed another *teensy* grope? If she pretended, just for a minute, that she couldn't get her balance?

Ill-advisedly, Danielle dropped her hands and did just that. *Mmm-hmm.* Based on a surreptitious, exploratory fondle, Jason was built like one of those superhot male models . . . all hard angles, interesting bunched-up muscles, and acres of warm bare skin. Did he have some chest hair?

she wondered. How much? Or did he keep everything bare to show off his sculpted chest?

The moment she found herself contemplating *that* personal detail, she knew she'd gone too far. With effort, Danielle levered backward to restore some much-needed personal space between them. It turned out not to be enough. She still wanted him.

She *had* to keep from touching him! It . . . did things to her.

"Thanks for the assist. I'll just go check on our table," she said perkily. "You start schmoozing. I'll be right back."

When leaving Moosby's, Jason had thought that getting outside into the frigid air would stall his libido. He'd been wrong. When arriving at the Galaxy Diner, he'd thought that hosting an impromptu meet-and-greet with half of Kismet's pie-loving population would demolish his fantasies. It hadn't.

Now more than ever, he wanted Danielle. Every time she touched him—innocently and accidentally—he wanted her more.

This was bad. Danielle was doing her best to turn him into Mr. Goody Two-shoes, up to and including letting her townie reputation lend him instant trustworthiness, and all he'd been able to do was replay, over and over in his mind, the moment when she'd stumbled into his arms and inadvertently touched him.

He'd stiffened as if he'd been sucker punched. In a way, he had. Because nothing in Jason's life had prepared him for this.

He'd never been more bowled over by a woman in his life.

Why did the one woman who accomplished that feat have to be someone he needed to stay on a hands-off basis with? For all he knew, Jason reminded himself, Chip's spy was still skulking around, waiting to catch Jason red-handed. Being bad. Again.

To keep himself occupied after his spontaneous public appearance had wound down and he'd slipped into a booth across from Danielle, Jason directed his attention to the diner itself.

A metal roll-up service-bay door—an obvious holdover from the property's past—formed one exterior wall. Antique auto lifts made up the bases of three of the tables. Several dinged-up, hand-painted metal FILLING STATION signs hung on the walls beneath the holiday garlands and lights. The place's remodel was an unequivocal success. Jason couldn't say the same for his own pathetic attempts at diverting himself. He could still feel Danielle across from him, exuding warmth and intelligence, tempting him to forget everything except her big blue eyes and the cute, telltale way she crinkled her nose while fibbing.

Come to think of it, she'd done a lot of nose crinkling while discussing her ex-husband. Did that mean she still had feelings for that jerk? Unreasonably, the idea annoyed him.

Now he needed a distraction from that, too. Frowning, Jason pulled the table's spotless antique auto ashtray—now filled with multicolored packets of various sweeteners—closer. He plucked out a few packets. He set them alongside his plate of pumpkin streusel pie-in-a-jar, then added some toothpicks to the pile.

Absently, he fiddled with them while Danielle talked about seasonal Moosby's specials, seasonal pie specials, and growing up as a full-time resident in a resort town that specialized in holly-jolly seasonal cheer. He slipped the paper napkin from beneath the wide-mouth Mason jar on his plate, then folded it.

"So, you know all about me." Danielle rested her elbows on the table, made a cradle of her interlaced fingers, then propped her chin in her hands. "It's time for you to tell me about you."

He disagreed. "I don't like talking about myself."

"That explains why there's a tell-all unauthorized bio in

the works about you," she said. "You know, if you give people some information, they don't have to make up stuff to fill that vacuum. Maybe if you cooperated with the press a little more—"

He stopped fiddling. "How do you know about that?"

She named her favorite Internet search engine. "You'd be surprised how much a person can find out online if properly motivated. Say, after they've been ambushed by protesters."

"Betty and her friends weren't protesting that book."

"It might have been nice if they had been. That's what real fans of yours ought to do," Danielle insisted. "Rise up to protect your privacy, if that's what you're all about. Why not?"

"Because it would be preposterous. People don't care about me. They care about who they think I am. It's not the same."

"I bet you wish it was."

He did. But there was no reason in the world Danielle ought to have known that. *Fold. Fold. Crease.* The origami-style shape he was making came into focus. He flipped the napkin. "Nope."

"Mmm." She watched him. "You have a tell, too."

"Like hell I do."

"Believe what you want." An airy wave. "But telling me a little about yourself doesn't feel so bad now, does it?"

"As an alternative to discussing an unauthorized biography that pisses me off every time I think about it?" She had him there. Jason couldn't help grinning. "You're not wrong."

"So?"

"So you're untrusting *and* pushy."

"You forgot unrelenting. And crazy about cranberry pie."

Ardently, Danielle nodded at her jar of cranberry-pecan pie and its accompanying orange-scented whipped cream. She'd dived into it like a woman possessed. All that remained were crumbs.

"You forgot to lick the plate."

"I didn't forget. I'm waiting for you to look away first."

He laughed. "You're not serious."

"No? Try me."

For an instant, something . . . *sensual* and inviting glimmered in her gaze. Jason could have sworn that Danielle wanted him to *try her* in a sense that went way beyond pies and plates.

Unwisely, he was up for it. "Go ahead. I dare you."

She actually chortled. "Your mistake, buddy. You don't *ever* want to dare a woman like me." In preparation, she cracked her neck like a boxer headed for the ring. "Get ready to lose."

He gave a blasé shrug. "Big words. Not much action."

"Oh yeah?" Arching her brow in a way that definitely foretold mischief, Danielle delicately removed the cutlery from her waiting plate. She set aside the napkin. She lifted the plate, eyed the crumbled remains of her pie with anticipation, and then, to Jason's disbelief . . . "Hey, what's *that*?"

He swiveled his head to look. Nothing seemed amiss.

Hey. Knowing he'd been tricked, he looked back just in time to catch the final hasty lick that Danielle gave her pie plate.

Their gazes met. Her eyes sparkled at him again. He had an instant, reckless image of what Danielle might look like while licking *him* that eagerly and felt himself harden on the spot.

Unaware of that fact, Danielle winked. "Gotcha. Sucker."

Her merry laughter rang into the diner as she put down her plate. As she did, her gaze fell on Jason's depleted pile of toothpicks and sweetener packets. Her attention moved to the napkin he'd folded. "Interesting. What do you have there?"

A mistake. Usually he kept his tinkering habit private. He was really off his game today. Knowing he was caught, Jason glanced at the makeshift object he'd absentmindedly constructed.

"It's a toy race car." He gestured at it. "The folded napkin is the body. The toothpicks are the framing and supports. The sweetener packets are, obviously, the wheels."

"'Obviously'? You made rectangular packets round."

"Folding. Plus sugar glue. It doesn't last forever, but it's easy and cheap—just white sugar melted in a little water."

"That's amazing." Danielle peered more closely. "If I didn't know better, I'd swear this was a tiny Formula One car."

It was. Duh. "That's what a race car is."

"You made a specific type of car out of toothpicks, sugar packets, and a napkin?" She shook her head in amazement. "My mom would *love* you. She's an artist. She's always wanted me to be one, too, but—" Halfway through that telling sentence, Danielle broke off. She dragged over the saltshaker, tied a scrap of teabag around its neck, then pushed it next to Jason's race car. She beamed. "There. I helped. Now your car has a driver, too."

No one had ever joined him in creating something. Not like this. Not this clumsily . . . or this poignantly. Irrationally, Jason felt moved by Danielle's efforts. She hadn't made fun of him or tried to profit from him. She'd just . . . *gotten* him. Effortlessly.

It had been a long time since he'd felt that way.

Not that he intended to say so. Gruffly, he cleared his throat. "Your 'driver' is twice the size of my race car."

"Perspective isn't my forte. My mom's the artist, not me."

"I bet she can't make a to-do list to save her life." He squinted. "What's that supposed to be hanging around his neck?"

Danielle looked insulted. "It's a winning medal!"

"Really?" He peered closer. "Hmm. If you say so."

She sighed. "Go ahead. Suggest I re-enroll in art school. Recommend I take up sketching or journaling or performance art."

"Why would I do that? I'd lose a brilliant store manager."

"Because making art is superior. It's a gift. A calling."

"I guess so. The world needs clipboard-wielding librarian

types, too. Otherwise, it would be chaos. Haiku all around. Disaster. You're too good at what you do to change now."

Danielle smiled. "Well . . . that's true. You've got me there."

But now *she* seemed inexplicably touched by something, too.

"For a long time, I felt sure I must have inherited some artistic ability," she said. "Or soaked it up via osmosis, living in this artsy-craftsy burg year-round. But no matter what I did—coloring graphic novels in college, enrolling in musical theater, sculpting, dancing, making a hugely unsuccessful foray into mystery writing, and helping to start not one but *two* indie bands—I had to admit the awful truth. And the truth is—"

"You'd rather be organizing inventory or helping customers find the perfect toy than getting your artsy fartsy on."

Her job dropped. She gave a bewildered nod. "Yes. *Exactly.* Most people don't believe me when I say so. How did you know?"

"The same way you knew my race car needed a driver."

Even when no one else ever had. He looked at her ungainly saltshaker "driver" and felt his heart stupidly expand.

"But that *can't* be true," she protested. "It's so—"

"Dangerous. Unadvisable." He frowned. *"Romantic."*

"—unlikely! I mean, the odds of you just 'getting' me—"

"And you 'getting' me," Jason felt compelled to put in.

"—have got to be astronomical." Danielle gave him a cagey look. "You're pulling my leg. You have a spy who investigated my checkered failed-artist past. Or something."

Her unwitting reminder of Chip's (potential) spy briefly dimmed Jason's newfound sense of synchronicity with her.

All the same, he knew this feeling wasn't going away anytime soon. Because even now, he felt all too aware that . . .

"You're dying to calculate the *exact* odds of this happening between us, aren't you?"

She laughed. "The instant I find a pencil and three minutes to spare."

He'd known that about her, Jason realized. "That's cool."

"Believe me, nobody else thinks so. Math geeks are very misunderstood." Marveling at him, Danielle shook her head again. "I wish I'd met you under different circumstances."

Jason did too. Things were so screwed up right now.

"I wish I'd brought my taxes with me. I could use the help."

"Come on." She blushed. "You have expert paid tax help."

"It's harder than you think to find people to trust."

"Tell me about it." Danielle gave him a guarded look. "Which reminds me . . . there must be something else going on here. Nobody finds organizing and toy selling endearing."

Jason did. For the first time in his life.

"So just hand over the dossier your spy has compiled," Danielle urged him with a facetious grin, "and I'll—"

"Check it for errors? Red pencil the grammar?"

"Of course! Why else would I want it?"

It was his turn to laugh. He'd been right earlier. This *was* dangerous between them. It had been bad enough when he'd been hot for her. Now he was also in sync with her? What the hell?

"So, this has been fun," Jason made himself say. "But we've got a long day ahead of us tomorrow, and I've got lipstick to shower off my neck." Jokingly, he showed her the remnants left by his enthusiastic, adoring public during today's dual meet and greets. "Would you mind driving me back to my car? I'd better find my hotel and check in before it gets too late."

At that, Danielle seemed . . . stricken? Surprised? Relieved?

Probably relieved. This was getting pretty intense between them, all of a sudden.

"Sure. No problem." Brightly, she scooted out from the diner's booth. "You're right to check in early. In Kismet, they roll up the sidewalks at dusk most of the time." Danielle cast his makeshift race car a final wistful look. Then she gave him a sassy look and wiggled her fingers. "Just fork over your fifty bucks for gas money, and we'll be on our way."

Chapter Eight

"Gigi!" Keeping her voice low, Danielle huddled in her bedroom closet with her cell phone to her ear. It had been four days since she'd shared pie and an imaginary race car with Jason at the Galaxy Diner. Now, at the dawn of day five, she felt even less prepared to deal with the situation than she had when she'd first sneaked Moosby's CEO out of her toy store and into her car for an unwise getaway from the press. "Pick up, pick up . . ."

Impatiently, Danielle listened to her friend's phone ring. And ring. And ring. Probably, Gigi was still asleep. Unlike Danielle, Gigi had the luxury of long, unbroken hours of peaceful slumber, undisturbed by an eight-year-old's bad dreams, a ten-year-old's habit of sneaking extra e-book reading time under the covers, or a six-year-old's determination to set a world record for staying up way past bedtime in the first place.

On the other hand, Gigi didn't have Zach, Karlie, or Aiden to love. So those were trade-offs Danielle was more than willing to make. She'd sleep in someday. After things settled down.

Giving up on her phone call, Danielle sent a hasty text

instead, making sure that Gigi was keeping up with the store. Now that she was busy trying to impress Jason with her management acumen and general suitability for the upper echelons of Moosby's HQ, she was relying on Gigi more than ever. Henry had gone above and beyond, too, as had the rest of her staff.

So far, they'd avoided the requisite yodeling store greetings, goofy yellow hats, and hideous Marky Mark and the Funky Bunch aprons. They'd amassed record sales, too—thanks in part to the irrefutable novelty of having a famous, charming, exasperatingly unrepentant expert toy seller in their midst.

To Danielle's surprise, Jason was utterly adept at working with customers. Another millionaire tycoon might have remained aloof. But Jason had seemed happy to jump right into the fray.

In fact, he'd seemed more than happy. He'd seemed at home.

But Danielle knew that was probably wishful thinking on her part. Because the only thing better than a superhot fling with a superhot stranger was a superhot *relationship* with a superhot long-term *partner* who would stay in Kismet long after the tinsel and wrapping paper were packed away. Not that that was in the cards for her. Because despite the surprising synchronicity she and Jason had discovered while at the Galaxy Diner, they'd both kept things strictly platonic over the past few days.

Danielle figured she deserved a medal for doing *that*.

On the other hand, she *had* accidentally made things more difficult for herself. Back when she'd expected to be immune to the appeal of Moosby's famed CEO—back when she'd reasoned that Jason's charisma and good looks were exaggerated and would pose absolutely no temptation for her while he was in Kismet on a part-time basis—Danielle had . . . well, let's just say she'd pulled a few strings. She'd done a little advance manipulation of the situation. Just to be on the safe side. Just to ensure she'd have every advantage when it came to battling for her promotion.

Unfortunately, her machinations had come back to bite her.

Even now, the proof of that misstep was sprawled on her pullout sofa, sleeping off another day of selling, schmoozing, posing for fan photos . . . and *not* apologizing to the Moosby's board.

That's right—Jason Hamilton was staying at her house. For the duration. And Danielle had no one to blame but herself.

"I'd better find my hotel," Jason had remarked innocently at the diner five days ago, "and check in before it gets too late."

Danielle had wanted to kick herself, right there amid the flashing holiday lights and the Christmas music and the pie.

Because she, like the overconfident dummy she was, had used her townie connections to make sure that what happened next was . . .

"It's the weirdest thing," Jason had explained to her two hours later. "My hotel was booked solid. I guess they lost my reservation. Every other hotel and B&B is completely full."

"Really? No kidding?" Danielle had stammered, casting a glance at his full contingent of luggage—one duffel bag. She'd forced out a shrug. "Well, Kismet is ridiculously popular this time of year. I'm surprised you got a reservation at all."

"Apparently, I didn't." He'd shaken his head. "I can't believe every place is full. Even my admin couldn't help."

When she'd envisioned that moment—one purposely engineered by her, less than twenty-four hours earlier—Danielle had imagined feeling triumphant. As it happened, she merely felt . . . dishonest.

"Well," she'd made herself tell Jason, just as she'd planned to, "you're more than welcome to stay with me for a few days. My place isn't very big, and it's not fancy, but—"

"But it'll only cost me a thousand dollars a night?"

His wry grin and good sportsmanship about her constantly overcharging him for simple necessities only made things worse.

"I won't hear of you paying me," Danielle had told him warmly. "Not a dollar more than five hundred, at least."

His grin had broadened. "What a deal. You *do* like me."

She did. The trouble was, she genuinely hadn't expected to.

She'd expected to be playing reluctant host to a frivolous playboy CEO. She'd expected to be saving the day, complete with fanfare and a grateful promotion-bestowing boss, when the manufactured "emergency" of Kismet's overbooked lodgings had arisen and then been expertly solved by her—despite the fact that she'd made it happen by calling in favors with her local hoteliers, who'd all gamely agreed to refuse Jason a room.

An hour later, he'd officially moved in with her.

Four hours after that, Danielle had tiptoed into her tiny, darkened living room, crept closer to the pullout sofa where Jason was temporarily sleeping, and pinched herself to make sure *she* wasn't the one who was currently sawing logs. But as she'd rubbed her arm to take away the resulting sting, Danielle had had to admit the truth: she'd outsmarted *herself* this time.

She had no one but herself to blame for her predicament.

So when Jason padded around her house at night in his hip-slung pajama pants and no shirt, *she* was accountable for her own hubba-hubba swooning. When Jason smiled at her over their shared AM coffee and unintentionally made her imagine the two of them were really coupled (and loving it), *she* was accountable for her own naïve yearning. When Jason showered each morning and the running water made her imagine soapsuds and water jets cascading all over his wet, flexing muscles, *she* was accountable for her own racing heartbeat and breathless fantasizing.

Jason couldn't have been nicer. When he helped her erect

her oversize Christmas tree, it wasn't his fault that she longed for him to take her—instead of that big Douglas fir—into his arms. When he helped unsnarl her rickety Christmas lights, he didn't purposely make his adroit untangling seem sexy; he just picked apart the strands. When he caught her getting ensnared in those same light strings as she prepared the tree for her traditional tree-trimming party with the kids, Jason didn't *mean* to back her into the corner with both hands full of lights . . . then gaze down at her with every appearance of wanting to kiss her.

He couldn't have meant to do any of *that*. That was all Danielle's overactive imagination at work. Because Jason had been nothing but polite and professional . . . while she'd been wondering what it would be like to play house with him for real.

Because unlike Mark, Jason appreciated her idiosyncrasies. Unlike her parents, he accepted her for who she was. Unlike Crystal, one nit-picky dad at school drop-off, and occasionally her mom, he thought she was a fantastic mother, too. Not that he had much to base that on—just a few cherished photos, a fridge covered with kiddie artwork, and what he claimed was "the way you light up when you talk about your kids." Jason seemed to find the nurturing side of her personality fascinating. Maybe because, as Gigi insisted, he already knew she was a dynamo at Moosby's and wanted to glimpse the other sides of her, too.

"A man like that, he does not care if you are a worker bee, only buzzing and buzzing all the time," her friend had asserted. "A man like that, he wants to know you can *play hard*, too. He wants to know you will play hard with him. Show him!"

Danielle had demurred. "This isn't France, Gigi. We don't have the same attitude toward flirting. Jason will think I'm irresponsible. He'll think I want to play all day with him."

Gigi had winked. "You do! I can tell. You are blushing."

Even remembering it now, Danielle felt her face heat.

She was guilty as charged when it came to wanting Jason. Fortunately, their time together was coming to a close. He was scheduled to embark on the next leg of his Midwestern Moosby's tour tomorrow morning. If she failed to get him to publicly apologize before he left, she didn't know what she would do.

Heaving a sigh, Danielle grabbed some clothes and left her bedroom closet. Passing by her bureau, she glimpsed the race car Jason had MacGyvered together at the Galaxy Diner. She smiled.

"Thanks," Jason had said, tapping her on the shoulder as she busily made up the sofa bed for him. "This is for you."

She'd turned. Caught sight of that race car. Smiled.

She didn't know why his giving it to her affected her so much. But it did. Having that improvised toy race car parked next to her jewelry box and her car keys was like having a handmade piece of Jason nearby. It was just as full of charm as he was. It was likely to stick around for about as long as he was, too.

Meaning, hardly anytime at all.

"I thought you left this behind," Danielle had said as she'd accepted it, admiring its ingenuity. "I didn't see you take it with you. You've got a future as a magician."

"Or a past as a thief." He'd grinned at that. "Sorry I couldn't take your saltshaker driver. That really would have been stealing."

And mooning over a hunk of napkin and some toothpicks really was embarrassing, Danielle told herself as she realized what she was doing. She and Jason weren't dating. They were colleagues. Colleagues and temporary roommates. That was all.

A sudden racket erupted from the living room. The front door banged open. Childish voices rang out. Footsteps sounded.

Her kids were home. They were supposed to be at their

dad's house until tomorrow evening. Why in the world were they here?

A girlish scream rent the air. Then . . . *thumping*?

Dropping her clothes, Danielle dashed barefoot toward the living room, berating herself all the while. She should have planned for this. She should have prepared Aiden, Zach, and Karlie for the possibility of a houseguest. She should have . . .

. . . eased up on the martial arts lessons for her daughter?

In a heartbeat, Danielle sized up the situation. Jason stood frozen in the living room, gorgeously shirtless (as usual) and wearing pajama pants that made the most of his hip bones and musculature. Ten-year-old Karlie crouched in a ninja pose nearby him, arms outstretched and eyes squinting, still holding the backpack she'd clearly been using to make the thumping sound with—in coordination with Jason's torso. Zach gawked at his sister. Aiden stood contentedly nearby, explaining the situation to a bag containing murky water, fish food, and one goldfish.

"It's a *home invasion*!" her son told the fish, his eyes as big as his fishy friend's. "Don't worry. Karlie knows karate!"

"How do *you* know about 'home invasions'?" Danielle demanded, momentarily diverted from the crisis at hand.

"Oh. Hi, Mom!" Aiden waved his chubby free hand. He raised the bag, making the goldfish sway. "Look! We got a new fish!"

"I asked, how do you know about—"

"Crystal watches the True Crime channel," Zach volunteered sunnily, still keeping a cautious eye on Jason. "Crystal lets us watch it too sometimes. *Crystal* treats us like grown-ups."

That was because, to barely post-collegiate Crystal, the children weren't too far removed from her own friends, Danielle knew. But she wasn't about to say so. Not to her own kids.

Not even if Zach *was* baiting her with his tone of voice. It wasn't news to her that kids liked being given whatever they wanted. It was just that, as their mother, she had to be firm.

Ergo . . . "That's it," she decreed. "No more True Crime channel. For anyone. I mean it. No matter what Crystal says."

"Speaking of true crime . . . does *no one* else care that I've cornered this guy?" Karlie's voice quivered, alerting Danielle that her take-charge daughter was running out of adrenaline. Clearly, she'd used up plenty of bravado already. Karlie shifted. She nudged her chin pugnaciously toward Jason. "I caught him *stealing* our Christmas tree! I caught him red-handed!"

Biting her lip, Danielle glanced at Jason. His attention, though, was directed at her legs. Specifically, at her bare legs, Danielle realized. When she'd bolted from her bedroom, she'd forgotten that she was still wearing her PJs—a pair of soft plaid flannel shorts, a ribbed cotton camisole, and a shortie polka-dot robe. Plus a case of raging bed head.

Not that Jason was looking at her unruly long dark hair. He was too busy sliding his attention slowly past her knees, over her thighs, up toward her midsection, all the way to . . .

. . . her perky, extra-alert nipples. Damn it!

Hastily, Danielle covered up. But not before she caught an unmistakable flare of interest and appreciation in Jason's face.

Dumbfounded by it, she gawked back at him.

Did Jason want her, too? Because if he did . . .

Well, that might change everything between them.

"I wasn't stealing the Christmas tree." Jason's voice was level and friendly. His attention was focused on Karlie. He added a genial grin. "I was moving the tree, temporarily, so I could fix the wiring on the lights. I didn't want your mom to burn down the house." He cast a heartening glance at Danielle. "Don't worry," he assured her confidently. "Kids *love* me."

In response, Karlie kicked him in the shin.

Zach kicked him in the other shin.

Aiden saw what his big brother and sister were up to. He stuck his tongue out at Jason, then struck a defiant pose.

"*We're* not just any old kids," he informed Jason.

"Yeah." Zach crossed his arms, making himself look equally rebellious. "We don't need some stranger to fix our tree, either. Because my mom hardly *ever* burns down anything!"

"'Hardly ever'?" Danielle protested. She scurried over to where Karlie was readying herself for another strike. "Come on!"

"There was that time with the burnt toast," her daughter reminded her, hands on her hips. "You had to beat the smoke alarm with a T-ball bat to make it quit screeching so loud."

Jason appeared unfazed by their pint-size belligerence.

Danielle admired his equanimity . . . even as she felt a new sense of foreboding overtake her. A few seconds later, she realized what had incited it: the telltale sounds of giggling, kissing, and baby talk moving closer from her front porch.

She barely had time to prepare herself before the new Mr. and Mrs. Rausch-Sharpe appeared in her open front doorway.

Mark had affixed Crystal's name to his when he'd remarried. He'd also borrowed his new wife's youthful fashion sense. At thirty-two, Mark wasn't too old to look current, of course, Danielle knew. But he was, in her opinion, too old to sport a hipster mustache, unisex black skinny jeans, *and* an "ironic" bow tie, all at the same time. Plus a still pink *Crystal* tattoo.

He and his tat's namesake squeezed themselves inside in a bumptious combination of arms and legs and giggles, unwilling to be apart even for the time required to navigate the doorway separately. Amid a burst of wintry air, they shut the door behind themselves. Then they resumed canoodling. As usual.

In one swift glance, Jason took in the arrival of Mark and Crystal, the resigned way that Danielle reacted to their showy smooching, and the suddenly tense atmosphere in the room.

His reaction was not what she would have expected.

"Come on, babe," he said. "Let's go make some coffee."

Babe? While she stood there baffled by that endearment, Jason merely gave her an inescapably inviting look . . . just as though they'd been roused from their bed by the kids' arrival.

"I'm going to need the energy," he added. "For later."

His eyebrow waggle and seductive tone weren't lost on any of the adults. Especially not Danielle. Jason was pretending they were a couple, too. He was trying to come to her rescue.

This would *never* work, Danielle knew. Mark was too smart.

As proof, Mark ripped his lips from Crystal's, his attention snared by the unexpected sound of an unknown adult male in his ex-wife's company. "Huh?"

"Hi." Jason held out his hand. "I'm Jason."

"Huh?" Mark repeated. Maybe he wasn't so smart after all.

"You must be Mark, Danielle's ex." Jason pumped his hand.

Mark appeared baffled. But he duly accepted the handshake.

Seeing the two of them together went a long way toward making Danielle feel better. Frankly, Jason bested Mark in every way. He was taller, studlier, friendlier, and sexier. He was smarter, more muscular, and more considerate. Plus, seeing Crystal give Jason a bedazzled, obviously astounded once-over felt *great*.

Crystal would never believe Jason was with her, Danielle knew. However ditzy Crystal was, she couldn't be *that* credulous.

"Wow!" Crystal giggled. She all but pushed past Mark

to shake Jason's hand herself. "Aren't *you* a lucky girl, Danielle?"

Or maybe she wasn't so smart after all, either.

She and Mark deserved one another.

"And you must be Candy," Jason said. "Nice to meet you."

She deflated. Her smile quavered. "Uh, it's Crystal."

"Of course," Jason agreed warmly . . . but his attention had already returned to Danielle. Even as he gazed at her, giving her a double dose of sex appeal, Danielle knew darn well that he remembered Crystal's name. She'd never once known him to forget anyone's name, from Moosby's frequent shoppers to their staff.

If Danielle had been a better woman, she would not have found it so sweet to see her ex and his insufferable new bride knocked off balance. But she wasn't a better woman. So she did.

However, now that the fun was over . . . "Thanks for the drop-off, you two." Probably, Mark had gotten mixed up about their visitation schedule again. "I guess I'll see you around."

"What's the hurry?" Mark swerved his suspicious, resentful-looking gaze away from Jason's visible six-pack abs. He sucked in his gut. "There's no need to give us the bum's rush, Dani."

Crystal eyed him, clearly peeved at hearing him use his pet name for Danielle. So she flounced to Jason, then put her hand on his forearm. "I think we were invited for coffee, sweetie."

The Rausch-Sharpes sulked at each other, clearly spoiling for a "who can flirt more recklessly" showdown. Danielle had never seen this childish side of their relationship before.

For the first time, she truly felt glad to be free. Maybe she really was a merry divorcée, just as she'd told Jason.

"You're right," Mark agreed, breaking the stalemate with

a glance at Danielle. "Thanks, Dani. I guess we can stay awhile."

"I guess we *can* stay awhile," Crystal cooed to Jason.

What? Danielle didn't want them to stay awhile. Doing that would be courting disaster. There were too many variables. Too many loose ends. Too much potential for failure. But Jason only nodded, perfectly at home with continuing their ruse. Thank God for his habit of folding and putting away the bedding he used on her sofa bed every night. And for his diligence in muscling away the pullout mattress, too. That meant there wasn't any evidence to contradict the idea that the two of them were a couple.

All the same, Danielle stared at the expectant faces of everyone around her and found herself unable to cave in to peer pressure. It wouldn't be fair to embroil Jason in her personal life. It wasn't up to him to help her feel better. Also—and more pressingly—she'd rather shave her own head than host a neighborly coffee klatch for two people who'd betrayed her.

Maybe she should have been more forgiving. She wasn't.

That didn't mean she needed to indulge in an unnecessary, immature, jealousy-inducing pretense with Jason. Did it?

Even if—as she couldn't helping thinking—it might be fun.

"Hey, can you guys move away from the TV, please?" Karlie piped up. She'd abandoned her vigilant watch over Jason now that all the grown-ups were present, and dragged out a video game console. "I'm trying to play this new game Crystal got for me!"

Danielle caught a glimpse of the *Fashion Makeover EXTREME!* video "adventure" her daughter brandished and changed her mind about her stringent antipretense principles. Maybe she *shouldn't* rise above all this. Because ordinarily, Karlie preferred quest games or puzzle games—not pink, sparkly, makeover "adventures" wherein the biggest challenges were taming unruly eyebrows and dieting off five pounds in time for the big swimsuit "finale." As it happened,

Danielle had already refused to get Karlie that particular "adventure" video game for Christmas.

Evidently, Crystal had overruled her. She enjoyed doing that. At birthdays, at Disneyland, at Halloween . . . and especially during the holidays, when she could score extra kid points.

"I'm going to make a robot!" Zach announced. With relish, her son wrestled a box of expensive Legos and electronic parts out of his overstuffed overnight bag. "Crystal got it for me!"

Grr. Danielle had vetoed that particular Christmas gift for her son, too. Invariably, Zach lost interest in toys with lots of gears and small parts. They only wound up underfoot, with the only remaining piece—the beeping, shrieking motor—in his hands for days, bleeping out its owner's every electronic whim.

Crystal wouldn't have to live with that racket. Danielle would. But Zach loved it right now. Clearly, this was another volley in Crystal's game of holiday one-upmanship with Danielle.

"My goldfish just made a poop that's longer than he is!"

Visibly mesmerized, Aiden flaunted his bag full of murky water and overfed fish. His last three fish had met tragic toilet bowl ends after being generously overfed by their keeper. Aiden had begged for another fish for Christmas, but Danielle had done her best to discourage him. Every time another guppy or neon tetra met its untimely demise, her son was devastated.

But Crystal didn't know that. All she knew was that giving Aiden a goldfish made him look at her as if she were a hero.

Danielle was familiar with the urge to be on the receiving end of that look. But that didn't mean she was okay with

Crystal constantly making end runs around her parental authority.

She inhaled. "Crystal? Can I talk with you in the kitchen?"

Her tone must have been more Terminator-like than she'd planned, because Jason gave her an alarmed look.

"First, let's get that coffee going, babe." He smiled and touched her hand . . . and it was all over with. Danielle forgot her ire altogether. Keeping up their deception, Jason gave a knowing chuckle. "You know how you are before the caffeine kicks in."

Mark knew, too. That detail seemed to convince him that Jason and Danielle truly were coupled. He gave a puzzled frown.

Nearby him, Crystal only preened, knowing that even if the hot new man in Danielle's life had gotten her name wrong, she had still won the latest skirmish in the ongoing Christmas war.

But a second later . . . "Candy, you look like the fun type." Jason nodded toward Karlie and the video game console. "I'm pretty sure *Fashion Makeover EXTREME!* is a two-player adventure. I bet Karlie would love it if you would play it with her."

The look Crystal gave him should have made him combust.

"Ooh! Would you? Would you?" Excitedly, Karlie bounced to the side, making room on the floor for her stepmother. She gulped in a breath. "You can be the Master Aesthetician. When she gives the players a bikini wax, they get extra va-va-voom!"

Hearing that vapid description made Danielle hate that game twice as hard. But she'd allow Karlie to play it—for now—if it meant seeing Crystal sit on the floor for a makeover marathon.

"I dunno, sweetie," Crystal demurred. "These are new

white pants. From Juicy Couture. They might get linty on the floor."

"Please?" Karlie begged. "Please please please please—"

With a sigh, Crystal relented. One down. One to go.

"Mark, a smart guy like you would probably be just the man to build that robot with Zach," Jason urged affably. "After all, it does say ages twelve and up on the box. Companies don't label things that way just for laughs. Zach's ten. He'll need help. There's plenty of room to set it up on the coffee table."

Grumpily, Mark eyed the table. He didn't like building things. He didn't have a knack for following directions. With him at the helm, the robot would wind up with four legs, no head, and much of its innards still unassembled. He knew it.

He would look like a bumbling fool. In front of Jason.

At the prospect, Mark seemed to shrink a few inches.

"Will you, Dad? Will you?" Eagerly, Zach ripped open the set's first bag. He poured its contents onto the table in a torrent of plastic bricks and gears. "It's got 972 pieces!"

At her ex-husband's stifled groan, Danielle grinned.

She'd probably go to hell for enjoying this so much.

"As far as you and your wonder fish go . . ." Jason hunkered down to admire Aiden's incredible pooptastic goldfish. "After I help your mom make coffee, I'll help you set up the fishbowl. I'm pretty sure I saw one in the garage the other day."

Mark scowled. Deeply. "He's been in my garage?"

"He's been here for *days*?" Crystal added, dumbfounded.

But Danielle's six-year-old son only beamed up at Jason.

"I'm glad *somebody* can see how *awesome* this fish is."

With that, Danielle realized, Jason won over at least one of her children. He really was, she realized, good with kids.

An instant later, Jason turned his smoldering gaze on her. If she hadn't known better, she'd have sworn he was really into this whole charade—kids, mayhem, imaginary sexual romp, and all.

"I'm not kidding," he said, "about that coffee."

But his deep, husky tone suggested he hadn't been kidding about all those erotic intimations, either. Dizzily, Danielle didn't know what was real and what was pretend anymore.

Then Jason took her hand, and she knew.

The magnetism between them was real. *Really* real.

She didn't care about fighting it anymore.

Grateful for the camaraderie they shared, however improbably and however briefly, she squeezed his hand—his big, slightly callused, infinitely amazing-feeling hand.

What the hell, Danielle thought. "I like coffee."

Then they headed into the kitchen and prepared to take their unlikely synchronicity to a new and unanticipated level.

Even if it was, for the moment, just pretend.

Chapter Nine

To Jason's disappointment, Danielle slipped her hand from his the minute they entered the kitchen. Once they were out of sight of everyone in the living room, she stepped away from him. She put up a barrier of caution and reserve, one he knew had to be about as substantial as her flimsy robe and sleepwear.

When he'd seen her burst into the living room dressed so skimpily, with her hair all pillow-tousled and her body scarcely covered by her sexy shorts and soft-looking tank top, it had been all he could do to tear his attention away from her—especially from her long, lithe legs and her budded nipples.

He still wished Danielle hadn't covered up. It was a crime to conceal a body like hers beneath humble polka-dot fabric.

She hadn't had much choice, though—not with the unexpected company they'd had. Jason couldn't believe the thoughtless way Danielle's dumb jock ex and his bimbo of a bride treated her.

He didn't like anyone who upset Danielle. Period.

"Bravo. Well done." Danielle broke into his thoughts by making a teasing curtsy. "You've effectively put everyone in their places. I could have done that myself, though."

"You never would have. You're way too nice."

"My kids wouldn't agree with that." *Not today, at least.*

"Why not? Because you won't buy them everything they want?" Jason shook his head. "Kids don't need what they think they want. They need what they need. Parents have to decide which is which. I have two younger sisters and a younger brother. Believe me, none of us needed to be bribed into loving our parents."

It was a good thing, too. Tommy and Susan Hamilton couldn't have afforded to bribe anyone. These days, they were doing very well, partly thanks to Jason's help. He liked giving it.

Danielle's mulish expression told him she wasn't convinced. "Crystal is piling up a pretty big fan club by doing exactly that," she informed him as she pulled out a canister of delicious-smelling coffee. "I think she's doing it on purpose."

"Of course she's doing it on purpose." He couldn't see any other scenario. Especially given who they were talking about.

But Danielle was kind enough to give her self-involved, PDA-loving nemesis the benefit of the doubt. "I dunno. Maybe. Sometimes I think so." She sighed. "I'm doing my best to get along with Crystal, for the kids' sake, at least, and we've never actually *acknowledged* the Christmas wars—"

"And, I'm guessing, the birthday wars, the vacation wars—"

"—but they're happening anyway." Danielle glanced over her shoulder at him just as his comment registered, inadvertently confirming his guess. "I don't exactly have a bottomless bank account, either. I can't compete with all these gifts."

"You don't have to compete." Jason came closer, wanting to ease her worries. He stopped a few inches from Danielle, watching her assemble coffee fixings. "That's why Crystal is so worried. You've already won. You'll win every time."

She scoffed. "I don't feel as if I've won."

He came even closer. Danielle's back was to him now, but as she put down the coffeemaker's carafe, Jason noticed the tension in her shoulders. He caught the faint fragrance of the peppermint body wash she showered with, too. *Mmm. Christmassy.*

With incentives like this, he could learn to love the holidays again. He already felt more like himself these days, and he'd hadn't yet spent a week on the Moosby's sales floor.

His return to his old form was all thanks to Danielle. In between appearances and advertising photo shoots, she'd pushed him to work. He'd acquiesced. Now that all was said and done, he was grateful to her for reminding him of the truth. He felt *at home* at Moosby's. He'd let himself get sidetracked by corporate bullshit . . . just the way he was currently getting carried away with liking her, despite all the reasons he shouldn't.

But no one was there to see them. And this was borderline pretending anyway. It was safe. In fact, it was essential.

Deliberately, Jason put his hand on her robe-covered shoulder. It would be easy to slip away those polka dots, bare her skin, lower his mouth, run his lips over her soft shoulder . . .

Instead, Jason gave her a reassuring squeeze. Making her feel better meant more to him than anything else. When all else failed, he knew, it was a good idea to listen. That meant . . .

"You don't feel as if you've won? How do you feel?"

"Well . . ." Her shoulders expanded as she breathed in. Her long hair threatened to tickle his nose. "I feel . . ."

Breath held, Jason waited. But he felt all too aware of how close they were. Without really meaning to, he'd situated them both against the counter near the coffeemaker, with no escape available—and no distraction from his desire for her.

He was moving on to another Moosby's tomorrow, Jason reminded himself. He didn't have to be 100 percent diligent.

". . . like I want something special for Christmas this

year," Danielle went on. Her voice sounded breathy, her tone tight. Was she nervous about something? "Something really special."

Jason wanted something special, too. He wanted her.

Somehow, he mustered enough chivalry not to act on that wanting. Instead, he contented himself with gently stroking his thumb over Danielle's neck. Even that much contact made his heart pound. Her skin felt so soft, her body so warm.

"I want *you*," Danielle told him. "For Christmas."

Shocked, he stopped moving. He'd thought he was the only one who felt that way. When he'd helped Danielle untangle her Christmas lights, when they'd accidentally wound up nose-to-nose, *he'd* been the one who'd almost kissed *her*. He'd felt sure that Danielle knew it, too. But she hadn't acted. Even with their uncanny compatibility factored into the equation, Danielle had behaved with complete propriety. Whereas he, unbeknownst to her, had gone on to enjoy his favorite daily treat: the sexy view he had of Danielle as she bent over with her delectable derrière in the air while making up the sofa bed for him.

He'd never met anyone more generous. More fascinating. More willing to repeatedly extort a man for gas money.

"*I want you*," she repeated, turning around. Her gaze met his, searching and certain. Her attention dropped to his mouth. Lingered. "If that means I won't get promoted, I guess I can—"

It didn't, of course. All the same . . .

"You don't really want to get promoted." Even as that unlikely insight struck him, it felt inarguably right. "I don't think you want to leave Kismet at all." As Danielle's eyes widened in imminent protest, he added, "I think you're just sick of watching Mr. and Mrs. Rub It In Your Face have all the fun."

"Mark and Crystal?" Danielle laughed, momentarily relaxing against him. "Sure, they're annoying. But that doesn't mean I don't want to get promoted. I'm really good at my job."

"I know you are. Maybe that means you should keep your job." Was he crazy? She wanted him . . . and he was debating career strategies with her. "Not get a new one. I've seen you with your customers, Danielle. You love them. They love you. You wouldn't be happy somewhere else—especially not at Moosby's HQ."

"It can't be that bad."

He thought about it. "It's worse. It's soul crushing."

Jason only wished he had an alternative to it. He didn't.

"You're just trying to make me feel better in case I don't get promoted. Because you won't apologize and make the board—"

"I won't apologize for wanting to kiss you, either."

Danielle blinked. "Kiss me?" She gave a vague frown. "But you let go of my hand when we came in the kitchen, so—"

"No, you let go of *my* hand."

"I thought you were only pretending out there." She aimed her chin illustratively toward the living room. Her gaze returned to his, tremulous and hopeful. "If you weren't—"

"I wasn't."

"I wasn't either."

Jason waited for her telltale sign: a nose crinkle.

It never came. She was telling the truth.

A moment ticked past, full of mutual confusion.

The reality of the situation struck them simultaneously.

"You want me," Danielle breathed.

"You want me," Jason echoed, light-headed and triumphant.

A heartbeat later, they lunged at one another. Their bodies met in a squashed union of arms and legs and torsos, hot and eager and long overdue, and it was all Jason could do not to moan aloud and alert everyone in the next room to what was happening. He was kissing Danielle. Incredibly, she was kissing him back. With fervor and enthusiasm and mind-bending skill.

He didn't care that she might still be playacting to make her ex jealous. He didn't care that he was technically her boss and she was officially off-limits. All that mattered were her, him . . . and the inconceivable pleasure that coursed through him as their lips met for the first time. Instantly, he needed more.

Kissing Danielle, Jason realized, was like eating gelato with one of those preposterously small spoons they favored in chichi Italian places. He couldn't possibly get enough. Not with the meager tools at his disposal. Because he was only a man—a flawed, unremarkable man with a disreputable past and a hole in his heart where his love of Christmas used to be. But with Danielle in his arms—with her in his heart—everything started to fill in. Like the toothpick-and-napkin race car he'd given her, he started to feel a lot more cherished than he had a right to.

He couldn't believe the way she'd looked at that damn thing when he'd given it to her, Jason remembered crazily as he delved his hands in her hair and kissed her again. Danielle had reacted as if he'd offered her something shiny and expensive from Tiffany, not a dumb handmade toy that would fall apart in days.

Time was, his handmade creations had lasted longer, he knew. But at least his knack for ingenuity had endured. Driven by poverty and love, a much younger Jason had turned empty boxes and piles of gravel into thrilling playgrounds for himself and his brother and sisters. He'd turned abandoned lumber and pilfered wheels into makeshift skateboards. He'd morphed cast-off shoes and threadbare pillowcases into lovable, lumpy dolls with hairdos made of orange carpet remnants—dolls his sisters had loved. Wrong-side-of-the-tracks kids like them couldn't be picky, of course. It was an admittedly weird talent he had, making things the way he'd done in those days. But without Jason's knack for improvisation—without the occasional five-fingered discount he'd used to get supplies for those improvised toys—the Hamilton kids would have gone without more often than not. Even at Christmas. Thanks to Jason and his not-so-secret talent for making something from nothing, they hadn't had to.

Those were the kinds of sappy, sentimental details Jason *didn't* want winding up in an unauthorized biography of himself. Those details made him seem destined to have become the man he was, with a retailing empire and an audacious net worth and honest-to-god squealing fans. But while living it—while struggling and scraping by the way he'd had to for years—nothing had felt destined. His net worth had been nonexistent. No one had been his fan. It felt dishonest now to give people the idea that his good fortune could ever be duplicated.

Jason didn't have a 1-2-3 manual for success. He couldn't. The funny thing about details like his toy-making past was that they were self-selecting. He'd gotten into a lot of fights, too; no one would have said he was destined to be a championship boxer. He'd done a lot of skipping school; it hadn't turned out to be his destiny to be a truant officer. By the same logic that people applied to his toy-store success, he should have had any number of diverse careers, all of them predestined and perfect.

It wasn't fair to suggest to people that success worked that way. Not when the only things that mattered were work, luck . . . and picking up the pieces to try again after failing.

So his race car wasn't perfect. But it was emblematic of *him*. His days of Dumpster diving for supplies and handmaking toys were behind him now, but Jason still liked the idea of something he'd made staying close to Danielle. Even after he'd left Kismet, his race car would be right there on her bureau.

The idea of his leaving made Jason grip her even tighter. He had less than twenty-four hours to get enough of Danielle's mouth, her hands, her expressive eyes and her evocative movements and her amazing way of pressing against him, undulating and moaning and burying her hands in his hair.

It was, he realized with a thrill, as if she had been wrapped up too tightly for weeks . . . and he was the lucky man who would get to uncover her on Christmas morning.

Uncovering Danielle would be . . . *remarkable*, Jason knew. For days, he'd followed her with his eyes, with his imagination . . . with everything except his hands. Now they could get in on the act too. The sky was the limit. Giddily proving it, Jason slid his fingers lower. He encountered Danielle's slender neck, her delicate collarbones, her soft, warm skin . . . her cumbersome robe.

That had to go. Deliberately, Jason clenched its lapels in both hands, preparing to pull it away. With her robe gone, Danielle would be that much closer to naked. Except doing that might mean not kissing her. Even for an instant, that seemed too high a price to pay. So he only gave a low, impatient moan of his own and then kissed her more deeply, pressing them both against the counter and the cabinets. Something fell. It didn't matter. Because Danielle was kissing him, and she wanted him.

He wanted her. He knew he could have her. Soon. *Soon* . . .

A sudden boisterous scuffle at the doorway broke the mood.

Jason glanced up just as Aiden skipped into the kitchen.

"Hey, look! I found your shirt!" The boy whirled it overhead like a cowboy's lasso. "It was in my room along with a whole bag of stuff. Your stuff, I think." His cherubic face took on a canny look. "You'd better not be sleeping in *my* bed. Because it's mine. It's not yours. You can't have it."

Zach came in just as Aiden said so, further obliterating the moment of privacy Jason and Danielle had been enjoying.

"He's not sleeping in your bed, dummy," Zach informed Aiden. "He's sleeping in Mom's bed. Just like Dad used to do."

"Don't call your brother names." Flushed and mussed, Danielle gave Jason the merest push away from her. She straightened her robe, then broke his heart by belting it.

All that lusciousness, locked away from him. Too bad.

"Adults," Zach went on, undeterred, "don't like sleeping by themselves. For them, every night is a sleepover."

His worldly wise tone brooked no argument. Jason wasn't interested in offering one. If there was a chance this ruse could land him in Danielle's bed, he was all for it.

So far, he'd enjoyed pretending to be Danielle's new man—close encounters, kid attacks, kooky exes, and mayhem included. He'd always liked kids. Although Danielle's brood was a little hostile toward him right now, Jason knew that was temporary.

He really *was* great with kids. He always had been.

His mother always said that was because he was a kid at heart. Jason knew there was more to it than that. He liked kids for themselves, as people, of course. But he also liked the idea of settling down, making coffee on a Saturday morning with his sleep-tousled paramour, feeling a part of a close-knit brood like the one he'd grown up in. It wasn't macho to admit it. But it was true. And that was *another* thing that didn't need to be published about him in the pages of a damn tell-all biography.

He hadn't glimpsed Chip's spy for a few days. But that didn't mean he wasn't out there, monitoring Jason's every move, from his time on the Moosby's sales floor to his daily visits to the bakery next door, which specialized in whoopie pies. He'd never experienced those cakey sandwich cookies before coming to Kismet. Now, Jason was pretty sure he was addicted to them.

"You're *sleeping together*?" Karlie came in next, obviously having overheard. "Mom! You told us you'd always love Dad!"

"I *will* always love your dad." Looking trapped, Danielle cast a flustered glance at Jason. Determinedly, she regrouped. "But just the way Dad has moved on to be with Crystal, someday I might want to move on to be with someone else, too."

All three children scoffed. Well, except Aiden. He was busy slinging Jason's T-shirt over his shoulders. He tied it like a superhero cape, then gave a self-satisfied twirl. "Cool!"

Karlie gave her mother a no-nonsense look. "Dad's fling with Crystal is only temporary, Mom. We all know that."

"Yeah," Zach agreed. "He's just sowing his wild oats."

"Wild oats?" Danielle frowned. "Where did you—"

"Grandma Benoit," her son clarified. "She said that Dad was just sowing his wild oats. She said he'd come crawling back."

"Crawling back? To me?" Danielle seemed surprised at that. Also, definitely amused. "Maybe that was true at one point," she told her children in a careful tone, "but now your dad and Crystal are married. They're going to stay together."

Her children shrugged. "Nah. I doubt it," Zach said.

"With *you* as the alternative?" Karlie asked. "No way."

At their insistence, Danielle seemed flabbergasted. She gazed at them all in turn. "How long have you felt this way?"

"Since . . . forever!" Aiden gave another superhero twirl.

Danielle bit her lip. "We're going to have to talk about this, you guys. Because the truth is, your dad and I are split. We're not going to get back together." Her tone was gentle. "We've moved on with our lives. Dad with Crystal, and me—"

"*You* haven't moved on," Zach disagreed.

"At least you *hadn't*," Karlie clarified with an evaluative glance at Jason. "Until *he* showed up to ransack our tree."

"Is it time to set up the fishbowl yet?" Aiden asked.

Jason realized, in that moment, that he was going to have to step in. Because Danielle obviously needed help. He could tell by her bewilderment. She probably believed she *had* moved on. But if the hungry way she'd kissed him was any indication, she hadn't yet moved on with anyone who was worth her while.

He had to help Danielle. For real this time. He had to show her that life without her ex-husband could be wonderful and fun and well worth experiencing. Not as a ruse to fool her blockheaded ex and his juvenile bride, either. Jason had to make sure that Zach, Karlie, and Aiden knew the truth: their mother wasn't going to reunite with their father. For one thing, Danielle was too good for that chump. For another . . . well, it was obvious that Mark really *did* plan to stay with Crystal.

They deserved one another.

He and Danielle had to go further, Jason realized. For her kids' sakes. For hers. And for his, too.

Because, after all, he *was* trying to be good, right?

What would be a better good deed than helping Danielle? She deserved it. After all, she was the only person who'd asked him for an explanation about the Bethany debacle. She was the only one who'd had enough faith in his integrity not to freak out—not to overreact the way the media and his board of directors had.

A good way to thank Danielle, Jason knew, would be by spending time with her and her kids. By making sure that Aiden, Zach, and Karlie saw their mom actively moving on. With *him*. The new Mr. Nice Guy of Christmasville, USA. Starting now.

Being seen with her and her three adorable moppets would only augment his new board-mandated, family-friendly image. Even Danielle would have agreed with that. It was a win both ways.

"Yes, it's almost time to do the fishbowl, buddy," Jason told Aiden. He loved watching the six-year-old's face light up in response. "After that . . ." Jason cast an eager glance at Karlie and Zach, getting more into the plan he'd just hatched with every passing minute. "Who wants to go on an amazing Christmastime sleigh ride?"

Chapter Ten

"I hate sleigh rides," Karlie said with a sniff.

"Yeah," Zach agreed loyally. "Sleigh rides suck."

"Language," Danielle cautioned. Whenever her kids came home from a stay at their dad's house, they always tested her rules.

"*I've* never been on a sleigh ride," Aiden said, "and neither have *they*." He hooked his thumb toward his siblings in an exaggeratedly world-weary fashion. "I think we should do it."

Zach and Karlie offered a united groan of protest.

"Come on, guys," Jason urged. "It'll be fun!"

Karlie examined her fingernails. Zach squinted in perplexity at the kitchen, as though fascinated by the concept of walls. Noticing their reluctance, Jason looked puzzled. Danielle felt sorry for the way her brood was shutting him out. Given his eager invitation, he must be more keen than she'd thought to experience that sleigh ride. She *had* promised him one. It didn't have to mean anything . . . *special* . . . was going to happen between them.

She wasn't going to fall in love with him in one day, was she?

"I think we should catch up on some chores today,"

Danielle told Karlie and Zach. "I know a few kids whose rooms need cleaning up. This kitchen floor is looking a little dicey, too."

Just as she'd expected, her kids looked horrified.

"I'd love to go on a sleigh ride!" Karlie said.

"Me too!" Zach added. "I can make my robot later."

Oh yeah. Jason had set some unwanted chores for Mark and Crystal, too. "Is your Dad still working on that, Zach?"

Her son nodded. "He's sweating and squinting at the directions. It looked a lot easier on the commercial."

"What about your video game, Karlie?"

Her daughter made a face. "Crystal is *way* too into winning that game. She pushed my player off the fashion-show runway!" She pouted. "Thanks to her, I lost four fashion points and a star."

"Oh." Danielle hugged them. "I'm sorry, you two."

They shrugged, clearly not blaming her.

Danielle glanced at Jason. "Are you serious about this? Because I did plan to do a sleigh ride sometime anyway . . ."

Neither of them had to be at Moosby's today. That's why she'd been calling Gigi—to make sure the weekly inventory switcheroo would take place with the regional toy store managers in her absence. With that arranged, Danielle had the whole day free to be with Jason. She didn't think he was suspicious about their newfound freedom (which would handily allow her to carry out her usual subterfuge *and* maximize her time with Jason on his last day in Kismet). Just in case, she'd told him last night that she was arranging for them to be free of their sales-floor responsibilities in case he had to make another in-person appearance or dazzle everyone with a last-minute photo shoot.

Her own contributions to those photo sessions and the resulting Moosby's ad initiatives had been minimal. She'd put on her assigned wardrobe—which involved mousy khaki pants, sensible shoes, and a frumpy flowered blouse for that lucrative "mom next door" look—had her hair straightened, and tried to look as amped up as possible while standing next to Jason like a game-show hostess, displaying toys from Moosby's big-brand partners.

Years ago, Danielle knew, Moosby's toy selection had been carefully curated. It had been unique. These days, though, most of their stock was composed of the same mega brands that overflowed the shelves at nationwide discount stores. If, as Chip Larsen claimed, Moosby's was suffering from lagging sales, Danielle thought the solution was obvious: refocus on their *More More Moosby's!* exclusives. HQ disagreed—hence, the ad campaign.

So far, the ads had failed to catch fire, though. HQ were diligently pushing them via their social media channels, but Danielle could tell their performance had been a disappointment. On the other hand, what had they expected? Some kind of Old Spice Guy phenomenon? The birth of the new GEICO gecko? Another "Just Do It" mantra? The new ads were so staged and phony that they weren't at all engaging—no matter how much research HQ's experts had done or what their focus groups had predicted.

Not that Danielle had been able to bear looking at all of them—not since seeing her own purposefully dowdy image staring back at her from the tear sheets on the very first ad. Ugh.

"Of course I'm serious." Jason gave her an enthusiastic look. "This could be my last chance to experience snow."

Danielle relented. Happily. "Okay, kids. Get your hats and coats and gloves and scarves—and Aiden, you need snow pants."

As Zach, Karlie, and Aiden ran off to collect their winter wear, Jason blanched. "All that gear just to go outside?"

"That's right, California. It's December, remember?"

He shuddered. "This is why I'm having Christmas in Antigua."

"All by yourself?"

"No, with a team of beach bunnies." He frowned. "A

squad? A crew of beach bunnies? A unit? A cadre? A troop? A gang?"

"I think the official term is herd. Herd of beach bunnies."

Jason grinned. "Actually, I'm going to Antigua with my family—my mom, my dad, my two sisters, and my brother. Every year, we rent a house someplace scenic. I fly everyone out to spend the holidays together. My mom and my brother cook, my dad goes fishing, my sisters catch up on reading. It's nice."

"It sounds nice." Danielle was impressed—and more attracted to him than ever. Family was important to her. She cherished her children and her parents. Even though Jason had been successful, he hadn't forgotten where he'd come from. He'd remembered his family and shared his wealth with them. "If the media and the Moosby's board could hear you now, they'd be wildly impressed."

Jason didn't look happy that she'd brought up work. "Tell them any of what I just said and I'll deny everything."

"Come on. Maybe you should be a *little* less private," Danielle urged. She wanted everyone to see that Jason was more than a guy who'd been caught on camera in a racy situation. "It could be an alternative to apologizing." *Or an adjunct.* "If you made some of your finer qualities public—in your next interview, for instance—it would endear you to the board and to shoppers."

He appeared unconvinced. "I don't want to endear myself to anyone. My private life is no one's business but my own."

But Danielle wasn't ready to give up. "I know you're hoping that your stellar work on the sales floor at Moosby's will save the day," she said, knowing she'd helped him with that, as promised, "but maybe it's time you did even more. You know, on a personal level." *Like kiss and make up with the Moosby's board of directors. So I can finally get promoted.*

She wasn't ready to let go of that dream. But she couldn't deny that Jason's comment about her not really wanting to leave Kismet bothered her. She didn't *think* he was right. Probably.

However, her life wasn't the issue here. Jason's was.

Danielle had already taken every chance she'd had to make sure her own work ethic subtly transferred to Jason. She'd e-mailed daily progress reports to HQ detailing Jason's efforts on the sales floor. She'd allowed the *Kismet Comet* to return to her store and photograph Jason setting up festive holiday windows (while she lingered nearby lending a sense of diligence to the proceedings). She'd assured Chip Larsen—during his single terse follow-up phone call with her—that she believed Jason should apologize and would do what she could to make that happen.

"I like being on the sales floor," Jason assured her, oblivious to her behind-the-scenes efforts on his behalf. "I think I'm going to like going on a sleigh ride even more."

Danielle relented. "Work hard, play harder?"

Another grin. "Something like that."

So Gigi was right. Maybe what (to Danielle) looked like indifference to the board's concerns was merely (to Jason) a different approach. After all, he *was* a toy store mogul. He hadn't exactly gotten where he was by being a gloomy Gus.

Well, she could go along with that, Danielle decided.

"You know, I saw what you did just now." Jason lifted his shoulder in the direction her children had scampered. "Karlie and Zach were blowing me off, big-time. You stepped in with that room-cleaning threat and made my offer to go sleigh riding look like a day out at Disneyland."

"I had to. You looked as if you might cry."

"I did not."

"Did too."

"Did n—" Jason broke off. Grinned. "Aha. Got me."

This time, it was her turn to smile. "I had to," Danielle told him more seriously. "After all you did for me with Mark and Crystal—the way you stepped in without a second's hesitation—"

"That's just the way I do things."

"Well, I appreciate it." She made a face. "Even if it's not really your responsibility. Even if it's immature of me to try to exact a little revenge for all that canoodling. I mean, I'm the mother. I'm supposed to take the high road."

"Says who? You're only human. No matter how deliriously happy your ex is, it's not cool of him to rub it in your face."

"He's not doing it on purpose. He's just happy."

"He's an adult," Jason said firmly. "He can be happy in a less obnoxious and hurtful way. Or I'll know the reason."

It was sweet of Jason to be concerned for her. That was one thing Danielle had hoped to find in her marriage—a person who would have her back at all times. A person she could count on.

A person she could trust. To her surprise, Jason was looking more and more like that kind of person every day.

Maybe her instincts about men *weren't* irrevocably flawed. Speaking of which . . .

"Hey, Dani?" Mark yelled from the living room. "What's going on in there? Where's that coffee, anyway?"

Guiltily, Danielle glanced in her ex's direction.

Utterly unrepentantly, Jason pulled her back into his arms. He caught her eye, gave her a sexy smile, then arched his brow.

"Showtime," he murmured conspiratorially, "in three . . . two . . . one . . ."

His mouth met hers just as tromping footsteps reached the kitchen. Dimly, Danielle heard her ex-husband give a mumbled, apologetic grunt. He stomped away, muttering to himself.

Aha. *That's* why Jason had decided to kiss her again.

This was another reprisal kiss, Danielle realized belatedly. It was intended to help even the score between her and

Mark. But even though she knew that to be true—even though she knew that Jason was probably just pretending to want to kiss her because he liked the challenge or the competitiveness or the raw machismo involved in their ruse—she couldn't help . . . *loving it.*

Jason kissed the way he did everything else: with a full dedication to enjoyment. His arms cradled her close to him. His mouth roamed over hers with purpose and pleasure, now nipping her lower lip, now sliding his tongue inside to meet hers, now moaning as he deepened his kiss and made her hungrier, happier . . .

I could really get used to this, Danielle thought as she twined her arms around Jason's neck, then gave as good as she got. It had been *so* long since she'd indulged in a real kiss—in real erotic contact of any kind. She felt like a starving woman who'd just stumbled upon a lavish buffet—like a frostbitten outdoor adventurer who'd just happened upon a roaring fire.

Kissing Jason incited every sensual impulse she'd ever had, plus a few new ones. She wanted to kiss him back, to bite his neck, to push her hips against his. So she did. She wanted to drag her hands along his hot bare skin, savor the acres of rippling muscle that covered his back and his torso, thrust her fingers in his hair and muss up all that dark waviness . . . because doing so kept Jason right where he needed to be: against her. So she did. She did *almost* everything she wanted to. It was great.

Jason was *really* good at kissing. Breathless and needy, Danielle forgot about Mark, forgot about her impending sleigh ride outing, forgot about making coffee and everything else. In that moment, all that existed were her, Jason, and all the tingly, rapidly overheating parts of them both that made contact as they writhed together against her kitchen counter. With Jason there, Danielle's commonplace kitchen was transformed into an erotic play zone. Her ordinary PJs became lingerie of the most tempting kind. Her body became something that brought her more and more and *more* awareness. More and more and *more* pleasure.

It wasn't just toothpicks and napkins that Jason could transform with his dexterous hands and his nimble imagination. It was *her*, Danielle realized as she went on kissing him. In his arms, she felt born again. She felt like a woman who could conquer anything—even the Christmas wars, her challenges at work, her argumentative children, and her own uncertain future.

Speaking of her children . . . Danielle was worried about them. She hadn't known they'd believed, all this time, that her split with their dad was only temporary. She had to do something about that. She had to help them adjust. But in the meantime . . .

Jason ended their kiss. "What's wrong?"

Had he really sensed her mind wandering? "Nothing."

"It was something." His expression was serious but not foreboding. Intent. Caring. Just as he'd done a while ago, while asking her how she felt about her battles with Crystal, Jason was listening to her. *Really* listening. "Tell me."

"Have I ever told you how sexy a man who listens is?"

He smiled. "Listening is no good if you're not talking."

Touché. "I'm just worried about my kids."

"There's no 'just' about that. They're important."

She loved that he realized that. "You know, you keep pretending you're just a goodtime guy. But underneath it all—"

"I'm a naked goodtime guy."

His sexy grin promised that was true. Danielle didn't doubt it. She couldn't help imagining it, either. She dropped her gaze to Jason's sculpted chest, lowered her attention to his abs, let it wander all the way down to the waistband of his pajama pants.

Hubba hubba. If only she could unwrap *him*. Looking at him, Danielle felt like someone who'd been given an incredibly longed-for and amazing gift for Christmas . . . then been told she'd have to wait until *never* to open it. The anticipation was killing her. She'd never get to fulfill all these yearnings.

On the other hand, Jason *was* leaving Kismet tomorrow. Given that, maybe it was safe to indulge a little?

"Danielle? Do you have a lint roller? Because my pants are absolutely *covered* in something. Cat hair, maybe? Who has a cat, any—" Crystal burst into the kitchen next. Her gaze swerved to the clinch that Danielle and Jason were currently entangled in. Her eyes widened. Her mouth tightened. "That is *not* appropriate, you two. What if I'd been one of the kids coming in here?"

Left speechless by the irony, Danielle gawked at Crystal.

Jason let his hand wander to Danielle's backside. He gave a cheeky squeeze, making her yelp with surprise. She blushed.

"Oh, never mind." Her onetime nemesis waved. "I can see neither of you gets it. Your behavior *does* affect other people, though, you know. Yours does, Dani. So does yours, Jackson."

At Crystal's sly, semitriumphant look, Jason grinned. If she thought she was going to turn the tables on him, she was mistaken. It was obvious he could see through her machinations.

All at once, so could Danielle. In a flash, she could see that Crystal wasn't worth getting upset over. Yes, she had Mark now—but Danielle didn't want him anymore. Yes, she'd won over the kids with new toys and treats—but Danielle had their love without bribery and cajolery. No wonder Crystal acted the way she did. She'd had to steal Mark's love and probably wasn't sure she could do the same with his children. She was scared.

She was also way too dense to stay angry with. Danielle was over it. Just like that. With Jason's help and his timely intervention earlier, Danielle had had a chance to step outside her own knee-jerk reactions to Crystal and Mark's antics. She'd had a chance to recognize that she could do better. Whereas before today she'd have tumbled face-first into a pile of iced-and-sprinkled Christmas sugar cookies for some much needed distraction, now Danielle felt absolutely free.

She didn't need to compete with Crystal.

She didn't need to be "the nice one." Not this time.

"Sorry, Crystal. I don't have time to hang around and discuss this." Just as Danielle said it, Aiden, Karlie, and Zach returned, duly kitted out in their kid-size cold-weather gear. "I have a Christmastime sleigh ride to enjoy. See you later!"

Then she ushered out her ex and his bride from her house, put on something much warmer than flannel shorts, a cami, and a robe, and got ready to find out exactly how far Jason would go to "play hard," determined to meet him from one impulsive moment to the next, for as many hours as remained to them.

The sleigh ride, courtesy of the staff at The Christmas House B & B located on Kismet's lakefront, was *amazing*. Jason had never experienced anything like it. Even as their packed-full sleigh coursed over snowy hills and through valleys bordered by snow-flocked pines and white-barked birch trees, he couldn't believe he was there. In an authentic sleigh. With metal sleigh runners *whoosh-whooshing* and actual jingle bells jingling and a pair of huge shaggy Clydesdales (named Holly and Ivy, no joke) pulling the whole conveyance at a trot. It was like something out of an old-timey greeting card. The people running the B&B, Reid Sullivan and Karina Barrett, had even gotten the rig out of their barn (an actual barn!), shortly after offering everyone peppermint hot cocoa and apple cider doughnuts "for energy."

He had to have mementos of this experience, Jason knew. The B&B had mounted miniature, remotely operated cameras to the hand-painted sleigh, so they could give riders video and still footage of their rides, à la Disneyland. Ordinarily, the sleigh rides were part of The Christmas House's famed all-inclusive holiday experience, which included family receptions, cookie-baking sessions, shopping excursions, gift wrapping, and an overall ambiance that was as Christmassy as Santa on steroids.

Because Danielle knew her fellow townies, the Sullivans, so well, she'd arranged for a special excursion for Jason and her kids to enjoy. It was a kick seeing Danielle flex her special insider influence—something Jason hadn't known she possessed. Afterward, along with Nate Kelly, the burly former NFL lineman who volunteered at the B&B, they'd all piled into the sleigh for a scenic ride that left Jason's face wind-chapped, his feet numb . . . and his heart as light as a kid's on Christmas Eve.

He only wished that Nate had driven the horses even faster. Jason had been hoping for a thrill ride. Instead, he'd gotten something that had felt like stepping into a Christmas carol.

All the same, as Jason sat in that sleigh bundled up between a whooping Danielle and an accidentally grinning Karlie (who still insisted she *hated* sleigh rides), he actually felt part of something. Something good. Something he wished could be lasting. Maybe that was why, afterward, he approached Nate.

"Hey, thanks for the ride," Jason told him.

"No problem." Nate patted Holly's shaggy flank. "These old gals like getting out in the snow. They love this time of year."

"Being outdoors, running wild, getting all the carrots they can eat?" Jason guessed, casting a glance at everyone else. Led by Danielle, they were currently collecting carrots from the old ribbon-bedecked bucket nailed at the edge of the barn's picturesque corral. "Not too bad a life for a horse, I guess."

"Nope." Nate shook his head. "Not too bad for anybody. Most of the year, I teach industrial arts and home ec at

Kismet High School. But when December rolls around, I volunteer here."

"Volunteer? As in not getting paid? I'm surprised."

"That's because you're not from around here." Nate watched the kids sword-fight with their carrots. Convivially, he gestured for them to come closer to Holly and Ivy instead. "Around here, we stick together. There's no place like Kismet."

"You're a lifer too?"

"You mean a townie? Yeah." Nate grinned. "So are my wife and stepdaughter."

"You never wanted to leave?"

Nate shrugged. "I tried once. When I was drafted into the NFL. Same draft class as Reno Wright. But it wasn't for me."

"Danielle wants to leave. To take the kids to L.A."

"Really?" Nate seemed genuinely taken aback. "Everyone loves her here. Especially now that she's working at Moosby's. She's helped just about everyone in town find toys and gifts."

"Yeah. I was surprised, too. Maybe she'll change her mind." *Maybe she'll let me stay with her.* Wait. What? Jason stuffed his hands in his pockets. He nodded at the sleigh's multiple state-of-the-art cameras. "What happens to the camera footage?"

"Usually our guests opt for photo and video packages. It's part of the experience the B&B offers. I didn't check with you guys, since you're not guests, but I can ask Danielle—"

"Don't do that." Jason glanced at her. "I'll take one."

Nate gave him a curious look. Then, "Aha. I get it."

"Get what?"

"You want the pictures and video," Nate guessed, "but you don't want Danielle to know you're a big ole softy at heart."

Jason started to object. He wanted the footage as a keepsake, sure. But if he was smart, he'd use it to bolster his image rehab efforts, too. What could be more wholesome than a sleigh ride? What could be more public pleasing than that?

Danielle would be happy, right? Just a couple of hours ago, she'd pestered him to let the world see the real him. Well, video and still footage of him frolicking in the snow with three loveable children and their small-town mom *was* the real him.

"Caught me." He shrugged. "No man wants to be a softy."

Nate laughed at that. He nodded. "It's yours. I'll sneak it to you." With that settled, he started adjusting the harnesses.

"Before you put away the horses," Jason interrupted, feeling inspired and hopeful, "can I ask you another favor?"

Nate listened to his request. Then, a few minutes later . . .

"This is *sick*!" Zach chortled, sitting in the driver's position on the sleigh's big bench seat with Jason protectively behind him as they flew over the packed snow, runners squeaking. The boy kept both mittened hands clenched on the horse's reins, staring straight ahead. "Mush, horses! Mush, mush!"

Beside them as the only other occupant of the sleigh—since Danielle, Aiden, and Karlie had opted out—Nate laughed. "Mush is for sled dogs, junior. But maybe you should slow down a little?"

Decidedly *not* slowing down, Zach guided the sleigh downhill. Bucolic scenery flashed by, bumping along in Jason's vision. He could have sworn he glimpsed a vivid blue jay in the snow, but they whooshed past it before he could be sure.

"Slow down? No way!" Zach yelled in a jubilant tone.

"Slow down?" Jason shouted at the same time. "Ha!"

Startled by their shared views on the necessity of making the sleigh go faster, he and Zach stared at each other. They joggled silently up and down on the hard, cold sleigh seat, measuring each other's response. Since Zach was effectively hemmed in by Jason's sheltering arms as he helped the boy control the horses, anything less than honesty was impossible.

"You're doing a great job," Jason said.

Zach grinned. All his former animosity melted away.

The boy didn't say anything. He didn't have to.

"Whoa! I think they just spotted the barn!" Zach whooped, then did his best to control the horses. Jason helped. They both bounced up and down on the seat, laughing as the big Clydesdales increased their speed, jingle bells tolling. "This is better than a roller coaster ride!" Zach shouted. "Whoopee!"

Behind him, Jason grinned. The wintry wind whipped up his hair and froze his cheeks. His eyes watered. He couldn't feel his knees anymore. He was pretty sure his fingers had permanently clenched into a horse-controlling position.

All the same . . . he loved it. This feeling—of making someone happy through his own efforts and ingenuity—was what had made Jason enjoy being part of the toy business in the first place. It was what had made it so rewarding for him to make all those lame homemade toys for his sisters and brother as a kid.

It was what he'd lost when he'd transitioned to CEO.

Beside him, Nate saw his expression. "Softy," he mouthed.

But Jason couldn't argue. Not when it was true.

He wished he had more time with Danielle. More time with Zach, Aiden, and Karlie. More time in Kismet, at Moosby's, and at the whoopie pie bakery next door to the toy store, too. There was still so much more left to do.

He still had to win over Karlie. He still had to finish setting up that fishbowl with Aiden, which they'd only partially done to allow the goldfish time to adjust to his new digs and clean water. He still had to branch out from gingerbread spice whoopie pies to chocolate peppermint crunch whoopie pies to cranberry orange pecan whoopie pies. He still had to find out if Danielle looked as misty-eyed and alluring while she was being made love to in a big, comfy double bed as she did while being kissed senseless in a typical, cluttered kitchen.

Maybe, Jason thought, he could finagle more time. Somehow . . .

"Just make sure you give me those photos," Jason told the hulking former NFLer as the sleigh pulled closer to The Christmas House's grounds. He spied Danielle waiting, bundled up in her fuzzy orange coat and hat, and experienced a weird sense of longing. For her. "Then you can call me whatever you want."

He told Nate where to send the digital footage. He promised to pay up with his credit card later. Then, with his secret mementos duly secured, Jason smiled and waved at Danielle.

If everything went well, they'd have more than just today to spend together, Jason knew. If everything proceeded the way he hoped, they'd have all the way till Christmas.

Chapter Eleven

Jason had done it again, Danielle realized as The Christmas House's big custom sleigh, decorated with its traditional holly-wreathed, hand-painted logo, veered around the corner and came to a snow-spewing stop near the B&B's open barn doors with its jingle bells chiming. He'd won over another of her children.

There was no other explanation for Zach's mile-wide grin. It didn't let up, either—not even as her son relinquished the reins to Nate Kelly. Evidently, her little boy had a need for speed . . . and a brand-new friend who was happy to indulge his budding machismo. Because Jason, too, was wearing a wall-to-wall grin as he jumped out of the sleigh, then held up both arms to help Zach out. For an instant, their smiles met and mingled.

They liked each other. Somehow, they really liked each other. Danielle could have sworn her heart did a happy dance.

She'd been so worried that, someday when she did find someone to try postdivorce dating with, the process would be awkward and difficult for her kids to handle. But Jason made the whole endeavor look easy. Zach chatted nonstop with him, waving his arms animatedly, as they patted the horses. Aiden ran up to him, ungainly in his snow pants, and he joined in, too.

The lone holdout at joining the Jason Hamilton fan club was Karlie, who stood nearby stubbornly toeing the snow with her boot and pretending not to notice anyone else. As the oldest, she was the least naïve—and clearly the most resistant to change, too.

Dad's fling with Crystal is only temporary, Mom. We all know that.

Remembering her children's stalwart belief that their parents' divorce was only temporary, Danielle bit her lip. She had to make it clear to Karlie, Zach, and Aiden that she and Mark weren't reconciling. She had to help them adjust to the idea of her dating again, too. So far, this outing with Jason was acting as a convenient test run—and so far, it was a roaring success.

All except for Karlie. She folded her arms and sneaked a glance at the jolly conversation happening near the sleigh, then made a grumpy face. She huffed toward The Christmas House B & B, her footsteps crunching a telltale path in the sparkling snow.

Danielle let her go. She could see that the B&B's proprietors, Reid and Karina, were waiting at the main house's light-and-wreath-bedecked back porch, along with Danielle's friend Vanessa Sullivan, who helped manage the place. Unlike Danielle, Vanessa embodied Kismet's artsy side, from her thumb rings and tattoos to her almost-Mohawk haircut and cutting-edge wardrobe. At one time, Danielle had thought she could be as free to express herself as Vanessa was. Now, though, she was happy to have opted out of an alternative lifestyle. Inventory and spreadsheets suited her much better than oil paints and artist's clay.

As Karlie stomped away, Jason approached Danielle. Behind him, she glimpsed Zach and Aiden helping Nate put away the horses. Jason had a moment free, then. Thanks to

Karlie's sulky retreat, Danielle did, too. What a wonderful coincidence.

She could get used to watching a handsome, muscle-bound man striding toward her through the snow. It was . . . thrilling. Because it was Jason. Because he was, Danielle had to admit to herself, the most arresting man she'd ever met—even now, when he'd swapped his fancy coat for a toasty ski jacket bought at Reno Wright's sporting goods store, and his citified, not-quite-appropriate wing tips for a pair of rugged snow boots from the same supplier. The two men had hit it off, Danielle had learned. That wasn't surprising. After all, given two minutes and an introduction, Jason was capable of making friends with anyone. And Reno, as the town's NFL conquering hero, had the confidence and ease to welcome any newcomer to Kismet . . . no matter what scandals that new arrival was supposed to have been involved in.

After all, Reno had a little experience with scandalous people. His own wife, Rachel, had stirred up a whopper of a scandal herself, during her time in L.A. Thinking about the mass overreaction to Rachel's sartorial showdown with one of her former Hollywood clients, Danielle frowned. All this time, she'd been thinking of L.A. as the epicenter of Moosby's HQ. But it was better known for frivolous celebrities, gossip, media mania, sunshine, smog, and gridlock. Would moving herself and her children there *really* be an improvement? Sure, Kismet could be unsophisticated. It could be limiting. The townspeople could be a little nosy. But it was also cozy, friendly, and familiar.

Those were a few of Danielle's favorite things.

Was it possible, she wondered as Jason neared her, that she was chasing another impossible dream? That just as she'd tried to convince herself she could be an artist like her parents and Vanessa—forcing herself through years of drawing, painting, acting, singing, and more—she was now trying to convince herself that she was a corporate-climbing, big-city dweller at heart?

If Jason was right about her not wanting to leave Kismet . . .

But he wasn't, Danielle told herself resolutely as Jason arrived and took her gloved hand in his. He *couldn't* be right about her. He barely knew her. As far as Moosby's HQ being "soul crushing" went, as he'd claimed . . . well, his own lack of effort had to have something to do with that perception. He needed to cooperate with the board, not fight them on every decision.

To that end, Danielle smiled. "You look like you're having fun." She took in Jason's shining eyes, his beard-shadowed jawline, and his eager expression . . . and wanted to sigh over all the handsomeness within her reach. He was *so* irresistible. But she needed to be firm. "If the board could see you now—"

"They'd pee their pants," Jason said. "My going on a high-speed sleigh ride is a definite liability risk. The lawyers would go crazy. I'd have to have a meeting first, sign waivers—"

Troubled, Danielle frowned. "Surely they wouldn't demand all that just so you can go on a Christmastime sleigh ride."

"Surely they would. You don't know them. Not like I do."

Actually, Danielle did know Chip Larsen a little, thanks to the phone calls they'd shared. But she knew it wouldn't exactly enhance her day off with Jason to discuss his alleged corporate adversary. In fact, just then, it felt a little like betraying Jason to have filed those reports with Moosby's corporate at all. But she had to do *something*. Jason certainly wasn't.

"But today," Jason went on, visibly shaking off those work-related details, "I'm not a CEO. I'm just a guy. A guy who's really getting into all this wintertime snow stuff. Zach was telling me about an excellent place nearby to go sledding. And Aiden wants me to build a snowman with him. But first—"

He broke off. Still holding her hand, Jason scanned the snowy horizon. Danielle gazed sappily at his face while he did, feeling herself get caught up in a daydream where *this* was her regular Saturday afternoon existence—doing something fun as a family, enjoying spending time together . . . stepping nearer to her man so she could greedily inhale the scents of leather and cold and faint musky maleness that clung to him.

As Gigi would have said, *Miam-miam*.

Danielle wasn't cut out for singlehood, she knew. She liked closeness. She liked working together to build a routine. She liked feeling that she had someone to care for—someone who would care for her, too. After her divorce, she'd pushed down all those longings and tried to forget about them. But just like her long-lost libido, her yearning for love and connection had resurfaced with a vengeance, called to the forefront by Jason.

By Jason and his broad shoulders, dark brows, sensual lips . . .

"Where's Karlie?" he asked, interrupting her latest enjoyable fantasy about kissing him . . . and then undressing him.

"She went back to the B&B." Danielle gestured in the direction of the place's three-story, white-painted main house. "They're hosting a gingerbread-house building session today."

"Does Karlie like baking?"

"She likes icing cookies. And eating them. And petting the B&B's mascot, Digby the dachshund. Every year, the Sullivan's outfit him in little holiday sweaters. It's adorable."

"Does Karlie want a puppy?"

Aha. Belatedly, Danielle understood what Jason was doing.

"I can't let you buy her a puppy."

"This from the woman who's extorted a small fortune

from me for gas money?" He grinned. "I could have hired a private helicopter for what you've charged me to get around town."

"That's different." Principally because Danielle didn't intend to keep any of that money. Especially not now that she and Jason had—however momentarily—become personally involved. "I mean, I should probably not let Karlie have a puppy right now, in case we all wind up moving to the big city."

"You won't like it in the big city. I promise." Jason looked around, taking in the scenic B&B grounds, the distant iced-over lake dotted with rickety fishing shanties, the towering pine trees and the overall sense of peacefulness. "You working at Moosby's HQ would be worse than you going back to art school. Or starting a third band. Or taking up acting again."

As Jason went on listing her less-than-successful artistic pursuits, Danielle gawked at him. He'd really been listening to her the other day. *He'd remembered.* Also, he'd just succinctly enumerated the very same reservations she'd been thinking five minutes earlier. How did he keep reading her mind that way?

". . . or coloring graphic novels," Jason finished. "If I had it to do over again, I'm not sure I'd work at Moosby's HQ either."

"If you didn't do that, you couldn't afford helicopters and puppies. And you know how the ladies love a man with deep pockets," Danielle joked, hoping to change the subject from her own unwanted misgivings, "so you can't possibly quit now."

"Ah." Jason appeared enlightened. *Too* enlightened. She hoped he knew she wasn't serious about wanting to date someone wealthy. "The truth comes out. You want a rich man. Well, babe . . ." With a smoldering grin, he stepped nearer. He dipped his head to the side, gazing at her mouth.

"I've got millions. Anytime you want it, you just come right here and get it."

Danielle wanted it, all right. She wanted *him*, as usual. Morning, noon, and night. Feeling her heart rate triple at their nearness, she inhaled. She looked up at Jason. The pull between them couldn't possibly be as strong as it felt just then.

Except it was. "I do want it. Where do I get it again?"

Her teasing tone made his lips quirk in a fresh smile. Jason puckered up. "Right here," he told her. "Right now."

"I don't remember asking for a timetable." Not when she was so busy savoring the anticipation between them. "As far as 'right here' goes, I'm a little confused. Do you mean your mouth? Or somewhere else? I thought I saw your lips move, but—"

"Oh, the rest of me is interested, too. Believe me."

She did believe him. She was also intrigued by that "rest of him" business. Because from where she was standing, the rest of him looked *fine*. "Let's start up here." Gently, Danielle touched her mouth to his. She *loved* the feel of his lips against hers. "And we'll just see where it goes from there."

"So slowly?" Jason stifled a frustrated moan. He kissed her again. "Let's keep going. We don't have time to dawdle."

"Oh yeah." Feeling herself become twice as overheated in her fuzzy orange jacket and hat, Danielle sucked in another lungful of crisp, icy air. "You're leaving soon. Well, maybe, since you're the boss, you can find a way to fix that. Hmm?"

She augmented her suggestion with another kiss. Responding instantly, Jason swept his hands over her jacket, over her shoulders, up to her hat. He clasped the back of her head, holding her closer and closer. Danielle opened her mouth wider. On a helpless moan of her own, she deepened their kiss. *Ah. Yes.*

Kissing Jason was like everything she'd ever wanted. It was liberating, exciting, and *very* unexpected, all at once. It was fantastic . . . yet it always left her wanting more. Maybe it always would. Unless Jason really could find a way to stay longer.

"With an inducement like that one," Jason told her breathlessly, breaking off their kiss to rest his forehead against hers, "I'll definitely find a way to get us more time."

"You could do that," Danielle agreed blithely, not wanting to break the spell by demanding a promise he couldn't keep. "Or we could just enjoy the time we have available right now."

Because, honestly, part of the appeal of being with Jason was that it was free of risk. If she hadn't known he had to leave for the rest of his public-appearance tour the next day, she might have been hesitant to move as quickly as she had.

Ordinarily, Danielle knew, she wouldn't have allowed a new man to meet and spend time with her children as readily as this. She wouldn't have allowed someone she'd been dating to move into her house, even temporarily. She wouldn't have gotten caught up in kissing a man—in public!—so easily. She had, within seconds, become the new queen of Kismet public displays of affection.

Hmm. Maybe she'd been a little too hard on Mark and Crystal. If they felt anywhere near the connection Danielle did with Jason, it was a miracle they ever got out of bed.

"You're right. Time's wasting." Jason squeezed her hand. He stepped away, then inhaled. He appeared to be mustering strength for . . . something. "We can't just stand here kissing all day."

"We could sneak into the barn and keep kissing all day?"

"Sounds good, but . . . no." He squared his shoulders. "We have things to do together. Fun times to enjoy. A certain balky ten-year-old to find and get a puppy for."

Endearingly, Jason's eyes gleamed with eagerness at the idea. Danielle loved that he wanted to be so generous. All the same, she had to say . . . "We're *not* getting a puppy."

"But if Karlie would like it—" After mulling it over for

all of a nanosecond, he nodded. "We should totally get a puppy."

"You're not supposed to bribe children, remember?"

"I've already committed a public scandal." Jason shrugged. "How much worse could a simple bribe make things?"

"I don't want to find out." He might not be dedicated to working things out with his board of directors, but Danielle was. "Let's just nix the puppy idea and go on from there."

"Okay." He scanned the skyline again, obviously considering other ideas. "Ten is too young for a sports car, right?"

"Jason!"

Another shrug. "The trouble with being ridiculously wealthy is that you lose all sense of proportion."

"I'll say, you do." The trouble with being kissed by a gazillionaire, she'd learned, was that it was difficult to quit. "Besides, if anyone needs a new car, it's me."

"Really? Because if you're in the market—"

"Kidding. I don't want you for your money."

"Everyone else does."

"Karlie doesn't. She's stubborn. Like her mother."

"You Sharpe women know how to keep a man on his toes."

"The truth is," Danielle mused, "you don't *have* to impress Karlie. She's a tough nut to crack. Besides, you've already added Aiden and Zach to your fan club. That couldn't have been easy."

Jason disagreed. "Aiden already invited me to have a sleepover in his room tonight, instead of sleeping with you."

Oh. She probably should have been focusing on the pertinent part of that statement—that her son had already awarded Jason the high honor of a sleepover invitation, something Aiden didn't issue lightly—but Danielle couldn't concentrate on that part at all. All she could do was imagine her, Jason, her comfy double bed with its Christmassy patterned flannel sheets . . . and all three of them in a ménage à trois to remember. If Jason slept in her room,

Danielle mused, that would *really* convince her kids that she'd moved on—exactly the way their Dad had done with Crystal.

Except with 100 percent less inane giggling and groping.

"Well," Danielle said, sidestepping the question of who was sleeping where for the moment, "Karlie is different. If you want to impress her, you'll have to let her impress you."

"Huh?"

"She's the oldest. She likes to be the leader," Danielle explained. "She likes to feel that she's in charge of things."

"She probably *is* in charge of things. Older siblings rule!"

Aha. Danielle grinned. "I forgot you're the oldest, too. You have two younger sisters and a younger brother, right?"

Jason nodded. "Jennifer, Janelle, and Jeremy. But they've always needed somebody like me to be in charge. They need me to take care of things. To lead by example. To blaze a trail."

"If you say so, Lewis and Clark." It was ironic that Jason considered himself to be an exemplar in his personal life, when his work life seemed so uninspired. Maybe the problem was that he didn't feel sufficiently *needed* at Moosby's HQ? "All I'm saying is that, if you want to win over Karlie, you're going to have to fall in line. You're going to have to let *her* lead."

Jason seemed baffled by the very concept. "How?"

Danielle thought about it. "Let Karlie teach you something. Let her show you something. Let her be the one in charge."

"Well, if we were in California right now, she could show me how well she can learn to surf," Jason said in an obvious (and off the mark) attempt to tackle the idea. "Or scuba dive. Or paddle-board. Because I could absolutely teach Karlie how to—"

"No. *You're* supposed to be the student here."

"I'm not sure you're right. That sounds wrong to me."

Danielle grinned. "Spoken like a true CEO."

At that, Jason frowned. "You think I'm a true CEO?"

Confused by his suddenly fraught expression, Danielle tried to backpedal. "You head up a successful multinational corporation," she pointed out. "You are, as they say, the boss."

"But I'm only the CEO because I have to be. Because without me holding the line, Mr. Moosby would lose everything."

Danielle blinked at him. "Alfred Moosby? The founder? Is he still involved with the company?" Moosby's HQ had always tried to keep a low profile in the media—except when taking advantage of Jason's charisma to stir up positive press. After going public, they'd downplayed the involvement of Moosby's original—but less dazzling and youthful—entrepreneur. "I had the impression he retired years ago."

"He did retire. But he entrusted Moosby's to me. He still cares what happens to it." Jason broke off. He squinted across the snowy landscape toward the B&B. "I've got it!" he said. "Ice-skating! I've *never* been ice-skating. Hell, I've never even been roller-skating. Or Rollerblading. I'm probably terrible at it." He brightened. "Karlie can teach me how to ice-skate!"

"Um, I'm not sure you ought to do that."

But Jason was already gesturing toward the boys, to make Aiden and Zach join them. Excitedly, he grabbed Danielle's hand.

"She's bound to feel like an expert," he explained. "Because I'm going to look like the rank beginner I am."

It was gutsy, Danielle had to allow. Still, for a die-hard California man like him, maybe ice-skating wasn't a genius idea.

"If you break your leg," she told him discouragingly, "you won't be able to finish your Midwestern Moosby's media tour."

Jason cheered up even more. "It's a win-win!"

Hmm. Maybe he had a point. A broken leg would be

problematic and painful, of course. But it would also require an extended in-town recuperation period. Wouldn't it?

Also, did that mean Jason *wanted* to stay in Kismet awhile?

No. She couldn't hope for that. "Karlie is a really good ice-skater," Danielle warned Jason as their foursome crossed the B&B's glittering snowdrift-dusted grounds. "She's taken figure-skating lessons for the past six years. She plays on Edna Gresham's peewee ice-hockey team. She can do a double lutz!"

"Sounds cool." Jason kept going. "I can learn that."

"No, you can't. It's a toe-pick-assisted counter-clockwise jump. The best you could even hope for is a flutz. Even then—"

"Look, I get it," Jason said patiently. He glanced at the boys, making sure they followed. "Ice is hard. Skates are sharp. Falls are inevitable. But I like the sound of that flutz thing."

She didn't want to say it, but . . . "A flutz is the cheater's version. It's not supposed to happen in correct figure skating."

"With a name like that? It sounds like fun!"

"Of course it does. To you."

She didn't mean to sound disapproving. But Danielle knew she did, thanks to the defensive glance Jason tossed her.

Well, that was the story of their (admittedly transitory) relationship, wasn't it? Danielle tried to be the voice of reason, while Jason went right on behaving irresponsibly.

She sort of loved his enthusiasm, though. Especially since it was aimed at making her daughter feel content with things—specifically, with her mother moving on with dating.

Tardily realizing that must be Jason's motivation for all this, Danielle experienced a fresh wave of affection for him. No wonder people melted whenever Jason came near. He couldn't help wanting to give people exactly what they needed—attention, praise, excitement . . . or, in her case, new hope for the future.

"All I mean is," she amended, "you ought to be careful."

"Or what?" Jason grinned. "I'll get hurt?"

"Yes!" It was unfathomable to her that someone wouldn't want to do all they could to avoid being hurt. "Of course."

He only shrugged. "You can't live life in a box."

That felt like a dig at *her*. At her "plan first, then plan again, then act, then feel haunted by regret" way of living.

Well, Danielle couldn't help that. She'd been hurt.

Jason had obviously never invested himself in anything long enough or seriously enough to get similarly hurt. Which was nice for him, of course—and only made him an ever safer choice for a fling. A nice, jingle-bell-jangling, under-the-mistletoe fling.

"Fine," she agreed as they reached the B&B and clomped up its back porch steps in unison. "Don't say I didn't warn you."

"You warned him, like, six different ways, Mom," Zach informed her. "If he doesn't get it by now, he's an idiot."

"He's not an idiot!" Aiden declared indignantly. "He knows all about fish and how *awesome* they are when they poop!"

At that, Jason grinned. "See? My wingmen have my back."

"We're your wingmen?" Zach asked. "That's sick!"

"I like wingmen," Aiden said loyally. "They're the best."

Danielle doubted her younger son had any idea what that meant. But his allegiance to his new buddy apparently ran deep.

Despite her wariness, she couldn't help liking that. Zach and Aiden's reactions to Jason only proved that they would be okay when, someday, she decided to date in earnest. Until then . . .

"Let's warm up inside the B&B first," Danielle suggested. "We can see the decorated Christmas trees"—The Christmas House boasted several different kinds and sizes of holiday evergreens situated around the property—"look at the snow globe collection, check out the gingerbread houses . . . maybe even have lunch in the B&B's dining room. Every year, they decorate it with candles and fancy linens and dozens of snowy white amaryllis flowers."

Jason winked at her. "I know where I'm taking you for Christmas next year. Judging by the way you looked when you just described all that, The Christmas House is *your* Disneyland."

Snapped from her reverie, Danielle shook her head.

The Christmas House wasn't her Disneyland. It couldn't be, because she—as a townie—was inured to all the holiday hoopla in Kismet. Even if she *had* begun feeling a little bit jollier lately.

Also, Jason wouldn't be in Kismet with her next year. He would be back to his regular life of traveling the world, making executive decisions, behaving like a playboy, getting into trouble . . . and *not* settling down with a small-town divorcée.

This fantasy was going a little too far, all of a sudden.

"Hey, I see Karlie!" Danielle waved toward the B&B's parlor, where her daughter sat beneath a Christmas tree with a few other children. Digby the dachshund had flopped on her lap with his traditional holiday sweater on. "Let's get this party started."

Chapter Twelve

Jason tried not to feel bugged by the way Danielle had shut him down when he'd joked about taking her to The Christmas House next year. But he couldn't help it. He did feel bugged.

What kind of woman didn't want to be treated to a special experience in a special place at Christmastime? What kind of woman didn't want her dreams to come true, no matter how potpourri-scented and over-the-top they were? What kind of woman, most of all, wasn't wowed by big, showy gestures?

Those were his failsafe. Jason had always known, in the back of his mind, that he could use his millionaire card, if he ever needed to, to get the interest of almost any woman.

Except Danielle.

What use was his fortune if it didn't even impress her?

He knew damn well that she'd sidetracked him on purpose, too. She'd hustled him and the kids into the B&B's parlor as though her snow boots were on fire, refusing to even entertain the idea of Christmas next year. Or the year after that. Or, you know, *forever*. Which was what was sounding pretty good to him.

Not that an overblown attitude like that made sense.

Clearly, all the sentimental Kismet coziness was getting to him, because Jason had never before felt so smitten with a woman. Even now, more than an hour after they'd all left The Christmas House together, he was proving his devotion by strapping ugly boots equipped with steel blades to his feet—all for the express purpose of making a good impression on Danielle's daughter.

This had better work, Jason told himself as he yanked his skates' laces tighter. Because he was forgoing a whole lot of potential kissing with Danielle in order to bond with Karlie.

Still, as he watched Karlie skate along the ice at Kismet's outdoor rink in front of the old-fashioned white stone courthouse, Jason couldn't help feeling sympathetic toward her. It wasn't easy being a ten-year-old girl. Karlie reminded him of Jennifer and Janelle at the same age—all coltish arms and legs, messy braided hair, and uncertainty covered up with girlish bravado. He liked Karlie . . . but she didn't want to like him.

Wearing an affectedly blasé expression, Karlie skated past the bench where everyone else was getting ready. Jason couldn't miss the hasty peek she cast them all, though. She didn't want to be seen needing attention or confirmation of her skills. But, just like everyone else, she craved them. Seeing Karlie's hopeful glance made him feel twice as determined to make this work.

Beside him, Zach got up from the bench. Wearing his skates, he took a few careful steps on the rubberized mat bordering the space between the outdoor benches and the ice-skating rink.

He stepped onto the ice. Several bigger kids almost veered into him. Jason leaped to his feet, worried about Zach. "Hey!"

The kids missed him. Expertly, Zach pushed off.

He swerved into a backward skate, then gave Jason a

quizzical glance. Obviously, he'd overheard his alarmed shout.

"Good job!" Jason held up both thumbs. "Keep it up!"

Zach saluted him with one mittened hand, then skated away. Jason watched him for a second. Then the truth hit him.

"Zach is on Edna Gresham's peewee ice-hockey team, too, isn't he?" Jason asked Danielle. "He wasn't ever going to get mowed over by all those big kids out there. Or the adults."

The ice-skating rink was popular—and it was understandable why. The rink was located in a scenic, historically significant spot, bordered by twin sets of bleachers for spectators and a light-bedecked retaining wall to contain the skaters. It was decorated with garlands and huge municipal ornaments strung overhead, and lit by more rows of white globe lights. Now that dusk was starting to fall, the whole place looked ridiculously picturesque. Christmas carols played over the loudspeakers, vendors sold hot chocolate, spiced mulled cider, and pies-in-a-jar from the Galaxy Diner. Cinnamon-scented deliciousness wafted over everything.

"No, Zach was fine all along. He's a good skater." Danielle smiled up at Jason from her position fastening Aiden's double-bladed beginner skates. "Welcome to my world, though."

"Your world?"

"Of worrying about these guys over every little thing."

Oh. Jason wasn't interested in doing *that*. He'd only just met these rug rats. As much as he liked them, he wasn't—

"Karlie, look out!" Jason yelled, catching a glimpse of the girl spinning in the middle of the ice. A pair of unsteady skaters were about to crash right into her. "They're going to—"

Hearing him, Karlie lost her balance. She wobbled.

She swept sideways out of the way, narrowly escaping a collision.

"Whew." Jason breathed again, casting a hasty look of concern at Danielle. "That was a close one."

But Danielle, having equipped Aiden and set him on his feet, wasn't looking at Jason. She was looking at her daughter.

"Uh-oh. Now you've done it."

"Done what?" Jason looked. At the storm clouds gathering on Karlie's pert, hat-topped face, he blanched. "I see. Uh-oh."

"Yeah. I'm just going to leave you two to it. Aiden and I will be out on the ice." Danielle held out her gloved hand to her son. He clasped it. In a well-practiced maneuver, the two of them trod gingerly to the rink. "Good luck!" she yelled.

Spying Karlie approaching, Jason knew he needed it.

Breathless and pink-cheeked, the girl stopped in front of him. She put her hands on her hips. She gave him a mighty scowl.

He was impressed. It was a pretty fearsome scowl.

"You have a future as somebody's boss someday," Jason told Karlie good-naturedly. "You're going to be indomitable."

She sniffed. "If you think I don't know what that means, you're wrong. Also, you can't sweet-talk me. I'm not my mom."

Oookay. Rallying, Jason gave her a serious look. "Sorry about distracting you out there. I was worried about you."

"*You* don't have any reason to worry about me."

Her implication that he wasn't part of her family was obvious. "I'm impressed. You look like a really good skater."

"Tell me something I don't know, temp."

Jason angled his head. "Temp?"

"Yeah. Temp. It's what we call people like you." Karlie gave him a dismissive look. "People who aren't from around here."

Ah. "From what I can tell, most people in Kismet aren't from around here. It's a tourist destination. A resort town."

Karlie lifted her chin. "That's why it's better to be a townie. People like *you* crowd up all the good spots. Like here."

She glanced over her shoulder, indicating her disdain for all the vacationers currently on the ice-skating rink. That was interesting. Unlike Danielle, who insisted she didn't want to stay in her hometown, Karlie was apparently proud to be a townie.

He wondered if Danielle had told her kids about her plans to move them all to L.A. There, *they'd* be the "temps."

"Has it ever occurred to you," Jason said, "that if there weren't any vacationers to 'crowd up' the ice-skating rink, the town might not set up the ice-skating rink at all?"

For an instant, Karlie looked uncertain. Like a typical ten-year-old, she recovered quickly. "That would *never* happen. For one thing, all these food places would protest."

"They might not have enough customers to be here either."

Her expression darkened. "Are you trying to *completely* ruin Christmas for me? I don't even know what my mom was thinking, bringing you here with us. This is the *worst* time of year for her to have some stupid new boyfriend."

Jason tried to take heart from that. At least Karlie was convinced he and Danielle were dating. That was progress, right?

"I might be a little *less* stupid," Jason said in a conciliatory, leading tone, "if I knew how to ice-skate."

"You don't even know how to skate?" Karlie blurted. She rolled her eyes, hands still on her hips as she gave him an incredulous once-over. "Were you born with flippers for feet?"

He almost laughed. This was too serious to make light of, though. Jason deliberately sobered his expression. "I'm pretty sure they're normal feet. I wedged them into skates, at least."

"Sheesh." Karlie cast an exasperated glance at the festive light strings overhead. Behind her, skaters whizzed and/or wobbled by, including Danielle and Aiden and (more quickly) Zach, who'd found some of his friends to skate with. "That's really pathetic. No wonder you're overreacting so much to every single person coming anywhere near me and Zach on the ice."

"Yeah," Jason agreed. "No wonder." He stared with open dismay at his laced-up black ice skates. "I didn't want your mom to know, but I'm running out of reasons to sit here."

He saw the craftiness enter Karlie's eyes and knew he'd chosen the right approach. If Karlie wanted to sabotage her mom's "stupid new boyfriend," her opportunity had just arrived.

"You do look pretty stupid sitting there," Karlie agreed.

Jason tried to appear as forlorn as possible.

If anyone who knew him could have seen him then, they would have laughed their asses off. Jason Hamilton was anything but forlorn—at least he was when he wasn't at work at Moosby's HQ.

He'd really been hoping his vacation would restore his work mojo. Instead, his trip had been cut short by his accidental scandal—and he'd found more inspiration and hope working here at the Kismet Moosby's store than anywhere else.

"I could, you know, like, teach you," Karlie offered grudgingly.

There it was. Jason brightened. "Teach me to ice-skate?"

She examined the end of her pigtail. Shrugged. Nodded.

"That would be great. Thank you, Karlie."

At his relieved, grateful tone, Karlie seemed uncomfortable. She gave another shrug. "Whatever. Just don't shout at me anymore. You sound like a freak. I have friends here, you know."

Jason nodded. "What do I do first?"

"Fall down."

Affronted, he frowned. "Hey. I *might* be good at this."

"No, I mean, falling down is the first step of learning."

"You're making that up." Jason was willing to look like

a patsy if it made Karlie warm up to him. But when it came to actually *being* a patsy . . . he wasn't down with that. "Come on."

In the distance, Danielle blew him a kiss. With her other hand, she held on to Aiden as they carefully circled the rink.

"If I'm going to teach you," Karlie said, "you have to do whatever I say. Whenever I say it. Exactly how I say to do it."

Wow. Junior Control Freak was on a roll. He'd really started something here. But he really wanted to make this work.

"You know, I'm a big brother myself," Jason began, "so I know what it's like to be the leader. That means—"

"Stand up," Karlie barked.

Oh boy. Obligingly, Jason made himself stand.

His ankles threatened to cave in immediately.

"My skates must be defective." He frowned at them. "I'm really strong, but these are doing something to my ankles."

He took a tentative step, hoping to muscle through it.

His knees momentarily buckled, joining the *screw you* party being hosted by his ankles. Suddenly, it felt as though his non-ice-skating body was staging a full-on rebellion. But he hadn't become the man he was by quitting easily. So he kept going.

"Stop!" Karlie ran toward him. She grabbed his arm, then peered into his face with real concern. "You're going to break your leg if you just blunder onto the ice like that, dummy."

"What is it with you Sharpes and your broken leg fixation?" Jason asked, remembering discussing that same dire scenario with Danielle earlier. "I'm tough. I'll be fine."

"It's everyone else I'm worried about," Karlie informed him. "If you collapse on the ice, you become a human hazard."

"You mean I might cause someone else to fall?"

"Or make them accidentally run over you and slice off a few fingers," the girl said with gruesome delight. "You can't go onto the ice until you learn how to fall properly."

Jason scoffed. "I know how to fall."

Karlie shoved him. He pinwheeled to regain his balance, refusing to fall before he'd even gotten onto the damn rink itself.

Or not. In one unlikely instant, Jason landed in the snow. On his ass. With both arms flopping uselessly to his sides.

Karlie loomed over him, all pink coat and pigtails, wearing a smug expression. "You were saying?"

This was going to be more difficult than he'd thought.

Humbled, Jason nodded. "Fine. Teach me how to fall."

"My pleasure!" Karlie gave him a hand up. Jason allowed her to believe she was hoisting all six-feet-plus of him to his feet. "Now, flex your knees in a squat, like you're sitting in a chair," she instructed. "Hold out your arms. Clench your fists to protect your fingers from passing skate blades. Now fall."

With concentration and gusto, Jason did. *Whooomp.*

It was a good thing he'd invested in better cold-weather gear at Reno's sporting-goods store. He was going to need it.

"Good!" Karlie applauded. "Now practice it again."

Jason did, ignoring the stares of curious onlookers.

"Okay. Now, wait for it . . ." Karlie paused. "Again! Fall!"

Suspiciously, Jason did as he was told. He moved from a deep, CrossFit-worthy squat to a near face-plant in the snow.

Karlie had been waiting until her mother was looking, he realized belatedly. She'd timed his practice flop perfectly.

From the snowbank created by a recent snowplowing, Jason glimpsed Danielle ice-skating by in a graceful line composed of her, Aiden, and Zach, all holding hands. Aw. They were sweet.

And he was a sucker. Because he was letting a four-and-a-half-foot tyrant dictate his every move. He must *really* like Danielle, Jason realized, to put up with all this.

"So, temp . . . how do you like my indomitableness now?"

Indomitableness? Karlie really had known what he'd meant.

She caught his surprised look and shrugged. "I read a lot."

"Let's go onto the ice now," Jason suggested. "I'm ready."

"Well . . . okay." Karlie squinted menacingly at him. "But *don't* try to hold my hand. If you really have to, you can clutch the wall. But if you try to grab me, I'll body check you."

Jason got up. "What kind of peewee hockey league do you play in, bruiser? I'm not on the opposing team, you know."

"Says you. And I'm on the *winning* kind of hockey team."

He admired her gumption. Even if Karlie was a tyrant (and she was), she was also determined, loyal, and ingenious. Those were all positive qualities. Jason didn't want to see them crushed by a world that sometimes boxed in women too tightly.

"Then I couldn't have picked a better teacher," he told her. He smiled. "Thanks again for helping me impress your mom."

Karlie looked away. Shamefacedly. "Don't thank me yet. You haven't made it around the rink a single time."

Jason wasn't worried. He'd started making inroads with Karlie, and that was all he wanted. "I'll get there eventually."

"My mom hates bad ice skaters."

"I'll keep trying until I get better."

"She hates positive thinkers, too."

"You can only fail if you stop trying," Jason insisted.

"Ugh." Karlie frowned at him. "That's what my mom says all the time. Like, when I have to redo a homework problem."

"Practice makes perfect."

"She says that, too!" Karlie's mistrustful gaze pinned him midway to the ice-skating rink. "What's up with you two, anyway?" she asked. "Because even my dad isn't that good at sounding *exactly* like my mom." She shuddered. "It's spooky."

Jason grinned. "I like it."

"You would." Karlie frowned elaborately. "Temp."

But this time, her epithet held a little less animosity.

"Let's ice-skate, townie." Jason grabbed the wall. He stepped onto the rink. He felt crisp wintry air rush past him, pushed by the more expert skaters. "I'm ready to go."

"You're going to fail," Karlie predicted glumly.

But just at that moment, Jason caught another glimpse of Danielle in the distance. She was moving backward as she ice-skated with precision slowness, towing Aiden with both hands.

The little boy whooped with glee. Jason smiled.

"I'm not going to fail. Not when I want this so much."

Then he boldly pushed off, veered onto the ice, and crashed.

Danielle had never seen anyone fall so much.

Again and again under the glowing lights of the Kismet municipal ice-skating rink, Jason pushed off on his rented skates, wearing a tenacious expression that only enhanced his incredible good looks. Once or twice, he actually got some momentum going. Then, just when it appeared he might finally be getting the hang of things, he'd inevitably tumble to the ice.

He didn't exactly do any of those things privately, either. Almost everyone in Kismet either knew Jason or knew of him by now. The local residents were as quick with their heckling and grins as they were with their encouragement and helpful hints.

It was endearing, really. Jason tried his best to let Karlie teach him to skate—something that clearly didn't come naturally to him—and her daughter didn't take it easy on him, either.

Finally, Danielle couldn't stand it anymore. Jason would

keep going until his kneecaps cracked. Karlie would gleefully let him. So Danielle called an end to their ice-skating outing.

"That's it, you guys. Time to head home," she announced long after dark. "Look at Aiden. His lips are turning blue."

"They are not," her son argued, looking vaguely Smurf-like.

"Zach's teeth are chattering," Danielle persisted.

"Nuh"—*chatter, chatter*—"uh," Zach disagreed, shivering.

"Karlie is one whip and a chair short of joining the circus." Danielle leaned in. "Lighten up on Jason, okay?"

"I'm not done teaching him yet!" her daughter objected. At least she had the good grace to seem discomfited by her own heavy-handed "teaching" routine. "He's still *horrible* at it!"

"Jason is getting pretty banged up. It's time to go."

On the ice, her temporary boyfriend gave her a cocky wave. "I've almost got it!" he shouted. "We can't leave yet."

Great. They'd all banded together to oppose common sense.

But as soon as Karlie saw that Jason wanted to stay, she changed her mind . . . of course. "Okay. I'm ready to go."

With a smooth sideways swoosh, she brought her skating to a stop at the rink's exit. Her departure made her brothers sigh.

Their only hope had been sticking together. They knew it. Once Karlie abandoned the cause, it was only a matter of time.

"Can we get whoopie pies?" Zach came in as well to join Danielle at the rink's edge where she'd stopped. "They're selling them at the concession stand. My friends got some."

"Me too! Me too!" Aiden clomped in in his brother's wake.

"Do they have those pumpkin chocolate chip ones?" Karlie asked, never too grumpy for sweets. "Those are the best kind."

In their wake, Jason kept skating. He was so muscular—and usually so agile. It surprised Danielle to see him struggling.

"If you both take Aiden with you, and you all stay together, that's fine." Danielle pulled out the cash she'd stashed in her pocket. "This should be plenty of money."

Karlie took it. "You're not coming with us?"

"I'm going to wait here for Jason. Just in case he needs help off the ice. Sometimes stopping isn't easy."

"He made it look easy," Zach said. "With his butt."

Aiden chortled. "Zach said butt!"

Karlie looked . . . guilty. Jason hadn't won her over yet. But he was closer than he'd been that morning. That was something.

"He's trying," Danielle told them. "He's from California. He's never been ice-skating before. They don't have ice there."

Zach and Aiden looked baffled by that.

"They have snow, though, right?" Aiden asked.

"No. They don't have snow. But they have sunshine, nice weather, swimming pools, high rises, the Pacific Ocean—"

"I like snow better," her younger son said decisively. "You can't build a snowman with any of that other stuff."

"You could build a sandcastle," Danielle told him. "That might be fun. You never know—you might like it in California."

"You can swim *here*," Zach reminded her. "We have a whole lake, remember? Kismet is so good, we're a tourist attraction."

Danielle couldn't argue with that. Thwarted in her initial attempt to help her kids warm up to the idea of moving away to L.A., she looked at them. All three of them were bundled up against the cold, pink-cheeked and exhilarated by ice-skating.

Was it really fair to take them away from things they loved? Like ice-skating? And sleigh-riding? And sledding?

"*I* think it would be exciting to live someplace new,"

Danielle ventured. "If I got promoted at work, Moosby's would probably ask me to move to L.A. But I'd have lots more money—"

"Without us?" Zach wailed, looking worried.

Aiden's lip quivered. "I don't want to live with Daddy."

Karlie appeared no less concerned . . . but she was craftier.

"Jason likes it *here*," Karlie pointed out with a sly look, probably intending her statement to be an inducement for Danielle to nix her new move-to-Los-Angeles idea. Her daughter nudged her chin in Jason's direction. "See? Just look at him."

Danielle did . . . just as he executed a sweeping turn around the rink's outer edge. He looked steady. Composed. Athletic.

He caught her looking. He belly-flopped to the ice.

All four of them sighed. Karlie shook her head. "He might be hopeless, Mom, but he wants to be hopeless *here*. Not in L.A."

It was obvious that Karlie thought Jason's newfound fondness for Kismet was a strike against him. That she believed Danielle might change her mind about going to L.A. for Jason's sake.

It was proof of how much Karlie didn't want to move elsewhere, if she would rather have her mom paired up with someone other than her dad instead of move away from Kismet.

"No. I wouldn't move without you. *With* you!" Danielle hugged them all to reassure them. "I would only move with you."

"If we move away," Zach said, "how will we ever see Dad?"

That was another wrinkle, Danielle realized. She couldn't move everyone three thousand miles west without talking it over with Mark. It wouldn't be fair otherwise. He was their father; he'd want to be involved. They were kids; they needed their dad.

Danielle was the only one who wanted to get away from Mark. And Crystal. And all the annoyances their relationship caused.

Maybe Jason had had a point about her wanting to avoid Mr. and Mrs. Rub It In Your Face. Maybe she needed to work on that.

But not tonight.

"We don't have to decide all the details right now," Danielle told them. "I don't even know if I'll get the job yet."

All three of them stared at her. Mutinously.

"Didn't somebody say something about whoopie pies?"

That did the trick. It was a good thing kids had short memories. Karlie cast Danielle a final suspicious glance, then corralled her brothers to help them hastily remove their ice skates, don their snow boots, then make a joint trip to the concession stand at the edge of the ice-skating rink.

Danielle watched them go, feeling torn. It was evident there was no long-term harm done because she'd brought up the idea of moving. Aiden skipped along cheerfully, arms waving as he described something. Zach tromped beside him kicking up snow, looking bigger and ganglier every day. Karlie brought up the rear, typically keeping a watchful eye on her younger siblings.

Well, she'd had to broach the subject sometime, Danielle knew. She couldn't exactly pick up everyone from school in a rented moving van one day and pull off relocating as a fabulous surprise. She had to prepare Karlie, Aiden, and Zach.

She had to prepare herself, too. Because, all of a sudden, the usual Kismet schmaltziness held a whole new appeal for her. Given the way she felt just then, she might have a difficult time leaving it all behind herself someday. Standing there beside the ice-skating rink, with the lights shining down in the velvety darkness to create a cozy cocoon, and

Christmas carols playing over the loudspeakers to goose the holiday ambiance, and smiling, happy skaters all around, Danielle felt . . . *happy* to be in Kismet for Christmas. She hadn't felt that way for a long time.

An announcement interrupted the start of the next carol.

"Couples' skate, everyone," the volunteer DJ announced. "This is a couples' skate. Singles, please clear the ice."

Couples' skate? Danielle *loved* the couples' skate.

At least she had, years ago, when she'd been visiting this same ice rink with her mom and dad. Not that they'd ever skated. Usually, Blythe Benoit had set up an easel and oils to paint the skaters. Forrest Benoit had hunched on the bleachers with his notebook, capturing whatever fleeting impressions helped him write poetry. Danielle had skated with her friends—or sometimes when it got late, as it had tonight—skated by herself, imagining that she was a graceful Olympic champion circling the rink.

Couples' skate had been only for adults. It had been special and romantic and fascinating, with its end-of-the-night hush and its couples-only status. During the couples' skate, special music played. Some of the main lights were turned off, leaving only the white strings overhead to provide a glow for the skaters. Volunteers cast spotlights on the couples, Danielle remembered, highlighting them as they glided around on the ice.

Anticipating it, Danielle hugged herself. All those years she'd spent waiting to be old enough and coupled enough to join the couples' skate . . . and Mark had never actually donned ice skates while at the rink. He'd always kept on his boots and hung out with his buddies instead, talking about ice fishing and football and tossing an occasional "Attaboy!" or "Attagirl!" to his kids.

Mark hadn't been a bad father. Or a bad husband. But he'd lacked a certain sense of imagination. Of tradition. Of *romance*.

"Excuse me," someone said. "Can I have this skate?"

Danielle looked. *Jason.* He stood bundled up just a foot or so away from her, holding out his gloved hand in invitation.

She wanted to take his hand. But her gaze slipped lower, to his snow-caked knees and beaten-up skates, which only reminded her of how truly terrible Jason was at ice-skating. Taking part in the couples' skate with him would not be the realization of a cherished romantic dream, Danielle realized. It would be an uncomfortably public act of charity designed to cripple her.

Accidentally, of course. She knew that. Jason wouldn't have hurt her on purpose. He truly didn't seem to recognize how inept he was at wintertime sports. His face actually *shone* at her.

She didn't have the heart to refuse him.

And that's how she knew she was really falling for him.

Danielle inhaled for bravery. "Of course!"

He seemed pleased. He gestured to the rink. "After you."

With Jason's hand at her back in a show of chivalry, Danielle reached the ice rink just as the couples' skate song—a soulful rendition of "Please Come Home for Christmas" began to play. Maybe this wouldn't be too bad, she thought. Jason had been practicing all night. He must have improved by now.

With a warm smile, he took her hands. She wished she could have whisked away their gloves. At least then she would have had the benefit of enjoying his touch, skin to skin. As it was, Danielle had to content herself with gazing raptly at his face.

Jason betrayed no knowledge of the public atrocity he was about to commit. Folks in Kismet took their ice-skating seriously, Danielle knew. Children ice-skated not long after they learned to walk—the better to practice their hockey moves. Adults ice-skated as a matter of course, the same way they went dancing or bowling or down to The Big Foot

Bar to celebrate the Lions football wins. Ice-skating was Kismet's unheralded talent.

Still holding her hands, Jason performed a careful swivel on the slippery ice. Oh no. Gallantly, he was planning to lead, Danielle realized too late. That meant skating *backward*.

"Oh! I can do that," she offered. "I'll lead. Let me."

"I've got this," Jason assured her. "Just relax."

His cocksure look actually fooled her into thinking he knew what he was doing. For a nanosecond. Then she panicked again.

How could she relax? She might be in traction by tomorrow.

"Are you ready?" Jason smiled down at her, brimming with foolish certainty. It looked good on him. She had to admit that.

Swallowing hard, Danielle nodded. She was nothing if not courageous. She only hoped her children weren't watching this.

"Here we go," Jason said . . . then he skated them both backward.

Stiffly, Danielle braced herself for impact.

Instead, all she felt were Jason's hands, her own shaky legs, and the gentle caress of the wintry evening air as it flowed past them both. Briefly, the breeze ruffled her scarf.

Imagining it fluttering, Danielle could almost envision herself part of one of the couples' skate duos she'd dreamed of.

"You can open your eyes now." Jason's wry voice interrupted her fanciful trip down memory lane. "It's safe to look."

Warily, Danielle did. "I'm sorry." A spotlight glanced over them, then graciously moved on. Probably the volunteer steering it recognized a disaster in the making when she saw one. "I didn't even realize I'd closed my eyes." *And braced for impact.*

"You can stop fighting me for the lead, too. I've got it."

Danielle gawked at her own hands and arms, firmly wedged in a battle with his. "I didn't realize I was doing that, either."

"You almost broke my arm trying to 'nudge' us into a different position." Jason's smile touched her. "Trust me."

Valiantly, Danielle sucked in another lungful of cold air. Around them, agile, experienced couples swirled across the ice. A few of them were almost ice dancing to the holiday music.

"Don't trust me to do *that*," Jason warned good-humoredly. "I'm still a beginner at this. But you looked so wistful standing there when the DJ announced the couples' skate. I knew I had to give it a try." He smiled. "You know, for you."

His casual tone didn't change the content of his words—or the impact they had on Danielle. Jason wanted to do something nice for her. Once again, he'd recognized one of her secret longings . . . then set about making it come true.

She could really get used to this. If she survived.

All the same, she couldn't just *trust him*. She was still *her*.

"Relax," Jason urged with his mouth next to her ear. His warmth sneaked over her, even as his deep voice rumbled past her hair and her hat, making her shiver—but not with cold. His big, strong body felt perfect against hers. "Just let go. Trust me."

Danielle doubted she could. But just as an experiment . . .

Tentatively, she eased her viselike grip on Jason's hands. She leaned ever-so-slightly into his arms. She let her legs carry her over the ice smoothly—not in a struggle for control, but as part of a sinuous shared experience with Jason.

To her astonishment, she did not immediately crash.

An instant later, she realized . . . "You're *good* at this."

Smiling, Jason steered them both around the next ice rink corner while the music begged them to come home for Christmas.

"You don't have to sound so accusatory," he said.

"But you said you were a beginner! You said you'd never ice-skated before."

"I hadn't." Jason shrugged. "I'm a quick learner."

Danielle gave him a suspicious look. "I saw you fall down."

"Yeah. You almost got me that time. I got carried away making that turn and almost forgot to flop when you looked."

"I saw you fall down over and over again!"

"Well, there *was* a learning curve to conquer."

"You practically let Karlie humiliate you!"

"There's no humiliation in learning." Jason squeezed her hands in his, then kept skating. "I think I've got it now."

"I'll say you do." Full of disbelief, Danielle skated with him, actually doing the thing she'd so wanted to do—join in the couples' skate. "I'm not convinced you were ever a beginner."

"I would never lie to you." He seemed serious about that. "I guess since I already know how to surf, paddleboard, water-ski, and do dozens of squats in CrossFit, I already had some of the skills I needed to ice-skate. It's fun."

"You should have told Karlie."

"Told her what? That her teaching was working?" Jason shook his head. Amiably, he nodded at one of her neighbors. "If I'd let her know I'd mastered it, she couldn't teach me anymore."

"That's the idea." Danielle smiled. "It's called learning."

"It's called forging a bond with someone," he disagreed, "and mine with Karlie wasn't finished yet. It still isn't."

Thinking about that, Danielle let herself be whirled around the ice-skating rink in Jason's arms. She was happy that Jason was dedicated to winning over her daughter, but . . .

"Sometimes it's better to admit defeat."

"Nope." Jason swayed slightly, then righted himself—and her. "I never said I was perfect," he added. "But I'm trying."

"You're doing all right." With that massive understatement, Danielle relaxed a little more. Jason was right.

Neither of them had to be perfect. Including her. She intended to enjoy this imperfect night with Jason, because it was all they had.

Unless she could somehow wrangle them both more time . . .

She was cooking up a way to do just that when Jason spoke up again. "Hey. Quit daydreaming and enjoy this, will ya?"

How had he known? Again? "I'm sorry. I will."

"If you need an incentive," Jason added nonchalantly as the music whirled around them, "I can promise a kiss at the end."

Mmm. That sounded good. "What's wrong with right now?"

"I'm good. But I'm not *that* good." He laughed. "I think a collision with the wall, the ice, or each other would be bad."

"Then let me lead," Danielle invited, "and you trust *me*."

Unexpectedly, Jason nodded. He whirled them around until she was leading by skating backward. Then he closed his eyes.

"Go ahead," he said. "Take me wherever you want to go."

So, with the Christmas carols playing and the holiday lights shining overhead and the moon looking down on all of it, Danielle took over. She brought her mouth to Jason's, and she kissed him with all the affection and longing in her heart.

A spotlight played over them. Once. Twice.

Raucous cheering erupted from the locals.

It was magical, Danielle thought. It was exactly the way she'd always imagined being part of a couples' skate would be.

That, of course, was when the universe laughed at her. Because that was when Danielle closed her eyes, just for an instant, to savor the incredible connection between them . . .

. . . and steered them both right into the nearest wall.

While in the spotlight. In front of everyone. Whoops.

Argh. I should have known better than to start trusting Christmas, Danielle told herself as they both got up, dazed and unhurt. What she'd always said was right: trusting was not for her. Even if she was, just then, ready to make another kamikaze run at the ice-skating rink wall, if that's what it took to get another one of Jason's kisses or another one of his smiles.

Because that's what he gave her as they stood. He held her hand while they both took a cheerful, unified bow for the (even more loudly cheering) crowd. And in that moment, despite everything, somehow, to Danielle, it all seemed worth it.

This year, Christmas had *definitely* driven her crazy.

Chapter Thirteen

The proof of Danielle's new Christmas craziness arrived not long after she returned home with Jason and her children in tow.

None of them could quit talking about the tumble she and Jason had taken on the rink—or about the way the two of them had rallied back from it in the end—but Danielle had other things on her mind besides ice-skating and kissing and getting carried away beneath the romantic lights of the courthouse-side rink.

Those other things began with shuffling her kids off to start their bedtime routines, continued with warning Aiden, Karlie, and Zach that she had to make an important telephone call . . . and ended with Danielle slipping away, phone in hand, while Jason was soothing his sore muscles in a nice, hot shower, to enact the plan she'd devised to snare them more time together.

The only way to make sure Jason wouldn't have to leave Kismet tomorrow for the rest of his Midwestern Moosby's tour was to make sure the board of directors didn't believe a Midwestern Moosby's tour was necessary. That was why, with her heart in her throat and her mind boggling at the chance she was about to take, Danielle slipped into her bedroom and dialed Chip Larsen.

Fortunately, it was earlier on the West Coast. She caught him on the third ring. His terse, unpleasant voice rang over the line and almost made Danielle give up on this whole gamble.

Because that's what it was: a gamble. She was about to gamble an opportunity in her future for a chance with Jason today. Danielle hoped it worked. She also hoped she wouldn't regret it. But there wasn't any time to contemplate that.

"Chip Larsen here," he barked. "State your business."

Wow. He probably didn't win a lot of friends with that phone opener. "Hi, Mr. Larsen. It's Danielle Sharpe."

"Who? If you're calling about an admin position, you should check with the HR department," he huffed, clearly in motion toward someplace. "I don't know how you got this number, but—"

"It's Danielle Sharpe," she repeated patiently. "The manager of the model Moosby's toy store in Kismet, Michigan."

A tense silence filtered over the line.

She'd had to endure this weirdness last time, too.

"Did you think I was calling about an admin position just because I'm a woman?" she blurted incredulously, belatedly realizing the probable source of that taut silence. "Because I've been applying for management positions for months."

"Ah. Yes." Chip chuckled. "Ms. Sharpe. Danielle. Of the *model* Moosby's store. In the boonies. Right. Of course."

His words came out with lengthy pauses between them. Clearly, he was checking something to remind himself who she was. Danielle didn't find his absentmindedness reassuring.

She also didn't appreciate his snide remark about "the boonies." If she went to work at HQ, would they all view her as some kind of country bumpkin? *That* would be a hurdle, for sure.

"We spoke earlier this week about Jason Hamilton and

his media tour of the Midwest." Danielle darted a glance toward the hallway outside her bedroom. At the other end of it, Jason was luxuriating in a hot shower. All wet, soapy, and naked.

Why was she making a phone call again?

"Yes. Jason." Chip's tone sharpened. "How is he doing?"

"He's doing brilliantly," Danielle gushed. "He's doing great work on the sales floor. Our customers love him. The staff does too. He has a real eye for window displays. Did you know—"

—he can make homemade toys? she was about to ask as her gaze fell on Jason's toy race car on her bureau. As much as anything else, it was proof of his overall value to the company.

Jason could be so much more than a typical CEO. He could be a real asset. For instance, he could revitalize their *More, More Moosby's!* exclusives. He might even be able to create new ones.

She didn't know anyone who was more skilled with his hands.

"Fine," Chip interrupted. "Have there been more protests?" Strangely enough, he sounded . . . *hopeful?* . . . about the possibility.

"No. There was only the one protest on the first day," Danielle explained, "and Jason—I mean, Mr. Hamilton—defused it."

"Just one, huh?" A disgruntled *humph* came over the line.

Next came more sounds of walking. A squeaky door opening.

Then . . . distant *flushing*? No. *No*, Chip couldn't be . . .

"He's made a wonderful impression on everyone here in Kismet," Danielle said hastily and truthfully. She blanched as a faint splashing sound came through the phone line. "I've sent you some things as proof of that," she told Chip even more rapidly. If he hadn't read her e-mailed memos detailing Jason's work by now, maybe her mentioning them would make him look. "I hope you and the board will consider his future very carefully."

"We *always* consider the future very carefully," Chip told her with unconvincing distractedness. "Even when Jason doesn't."

"Of course. What I mean to say—if I can be absolutely frank with you, sir?—is that Mr. Hamilton is making such good progress here in Kismet, that I honestly don't think an expanded media tour will be necessary. When you've had a chance to review the materials I sent you, I think you'll be very pleased."

Chip gave a noncommittal grunt. Then . . . *unzipping*?

Oh God. He really *was* about to pee while on the phone with her. Danielle couldn't believe it. This was very unprofessional.

Did she *really* want to work more closely with him?

"That's all I wanted to say!" she chirped. "I'm afraid I have to run, Mr. Larsen. Thanks for speaking with me. Bye!"

She ended her call in the nick of time. Simultaneously relieved and disbelieving, Danielle stared at her phone. The corporate big leagues weren't what she thought they were, if phone calls like that one were par for the course. Yuck.

Experiencing an intense urge to wash her hands and apply a gallon or two of hand sanitizer, Danielle hightailed it toward the kitchen, feeling her heart pound as she went. This was risky. If Chip Larsen reviewed her memos and didn't agree that Jason was making good progress in Kismet, her credibility would be shot. But if he saw them and agreed with her, she might have just finagled herself and Jason a few additional days together.

Ordinarily, she wasn't one for keeping secrets. She liked to be aboveboard in all things (okay . . . except for her very necessary inventory manipulation at work). But this time, when Jason had seemed so downbeat about her mentioning his CEO status and about discussing Moosby's HQ earlier, she decided a little bit of light subterfuge might be in order. Just temporarily.

Just until she'd solidified . . . whatever this was between them.

It might, she knew, just be a fling. Realistically, it *had* to be a fling. Jason might be hinting about spending Christmas with her at The Christmas House B & B next year, but Danielle knew he couldn't possibly mean it. She was pretty fantastic, but she wasn't "date *People* magazine's 'sexiest man alive'" fantastic.

Almost as if to prove it, Karlie yelled out to her.

"Mom?" her daughter said from down the hall. "Zach's going to barf! You'd better come quick. Bring some towels, too."

Yep, Danielle decided as she hustled in that direction. Her life was pretty glamorous. Just the kind of thing a millionaire CEO really went for. In her dreams, that is.

Ten-year-old girls were not experts at hazing their mothers' unwanted new boyfriends, Jason realized as he stood naked in Danielle's bathroom clutching a hand towel to his groin. He could have sworn there'd been a full contingent of adult-size bath towels when he'd gotten into the shower. But when he'd gotten out again—on an emergency basis, because of Zach's upset stomach—Jason hadn't been able to find them.

Judging by the smug look on Karlie's face, she'd managed to sneak away with all the towels except the single letter-paper-size scrap of terry cloth currently clutched in Jason's hand.

"Your big, dumb, new boyfriend doesn't know how to take a shower," Karlie continued shouting down the hall in her mother's direction. "He got in without checking for towels first."

As tactics went, hers was pretty weak. It wasn't exactly a criminal-worthy failing to wind up towelless. Also, he *had* checked first. But even if he hadn't, Danielle couldn't possibly mind. Wet and irked, Jason grabbed a handful of shower curtain for additional coverage. His feet pooled water onto the bathmat.

"You know how you hate having to bring us towels in the middle of a bath," Karlie bellowed, going on with her tattling. "Especially when you're in the middle of an *important* call."

Judging by the newly triumphant gleam in the girl's eyes, *that* was the key. Danielle's phone call. She had friends. She chatted with them. She kept in close contact with Gigi and Henry and the rest of the Moosby's staff, too. So Jason didn't dwell on Danielle's "important call." Especially since poor little Zach was still slumped over the toilet bowl, waiting to heave.

"Are you feeling any better, buddy?" Jason asked with concern. He would have patted the kid's back for comfort, but he needed both hands to stay decent. "I opened the door as fast as I could when I heard you guys pounding on it to get in."

"I know. Thanks." Zach gave a weak nod. Then, gamely, he offered Jason a thumbs-up. "Too many whoopie pies. Ugh."

Danielle arrived, full of mingled competence and alarm.

She took in the situation in a glance. Making a sad face, she crouched beside Zach. She patted his back. "Are you okay?"

Zach nodded feebly. "Just a false alarm, I guess."

Danielle examined him closely. She gave a faint frown.

Aiden lingered in the doorway, watching with big, hopeful

eyes. He was wearing Abominable Snowman pajamas and carrying a copy of *How the Grinch Stole Christmas* for his bedtime story.

"Do we get to stay up late because Zach is sick?"

"Zach isn't sick. He's fine now." With an experienced air, Danielle lay the back of her hand against her son's forehead. She smiled at him. "How many whoopie pies did you eat?"

"Umm . . . four?" Zach grimaced. The color had returned to his face now. He seemed 100 percent recovered. "You did give us all that money, Mom. We figured we should buy a *lot* of whoopie pies. They were supposed to be for sharing with you guys, but . . ."

The boy shrugged elaborately, giving a sheepish smile.

"Next time, I want change. Okay? Karlie should have known better." Danielle looked up, her attention caught by something besides Zach for the first time: Jason. Her gaze landed on his groin first—since it was at eye level—then slid upward. Her eyes got bigger than Aiden's. "Aha. That explains why I was supposed to bring towels." Self-consciously, she said, "Sorry, Jason."

"It's all right." He'd nearly drip-dried now. "Z, I'm glad you're feeling better. You really toughed it out there."

"I did." Zach's gaze shone with hero worship. "Thanks, J."

Clearly, they'd forged a deeper instafriendship than Danielle had realized, if they already had nicknames for each other. All the same . . . "This would have been an excellent time to have two bathrooms," Danielle said apologetically. "If we did—"

"You couldn't have had two bathrooms!" Karlie swooped in to say. "Because you and Dad were practically broke when you bought this house," she reminded her mother. Her tone was rich with the echo of family lore. "You were newlyweds. You couldn't afford a fancy house with two bathrooms. You were young and in love!"

"We were young and naïve," Danielle disagreed, plainly

not embarking on the sentimental journey her daughter obviously wanted to encourage. "Turns out, two bathrooms is a necessity."

"Dad's new house with Crystal has three bathrooms and a hot tub," Zach volunteered, always willing to talk up Crystal. He poked around in the vanity cabinet, then withdrew something fluffy. "Hey, here are the towels. They're right here."

"How did they get wedged under the sink?" Danielle asked, her attention diverted from sneaking surreptitious glances at Jason's nude arms and legs and chest and . . . well, pretty much *all* of him except the most critical parts. "That's weird."

"Yeah." Karlie chuckled. "Really weird." She sniffed. "Maybe your dumb new boyfriend thinks that's where towels go. All bunched up in a heap next to the extra toilet paper. Weird."

Jason raised both arms in surrender. "Hey, I was just minding my own business, having a nice, normal shower—"

"Trying out my peppermint body wash," Danielle observed, stepping a fraction closer to sniff his skin. Her eyes gleamed at him with appreciation and good humor. And *desire*. "Nice."

"It's not nice!" Karlie's expression turned belligerent. "You told *us* that soap is off-limits. *We* can't even use it."

"—when everybody burst in here so Zach could spew," Jason finished. The truth was, he'd cadged some of Danielle's body wash because it made him feel stupidly closer to her. He was an idiot. "I stepped out to help, couldn't find a decent towel, and here we are. Z, if you'd just hand me one of those, please—"

"No prob, J." Zach tossed a larger towel. "All yours."

The boy's camaraderie-filled, man-to-man tone almost cracked him up. Divertingly, though, Jason realized he couldn't towel off with everyone in the bathroom. He wasn't trying to host a peep show. Meaningfully, he cleared his throat.

Danielle caught his expression. She grinned.

"That's it, everybody. Time to clear out." She clapped her hands like a maternal drill sergeant. "Your regular bedtime bathroom shifts will resume in a few minutes. Let's go."

Zach and Aiden obediently marched off to their rooms.

Karlie, however, slumped against the bathroom vanity with classic preteen exasperation. "But Mom! Jason broke the rules!"

Danielle blinked. "What rules?"

An infuriated exhalation. "About needing more towels? About interrupting you when you're on an important phone call? About being *naked* in front of three little kids? How about that, huh?"

Danielle hid a smile. "Jason isn't naked. He can't very well help being too big for that little hand towel, now can he?"

She'd noticed. Jason couldn't help preening.

"Mooom!" Karlie wailed. "I think I'm traumatized!"

"You're fine." Danielle cast another hasty up and down glance at Jason. He wished he knew what she was thinking. "As far as the rest goes . . . no harm, no foul. That's what I say."

"Argh! You *never* say that!" Karlie complained.

"I just did. Now shoo. Off to bed with you, sweetie."

"I need to get into the bathroom too, you know!"

"Just as soon as Jason is done. The sooner you leave—"

"Fine." Karlie whirled around, her long braid swinging. In the midst of preparing to storm away, she narrowed her eyes at Jason. "The only good thing about *you*," she informed him heatedly, "is that *you* like it here! Unlike my mom!"

Behind her, Danielle flinched. She looked concerned.

Evidently, Danielle *had* told her kids about their potential move to L.A. Just as evidently, the idea hadn't gone over very well. Jason felt sorry for that. He also felt sorry that Karlie wasn't ready to like him. Purposely, he smiled at her.

"I do like it here," he said, trying to fix that. "Kismet is nice. It's full of Christmassy stuff. Who doesn't like that?"

"Me." Karlie jerked up her chin. "I *hate* Christmas. This is going to be the worst Christmas ever. All because *you're* here."

Then she did storm away, leaving Danielle behind to gaze worriedly after her. Jason looked at them both, so alike and so upset, and knew that somehow, he'd really screwed up this time.

Unlike with Bethanygate, he felt awful about it, too.

"I'm sorry, Danielle." He clutched both his towels, no longer caring about his nudity or Danielle's reaction to it. Less lascivious events were more important now. "I really thought I could help your kids adjust to your dating again."

"You have," Danielle assured him, seeming to feel a little better as she glanced at him. "Do you think I don't know this would have been inevitable eventually? No matter who I was dating? To Karlie, nobody's ever going to measure up to her dad. I just didn't realize she was still hoping we'd reconcile."

Jason frowned. He steeled his resolve. "I'm not giving up, you know. Unless you want me to. If you want me to, I will."

"Just keep doing what you're doing." Danielle cast a racy, lingering look in his direction. "Including all of . . . *that*."

Hmm. She was more resilient than he'd given her credit for, Jason realized. At least she was if her gesticulating fingers indicating him, his nudity . . . and, he imagined, his overall willingness to bare himself to her meant anything.

He thought they did. They *definitely* did.

Danielle Sharpe didn't do anything halfway. Including looking at him, kissing him, confusing him . . . counting on him.

He must have been crazy, Jason realized, to have mixed himself up with a divorcée and her three children. This wasn't just some lark he could forget after a wild weekend. This was *real life*. For Danielle, Karlie, Zach, and Aiden, there would be no gallivanting off to Antigua to forget about this afterward.

The realization was sobering. Jason wasn't sure he was ready for so much responsibility. He hadn't been thinking long-term when he'd come up with this plan. On the other hand, he'd been shouldering big jobs since he was just a scrawny kid.

Nowadays, he had much bigger shoulders.

"I think *you're* the one who hid all the towels in the cupboard," Jason teased her. "Nice try. I'm on to you now."

"Are you? I doubt it," Danielle said. "I bet I can still surprise you." Then she did just that by tossing him another interested look—and, just when he expected her to say something mischievous, Danielle added, "You did a good job with Zach tonight, by the way. Usually he's really freaked out by getting nauseated, but you calmed him down faster than ever. Thanks."

Then, without waiting for his response, Danielle closed the bathroom door and headed down the hallway in pursuit of her sulky daughter, leaving Jason behind to towel off, admire her resourcefulness, and think about what she'd just said, too.

Maybe—just maybe—Jason thought, he *did* have what it took to survive small-town schmaltziness full-time. Maybe he even *wanted* to do that. He couldn't be sure he wasn't just trying to run away again, the way he'd done with his vacation. He couldn't even be sure he knew what the hell he was doing. The only way to find out was to go all in with Danielle . . . to snag enough time in Kismet with her to know if things were real between them.

He'd tried to do that earlier today. He wouldn't know if he'd succeeded until Chip Larsen deigned to look at the sleigh-ride video footage and photos Jason had e-mailed him.

The bottom line was, Jason needed more time with Danielle. If those photos of his sappy, happy, Christmastime family fun in snowy Christmas Town didn't do the trick to convince Chip and the board that Jason was a new and improved man, nothing would.

Twenty minutes after the very last "good night" and the very last lights-out for her three kids, Danielle crept into her quiet living room with two glasses of spiced mulled wine, a heart full of hopefulness, and an unexpected sense of surprise.

Jason had lighted the Christmas tree for her, she saw. He'd also, if the sight of him on all fours underneath that Douglas fir was any indication, taken it upon himself to water it.

Danielle loathed watering the Christmas tree. First, there was the ignoble, butt-wagging posture required (although Jason made that look *really* good). Next, there was the threat to her hair. Because every time she crawled in there to try to wedge a long-spouted watering can into the tree stand's basin, she got pine needles stuck in her curls. Finally, there was the reminder that if she didn't do it, nobody else would. Everything in her household was up to her to take care of now. All by herself.

Including Christmas.

Not that she couldn't handle that. She could. Of course. It was just that, sometimes, Danielle wanted to share those responsibilities. She wanted to feel she was part of a team.

A Christmastime team . . . that lasted all year long.

Shaking her head at her own gullibility, she stood there with her clove, cinnamon, and citrus-spiked Merlot for a minute, watching Jason do the tree watering. His arms were longer than hers. His tolerance for sticky sap, falling needles, and the threat of being crushed to death by a toppling tree (admittedly not very likely) was clearly much higher than hers was, too.

Jason was excellent at pitching in where needed. Whereas Mark had required something close to a bullhorn and a cattle prod just to make him notice something needed to be done around the house, Jason somehow noticed and then did things on his own.

"Would it be weird of me to imprison you here until all my Christmastime stuff is done?" Danielle joked, finally trading her view of his backside for his attention. "Suddenly I'm dying to find out if you're any good at baking cookies, wrapping gifts, and hanging stockings. Oh, and going Christmas caroling."

That was a tradition she hoped to establish with the kids. Starting this year. Maybe even with Jason, if he agreed.

"You'd have to let me out of the house for that last one." Wearing an agreeable grin, Jason backed out from beneath the tree. He got to his feet, dressed in a pair of jeans and a sweater that covered him considerably more than a hand towel had. Too bad. "But I promise not to run away." He aimed a curious look at the tree. "When are you going to decorate it?"

"A few days from now. The kids get bored if I don't string the lights beforehand. Why? Are you angling for an invitation?"

"Somebody has to reach those tall branches." Jason winked, then nodded at the wineglasses. "Is one of those for me?"

She handed him one. "You labor, I bring refreshments."

"Not a bad deal." Relaxed and content, with his dark, wavy hair combed loosely away from his face and his jeans slung low, Jason aimed his wineglass toward the sofa. "Join me?"

She'd thought he'd never ask. "For a glass. Or two."

Companionably, they moved onto the sofa, side by side. From the outside, Danielle guessed, they probably seemed totally at ease. On the inside, though, she was aflutter with anticipation.

Hoping to ease it, she knocked back her spiced wine.

All of it.

At the same instant, Jason turned to ask her something. He saw her chug and gave her a knowing grin. "Everything okay? That bedtime routine took a lot longer than I thought it would. I've never seen a kid demand more stories than Aiden."

"He loves them." Danielle resisted an urge to pound her chest. It turned out that spiced mulled wine had a kick. "You did a good job with that Grinch voiceover, by the way."

He laughed. "I'm naturally grinchy." His gaze dipped to her glass, then raised to her face. "I'll get you more wine."

He rose in an agile motion and whisked away her glass. A few minutes later, Jason returned with a refilled glass for her.

"You win," Danielle announced. "Mark couldn't be bothered to bring me anything, not even when I had appendicitis."

"Shame on him." Jason lounged next to her, then put down his own wine. "Let's make a deal," he suggested. "You make that the first and last time we talk about your ex tonight . . . and I'll do my best to make you forget he ever existed. Okay?"

"Um, okay." She gulped more wine. She nodded. "I mean, yes, please. Let's do that. Starting now." Another swig. "Go for it."

With a grin—probably in response to her babbling—Jason leaned nearer. He steadied her wineglass by covering her hand with his, then gave Danielle a kiss that made her feel twice as intoxicated as ordinary Merlot ever could. Jason's mouth was sweet and spicy. He coaxed open her lips with barely a breath.

His hands were nimble, setting aside her glass in a smooth gesture that Danielle barely noticed. Jason brought his hand to her jaw instead, then cradled her closer to him, losing himself in kissing her more deeply. His body leaned on hers, his hair brushed her cheek, and everything about him felt so perfect and so right that Danielle almost laughed with the sheer joy of it.

She wanted to be seduced. Jason seemed to be there to do exactly that, just the way he'd fulfilled so many other wishes of hers. Near the twinkling lights of her still undecorated Christmas tree, Jason kissed her and stroked her and whispered that she was beautiful, and thanks to the wine and the wanting and the very real magic of having holiday music playing nearby—how had that happened, anyway?—Danielle let herself be swept away. For several long, blissful moments, she lost herself in Jason's arms, in his smiles, in his big, strong body and the utter, unabashed revelation that he wanted her. Right *then*.

Suddenly nervous again, Danielle broke off their next kiss.

"I'm, um, happy we postponed your sleepover in Aiden's room," she blabbed with an anxious glance in that direction. All was still quiet on the kid front. No impediments there. "That means you're free to have an adult sleepover instead."

Her racy joke didn't go over the way she meant for it to.

"You know, I love that you're a mom." Jason gazed into her eyes. He trailed his fingers along her neck, down the V-neck of her sweater . . . all the way to her modest cleavage. He let his gaze follow the same path. "Right now, though, you're a woman first. Tonight, I want you to forget everything else—"

He caught her indrawn breath and gave a knowing smile.

"—yes," he went on, anticipating her next words, "even the fact that we have to get up early for work tomorrow morning—"

Gobsmacked, she stared at him. "How did you—"

"—and just *feel* us together. You and me."

Dazedly, Danielle nodded. *This is it*, she thought. This was the moment when she gave full rein to her libido and just went for it. With Jason. With the sexiest man she'd ever met.

Oh wow. She *had* to be dreaming this.

Except it didn't feel like dreaming as Jason smiled and slid his hand lower, cupping her breast and making her gasp. It didn't feel like dreaming as he stroked his thumb over her and made her nipples jut against her sweater in a quest for more. It *definitely* didn't feel like dreaming as he edged a little closer on the sofa . . . and she felt a certain hard, masculine, *immense* part of him barely graze the back of her hand through his jeans.

Holy moly. This was going to be even *better* than a dream.

"I wouldn't ordinarily do something like this," Danielle murmured, fighting the need to do more than just graze him. Her stomach felt light, her body languid, her mind awhirl. "But somehow, this feels different to me. *You* feel different to me."

"Nah," Jason rumbled. "I'm just a regular guy."

At that absurd understatement, Danielle almost laughed.

"I'm just a regular guy who's about to make you feel better than you ever have before." Jason leaned even closer, making the sofa's throw pillows cocoon them both. He gazed intently into her face, then stroked her again. "This might be our only night together," he reminded her. "We have to make it memorable."

Danielle nodded in agreement. She buried her fingers in his hair and gazed back at him, hardly able to believe she was there, in her own living room, with the "sexiest CEO alive."

"In my bedroom," she suggested boldly, ready to give and take and create a whole new batch of hotter-than-hot memories. "We can't do this out here. As nice as making out is—"

"It can't hold a candle to what's to come." Jason stood. He held out his hand to her, then smiled. "Come on," he invited. "Let's have a night to remember."

Breathlessly, Danielle took his hand. She stood too. Then they ventured down the hall and into her bedroom together, leaving their wineglasses behind along with their inhibitions.

For the next several hours, neither of them would need them. Just as they didn't need clothes, more spiced mulled wine, or anything else to ensure that when they came together—skin on skin and heart to heart—everything would be perfect.

Between them, it simply *was* perfect. Twice.

Not that either of them was counting.

Even if it was only for one night, Danielle knew as she snuggled afterward in Jason's arms, replete and content and marveling at the memory of every erotic intimacy they'd just shared, it *was* a night to remember. Judging by the macho, satisfied look on Jason's face, he felt the same way.

Now, if only they could somehow get more time together, things could be *more* than perfect. They could be enduring.

At least for another few nights, they could be . . .

Chapter Fourteen

Jason woke up with an armful of cuddly woman, a head full of sizzling erotic memories, and the dawning realization that he'd talked himself into doing something he shouldn't have last night.

In the warm glow of those damn Christmas lights, bolstered by days of wanting Danielle, he'd convinced himself that he was doing something good for them both. He'd convinced himself that he was a nice guy who only wanted to help Danielle move on from her ex . . . when really, in the harsher light of another December day, it was obvious to Jason that all he'd wanted was *her*.

Everything else was an excuse. He wasn't a nice guy. Not *that* nice, at least. He didn't begin to deserve her. He just didn't. The fact that he was thinking it proved it was true.

Last night, when he'd held Danielle in his arms and kissed her—when he'd stroked her—he hadn't been thinking about doing a good deed. When he'd slipped off her clothes, marveled at her incredible, unabashed nakedness, kissed her from her head to her toes and—lingeringly—everyplace in between . . . he sure as hell hadn't been doing it out of a sense of charity. When he'd made her cry out and clutch the sheets, when he'd done as she'd begged and thrust inside her, when he'd made them both shudder and moan, Jason hadn't been thinking of becoming a better man.

None of the things they'd done would help Danielle move on, Jason realized too late as he gazed down at her beautiful, slumbering face. Because none of the things they'd done would give her the future she wanted. But all of them would bond her even more tightly to him. Because of who she was, they would make her want him more. Need him more. *Rely on him more.*

He'd taken a woman who didn't want to trust anyone, and he'd made her trust him. On purpose. He'd done it with the best of intentions. But as Jason woke up and found Danielle willingly curled against him with her hand resting over his heart, he knew he should have reined himself in. He wasn't cut out for this.

He'd never experienced *anything* as all-encompassing as this. He'd had relationships, sure. But none of them had felt this way. None of them had involved togetherness plus Christmas plus Moosby's plus scandal plus three little kids—one of whom didn't even like him yet . . . and maybe never would.

Hell. What had he been thinking?

Well, he knew what he'd been thinking, Jason admitted as he felt himself stir beneath the sheets. He'd been thinking he could have Danielle—the sexiest and most beguiling gas-money extortion artist in all of Midwestern Michigan—all to himself. To have and to hold and to screw both their brains out, with no consequences and no future beyond the few additional days he'd probably already persuaded Chip Larsen to give them.

Thinking about his company's chairman of the board was the most effective boner killer imaginable—which was exactly what Jason needed to get his head on straight. If he wanted to be fair to Danielle, he couldn't linger in her bed for a cozy morning after. He couldn't give her the impression this meant more than it did. Because despite their unusual synchronicity—despite how much he liked her—Jason knew this couldn't last.

Eventually, he would go back to L.A. He would. Even if the idea of doing so made him want to bury his head under the covers and forget that L.A.—and Moosby's corporate—existed at all. But he didn't have another alternative. All he knew were toys.

Eventually, too, Danielle would realize she was staying in Kismet. Because Jason knew damn well she wouldn't disappoint Karlie, Aiden, and Zach by moving them away from home. Away from the snow. Away from the whoopie pies. Away from Mark and Crystal and all the things they loved about their rusticated burg.

That was why, when Jason heard Danielle's cell phone vibrate on his side of the bed—when he saw it light up to display an incoming text message—he grabbed it from the nightstand to avoid waking her. He glanced at Gigi's message.

Inventory emergency. Come to the store. Quick!

Hmmm. That would suffice as an escape hatch, Jason decided. So he pulled on his clothes, scribbled Danielle a note, and then headed downtown to the toy store to take care of the problem. Whatever it was, he knew, it would be less daunting than facing a sleepy-eyed, hopeful Danielle, her three cute rug rats, and a blissful Sunday morning spent making waffles, taking care of goldfish, building Legos, and playing video games with Karlie—all before carpooling to Moosby's with Danielle for another idyllic workday. Because with her, they *were* idyllic, weird as that was.

Especially for a man who'd gone on vacation to avoid working. Maybe he needed to live with Danielle to make his work life feel happier. Or maybe he was still thinking with his cock instead of his brains. Because he couldn't abandon his real job.

No matter how much, just then, he might have wanted to.

Bah humbug, Jason told himself as he reached his rented SUV and saw the snowfall and ice that had covered it overnight. He wasn't cut out for any of this. The sooner Danielle realized the kind of man he really was, the better for them both.

Danielle woke up with a smile, a languorous stretch, and a growing certainty that she'd chosen exactly the right man to trust. Despite the way Mark had betrayed her—despite all her fears that she'd been partly to blame, for believing in him—she *wasn't* incapable of choosing a good man, she realized happily as she pointed her toes and thrust her arms out from beneath her cozy flannel sheets. She was *excellent* at choosing a good man.

She'd chosen Jason, hadn't she?

He was a good man. Everything they'd done together over the past few days proved it. Last night proved it. Because Danielle would have done almost anything to satisfy the lusty craving that Jason had incited in her. But rather than take advantage of that, instead Jason had made their night together feel special.

When he'd taken her into his arms and kissed her, when he'd stroked her, when he'd called her beautiful and sexy, he'd made her remember that she *deserved* to love and be loved. When he'd slipped off her clothes, when he'd shed his own jeans and sweater and let her look her fill of his incredible nakedness, when he'd kissed her all over until she'd been trembling and groaning and begging him for more, *please*, he'd made her remember that she was a woman first and a mother second. When he'd finally, *finally* come inside her and made them one . . . well, he'd looked into her eyes and he'd let her come inside him, too.

After all that, Danielle knew, it wasn't fair to Jason to go on this way. Last night had been everything she'd hoped for and more—and that was why, now, she knew she had to reel herself in. All she'd wanted was a fun holiday fling. And maybe a way to help her kids move past their hopes for a reconciliation between her and Mark, too. But judging by Jason's reaction to their passionate night together, he wanted more.

That wasn't surprising, she knew. Their night together *had* been really fantastic. Jason had anticipated her every desire. Danielle had surprised him with a few inspired moves of her own. Together, they'd discovered a whole new level of synchronicity.

But now she had to face facts. The facts were that she still wanted her promotion and—just as Karlie had pointed out—Jason was enjoying Kismet more every day. It wouldn't surprise her if he decided to stay. If *that* happened—and their fling inevitably ended—it would be beyond awkward working with him. It would be better, Danielle knew, if she distanced herself now.

All the same, as she sleepily yawned and congratulated herself on her new resolve to keep things casual, she couldn't help thinking that maybe she could wait a few days to do that. After all, she might be overthinking things. For all she knew, Jason might still be moving on with the rest of his tour.

They might only have time for a single sexy AM quickie before saying their good-byes and moving on with their lives.

With a mischievous grin, Danielle reached for him.

She came up with a sheet of paper instead.

Snatching it from the pillow, she frowned in confusion. She read it, feeling stupidly fond of Jason's chicken scratch handwriting as she did. Then, she smiled.

Jason had gone to Moosby's to deal with a problem.

She was already having a positive influence on him! At

this rate, Jason would be genuine boyfriend material in no time.

Whoops. I mean, Danielle told herself hastily, *good for him! Now the board of directors will finally see how talented he is—and give me my promotion . . . all I really want from this anyway.*

With that thought firmly in mind, Danielle threw back the covers. She got out of bed, got the kids ready to go to Mark's, then prepared to head to Moosby's herself. There was no way she was letting her superstar boss make her look like a slacker—not now, when all her dreams were finally within reach.

"You can't leave Kismet," Chip Larsen told Jason over the phone. "Ever. Our social media accounts are going crazy!"

"Are you saying I need to lie low until the villagers put away the pitchforks and torches?" Jason asked. He couldn't think what he'd possibly done wrong now. "I'd think you'd want me right in the middle of things, getting strung up."

"Ordinarily, I would," Chip admitted. "But you being attacked by a mob wouldn't do our stock price any favors. And you know me—I'm all about the Benjamins. Even when it comes to you. So as much as I might *wish* you were getting strung up—"

"Enough said." *Greed wins again.* That sounded like Chip.

Standing alone in Moosby's back room amid all the latest boxed inventory, Jason gave the toys around him a curious look. With Danielle's tutelage, he'd familiarized himself with the Moosby's official employee handbook. It seemed to him that their inventory should have been more . . . diverse. "So what happened?"

"Good publicity for a change, that's what happened," Chip crowed. "You were holding out on me!" he added in a chastising tone. "You should have started sending me *usable* stuff like this days ago, you bastard. What a PR angle! Good work."

Aha. He'd gotten the photos and video footage. That was good. It sounded as if Jason now had carte blanche to stay in Kismet indefinitely, without needing to cajole the board onto his side first. But . . . "PR angle? What PR angle?" he asked. "I didn't send those pictures for PR purposes. I sent them—"

To show you how new and improved I am. But Jason didn't have a chance to say so before Chip interrupted him.

"Danielle Sharpe and her three kids—*that* PR angle. It turns out that all five of you together are a social media gold mine. Customers *love* it." Chip chortled. "We had the media monkeys amp up the storyline a little, of course. Play up the folksy angle. Boost the love-at-first-sight stuff. Show your supposed heart of gold, et cetera, et cetera. I've got to give you credit, though. Thanks to your smart use of Danielle and those kids—"

Whoa. "I didn't 'use' Danielle. Or her kids."

For a heartbeat, Chip was silent. Probably with disbelief.

Then, "Come on, Hamilton. I know damn well you picked this woman and her kids on purpose. They're adorable. They're squeaky clean. They're small town. They're relatable. They're—"

"They're *not* an ad campaign," Jason pointed out tersely, beginning to regret sending that footage. It had wound up on *all* of Moosby's social media accounts? Dizzy with an unwanted sense of déjà vu, Jason frowned. "You weren't supposed to post those damn pictures to the whole world! You were supposed to—"

Look at them and realize I'm a good guy after all, he was about to say. *Just the way Danielle hinted you would.*

But Chip interrupted again. "You, more than anyone, know nothing is private anymore. Of *course* we made those pictures public! Did you think I was just going to ooh and ah over them? Make a scrapbook? Tell the board how freaking *nice* you are now?"

Well . . . yes. He had thought that.

Being in Kismet had wrecked his ability to think straight.

"We both know better than that," Chip went on. "You didn't get to be CEO of a multinational company by being Mr. Nice Guy."

"You *wanted* me to be Mr. Nice Guy! That's why I'm here."

"Only in public." A pause. "Didn't I make that clear?"

Maybe he had. Maybe Jason had misunderstood. More importantly . . . "I don't think Danielle would want those pictures posted online. Especially with her kids included."

"Danielle Sharpe knows what's what," Chip said confidently. "She's smart. She's ambitious. She's a go-getter. She wants to get promoted, and she's doing what it takes to accomplish that. She knows those kids are prime assets. So should you."

"They're *kids*! Innocent, trusting kids."

"What are you, a bleeding heart, all of a sudden?"

"No." *Yes.* Jason swore under his breath. "Take them down."

His chairman of the board laughed. "The hell I will! In fact, we want more of the same. You know how easily the public gets bored. We need engagement. Thanks to this, sales are rising across the board. *Hashtag sleighride* is trending worldwide!"

"No." Jason paced. "No more pictures. No more video."

"Face it, Hamilton. Getting 'involved' with a hometown honey like Danielle Sharpe is the best PR move you've made all year. Especially now, at Christmas. It's heartwarming shit."

"Danielle will never agree."

"You're persuasive. Make her agree. Our sales and our stock prices are going through the roof. It's all because of *hashtag sleighride*."

This wasn't what Jason wanted. "I won't do it."

"You won't? Or she won't? Because if you're saying she won't, I'll call her. I'll make it clear her job is at stake."

Shocked, Jason stared at Moosby's back room. *Not that.* Losing her job would destroy Danielle.

"Danielle Sharpe is more useful to the company as part of your image rehab than she ever was as a store manager," Chip went on bluntly. "I want more photos. More videos. More footage of the five of you doing Christmassy things together. If you can't make that happen," he added ominously, "I can. And I will."

When Danielle arrived at Moosby's, she was hoping to run into Jason—all the better to luxuriate in the morning-after glow they'd been so unfairly denied. Instead, the first person she saw on the toy-packed, customer-filled sales floor was Gigi.

Her number-one salesperson gave her an impish grin.

"Aha! So you *can* still get out of bed." Gigi winked. "I thought maybe Jason had tired you out far too much for that."

Danielle's cheeks heated. "I don't know what you mean."

"*Oui*, you do. Your rosy cheeks say so."

"This isn't appropriate work conversation." Danielle nodded at a pair of shoppers. "I got your text. What's the emergency?"

Whatever it was, she hoped Jason had already taken care of it. Not because she didn't want to do the work herself, but just because she wanted him to be the responsible, go-to guy she knew he could be . . . especially after all the guidance she'd given him.

"There is no emergency." Gigi shrugged. "I just wanted to talk to you. I wanted to find out how it is going with Jason."

"It's going . . . fine." Unable to hold back a grin, Danielle rearranged a shelf full of stuffed animals as the toy store's usual hubbub swirled around her. She paused. "Are these new? Did you get them from HQ? You know what I told you about swapping out the inventory. If we keep all these stuffed animals—"

"—we will never sell them. I know." Gigi shook her head, unbothered by the potential snafu in their midst. "Believe me, we received many, many more than those you see. I already have sent boxes of stuffed animals to the other regional managers."

Danielle nodded. "Good. Thanks."

Her Moosby's store had no real control over their inventory. Initial ordering was centralized, as was replenishment. That meant that every week, she and her staff were stuck with merchandise they couldn't sell—items that didn't fit her store's demographics. Kismet drew a lot of tourists with school-age and older children, yet HQ sent her infant toys and plushies by the truckload. Her town was full of outdoorsy kids who loved to skate, snowboard, and play outside, yet HQ sent her indoor toys like books, dolls, and board games . . . all while simultaneously overloading the Moosby's stores in more urban areas with sports gear and other items that they couldn't use.

As the store's manager, Danielle was supposed to sell whatever merchandise was allotted to her. But she'd noticed early on that where she ran out of snowboards, other Moosby's ran out of board games. Where she couldn't get enough bicycles and skateboards, urban stores saw those same items languish on the shelves. That's when she'd devised her stock-swapping program, to better tailor all the regional stores' selections.

Not that HQ would have appreciated her efforts, of course. Moosby's corporate was all about making alliances with big-brand toy makers, "optimizing" order turnaround, and paying consultants big bucks to devise new inventory and ordering metrics. Danielle had tried to tell the people in upper management that they were wasting their money, but she'd hit nothing but dead ends.

That's why she'd taken matters into her own hands. She'd trusted Gigi to handle the system, but (so far) not Henry.

Speaking of whom . . . "How are things going with you and Henry?" Danielle asked. "Has he asked you out yet?"

"Henry? Bof!" Gigi gave a Gallic wave. "I got tired of waiting for him." Her expression turned puckish. "So I arranged to bump into him while closing the store one night. It all happened *very* accidentally, *bien sûr*. I had to hold on to him tightly to steady myself. Also, I happened to be wearing quite an attractive top at the time. *Et voilà*!" Animatedly, Gigi gestured. "Finally, Henry found the courage to speak to me about something besides 'Where do the baby dolls go?' or 'Which of us is doing the Silly Putty demonstration for *les enfants* today?'"

"Then you're going out? Together?"

"We have already been out together." Nonchalantly, Gigi examined her fingernails. "We have another rendezvous planned for tonight."

"Gigi! That's terrific!"

"Eh, I knew that I would triumph in the end. Women always do." Her friend pouted. "However, I do not see why I should talk about my liaisons when you will not talk about yours." She waggled her eyebrows. "If you want to know the scoop, g-friend . . ."

"Fine. Jason is . . . great," Danielle said, relenting. A smile bubbled up inside her, then broke free. "I mean, he's *really* great. Of course, this is all just temporary between us, but—"

"'Of course' it is temporary? Why is that?"

"Well, it's just a fling." Danielle plumped up a stuffed penguin. She put it back on the shelf. "We're not serious."

"Not serious? Is that really what you think?"

"Why? Did Jason say something to you?" Danielle grabbed Gigi. "Spill! What do you know?"

At her newly über-alert tone, Gigi laughed. "See? *That* is how I know you have really fallen for Jason."

Danielle scoffed. "I only mean that if he *did* say something to you, then it would be nice to know about it. That's all."

"He said the same thing you said. That you are 'great.'"

"Oh." Somehow dispirited by that, Danielle tried to switch her focus to the next pile of stuffed animals. Or to the holiday tunes playing in the store. Or to the adorable little kids who flocked the play table, getting ready for the next daily demo. "Well, 'great' is good, right? I mean, I couldn't possibly ask—"

Another laugh. "It was the way he looked when he said it," Gigi clarified in her usual playful tone. She waggled her eyebrows. "He said it as though 'great' was . . . *everything* nice."

Danielle couldn't help smiling. "Oh. I see."

"No, you do not see," her friend disagreed. "Any more than Jason sees. The both of you, you are pretending right now that you do not care too much. But you really do. You care a lot!"

Danielle relented. "He likes it here, Gigi. I think he might want to stay in Kismet. But you know me—"

"You always are wanting to leave Kismet. But if you were in love, it would be different! If you were in love, Mark and Crystal would not bother you anymore. Because for getting over a lost love, there is nothing as good as finding a *new* love—"

"That's not it." Not entirely, at least. "Really. I—"

"—and *smashing* it right in the face of the old love!" her friend continued with old-world relish. Gigi pantomimed a gangsta-rap pose. "How do you like me *now*, mother-effers?"

Her extra-enthusiastic delivery made Danielle crack up.

"I don't want to make Mark and Crystal pay," she insisted. Then, for veracity's sake, she added, "Much. But I don't want to lead Jason on, either. I'm not sure I can commit yet. I need . . ."

She spied Jason at the other side of the toy store's sales floor, talking with a pair of bundled-up kids. Her voice trailed off as she watched him, wholly unable to concentrate on words.

Gosh, Jason was dreamy. He was so nice, too. He was taking his time with those two little girls, explaining all about one of the *More More Moosby's!* exclusive toys. His face shone as he picked up one of those toys, then demonstrated how it worked.

If things *did* work out for them, she could really get used to having Jason in the store with her. The two of them were very in sync with their approach to helping customers. Just as they'd been in sync last night while kissing, undressing, stroking . . .

Gigi cleared her throat. "Yes? You need . . . ?"

Danielle started. Forcibly, she swerved her gaze away from Jason. "I need . . ." She frowned. "What was I talking about again?"

"You were telling me why you cannot commit to the man who has stolen your attention so thoroughly that you cannot speak."

"I can speak!" Hoping to prove that she could do that *and* look at Jason at the same time, Danielle shifted her gaze back to him. *Aw.* Now he was making a silly face while pretending to drive a *More More Moosby's!* toy race car along a toy shelf.

Hey. That particular race car looked a lot like . . .

"Yes?" Gigi prodded. "You can speak? Or do you mean you can stare at a handsome man and drool over his muscles? Because I do not want to burst your bubble, but *I* can do that one, too."

Danielle shook herself. "I need to go ask Jason something," she informed Gigi with dignity. Then she smoothed down her sweater, checked her hair, ran her tongue over her teeth to check for lipstick smudges, drew in a deep breath, and . . .

"That is a lot of primping for a simple conversation."

Argh. Caught, Danielle glanced at her friend. "Cut it out."

"You cut it out. I am only observing what you will not."

But Danielle knew that Gigi couldn't possibly know her better than she knew herself. Which was why, as she sashayed over to where Jason stood, she felt completely confident . . .

. . . about wanting to take him into her office and have her way with him. Nakedly. *That* wasn't professional, but it was true.

If Chip Larsen could have read her mind then, there would have been no quantity of carefully written memos that could have convinced him she was right about Jason *and* deserved a promotion. It was a good thing she had an insider on her side. Because she had Jason to put in a good word for her.

Just look at how diligent he was being on the sales floor!

". . . he doesn't really look like that, though," Jason was telling the two little girls as Danielle approached. He pointed at the cartoonified image of Alfred Moosby on the package for the *More More Moosby's*! exclusive race car. "For one thing, he doesn't have crazy, sticking-up white hair. For another—"

"He's *real*?" one of the little girls breathed.

"You *know* him?" the other asked, sounding skeptical.

"Know him? Of course I know him." Sounding introspective, Jason studied the packaging. "He's like a father to me."

"I thought he was made-up," one of the girls said.

"Yeah, me too," the other added with certainty. "Like Ronald McDonald. Or Chef Boyardee. Or Aunt Jemima."

Jason shook his head. "Chef Boyardee was real, too," he told them. "Except his name was spelled differently. Sometimes companies need mascots. Sometimes they start as real people."

One little girl crossed her arms. Doubtfully. "You're making this up. Mr. Moosby is just a cartoon. He's not real."

"He didn't used to be a cartoon," Jason explained in

an easygoing voice. "But the Moosby's board of directors decided they needed a 'friendlier' face to represent the company. They hired an expensive artist to come up with this cartoon"—he tapped it—"then they put the real Mr. Moosby out to pasture. He didn't want to retire," Jason went on, "but they made him. So—"

"So *that's* the real inside story of Mr. Moosby!" Danielle said brightly as she stepped in, giving Jason a "What are you doing, you lunatic?" look. Kids didn't care about corporate machinations. "How about that, girls? How would you like to have a cartoon version of yourself made? We're thinking of bringing in a local caricature artist for the next demo day."

"Cool!" the little girls breathed in unison.

They let themselves be led away from Jason to the play table where a seductive-looking Gigi and flustered-looking Henry were getting ready to lead the next demo session. After getting the girls settled in, Danielle made a beeline back to Jason.

Curiously, she looked at him. "What's the matter with you? That story started out so heartwarming and sweet, then it jumped right onboard the express train to Ranty Town."

"They don't even believe Mr. Moosby exists!" Jason waved his arm in exasperation. "The board has erased him. They pretended to value him at first. But the minute he got 'too old' to be relevant—in their eyes, at least—they turned him into a cartoon. They raked in big profits while doing it, too. I didn't like it then, and I'm not going to pretend I like it now." He glowered at the nearest cartoonified toy package. "If I hadn't stepped in when I did, Mr. Moosby would have been stripped of all his leverage in his own company."

Apparently Alfred Moosby still had *some* influence, then. That was fair. He and Jason were legends in toy retailing.

"Mr. Moosby is lucky to have you on his side." Interested in this unknown side of Jason, Danielle studied him. "Do you really know Mr. Moosby? Are the two of you really close?"

"I wasn't kidding about him being like a father to me." Idly, Jason rearranged a display of toy dump trucks. "If not for Mr. Moosby, my whole life would have been different."

"I thought you were the one who made a difference to him," Danielle said. "That's the way the Moosby's handbook spins it."

"I knew there was a reason I didn't like that thing." Jason frowned. As he stepped aside to let a trio of browsing shoppers pass by, his unhappy expression deepened. "Speaking of which, I was in the back office this morning, taking a call, and I couldn't help noticing that the boxes of inventory were all—"

Inventory? Suddenly on red alert, Danielle changed the subject. "You should tell someone the real story of Mr. Moosby. Maybe contact that biographer and set the record straight?"

As she'd hoped, Jason took the bait. "I can't do that," he told her. "It would make me look as bad as Bethanygate did."

"That's impossible. You looked pretty bad because of that," Danielle said. "Nothing in your past could make you look worse."

"Oh yeah?" Obviously interpreting that as a dare, Jason crossed his arms. He leaned nearer to her, as though to share a secret. Amid the bustling shoppers and the holiday ambiance and the underlying sugary scent of the vanilla Christmas cookies her staff were handing out as free samples that day, he confided, "When I was a kid, I had a knack for making things. Toys, mostly. I used to make them for my sisters, my brother, sometimes even the neighborhood kids. We were poor, so I had to scrounge for supplies. But sometimes, I couldn't Dumpster dive for everything. Sometimes, I had to be more creative than that."

Danielle wasn't sure where this was going. But at least it had veered directly away from her inventory manipulation.

"One year," Jason went on, "my sister Janelle wanted something special for her birthday. I didn't have all the supplies I needed, and I didn't have any money, so I did what I always did. I strolled into a local store, helped myself to a five-finger discount like the junior hooligan I was—"

"And Mr. Moosby caught you?" Danielle guessed.

Jason nodded. "I thought I was done for. He was scary! At least to a guilty fifteen-year-old, he was. But that crazy old man saw things differently than anyone else did. By then, I'd been in a lot of trouble. Fights, skipping school, a couple of busts for shoplifting. This time, I knew, there wouldn't just be a slap on the wrist. If old man Moosby turned me in—"

"But he didn't?"

"He didn't." A faint smile crossed Jason's face. "Not only that, but he looked at the beginnings of the toy I was making for Janelle—because I'd brought it along to match the parts—and he *liked* it. He said it was ingenious. I'll never forget that. *Ingenious.* Nobody had ever talked about me that way before."

Danielle glanced at the *More More Moosby's!* exclusive race car he'd been handling earlier. "I bet it *was* ingenious."

Jason shrugged. "Maybe it had the potential to be. To Mr. Moosby, *I* had potential, too." He frowned as he gazed out the toy store's gaily decorated picture windows. "He told me I could work off the price of what I'd stolen by sweeping and mopping and stocking toys. After I had, I just kept working for him."

"You liked it," Danielle surmised. "You were good at it."

Given his inherent charisma, she could easily imagine it.

"I was good at helping customers. Good at knowing what they needed. Good at knowing what they'd buy, even if they *didn't* need it." He gave her an almost embarrassed grin. "It didn't hurt that I was a cocky little punk. I was willing to charm people into buying, if I had to. The original Moosby's store flourished. Then it became two stores, then six, then a dozen."

Danielle touched his hand. "A legend was born!"

"That's what the corporate bullshit machine says. Yeah."

"Don't say that. It's true! You're good at what you do."

Jason shook his head. "I owe it all to Mr. Moosby." He glanced at that cartoon image again. "The board turned him into a clownish caricature of himself—and all because some corporate 'experts' advised them to. My friend deserved better than that."

"I'm not too fond of corporate advisers myself," Danielle couldn't help saying in a commiserating tone. "Sometimes they don't know what they're talking about. Sometimes things sound good in theory but don't work at all in practice."

Like inventory management schemes. Maybe, it occurred to her, Jason wouldn't object to her against-the-rules inventory routine. Maybe he would even applaud it, if he knew about it.

But for right now, she couldn't risk telling him.

"Hey." She nudged him. "Can you hook me up with the big guy?" She nodded at Mr. Moosby's image. "I'd like to meet him too."

With new contemplativeness, Jason gazed at her. He nodded. "You know, I might do that. I think Mr. Moosby might like to meet you, too."

"It would be almost like meeting the parents," Danielle joked. "You know, like people do when they start getting serious. Me, meeting your mentor. Him, giving us his blessing—"

She realized what she was saying and hastily broke off.

Meeting the parents? Getting serious? Ugh.

Wasn't she supposed to be trying *not* to encourage Jason to get carried away with their relationship? Wasn't she supposed to be keeping things Christmassy and casual between them?

Focus, she commanded herself. *Be smart*.

But it had never been more difficult to remain equable as

it was just then. Because, not surprisingly, Jason seemed wholly on board with the idea of taking things to the next level between them. Worse, Danielle really . . . *loved* that about him.

"Or not," she amended before he could reply. "I mean, what am I, pushy, much?" She gave a forced laugh. "Next I'll be inviting myself along to your beach Christmas in Antigua."

"You could come. Everyone would love you."

". . . and my rowdy kids, not so much, I'll bet."

"That's where you're wrong. Jennifer has two kids—"

But the last thing Danielle needed was to start thinking of herself as part of a big, boisterous, loving extended family.

No matter how much she loved that idea, too.

"—and I've got sixteen kids waiting for me to help out with a toy demo, right this minute," Danielle interrupted with an apologetic gesture. "Sorry. Do you want to help?"

Hard work. *That* ought to be enough to make a notorious playboy back off, she figured. It was a perfect strategy.

Except . . . "Sure." Jason rolled up his sleeves. "I'm on it."

Fifteen minutes later, Danielle discovered that Jason was as good at leading a toy demo as he was at everything else.

And *she* was as good at falling for him as she'd ever been. If this kept up, she'd never be able to rein herself in.

Worse, she'd completely forget why she wanted to at all.

Chapter Fifteen

At first, Jason couldn't quit thinking about Chip—and his obnoxious demand that Jason dish out a steady supply of photos and videos for Moosby's PR use. It shouldn't have surprised him that his chairman of the board wanted to take advantage of his chemistry with Danielle, though. After all, Chip was notoriously obsessed with increasing profits—and apparently, the sleigh ride footage of him, Danielle, and her kids had kicked off a major sales spike. That meant that Chip (and even Jason's board ally, Charley) couldn't quit talking about The Kismet Effect.

That's what the "social media monkeys" had deemed it: the Kismet Effect. Using it, they'd boosted the holiday allure of the small resort town to a whole new level. According to Chip, the whole world was smitten with the "fairy-tale story" of Jason and Danielle falling for each other. Because of those sleigh-ride images of him, Danielle, Karlie, Zach, and Aiden, everyone believed in the story that the Moosby's marketing gurus had concocted—a story that involved Jason and his new "family" doing Christmassy things while looking wholesome and adorable.

They were calling it a "new media" approach. Jason called it exploitative, misleading, and a few choice expletives, too.

He'd tried again to have that footage recalled. Chip had stubbornly refused. He'd said it was "out there already." In the end, Jason had been forced to relent. Thanks to his experience with Bethany, he knew how impossible it was to roll back anything on the Internet. All he could do was move forward.

And try to keep Danielle from learning about the footage, of course. Jason hadn't wanted to hide it from her. Not exactly. But he hadn't wanted to open her Web browser and put her face in front of that damning footage, either. So he'd settled on a middle ground of just . . . forgetting about it as best he could.

Two and a half weeks later, his strategy had worked.

By her own admission, Danielle was too busy to keep up with celebrity gossip—especially celebrity gossip that was broadcast via Twitter, Instagram, Facebook, YouTube, or any one of the (apparently) hundreds of "dream date" boards that users had made on Pinterest. So, because of Danielle's overall indifference to social media and without much effort on his part, Jason managed to forget all about Chip and his push for more pictures.

Instead, Jason did Christmassy things with Danielle and the kids. Not to generate photo ops, but just to do them. Together with Danielle, Aiden, Karlie, and Zach, Jason viewed the famous holiday lights show in Kismet's Glenrosen neighborhood. He took part in holiday shopping at the boutiques downtown. He ate more whoopie pies. He sipped eggnog, did more ice-skating, and helped Danielle wrap Christmas gifts with paper and ribbons and bows.

It was all really . . . *nice*. It was almost as nice as the extra-special Christmases Jason had imagined enjoying as a child—except now, as an adult, he had the bonus of sharing those special moments with a woman whose sex appeal, enthusiasm, and small-town openness made her irresistible to him. For Danielle, every moment they shared seemed exciting. Every cup of eggnog or turn around the ice-skating rink seemed filled with fun.

"For a woman who claims to be 'over' the whole Kismet Christmas thing," he teased her partway through those weeks together, "you sure seem to like all this schmaltzy holiday stuff."

"Nah. I'm doing it all for you," she'd claimed, doing an impromptu hip-swiveling boogie as she handed him another sparkly ornament while decorating the family Christmas tree. "I'm doing it so you can have the fully loaded holiday experience."

"Well, I *love* the fully loaded holiday experience." He'd accepted that ornament and hung it on the tree, then paused to admire all the crooked, crazily painted handmade ornaments the kids had created over the years. "I'm not the one who claimed to be immune to all of it, though. *I* think it's great."

"Typical temp talk," Karlie had grumbled nearby.

But Danielle hadn't heard her daughter's sarcastic comment, and Jason had learned to overlook those remarks. He still hadn't won over Karlie completely, he knew, but he had made a few inroads by intervening with Danielle on her daughter's behalf.

Evidently, Danielle didn't like Karlie's *Fashion Makeover EXTREME!* video game. She'd banned Karlie from playing it except at her Dad's house. But when Jason had expressed an interest in trying it, Danielle had relented. He'd quickly learned why Danielle had objected to it, given its blatant objectification, lack of interesting playable characters, and emphasis on beauty competition. But Karlie *loved* that game from the first heart-shaped pink pixel to the last, so Jason played it with her.

"Ha *ha*!" Karlie boasted every time. "Pwned you again. When are you going to learn you can't beat me at this, temp?"

Jason always pretended chagrin. "I guess I just can't get the hang of doing a good digital pedicure. Congrats, townie."

Over time, as they played, Karlie seemed bugged by the game's limitations, too. But she stuck to her guns and insisted she loved it. "If only my mom would let me play it with my friends instead of with her stupid new boyfriend," she'd groaned while putting away the game console after their last matchup. "I'm the only one who hasn't reached the Ultimate Diva level!"

"Ultimate Diva level is dumb," Zach had told her, not looking up from his handheld game. "But that's a girl game for you. Everybody knows girl games suck. They're not *real* games."

The ensuing squabble had almost toppled the newly decorated Christmas tree, chipped Zach's tooth, and made Aiden spill all the goldfish food he'd been clutching when the fight broke out.

"Hey!" the six-year-old had protested indignantly. "You almost made me spill all of the food for Rudolph."

Knowing what was coming, Jason had hurried over to help Aiden. The kid loved feeding his fish. If Jason and Danielle weren't vigilant, he eagerly sprinkled in more and more and *more* fish food, just for the fun of watching Rudolph gobble it.

"Hey, buddy. Let me help you with that."

"Okay." With a shrug, Aiden handed over the fish food. He waited with his palm outstretched while Jason measured out a tiny pinch. On his tiptoes, the boy levered over the fishbowl. He sprinkled in the food. Then he squatted with his face to the glass to watch Rudolph chow down. "Do you think my mom will let me get Dasher and Dancer and Donner and Cupid and, um, Nemo and, er, Justin yet?" Aiden asked. "You know, the other goldfish? So I can have all of Santa's reindeer in the bowl by Christmas?"

Jason had grinned, resisting an urge to explain that Nemo and Justin weren't reindeer names. "Pretty soon. Maybe."

He'd learned by then why Danielle had been dead set against Crystal getting Aiden a new goldfish for Christmas. Danielle had already known about her son's Fish Hit Man reputation. She'd also known about Aiden's tender soul and subsequent heartbreak after the accidental fish manslaughter inevitably occurred.

Pretty much, Danielle knew everything about her kids.

By the time Jason had stepped barefoot on his umpteenth stray Lego brick—just as Zach had happened by, gleefully toting around (just) the beeping motor from the 972-piece robotics set that Crystal had bought him (and Mark had failed to help assemble, and Danielle had strenuously objected to buying based on Zach's history with complicated sets that were beyond his age level), Jason had had to admit the truth. To her face.

"You know *everything* about your kids," he'd told Danielle. "If I ever try to contradict you, feel free to punch me."

"I think my kids would really benefit from living in L.A."

"Not necessarily," he'd argued automatically. "There's crowding, crime, smog, and traffic. There's no snow. There's—"

The punch in the arm he'd received shouldn't have surprised him. Even now, more than a week after that incident, Jason knew that Danielle would have insisted she was right about moving.

She was starting to weaken, though. When the five of them went downtown to see the unveiling of the thirty-foot-tall official Christmas tree in the Kismet town square, Danielle admitted that "a Hollywood tree" probably wouldn't be as nice. When they went to their neighborhood cookie-and-candy exchange, toting plastic containers of iced-and-sprinkled sugar cookies and homemade peppermint bark, Danielle remarked that she "might miss" her friends' annual parties. When they went sledding at the edge of town, and Jason and Danielle tumbled out of their shared sled halfway down, laughing all the way as they face-planted in the snow, she speculated that beach sand "wouldn't be the same." Every time, Karlie, Zach, and Aiden agreed with her.

The closer Danielle came to conceding that she might want to stay in Kismet after all, the more Jason wanted to stay too. Not that that was possible. He was a CEO. He had important responsibilities. People relied on him for their livelihoods.

To his disappointment, Danielle agreed with him about that.

"I bet no one else but you could keep Moosby's going so well," she said as they wound a red-and-green garland made of construction paper loops around her family's Christmas tree. "If you weren't the CEO of Moosby's, the toy stores would crumble."

Not really, Jason hadn't wanted to say. Because he knew damn well his most important contributions to the company had already come with the first expansions and gone with the final *More More Moosby's!* toy exclusives. His skills had been in bringing people onboard, generating enthusiasm, and curating a unique selection in their toy stores. None of those things were strictly necessary anymore. *He* didn't want to be cartoonified.

Or, "You must really love being in charge of everything," she said as they cut out paper snowflakes with the kids, then hung them—Karlie's featuring plenty of glued-on glitter—in her cozy little house's windows. "You can do whatever you want."

Jason hadn't had the heart to tell Danielle that, in most instances, the board had the final say. As combined majority shareholders, they had the right to steer the ship—even if he thought they were steering it straight into the rocks.

Or, "Without you, Moosby's wouldn't even be what it is today." Leadingly, Danielle had gestured at the fix Jason had been performing on one of Zach's old toys. "You're so creative."

But Jason had only scoffed. "Selling original toys isn't as lucrative as getting paid to display someone else's toys." That was what Moosby's had begun doing a few years ago as part of their ongoing partnerships with mega toy makers. "Selling shelf space is where it's at these days. We provide the tried-and-true, come-in-and-browse-awhile ambiance. Other companies provide the merch. We take on zero inventory. Zero risk."

Danielle had looked alarmed. "Do you think Moosby's will quit stocking unique toys altogether? Our customers love them!"

"Do they?" Jason had asked as he'd tightened a miniature screw. "Or do they have 'nonpaying nostalgia' for those toys?"

Because that's what the board and their consultants had decided. They'd assembled focus groups, studied market research, conducted comparatives, and concluded that their *More More Moosby's!* line of original toys was better treated an in-store "decorative element" than as bona fide profitable merchandise.

That particular decision still rankled Jason.

"Well . . ." In the midst of hanging Christmas stockings on her TV's entertainment center, her modernized stand-in for a traditional fireplace mantel, Danielle had paused. "I have to admit, most people who pick up the *More More Moosby's!* exclusives are adults, not kids. The kids make a beeline for video games. Plus, Moosby's exclusives are sort of on the expensive side . . ."

That was because they were made in the USA, Jason knew, without cheap overseas labor, in quantities too small to generate the usual aggregate economies of scale. In fact, it had been years since Moosby's had produced new exclusive toys. As far as Jason knew, the factory that made them had shut down.

"But they could be updated," Danielle went on. "I'll bet someone extra talented could take a fresh look at them."

"It's possible," Jason agreed, "that someone already is."

Then he'd joined Danielle at the entertainment center, taken a fond look at the familiar names stitched onto the stockings she'd been hanging, and kissed her—even as all the kids squealed, ran around, and made hilarious kissy-face sounds.

Predictably, Danielle forgot all about business after that. Just the way Jason wanted her to. Because he didn't want to think about work. He didn't even want to think about Christmas.

More and more, the approach of Christmas meant one thing: the end of his stay in Kismet and the beginning of his planned beach Christmas in Antigua with his family.

When he'd made those plans, he hadn't expected to be in love. But that's what had happened. Jason was sure of it.

How else could he have looked at a woman who was currently wiping Aiden's runny nose while simultaneously singing along to "Run Run Rudolph" . . . and actually found her actions *endearing*?

He was so far gone that, when Danielle glanced up at him, saw him watching her, and smiled, he volunteered for more.

"I hear The Big Foot Bar does a wicked peppermint hot cocoa," Jason said. "How about some adults-only time tonight?"

Danielle's smile broadened. "I think I could persuade Gigi and Henry to babysit. In fact, I'd *love* to see them try."

At her mischievous look, Jason loved her more than ever.

"It's a date. I have a few things to do down at the store first." For some necessary tasks, he needed access to a computer. He hadn't brought one for what he'd thought was going to be a short-lived media tour. "But after that, I'm all yours."

"I can't wait." Danielle gave Aiden a reassuring squeeze, then stood while pocketing her tissues. "Say, eight o'clock?"

Jason nodded. Aiden did, too. "I'll show Gigi and Henry how to feed my goldfish!" he said. "They're going to love Rudolph!"

"Gigi ought to be really good at *Fashion Makeover EXTREME!*" Karlie suggested from the sofa, where she was curled up with a book. A smile quirked her lips. "Unlike *some people* who suck."

"Maybe Henry can build robots," Zach put in. "My friend Lorenzo's big brother has the same set I got, and his robot is sweet!"

Jason had some plans of his own on those fronts, but it would be a while before he unveiled them. In the meantime . . .

"Eight o'clock is perfect," he told Danielle with a squeeze of her hand. "I'll be there."

Half dressed in a skirt, lacy bra, and chemise, Danielle heard the doorbell ring at 7:45 sharp. Startled, she glanced at her clock, then at the clothing, hosiery, and footwear trailing from her closet to her bed. Boots vied with booties and sandals on her bedroom floor; sweaters challenged silky tops and tees; her fluffy orange jacket surveyed the whole scene with smug serenity, knowing it would be called into action no matter what else happened that night, given the wintry December weather.

Pondering all those items, Danielle *still* couldn't decide what to wear. The Big Foot Bar wasn't fancy. It was a friendly but grungy watering hole that catered to locals. Probably, a skirt was overkill. Maybe a pair of jeans and a cute top?

Ding dong. The doorbell chimed again.

Feeling flustered, Danielle threw on her robe and belted it. She scurried to the front door, casting an evaluative glance at her children as she went. Aiden, Zach, and Karlie seemed fine. Danielle didn't hire babysitters very often. Given how much she worked, she liked spending her free time with her children as much as possible. Especially since her divorce. But tonight . . .

. . . tonight, she was going all out on the va-va-voom front.

"Woo-hoo! Look at you!" Gigi cooed as Danielle opened the door. Her friend sashayed inside with Henry bringing up the rear carrying some boxes. Gigi's gaze took in Danielle's hair, her makeup, and—lastly—her unfinished outfit. "All of the mêlée is catching up with you, I see. You are looking very fancy tonight." Gigi edged aside Danielle's robe and took a peek. "Right down to your lacy lingerie. *C'est parfaite!*"

"Hi to you, too." Danielle clutched her robe to shut it. She wasn't sure if her relationship with Jason qualified as a "mêlée," per se, but it had been a whirlwind, for sure. That's probably what Gigi meant. Blushing over the new bra her friend had noticed, Danielle nodded to Henry. "What are the boxes for? Wait—are those *Moosby's* boxes you're carrying?"

Gigi shrugged. "I needed for them to be out of the way before the Kismet Christmas Carol Crawl next week. We are going to have a lot of extra people in our store. Something had to give." She gestured at Henry. "Where should Henry put them?"

Since Jason was still Danielle's houseguest—and he still couldn't know about her inventory manipulation—that was a good question. "In the garage," she decided. "Right through there."

She pointed, indicating the way for Henry.

"I'll show you," Zach volunteered. He jumped up.

Ever since her son had begun spending more time with

Jason, he'd become twice as attentive as usual. Zach had always been a caring kid, but now he was even more helpful. Danielle guessed that all the Lego-building "J" and "Z" had been doing together was leading to good things. *Positive role model* things.

Jason Hamilton: CEO, playboy, role model. Who'da thunk it?

"How do you know when you have too much inventory?" Karlie asked Gigi. "How do you know which things to move? Because I've been getting interested in entrepreneurship lately, and I . . ."

As her daughter astounded her by launching a discussion of retailing with Gigi, Danielle reevaluated the situation in the living room. At first, she hadn't looked closely enough to realize it, but Karlie had been reading a book—something she hadn't done much of since getting interested in video games.

Maybe Jason had had a positive influence on Karlie, too. After all, Danielle had heard the two of them discussing the specifics of Karlie's *Fashion Makeover EXTREME!* video game in ways that Danielle simply couldn't have pulled off without inciting an instant knee-jerk rebellion in her daughter.

"Gigi, come meet my new goldfish!" Aiden tugged Gigi's coat sleeve, eager for her to see Rudolph. "He's right over here. See? Look at him! Maybe you can help me feed him later."

"Not too much food!" Danielle cautioned automatically.

But to her astonishment, Aiden was already one step ahead of her. "We can't feed him right now," her son was saying to his babysitter as he laid his hand protectively over the fish food Gigi had impulsively grabbed from beside the fishbowl. "Jason said if you feed Rudolph too much or too often, he'll explode."

At Aiden's matter-of-fact tone, Danielle boggled. She'd

tried to explain to her son in several different ways that it was important to carefully ration the goldfish food. It had never occurred to her to be quite as *graphic* as Jason had been. She hadn't wanted to scare Aiden by being too direct about all the fish deaths he'd accidentally caused over the years.

Evidently, though, where her gentle entreaties had failed, Jason's blunt warning had made an impression on Aiden.

"Ah. I see. We do not want to do that then, do we?"

"Nuh-uh. I *love* Rudolph!" A sly glance backward at Danielle. "Except he needs some other fish to keep him company."

Aiden's hint wasn't lost on Danielle. She knew that her son wanted more goldfish. Until now, she hadn't seriously considered giving in to his pleas—for his own good, of course.

Marveling at the changes she'd noticed in her children, Danielle watched them more closely. Zach was acting like a perfect junior gentleman. Karlie had started spending her video game time reading. Aiden had finally learned not to murder his hapless goldfish. *She* was about to go out for an adults-only *date*. That was something she hadn't done in years, because she and Mark had gotten married and started a family right away.

There was only one explanation for all these changes.

Still . . . could Jason really have made this much difference in only a few short weeks? Danielle knew that he'd affected her in a big way. It seemed that she hadn't noticed, until now, exactly how involved Jason had become with Karlie, Zach, and Aiden, too.

She couldn't have special-ordered a custom boyfriend more perfect than Jason had turned out to be. If only he were staying. Or she weren't going. Or things were just . . . different.

Because as an SUV door slammed outside and then

footsteps sounded up her snowy front porch, Danielle remembered that the man who'd engendered all these positive developments was only going to be with her temporarily. For a variety of reasons.

None of which seemed very critical as Jason opened the door and then came inside, brightening at the sight of her visitors.

Wearing his new cold-weather gear with tousled hair and another casually tossed-on GQ-worthy scarf, Jason greeted Gigi and a just-returned Henry. He fist-bumped Zach, ruffled Aiden's hair, then gave Karlie a genial, "How's it going?" nod.

Karlie grinned in response . . . then seemed to remember that she was annoyed at the mere existence of her mother's "stupid new boyfriend." Sighing mightily, she slouched on the sofa again.

Danielle caught Jason's quickly hidden downcast look.

She touched his hand, then drew him over to stand near the Christmas tree in a more private spot. "Don't take Karlie's attitude too personally," she told him in a low voice. "Even at the best of times, Karlie can be a little standoffish. She's a hugger, not a huggee. She likes to be the one who makes the first move."

"I get it." Jason let his gaze rove over Danielle's semi-dressed figure. Either he liked her current state of dishabille, or he was interested in helping her out of her clothes altogether. But all he said was, "Karlie's cautious. That's okay. She just needs time. Like mother, like daughter."

"Are you saying I'm acting like a ten-year-old?"

He grinned to defuse her defensiveness. It worked. "I'm saying everyone should get to decide their own limits. Kids too. When I was a kid, I would have been a lot happier if I hadn't had to hug my stinky old bearded uncle Oscar, that's for sure."

"It's not that Karlie doesn't like you."

"It's a little bit that she doesn't like me."

"She'll come around eventually."

"I'll keep trying until she does."

"I know you will," Danielle said warmly, "and I appreciate that. Really, I do. So—"

Gigi stepped in. "As heartwarming as this is, Henry and I are not here to listen to you two behave like parents."

Surprised, Danielle stared at her. "*Parents?* We're not—"

"—acting like parents," Jason finished for her. He cast Danielle a bewildered glance, then gave Gigi a decidedly uneasy-sounding chuckle. "I don't know anything about parenting."

"He doesn't know anything about parenting," Danielle confirmed. "Yesterday, he gave the kids cupcakes for breakfast."

Jason straightened. "Again—tell me the difference between a muffin and a cupcake. Because they seem the same to me."

"A muffin is breakfast. A cupcake is dessert."

"So if I'd scraped off the frosting, then it would have been okay?" Jason persisted. "Because the way you freaked out, anyone would have thought I'd fed the kids Doritos and beer."

"You're not *that* clueless." Danielle suppressed a smile. She'd loved that Jason had taken it upon himself to try to stir up some breakfast. "Besides, you did let me sleep in that day. That earned you some major points right there."

"I brought you a cupcake, too. Which you ate! So—"

A piercing whistle cut short their discussion.

Henry took his fingers out of his mouth. He grinned.

"We're here," he clarified with a besotted look at Gigi, "so you two can go have a date. So will you get going already?"

Gladly, Danielle did.

And that's how, with her friends' blessing and her children's cooperation, she got herself dressed, got herself out the door into a moonlit wintertime December night, and got herself onto her first real date . . . with her first fake boyfriend.

It was going to be *fantastic*. She just knew it.

Chapter Sixteen

To Jason, stepping into The Big Foot Bar with Danielle felt like coming home. The place was comfortable, welcoming, and a little raucous. It was full of pitted wood tables, beer-stained concrete, and liquor-company "stained glass" gimme lamps featuring logos of current and long-forgotten brands. There were neon signs on the kitschy wood-paneled walls, a jukebox in the corner, and several boisterous patrons. The only nod to the season was a limp felt Santa hat propped on a Jim Beam bottle.

It was a dive bar in the best sense. He loved it.

Clearly, this was where the locals came to unwind.

Beside him, Danielle looked around. "Sorry. You probably weren't counting on someplace so grungy. We can go across the lake to Lagniappe on the Lakeshore instead, if you want. They serve real scotch, good wine, and those chichi 'small plates' of food that are all the rage in the tourist places right now."

Jason inhaled the yeasty tang of beer. He examined the tables full of parka-wearing people just in from the snow.

He spied a waitress passing by with a tray loaded with peppermint hot chocolate drinks and shook his head.

"Not until I get one of *those*. This place is perfect."

Danielle blinked. "It is?"

"It's just like home." Jason caught her surprised glance as he put his hand to the small of her back and steered them both to a free table. "I already told you about my past. Did you think I was pounding foie gras and champagne in between Dumpster-diving expeditions? I was eating beef stew from a can and drinking cheap beer. I wasn't born a CEO, you know."

They settled in at one of the close-packed tables. Jason nodded at the people he recognized from the store and his meet-and-greets; Danielle exchanged hellos with her friends, too.

"I can't believe you like it here," she said. "You must be a townie at heart." She wiggled out of her fuzzy orange jacket and slung it over the back of her rickety chair along with her purse. "I guess that means you could be happy in Kismet."

"It looks that way." Jason signaled the waitress to bring two of those liquored-up peppermint hot cocoas. "Unlike you?"

"Well . . ." Seeming thoughtful, Danielle looked around. "I like it *here*," she admitted. "But that doesn't mean that Kismet is the best place for me overall. The job market is bad—"

"Your job isn't at risk." Not if he could help it.

"—even for folks working in the tourism sector," she continued, "which used to be unbeatable around here. And cultural events are few and far between in Kismet, unless you really like snowmobile races and the county fair—"

"Nothing wrong with a Tilt-A-Whirl and a livestock show." He grinned. "Plus, I'd like to try a snowmobile race. I think I could win."

"—and the schools don't have any of the advantages of big-city schools," Danielle added. "For instance, we don't have—"

"Overcrowding? Budget cuts? Discipline issues?" Jason

moved his arm to make room for the waitress to set down their drinks. Both were topped with whipped cream but no holiday sprinkles. This wasn't Starbucks. The high-proof alcohol wafting upward from those chocolaty drinks almost made his eyes water. "I hate to tell you this, but kids can be real terrors, no matter where they live or who their parents are. I'm proof of that."

"You're not so bad." Seeming to give up on her quest to convince him Kismet was subpar, Danielle leaned back. A holiday song from the '80s began playing on the jukebox. "You might have had a rough beginning, but you've succeeded big-time."

Her smile of approval made Jason want to launch an IPO or handcraft some new toys. Instead, he sipped his hot cocoa.

Extra-strength, boozy, minty chocolate was *delicious*.

"Except for your penchant for girly drinks." Danielle shook her head. "Aren't you supposed to knock back vodka shots? Swill a six-pack of beer? Drink a sophisticated 007-style martini?"

Jason scoffed. "I like this. You might have noticed by now," he told her, "that I don't care what people think of me."

"You must care a little. You're here, aren't you?"

Obviously she was referring to his on-demand media tour.

"I came here as a compromise with the board, yes. But once I'd spent a little time here . . . nope. I still don't care about the public at large." He hoped that, someday when Danielle heard about or saw those sleigh-ride photos—and the new images that had somehow been appearing over the past couple of weeks—she would remember his words tonight. She would know that he hadn't taken advantage of her—especially not for the sake of placating the public. "Believe me, it would have been easier to go along with the just-apologize playbook. But I did nothing wrong."

"Well . . . this morning I remember you were pretty naughty."

Her flirtatious glance made his pants shrink a size. But he was determined to give Danielle a long-delayed night out—not to whisk her straight back to her house for some private time.

"So scoff all you want at my drink choices," Jason said with a proud lift of his supersugary drink, "but *this* is the best thing I've had in my mouth since this morning."

Oops. Remembering Danielle's naked body, her urgent cries . . . the incredible way the two of them had felt when coming together . . . *that* wouldn't encourage him to stay in public with her. Jason knew that no mere boozy hot cocoa could compare with *that*.

Being with Danielle was a dream he hadn't known he wanted.

Now that he did, he wished things were less complicated.

Whoever was still sharing photos with Chip and the Moosby's media team *wasn't* Jason. Probably, it was the spy who'd been trailing him in Kismet. But Jason didn't know how to stop it.

For the moment, he settled, as he sometimes did, for pretending the ongoing Moosby's social media campaign wasn't happening. It was nicer to flirt with Danielle in a grimy bar full of regular Joes and girls next door, all of them getting ready for Christmas in their own unique, down-home ways.

"Oh yeah? The best thing you've had in your mouth since this morning?" Seductively, Danielle leaned nearer. She'd never looked prettier—or more beloved. "If you say that a little louder, the whole place will know what we've been up to."

"Screwing each other's brains out?"

"Mmm-hmm." A nod. Another touch. A trailing caress

up his arm. "I have to say, I didn't know sex could be . . . like *that*."

Jason couldn't help grinning. "Like what?"

Danielle's gaze turned faraway. "Like it is in the movies. You know, where everybody is tearing off each other's clothes, and they're kissing all over the place, and they're doing it standing up in an alley somewhere, breathing hard and—"

"Speaking of hard . . ." Jason took her hand. He lowered it to his thigh, wishing he could slide it the few necessary inches to the left that would let Danielle feel for herself how hard he was. He settled for giving her a passionate look. "*I am*."

"See? That's what I'm talking about!" She waved her free hand for emphasis. "This kind of thing *never* happens to me! It never has. We're here drinking grown-up drinks"—she took a swig of hers—we're out past nine o'clock, you're *flirting* with me—"

"It's more than flirting." Amid the noisy bar, Jason nodded toward the exit. "I'm pretty sure I saw an alley back there."

Danielle's gaze widened. She squirmed. "You don't mean—"

"That I would take you standing up in an alley? I do."

Jason hoped his smoldering gaze adequately conveyed how good an idea that seemed to him just then.

"We'd freeze to death," Danielle protested.

But her eyes sparkled at the idea. Interestedly.

"It wouldn't have to take long. Unless you wanted it to."

"With you? I *always* want it to take a long time."

"We'd only have to get minimally undressed," Jason said, feeling himself warming up to the idea. "That means it shouldn't be too cold. You're wearing tall boots. I'm wearing a scarf. My coat would be good cover for us both. And your skirt—"

"Is on top of a pair of tights. They're like Fort Knox."

"Have I mentioned I have a criminal past?" Jason gave her a self-assured look. "I'm capable of breaking in almost anywhere."

"Not in here. It's a spandex no-fly zone."

"Hmm. Maybe I don't like winter so much after all."

"See?" Triumphantly, Danielle sipped her minty cocoa. She lifted her eyebrows in an arch look. "I told you it's not so great here. For every charming piece of Christmas kitsch, there's an equal and less charming wintertime problem."

"Hmm. A compromise then."

"Such as?"

"Such as I make you feel good without taking off your clothes." Demonstrating, Jason lowered his hand to Danielle's knee. As predicted, he encountered the soft black tights she'd worn with her boots and skirt, but he didn't let that stop him. Keeping his gaze fixed heatedly on hers, he slowly slid his hand up to her thigh. "All I need are a few more inches, and then—"

Danielle gasped. She froze in surprise as his fingers slipped under her skirt hem, then toyed with her inner thigh.

"And then we're going to get arrested!" Belatedly, she slapped her hand atop his, ending the caress Jason had been enjoying. "I'm here for a date, not a night in jail."

"Spoilsport."

"Exhibitionist."

"Chicken."

"Froufrou drinker."

"Hey." Sternly, Jason regarded her. "It takes a strong man to admit his love of liquid chocolate and whipped cream. At least it doesn't come with an umbrella and a pineapple slice."

Danielle laughed. Camaraderie enveloped them, just the way it always did, whether they were on a snowboarding slope, in a bar, on the ice-skating rink, or at home. Jason . . . loved that.

"Hey, Jason!" someone called from the other end of the bar.

He looked up just as Reno Wright strolled over, wearing an amiable look with his arm slung protectively around Rachel, his wife. In Kismet, the two of them were like royalty—Reno with his NFL-star past, and Rachel with her prodigal townie status.

"And Danielle!" Rachel stepped away from her husband's embrace long enough to hug Danielle hello. "How are you?"

They traded chitchat about the holidays, their respective businesses, people they knew in town, and the Wright's new baby.

"I probably ought to be trying to drop a few postbaby pounds," Rachel admitted with a rueful pat to her midsection. "But Reno likes me a little cushier. And I don't actually mind being curvier. I'm not in L.A. anymore." She shrugged. "When I was pregnant, I couldn't get enough of Kristen Miller's cranberry-mincemeat pie down at the Galaxy Diner. So worth it!"

"We both put away enough pie to power a small army," Reno confirmed with a matching pat to his perfectly taut abs. He tossed his wife a love-struck look. "I wanted to be part of everything—pregnancy cravings, delivery, the whole thing."

Jason nodded. "That's the way to do it. All in."

He caught Danielle staring at him in apparent awe. Most likely, he knew by now, that was because Mark had been a jerk while she'd been pregnant. If she said anything about her damn ex-husband and his many unrelated-to-Jason faults, he might have to punch something. He wished Danielle would quit painting him with the same brush her ass-clown ex-husband had handed her.

"That looks like Mark and Crystal over there," she said.

Here we go, Jason thought. Being preoccupied with her ex-husband was Danielle's Kryptonite. He wanted that to end.

He started by not taking the bait or looking. Then . . .

"So . . . you two are out having a date night?" Jason asked, deliberately involving Reno and Rachel in his diversion.

His tactic worked. Reno grinned. "Date night? Sort of."

"It's a retirement party," Rachel explained, tossing an over-the-shoulder glance toward another table. "Kind of, at least. The factory on the east side of town is closing. I wanted to hire the employees to do some work for my clothing company, but I'm already committed to another supplier. I figured the least I could do was lend the workers some moral support."

"I know almost everyone who got laid off," Reno confirmed with a somber look. "I wanted to help, too, but I turned down a franchise offer last year. I don't have the cash flow I might have had if I'd taken it. I wish things were different, but The Wright Stuff can only absorb so much of the labor force."

"Still, it's better to stick to your conscience, right?" Rachel looped her arm in her husband's, giving him a supportive look. "Multicorp isn't exactly the most ethical company."

Danielle nodded. Evidently, she knew all about the franchise offer they were referring to, involving the unethical Multicorp and Reno's local downtown sporting-goods store.

Given the disapproving tone of their discussion, though, Jason couldn't help feeling singled out. After all, he'd been instrumental in opening Moosby's toy stores across the world.

"Franchising doesn't have to be bad," he pointed out. "It creates jobs and expands markets. Customers like consistency."

Reno only shrugged. "That's what they told me. In the end, I decided it was better to do something small with integrity, than something big with compromises. It would have been lucrative. But thanks to football, I've already got all I need."

So did Jason. Not thanks to football, but thanks to Moosby's. He had all he needed. More millions wouldn't matter.

He'd made compromises, though. He'd been making them since the day he'd taken Moosby's public. At the time, the world had applauded his actions. The press had called him "visionary." Even Mr. Moosby had been thrilled with the company's growth.

But that was then. And now . . . Jason shifted uneasily.

"But that's me," Reno said heartily. "I'm a beginner at business. I don't have your acumen, Jason. You're legendary."

He didn't feel legendary. Not then.

"He's *incredible*," Danielle said, stars in her eyes as she looked at Jason. She held his hand. "He's talented and hard-working and brilliant, and the knack he has with customers—"

"Is unrivaled except by my knack for buying rounds." Jason nodded at Reno and Rachel. "Do you think your friends would be offended if I ordered up a couple of rounds for the table?"

Maybe then, he thought, his conscience would quit squawking. Because it couldn't have been long ago, Jason knew, that another similar factory—a factory manufacturing *More More Moosby's!* exclusive toys—had been similarly shut down elsewhere.

Then, Jason had been one step removed from that decision. He'd tried to stop that closure. But it had been a single decision in a lifetime of decisions. He hadn't truly thought about the impact that closure would have on the employees.

"Offended? In Kismet?" Rachel asked. "At The Big Foot?"

"Over getting free drinks?" Danielle laughed. The two townie girls exchanged amused glances. "Not likely."

So, while Rachel joined Danielle at their table, Jason and Reno went to the bar to order more commiseration drinks.

"Hey." At the scratched up, well-loved bar, Reno nudged

him. "Sorry to get up on a soapbox back there. I don't like all the changes in this town. It's not the way it was when I was a kid growing up here. Or maybe it just sucks being an adult."

"It just sucks being an adult."

"Well . . ." Reno tossed an adoring look at his wife. "There are compensations for *that*." His famous grin—so familiar on ESPN—flashed at Jason. "For you and Danielle, too, it looks like."

"Yeah." Jason couldn't help grinning back as he peeled off several bills to pay for the rounds and settle his bar tab. "I might not be perfect at work, but I'm kicking ass at home."

"Oh." Reno looked surprised. "I knew you and Danielle were seeing each other. I mean, who doesn't, right? But I didn't know you were living together already. You're pretty serious, huh?" He gave Jason a mock threatening look. "You'd better treat Danielle right, dude. Don't make me come looking for you."

But despite Reno's warning—and the over-six-foot, former athlete's muscle he backed it up with—Jason was stuck on . . .

"What do you mean," he asked with a chill running up his spine, "who doesn't know Danielle and I are seeing each other?"

He hoped Reno meant that Kismet was a small town. That the people there gossiped. Or that Danielle had told Reno the whole story, from the moment they'd met in her office until now.

Reno stopped tapping his fingers on the bar. He gave Jason a curious look. "Surely *you* know about it. The Twitter thing?"

Uh-oh. Jason knew he should have anticipated this.

He hadn't. He'd been blissfully being with Danielle.

"*Hashtag sleighride*?" Reno specified. "That whole meme

with you and Danielle and her kids? The YouTube channel, the Instagram photos, the Vine videos? We *do* get the Internet out here in the boondocks, you know. When you two walked in here tonight, didn't you notice the hush that fell over the bar?"

Jason frowned, remembering it. "I thought that was a reaction to how smoking hot Danielle looks tonight."

Reno gave a knowing smile. "Spoken like a man in love."

Spoken like a dead man. If Rachel Wright started talking about *#sleighride* with Danielle, then he was done for. He hadn't even prepared an excuse, Jason realized belatedly. All this time, he'd been counting on Danielle caring enough about him not to mind that he'd basically allowed her to be sold out on social media for the advancement of his company.

Put that way, the situation sounded pretty bad.

"That awestruck silence in the bar was a reaction to knowing that whatever you two did in here tonight, it was going to wind up on TV tomorrow," Reno explained, giving Jason a puzzled look. "There was probably some primping going on among the bar patrons, too, I'd imagine. You didn't guess?"

"Wind up . . . *on TV*?" This kept getting worse and worse.

"Some of the infotainment shows are doing daily coverage."

Jason swore. How the hell did they keep getting footage?

"All right. This ends now." He threw down some money, nodded at the bartender, then headed back to Danielle. "Nice seeing you again, Reno. You too, Rachel. But we're leaving."

"Leaving? Now?" Danielle blinked at him. Then her gaze traveled past his face, down to his chest, lower to his groin . . . and lingered. She smiled. "Yep. We're leaving now."

While gathering her jacket, she said her good-byes to her perplexed-looking friends. At her placid expression, Jason wanted to jump for joy. *She didn't know yet.* Rachel hadn't blurted out anything about *#sleighride*. He was safe. For now.

Danielle obviously thought he was gunning for a stand-up quickie in the alley near The Big Foot Bar. That couldn't have been farther from the truth—especially now that Jason realized that the spy might have followed them there. With a camera.

But Jason also knew he'd dodged a bullet. If Reno's off-hand comment about Moosby's media onslaught had come at another time . . .

"Danielle?" a man blurted nearby. "Is that *you*?"

Halfway through bundling up and preparing to leave the bar, Jason froze. *Damn the snow and cold weather.* In L.A., he and Danielle would have already made their getaway. But here in Kismet, they were stuck preparing for near arctic conditions.

"Mark!" Danielle cooed. "And look, it's Crystal, too!"

Danielle sounded sort of . . . tipsy, Jason realized. Uh-oh.

Hastily, he finished helping her on with her jacket. Orange fuzz went up his nostrils and tried to get frisky with his nose hair. In his arms, Danielle teetered on her high-heeled boots.

"Imagine running into you two here!" Danielle gave her ex and his new wife an expansive, intoxicated grin. "Tonight," she said, "*I'm* having fun, too, for a change! Tonight, *I'm* going out to have an alleyway quickie with Jason. He's even chivalrous enough," she boasted loudly, "to make sure the sex won't take very long! He said the sex hardly has to last any time at all!"

That was the one detail that had penetrated the fog induced by her liquored-up peppermint hot cocoa? That Jason had promised they could have an extra-quick quickie, if she wanted to?

"It would take long enough," he couldn't resist clarifying in his most macho voice. "*Exactly* long enough to be satisfying."

But that wasn't the point, Jason knew. And even if he

hadn't known, Mark and Crystal's identically mystified looks would have brought home that truth to him an instant later.

If they knew about *#sleighride*, too, like Reno . . .

If they mentioned it to Danielle . . .

"But only if we get started right now, babe." With a hasty chuckle, Jason put his arm around Danielle. She had, he saw with a glance, finished both her minty hot cocoa and his. That was the likely equivalent of several consecutive shots of liquor. He knew Danielle didn't drink often. She was a lightweight. "Otherwise, if the temperature keeps dropping, it'll be too cold out there."

"Pfft." With that blustery exhalation, Danielle pulled out the chair she'd just vacated. She offered it to Crystal. "Don't be such a baby, Golden State. It's barely below freezing out."

Jason nodded good-bye to Reno and Rachel, who were on their way out of the bar. He looked at Danielle, knowing he had to get her out of there. Quickly. "Let's go. I'd rather not wait."

Victoriously, Danielle poked Mark in the chest. "Did you hear *that*, Mark? Jason would 'rather not wait' to have sex with me! He's dying for it! It's going to be like movie sex, too," she announced to her ex and Crystal, "with lots of kissing and heavy breathing and moaning *and* acrobatic positions."

Openmouthed, Mark and Crystal gawked at Jason.

"It's true. I'm strong. She's flexible." He shrugged. "Together, the two of us are—" *Hang on, idiot.* "—still leaving."

"Because *we're* going to have sexy sex!" Danielle crowed.

Jason had had no idea she'd felt so unwanted during her marriage. Obviously, she had. Either that or she'd felt *really* hurt by Mark's infidelity. Maybe both. Because right now, Danielle clearly wanted to prove that she was desirable.

Jason wanted to help her with that. He did.

Not the least because he *loved* being with her.

But he needed to get away. He needed to formulate a plan for dealing with the inevitability of Danielle discovering Moosby's social media footage. He needed to implement it. Right then, in The Big Foot Bar, Jason realized that the haze he'd been in had to end. It had to end before it was too late.

"But first, *before* all the supersexy sex starts," Danielle said as she grabbed Jason and shoved him onto a wobbly chair between Crystal and Mark, "I think we owe you two a show!"

Then she hiked up her skirt, flashed the whole bar a self-satisfied, tipsy grin . . . then sat on Jason's lap and kissed him.

She'd been right, Danielle realized giddily as her mouth met Jason's for a second time. This night *was* fantastic!

Already she'd escaped from the daily grind with Jason, the sexiest man she'd ever met. She'd gotten dressed up. She'd worn a fancy bra. She'd laughed with her friends, flirted with Jason, and knocked back plenty of yummy peppermint hot cocoa at The Big Foot Bar. The music was playing, the crowd was predictably rowdy, and the moment was right to finally get her payback.

That's right. Mark and Crystal were about to get a taste of their own medicine, Danielle vowed as she planted another kiss on Jason. Because she *was* desirable, even if her own husband hadn't desired her enough to remain faithful. And she *was* having fun tonight. She was going to do that with Jason's help.

On his lap. With another kiss. Then another. *Mmmm* . . .

Finally, Danielle levered away from Jason. Satisfyingly, her ex-husband and his new bride gaped. They looked . . . astounded.

Happily, Danielle brushed her hair from her eyes. The room was spinning a little, but maybe that was the uneven floor. The Big Foot wasn't exactly deluxe. Sure, she'd polished off her peppermint hot cocoa and Jason's too, and she'd quaffed both of those drinks pretty darn quickly, to boot, but that didn't mean she was *drunk* or anything. Sure, she didn't drink often, but . . .

. . . but *wow*, Jason felt good beneath her. He felt solid, strong, and wonderful. He'd wrapped his arms around her in a passionate embrace—or maybe, given how unsteady she suddenly felt—in something more akin to a secure fireman's hold—and he looked *so* handsome in his coat and scarf and fancy clothes.

Mark didn't look that handsome, Danielle couldn't help observing. Maybe Gigi had been right. Maybe pushing a new love into the face of an old love really *was* the fastest way to cure a former heartache. Why hadn't Danielle met Jason two years ago?

"How do you like me *now*, mother-effers?" she yelled.

"*Okay*," Jason said kindly. "It really is time to go."

"Go? No way!" Danielle wriggled away from his steadying grasp. She stood, playfully took his hands in hers instead, then gave her hips a seductive swivel. "Come on, Jason. Let's dance!"

"Dance to 'Blue Christmas'?" Crystal arched her brow. "You two really *are* into making this whole *hashtag truelove* thing happen."

"*Hashtag truelove*?" Confused, Danielle swayed. Maybe that was the name of the band who'd recorded the cover version of "Blue Christmas" playing on the jukebox. Bands had weird names these days. The weirder, the better. "Sure! You bet we are!"

"I didn't know you two were really serious." Mark cast a perplexed glance at Crystal, letting Danielle know that he and his new wife had discussed her recently. She was alert to all the telltale signs in him. "I guess I should have known you were," he added. "I mean, since you let all that stuff appear in the media, Dani, especially with the kids inv—"

"Dancing," Jason declared, "is a great idea."

He whisked her away to the area near The Big Foot's small stage, where local bands played live on weekends. With a smile and a smoldering glance, Jason pulled her into his arms.

Danielle stumbled in his direction. The room spun.

"Maybe I *have* drunk a teensy bit too much," she said.

But then Mark and Crystal followed them onto the dance area—all but declaring a Kismet dance-off—and Danielle forgot all about her dizziness, fuzzy-headedness, and wobbliness.

"Oh yeah? You want to bring it?" she asked. "Bring it on!"

She attempted a flamboyant flamenco. Jason chuckled and pulled her back to earth into a more manageable slow dance.

"Slow down, *Dancing With the Stars*," he murmured into her ear. His hips swayed. "We've got all night, remember?"

Danielle almost relented. That's how good Jason felt.

But Mark wasn't heeding any calls to reasonableness.

"Hey, is this stuff going to be on TV?" he asked as he leaned in while dancing with Crystal. "Or YouTube, at least?"

"That's got to be why you're acting so crazy, right, Danielle?" Crystal beamed as though seeing imaginary cameras.

They were both the crazy ones, Danielle knew. TV? YouTube?

Sure, Jason was famous. He was recognized worldwide. But it wasn't as if paparazzi had trailed him to Kismet and then followed him nonstop. She would have noticed that. She wouldn't have liked it, but she would definitely have noticed it.

Just the way she noticed his dreamy eyes right now. His handsome features. His steady hands and his fantastic sense of rhythm. Jason danced as though they *did* have all night to do it.

But she still kind of liked the idea of some movie sex.

"You're so wonderful," Danielle told Jason earnestly. "Thank you for helping me stick it to my ex and his wife."

He gave a somber nod. But his lips quirked, as though he thought her intentions to rub her happiness in Mark and Crystal's faces were silly. And maybe they were, Danielle knew.

They were also pretty darn gratifying. The parts of her that had been bruised and battered during her divorce loved getting their vengeance now. It was all possible because of Jason.

Feeling awash in affection and gratitude, Danielle raised her hands to his face. She meant to cup his jaw. Tenderly.

Instead, she slapped his cheeks like a towel-wearing man putting on Old Spice in an old-timey commercial. Whoops.

She covered her tipsy error by smiling broadly.

"I love you, Jason!" Danielle declared fervently, staring into his eyes. "I really, really love you!"

As Jason smiled back at her, the room spun even more.

"I love you, too," he said, as if from far away.

But he said it patiently, almost accommodatingly—the way Danielle sometimes told Aiden that his drawings of big-headed stick-figure people were magnificent. Was Jason humoring her?

"No, I *really* love you!" Danielle said as they turned, still dancing, but not to another *#truelove* song. "I do!"

It was true, she realized as she almost yelled it. She meant it. She *did* love Jason. She loved him in front of everyone, from her ex-husband to her friends to the bartender.

"I love you, too," Jason repeated, smiling broadly.

Because of that smile, Danielle wasn't sure if he was indulging her or not. But as she gazed into his eyes, there on the scruffy dance floor of The Big Foot Bar, she thought she knew. She believed that Jason loved her back. It was . . . *incredible*.

Then, horrifyingly . . . "I think I'm going to be sick."

Leaving Jason behind, Danielle ran to the ladies' room with her hand over her mouth, feeling overwhelmed by liquor, long-delayed revenge, and the significance of what she'd just said.

No matter what, though, she and Jason were officially in love now. From here on out, things could only get better.

Chapter Seventeen

Standing in the alley behind Moosby's, Jason tried for the sixth time in two days to reach Chip Larsen on his cell phone.

As usual, his chairman of the board didn't answer.

It was time for the next step, then.

"I want you to stop all this *hashtag truelove* bullshit," Jason growled into the phone as he left a pointed voice mail. "I never volunteered for any of this. I don't want it. I don't need it. I'm fed up with it. I know I said I'd do the goddamn media tour, but this isn't what I signed up for." He gritted his teeth, wishing this wasn't happening. "Just. Make. It. Stop."

Click. Jason disconnected the call, full of turmoil and frustration and—if he were honest—unexpressed terror, too.

It had been three days since he and Danielle had gone out to The Big Foot Bar together. Three days since she'd told him she loved him. Three days since he'd told her he loved her.

Three days since he'd snapped out of his dumb-ass love-struck fog of ignoring reality and awakened to the fact that if Danielle realized what had been going on, she'd be devastated.

On the other hand, Jason told himself as he gazed out at the snowy rooftops of Kismet's decorated downtown businesses, maybe Danielle would give him the benefit of the doubt. Maybe she would let him explain. Maybe, when she finally found out about the social media stuff, she wouldn't jump to conclusions.

After the Bethanygate scandal, Danielle was the only one who'd asked him to explain, the only one who'd believed him when he had. Maybe she would believe him again, about this mess.

Jason ardently hoped so. Because he hadn't been talking out of his ass when he'd told her he loved her the other night.

It was true. Even if they hadn't discussed it since then.

Clinging to his hope that, if everything went wrong, Danielle would be the one person he could count on to trust in his integrity and let him explain himself, Jason pocketed his cell phone. He drew in a big, bracing lungful of frosty, gingerbread-scented air, then opened the toy store's back door.

When he entered the back room, Danielle nearly jumped out of her chair. She flung out her arms, widened her eyes—then deliberately leaned sideways in a way that covered her computer screen. *Oh God.* Had she seen the social media footage?

Jason's heart stopped. His feet stuck to the floor.

But all Danielle said was, "There you are! What in the world were you doing in the alley? You hate the cold and snow."

She hadn't seen anything. Weak with relief, Jason grinned.

"It's not so bad now that I'm dressed properly." In a tone that teasingly matched hers, he added, "What in the world were *you* doing in here? You look . . ." How to put this? "Guilty."

She did, it occurred to him. But he couldn't think why.

She uttered an unconvincing laugh. "Pot, meet kettle."

"Why? I haven't done anything wrong."

The earth should have swallowed him up right then.

He might not have *done* anything, but he hadn't stopped anything, either.

He'd been too busy falling in love. Real love. True love.

"Me either," his true love declared. "I'm just . . . working."

"Oh yeah?" Good. A change of subject. "On what?"

"Just checking up on my promotion." Danielle didn't budge from her incriminating computer-screen-obscuring position.

Inwardly, Jason swore. "I've been meaning to act on that."

"It's okay. I've got it covered," Danielle assured him. "It's not as though I *need you* to get promoted. I mean, if you want to put in a good word for me, I won't stop you, but—"

"I absolutely do want to put in a good word for you. I will." *Hell.* He'd let that detail slip through his fingers, too. Love had morphed him into a total screwup. "Soon. Very soon."

"There's no rush. Chip's not in the office anyway, so—"

"Chip?" Alarm bells clanged in Jason's head. Danielle sounded so . . . *well acquainted* with that loser. "You know his schedule *and* you're on a first-name basis with the chairman of the board?"

Danielle's eyes widened. "Uh, isn't everyone?"

For a moment, silence fell between them. Jason contemplated the fact that Danielle seemed completely conversant in the up-to-the-minute particulars of Chip's busy schedule—and that she appeared to be pretty damn cozy with that jerkface, too.

Then he realized what was going on. He was feeling defensive because of the Moosby's social media mess. He'd omitted some facts he should have shared with Danielle. Now he was assuming that she was doing the same thing to him.

"You're right. Chip does like to cultivate a 'man of the people' vibe inside the company," he said. "It strokes his ego."

"Gross." Emphatically, Danielle shuddered. "Let's not put 'Chip' and 'strokes' in the same sentence ever again. Okay?"

Was she overcompensating? She still seemed . . . guilty.

Had she been . . . *colluding* with Chip somehow? Jason wondered with dawning concern. After all, Danielle was ambitious. Even Chip had pointed out that much. Jason wasn't entirely sure who he could trust anymore. He'd thought he could trust his pal Charley—and the intel he'd given him before he'd come to Kismet.

But all that reconnaissance had been proven wrong.

Edna Gresham hadn't been the Moosby's manager. Jason hadn't had a cakewalk media tour ahead of him while hanging out with a quilt-making grandmotherly type. Instead, he'd been ambushed by Danielle and all her supersmart, extra-hot awesomeness.

It was almost inevitable that he'd fallen for her.

In retrospect, he was fortunate that Chip and his unknown spy were focusing on the more wholesome angle of Jason and Danielle falling in love at Christmastime in Kismet. Another conniving exec in Chip's position might have tried for more salacious photos—something more akin to the snapshots of Jason with Bethany and her bare breasts. He was also fortunate that he'd realized what was going on before losing his mind and *really* having a stand-up alleyway quickie with Danielle.

Thanks to her sudden-onset nausea that night, the only thing Jason had done quickly was bring her cool compresses.

Still, despite his intentions not to mistrust Danielle, Jason couldn't help wondering . . . "'Gross,' huh? You've met Chip?"

Danielle went still. He could see her mind spinning.

Formulating an excuse? A fib? If Danielle was conspiring with Chip—if she was somehow in on Chip's oust-Jason plan . . .

Well, that would destroy him. He didn't even like thinking of Danielle being pleasant to the man who wanted to remove Jason from his own company, much less helping him do it.

As much as Jason told himself he was being paranoid, Danielle *was* taking an incriminatingly long time to answer him.

Maybe she wasn't being oblivious to her starring role in Moosby's social media. Maybe she was being calculatingly silent . . . all the better to secure the promotion she wanted.

He couldn't believe he was even thinking it about her.

Was this the kind of untrusting bastard he'd become, that he seriously doubted the woman he'd fallen in love with?

"Ohmigod!" Danielle exclaimed. "Look at the time!"

She switched off her monitor, then leaped from her chair. "It's almost time for the Kismet Christmas Carol Crawl."

Grabbing a hank of silvery tinsel from the coat hook that housed her fuzzy orange jacket, Danielle slung that shiny stuff around her neck like a gaudy feather boa. She added a headband with protruding reindeer antlers, a jingle-bell necklace, and a pair of red-and-white striped gloves. Then she turned to him.

The Christmassy eagerness in her eyes made him nervous.

"What are you doing?" Jason held up his hands to ward her off. "I don't like the maniacal gleam in your eyes."

"Everyone has to get dressed up for the Christmas Carol Crawl." Matter-of-factly, Danielle wrapped his neck with a felt scarf with appliqued gingerbread men on it. She smiled up at him. "Good thing you're already wearing your coat, or I'd hit you up with a hideous Christmas sweater or a bedazzled vest. We have plenty of those left over in the store's lost and found." A wider grin. "Lean down so I can put this Santa hat on you."

"What if I don't want to wear a Santa hat?"

"You can't go on the crawl without it."

"I'm pretty sure I can."

"No, getting dressed up is the tradition." Danielle waved

the Santa hat menacingly. "Don't make me get the elf shoes."

Jason swallowed hard. Agreeably, he leaned down six inches.

That goofy Santa hat landed on his head at a rakish angle.

"Perfect!" Danielle beamed up at him. "Some people go all out for this. Reno's sister, Angela—Nate's wife—is one of them."

"She can have my share."

"Don't be a buzzkill." Danielle adjusted his scarf, which might seriously have been crafted by Edna Gresham. "It's going to be fun! The Christmas Carol Crawl is sort of a traditional caroling expedition turned neighborhood block party turned Christmas-themed trick-or-treating turned pub crawl."

"Pub crawl?" Jason brightened. "That's more like it."

"Minus the booze," Danielle explained, "plus lots of kids, plus all the local businesses and their staffs. Everyone heads downtown, dressed in their Christmassy finest, and meets at the town square. They fan out from there, caroling as they go, stopping at all the local businesses to shop, play games, and collect treats. The crawl started as a way to support the locals when tourism took a dip a few years ago, but everyone had such a good time that it's become an annual event."

"Moosby's is one of the participating businesses?" Jason guessed. No wonder the toy store's inventory had looked peculiar to him. It had probably been shuffled to make room for the tables of treats and eggnog that Gigi and Henry had set up on the store's sales floor. "It's unorthodox," he said. "You probably should have gotten permission from HQ before signing up the store to be one of the participating businesses."

"Come on. You're not a stickler for rules . . . are you?"

At her hopeful expression, Jason couldn't disappoint her.

"Nah," he fibbed. If Chip had been there to see what they

were doing, his chairman of the board would have turned Jason's cooperation with an innocent carol crawl into a major corporate transgression requiring immediate removal as CEO. But Chip wasn't there. He was probably gallivanting around, scheming to have Jason replaced with one of his cronies, as usual.

"I'll make an exception this time," Jason joked. "Just as long as you don't break any more rules, you miscreant."

Danielle's smile wobbled. "Takes one to know one, hooligan."

Good. Everything felt (relatively) normal between them.

Jason hooked his thumb toward the sales floor. "I'll just go check on the Christmas Carol Crawl prep. Unless there's something you need me to do back here?"

Meaningfully, he shifted his gaze toward her monitor.

Show me what you're hiding, he commanded telepathically.

Sadly, he wasn't Professor X. His command didn't work.

On the other hand . . . "You can do *me*," Danielle offered.

Her flirtatious glance immediately switched him into *yes* mode. "Any place. Any time." Jason reached for his belt. "Now?"

"Mmm-hmm. I thought you'd never stop talking."

Danielle wrapped her arms around his neck, drew him closer for a kiss . . . then made Jason forget all about *everything* else.

Danielle hadn't even finished pulling on her sweater and reassembling her silvery tinsel boa before the doubts she'd been pushing away came roaring back. Full strength, meaner than ever.

Damn it. She didn't want to feel this way.

Not about Jason. Not about them together.

Not about herself.

But the truth was, Jason had caught her today in the midst of doing some very critical multitasking. She'd been (of course) taking care of some ongoing inventory manipulation. She'd also been e-mailing Chip Larsen, something she'd decided to do when she hadn't been able to reach him on the phone.

She hadn't wanted Jason to know about either of those things. But she *had* wanted to nudge Chip into making a decision about her promotion. Preferably without Jason's input. Danielle really didn't want to take advantage of their relationship.

She needed to know, though, if taking a new job and moving to L.A. was even a possibility for her. Because if Chip decided against giving her an executive position, there was no reason she and Jason couldn't take their relationship to the next level. There was no reason she couldn't love him all the way.

Even when she wasn't tipsy on peppermint hot cocoa.

Danielle didn't want to say so, though. Not until she knew something definitive. It wasn't fair to string along Jason—and that wasn't what she'd intended to do—but it was obvious, in retrospect, that that's what it *looked* as though she'd done.

She had, to be scrupulously accurate, used Jason to make her ex-husband jealous. She'd used him to entertain her children during the run-up to Christmas. She'd used him to fix things and do chores around her house. She'd used him for supersexy sex.

She'd done the latter not more than three minutes ago.

It had been heavenly, too. Quick, intense, and blissful.

But they couldn't keep skirting the real issues, Danielle knew. As much as she loved being with Jason, she was still keeping secrets from him—secrets like her inventory manipulation.

Today, she'd thought Jason had caught her at it. When

he'd come in from outside, her heart had practically stopped. He'd sounded so suspicious. He'd even said she looked guilty!

In that moment, Danielle had almost blabbed everything.

But she'd kept her head long enough to deflect attention from what she'd been doing. Then she'd nonchalantly positioned herself in front of her computer screen, and she'd bought herself enough time to figure a way out of her current jam.

She was smart. She knew she could do it.

Even if she hadn't, it occurred to her, ever managed to successfully reposition Jason on the apology-making front.

She'd pretty much given up on discussing the idea of his acquiescing to the board of directors' wishes. As their time together had grown more intense, Danielle had just sort of . . . started ignoring all the work-related details between her and Jason. She'd also quit contacting Chip, which was why she'd felt compelled to call him and try to schmooze today.

After all, Danielle knew she couldn't count on Jason to vouch for her. She was afraid to even try to do that.

Her experience with Mark had shown her that even the most idyllic relationships could contain shattering secrets. She'd thought she and Mark were happy together. She'd learned otherwise in the most painful, betrayal-filled way possible.

She did *not* want to have a similar experience with Jason.

It was ironic, Danielle thought as she wiggled into her jeans, zipped them, then stuck her feet into her boots while Jason got dressed nearby, that she was worried about him betraying her . . . when she was the one who'd been less than honest with Jason right from the beginning.

Determined to get her promotion—and eager to take advantage of her one-on-one time with Moosby's famous, big-shot CEO—she'd pulled strings to make sure Jason would have to stay at her house. Eventually, she'd have to come clean about that.

There was her "all the B&Bs are full" scheme. Her eagerness to show up Mark and Crystal by showing off her relationship with Jason. Her inventory shenanigans. Her (until recently) nonstop efforts to persuade Jason to give in to the board's demands.

Those would all have to be explained. Sooner or later.

Danielle only hoped that Jason was more forgiving than she'd proven to be. Because if she'd carried a grudge against Mark for this long, who knew how she'd react if things went south between her and Jason?

Probably not very well, given her recent history.

Unhappily reminded of all the slightly dishonorable, definitely out-of-character things she'd done with the hope of getting promoted, Danielle frowned. Chip Larsen had dangled the promise of being recognized for all her hard work—of joining the big leagues and securing a big-city life for Zach, Aiden, and Karlie—and Danielle had snapped at that bait instantly. But if getting that promotion was making her do things she regretted, was it really worth it? Should she really leave Kismet at all?

Probably, Danielle told herself as she watched Jason pull on a shirt that (sadly) obscured his fabulous midsection, it would never come to her leaving Kismet. If history held, Jason would leave town himself before she ever called a moving van.

Men left. They left her, at least. Those were the facts.

"Hey." Beside her, Jason touched her shoulder. "Why so glum? If you're bothered by getting frisky at work, remember I *did* take four seconds to lock both the doors so we were safe."

At his obvious concern, Danielle felt her worries sink away again. They retreated to wherever they went when she wasn't obsessing about her past, her future, or what might go wrong.

"I know you did. Thanks for that." She kissed him, then rolled her eyes. "God knows, I didn't have the wherewithal for that. Once you kissed me, I practically forgot my own name."

"Once you did that special thing you do with your hips, I *did* forget my own name." Jason's abashed smile touched her. "I forgot to be quiet, too. It's a good thing there are so many sound-dampening boxes in here for noise insulation."

"I should probably bring a long scarf next time," Danielle told him with a saucy lift of her eyebrows, "to keep you quiet."

"Ooh, kinky." Another grin. "I don't think you're really the gags, whips, and chains type, though. I'm not buying it."

Guilty. "Stop knowing me so well. It's disconcerting."

"That's because your lame ex-husband couldn't do it." Jason came closer, then swept his hand along her chin. Tenderly, he tucked a curl behind her ear. "Eventually, you know, you're going to have to stop expecting me to be him. I'm not him."

Danielle shrugged. "I know that."

But Jason didn't take her dismissal at face value. He grasped that errant curl in his fingers, then gave it a tug.

"I," he said fiercely, "am *not* your ex-husband."

"I know!"

He gave her a skeptical look. "I won't ignore you. I won't cheat on you. I won't make you feel like less than you are."

That sounded . . . *improbable*. But wonderful, if true.

"You forgot one," she joked. "You won't lie to me."

A funny look crossed Jason's face—probably because she'd doubted his integrity, just for an instant. He had a real issue with that.

He opened his mouth to promise not to lie, but at the

same instant, someone started pounding on the back office's door.

"Mooommy!" Aiden yelled. "Your door is broken. Hey!"

"Open up!" Zach shouted. "It's almost time for the Christmas Carol Crawl! Wait till you get a load of my costume!"

In unison, Danielle and Jason waited. Then . . .

"I'm here, too," Karlie said in a faux bored voice. "Come *on*, already. It's our first time! We can't be late, Mooom."

Jason raised his eyebrows. "First time? You've never done the Christmas Carol Crawl before?" he asked Danielle. "I didn't think you were *that* opposed to all things Christmas in Kismet."

"I'm not. Not really," she admitted, hustling to the door to unlock it. "In previous years, Edna Gresham was in charge at Moosby's. She never let any of us participate in the carol crawl itself. She wanted all the staff here, at the store, 'capitalizing' on the chance to make sales while everyone was downtown."

"And that worked?" Jason asked dubiously as she opened the door. The kids scampered inside. "Moosby's didn't participate in the crawl activities, but they raked in sales anyway?"

Danielle hugged Aiden. Then Karlie. Then Zach. Over the top of Zach's head—well, technically, over the top of the full-size papier-mâché reindeer headpiece he'd chosen for a costume—she gave Jason a noncommittal look. "What do you think?"

"I think this place didn't have model-store level sales until after *you* took over for Edna."

"Aw." Fondly, Danielle grinned at Jason. "I knew you were smarter than everyone in the press says you are."

Jason blanched. She felt immediately contrite.

It wasn't as though she followed the news anyway. Reporters could be saying Jason was from Mars. She wouldn't have known any better. "Sorry. I mean, let's go sing some Christmas songs!"

Then they all finished bundling up, grabbed their official Christmas Carol Crawl songbooks from the table in the front of the Moosby's sales floor, and headed to the town square.

On his way into town, Jason had driven past a sign on the edge of the lakefront: WELCOME TO KISMET: THE MOST CHRISTMASSY TOWN IN AMERICA! At the time, he'd bah-humbugged that sign.

But now, completely ensconced in the midst of the Kismet Christmas Carol Crawl, Jason knew that sign had been right.

In downtown Kismet, near the town's huge official Christmas tree, thousands of residents and tourists enjoyed the holiday ambiance. The air felt crisp with winteriness, redolent of spicy gingerbread and bracing pine. The wood-sided and redbrick local businesses gleamed with multicolored lights. Their eaves flashed; their roofs were frosted with ice and snow. The wrought-iron lampposts were ringed with holly; so were the old-fashioned freestanding mailboxes. An occasional breeze made the jingle bells strung along the sidewalks chime. Everywhere Jason looked, people were smiling. Young, old, in between—it didn't matter. Everyone seemed to love the Christmas Carol Crawl.

Participants departed in waves, like runners in a marathon, dressed in simple—or more elaborate—costumes, depending on the person. Jason spotted dozens of Santas in red and white, several elves and Grinches, a few reindeer in repurposed two-person horse costumes with added plastic antlers, and even a number of people dressed as Ralphie from *A Christmas Story* in cracked black eyeglasses and blond wigs. Children nibbled on sugar cookies or jealously guarded jumbo candy canes; adults swarmed the various cafés, bakeries, and other businesses nearby.

While awaiting their turn to depart, Jason, Aiden, and Karlie stopped at Kristen Miller's Galaxy Diner food truck.

Since her diner was too far away from the town center to participate directly, she brought her pies-in-a-jar to the square instead.

Inside the Mobile Galaxy Diner truck, Kristen and her staff dished out mini Mason jars full of delicious pies to an eager crowd. Almost unrecognizable in a ponytail and hardly any makeup was Kristen's celebrity pop-star sister, Heather Miller.

"Ohmigod, omigod, omigod!" Karlie almost hyperventilated as she belatedly recognized the songstress who leaned out the window of the Galaxy Diner's mobile truck to hand her a jarred apple pie with streusel and caramel. "You're Heather Miller!"

"Yes, I am. I was sort of hoping no one would recognize me, though. I'm just here to help out. What's your name?"

But Karlie was having none of it. "Not recognize you? *You?* Impossible! You're only, like, the greatest singer ever!"

"Thanks. You're sweet," Heather said. "But I do a lot more than sing these days. There's my charitable foundation, my—"

"You dance, too!" Karlie shoved her pie at Jason. Grinning maniacally, she executed a series of well-practiced moves. "See? I must have watched all your videos a hundred times!"

Kristen Miller came to the window, too. She grinned. "Hey, you're really good at that, Karlie." She elbowed her celebrity sister. "I think you might have some up-and-coming competition."

Danielle's daughter looked as though she might explode with happiness. Jason couldn't help wishing he could make Karlie beam up at him with that kind of joy. Unfortunately, he wasn't a glamorous, mega talented pop star. He was just . . . himself.

He was a man who couldn't help scanning the thronging crowd for glimpses of a satellite TV van, someone with a camera, or any other recording device that might turn his stay in Kismet into a holiday nightmare. He hadn't been able to keep Danielle away from the carol crawl, but he'd been tempted to try.

In the end, Jason's foolish optimism had won out. Because maybe, even if Danielle found out everything, she'd forgive him.

They were in love now, weren't they?

"Hey, what's the holdup out here?" A man came to the window with a kitchen towel slung over his shoulder. An attitude of jolly competence clung to the rest of him. "We've got a lot of tiny pies to move and a line down the block to get through."

Reflexively, Jason looked. Beside him, Aiden did, too.

He could have sworn he glimpsed someone short, suit-wearing, and shifty-looking near the end of that line. *Chip?* A second later . . . he was gone. Uh-oh. Could it really have been—

Next door at the festively decorated Torrance Chocolates food truck, Danielle caught Jason looking around. She eyed him questioningly. Jason shrugged, then went back to Karlie's fan crush. Fortunately for him, he realized, even if Chip did somehow show up in Kismet, Danielle might not recognize him.

Unless she'd been in cahoots with him . . .

Shaking off that thought, he returned to the conversation.

"Don't worry, Casey," Kristen told the new arrival. "We're not ruining your baby's inaugural outing." For Jason's benefit, she explained, "Casey had the idea for the Galaxy Diner food truck. He's kind of a genius when it comes to business matters."

"That's one way to put it," Casey agreed amiably . . . if cryptically. He glanced at the Torrance Chocolates truck, where Danielle and Zach were paying for their drinks—a Bandini Espresso caramel latte for Danielle and a white peppermint drinking chocolate for Zach. "At the moment, I just want to win."

"Win?" Jason asked, intrigued by the zeal in his voice.

"A friend of mine came up with the idea for the Torrance Chocolates food truck at the same time I thought up this one," Casey told him. "Fortunately for me, Shane is spending Christmas in Portland, thousands of miles away, so *I'm* going to win."

Beside him, Kristen shook her head. "You two become friends again and immediately start competing. That's so . . . you. And him."

Casey grinned. "You love it, and you know it."

"I love *you*," Kristen returned, nearly cooing.

Jason wondered if he and Danielle sounded that lovesick.

"Yeeech!" Karlie exclaimed, shaking her head. "All the adults in this town are acting totally weird. My advice to you, Heather, is to just get out of here before it happens to you."

"Before *what* happens to you, hon?" Another man strolled up, carrying a fresh case of assorted pies-in-jars from the diner.

Heather beamed at him. "Karlie, this is my boyfriend, Alex." She tipped her head toward Karlie. "Alex, this is Karlie."

"Hey, Karlie," Alex said. "How's it going?"

Karlie gave a disgusted groan. "Not you too, Heather!"

She threw up her arms in indignation, then gave her idol a final disillusioned look. "I guess all those songs about boys had to be inspired by somebody, right? Just typical!"

She snatched her pie-in-a-jar from Jason. "Let's go."

"I don't have my pie yet," he protested, torn between wanting to have a treat and wanting to get on Karlie's good side by storming off in a huff with her. Then he spied the stand sponsored by The Christmas House B & B and changed his mind.

Maybe, Jason thought, there was a way he could do both.

"Right behind you, Karlie!" He gave a jokingly exasperated headshake to the two couples running the Galaxy Diner food truck. Then, as Karlie marched off in anti-true-love protest, Jason leaned in. In a low voice, he said, "Good luck to you, Heather and Alex. Nice work, Kristen. I hope you win your bet, Casey." More loudly, Jason added in a sulky tone, "I'm going to The Christmas House stand for some of the gingerbread men they're selling. Let's go, Aiden!"

Feeling pleased with himself for his expert multitasking, Jason turned around with Aiden's mittened hand in his. He fixed his gaze on Karlie's retreating pink-coated figure—and on the more distant goal of The Christmas House's stand, where Reid Sullivan, Karina Barrett, and their blended family of five kids were serving up gingerbread men—then started walking.

Once everyone was duly snacked up and energized, he and Danielle would reconvene near the glittery town Christmas tree, just as they'd planned, and join the next wave of carolers.

Even now, Jason realized with a surge of Christmassy good cheer, the sounds of multistage Christmas carols floated into the air around him. They reached him from every quaint corner of the area dedicated to the Kismet Christmas Carol Crawl. It sounded something like a massive multiplayer version of "Row, Row, Row Your Boat" performed in rounds . . . except in this instance, "Deck the Halls" was the song everyone was singing together.

A few snowflakes drifted down on the breeze. Aiden snuggled his hand more securely in Jason's while they hustled toward those gingerbread men. And in that moment, Jason experienced a weird, wonderful, utterly welcome sense of rightness. Of belonging. Even, he thought, of fate. He'd been *meant* to come to Kismet at Christmas. He'd definitely been meant to fall for Danielle.

Happily, Jason cast her an over-the-shoulder glance.

He wanted, responsibly, to let her know where he, Karlie, and Aiden were going. He wanted, sappily, to share his newfound sense of Christmastime happiness with her.

Instead, Jason saw Danielle standing near the Torrance Chocolates truck with her caramel latte clearly forgotten, deep in what appeared to be a very serious conversation.

With Chip Larsen.

The bastard had found her.

Or, Jason thought with dawning dread, *she'd* found *him*.

Either way, he had to do something. Quickly.

So he sent Karlie and Aiden to rendezvous with Gigi and Henry, who were also coming along on the Christmas Crawl.

Then, with two of three children safely taken care of, Jason squared his shoulders and made his way through the crowd toward Zach—and eventually, fatefully, toward Danielle, too.

Chapter Eighteen

"I'm very sorry to tell you this here." Wearing a less-than-convincing apologetic look, Chip Larsen put his hand on Danielle's shoulder. He squinted into her eyes. "Now, during such a festive event." He chuckled. "The whole town must be here!"

"People who are 'sorry' don't generally chuckle." Danielle clutched her caramel latte like the lifeline it couldn't possibly be, unable to convince herself this was happening. "So you'll forgive me if I'm skeptical about what you've told me."

Maybe, she thought, she could bluff her way through this. It could happen. Chip was pretty out of touch. He couldn't possibly have any *real* proof of what he'd just told her.

"Skepticism won't change the facts." Chip attempted, even less successfully, to appear sorrowful. "Someone in your store is manipulating the inventory. That is strictly against Moosby's company policy. It's an offense that borders on fraud. You, of all people, must know that, Ms. Sharpe."

"Actually, I don't even know you are who you say you are." Inwardly quailing, Danielle nonetheless managed to put on her toughest demeanor. "There are reporters here for the Christmas Carol Crawl. People from local newspapers and TV stations like to cover Kismet as a special-interest story this time of year." She gave him another doubtful look. "For all I know, you're just an overambitious reporter who's fishing for a story."

As the Christmas Carol Crawl continued around them, showing off Kismet's kitschiest, friendliest, most holiday-loving side, Chip frowned at her. He seemed surprised that she'd argued.

He showed his teeth. "I like your gumption, Ms. Sharpe. I knew I would. I thought you'd recognize my voice from our phone calls, but since you didn't . . ." He flipped open his wallet. "See?"

It was him. Of course. *Oh no.* Danielle's heart pounded. Her vision went hazy. But she leaned closer and pretended to examine his ID anyway, all the better to keep up her cover story.

"We believe one of your sales clerks is the instigator in this fraudulent activity," Chip went on. "Gigi Marchand?"

Danielle gawked, her head swimming. *No. Not Gigi.* She couldn't let her friend take the fall for what she'd done.

Danielle swallowed hard. "This is hardly the time or place to discuss this, Mr. Larsen." With effort, she added as much crispness as she could to her voice. "If you'd told me you were coming to town, I could have made arrangements for you—"

"The kind of 'arrangements' you made for Jason Hamilton?" Chip shook his head. "Your little house isn't that big."

She was too flabbergasted to continue. How did he know about that? How did he know about the *size of her house*?

Had Jason let slip that information? She hadn't known he and Chip had been in contact with one another. If they had—if Chip had told Jason what she'd been doing with the store's inventory—it wouldn't look good for her.

Staunchly, Danielle tried to rally.

"No. Not those arrangements," she said smoothly. "That was a one-time thing, of course. But at the moment, I'm in the—"

"Middle of this goofy Christmas Carol Crawl thing. I can see that." Benevolently, Chip nodded. "But this might be your only opportunity to interface with me about this. If you're saying this event is more important to you than your job—"

It was, Danielle realized. Because it was important to Karlie, Aiden, and Zach. They'd really been looking forward to attending this year. But that was insane. She couldn't feed and clothe her children with holiday songs and Christmas cheer.

"—then I guess I misjudged you. That's my fault."

"No, my job is very important to me. It's just that—" Danielle broke off, desperately searching for another avenue. "Do you have any proof of this inventory manipulation?"

As she voiced that audacious question, her voice shook. *This is it. I've gone too far. I've been caught.*

Strangely enough, she felt oddly connected with Jason in that moment. He'd transgressed, too. He'd had to face the music, too. With Chip Larsen as the smug, frankly smarmy conductor.

That couldn't have been any fun. Where was Jason, anyway?

Danielle had no time to look around for him. Because Chip chose that moment to thrust his cell phone toward her.

On its screen, a video was playing. A video that clearly showed Gigi in the snowy alley behind Moosby's toy store, with Danielle's trusty clipboard in hand, overseeing one of their frequent inventory switch-overs with the other regional stores.

Seeing it, Danielle felt her heart sink. This really was it. Gigi had been caught, and Danielle was responsible.

The only good news was that the other store manager's

face wasn't visible on camera. Because of the cold, he was bundled up in a hooded parka while transferring clearly marked Moosby's inventory from her store's back room to a truck destined for his.

At least, Danielle thought dismally, she hadn't gotten any of the other participating regional store managers into trouble.

"This is a very serious offense," Chip was saying. "I'm the chairman of the board of Moosby's. I don't show up for every incident of stealing, cheating, or rule-breaking." He chuckled again. "If I did, I'd spend my life on a damn plane."

He was right. His presence there was unusual.

"I came here because I like you," Chip went on in a conciliatory tone. "I came here because I got the sense that the two us"—he gestured smarmily between them—"we see eye to eye."

He'd probably gotten that impression because of her. Because she'd assured Chip that she agreed with him about the need for Jason to apologize. Maybe wrongly, she thought now. Because Chip Larsen was, honestly, kind of creepy.

Still, facts were facts. Chip had incontrovertible proof of what she'd been doing. Maybe he'd been right about the things Jason had been doing wrong, too.

"I came here as a courtesy," Chip went on, sounding annoyed now—probably because Danielle hadn't found a way to reply yet. "A courtesy to the manager of our *model* Moosby's store. I wanted you to be the first to know, Ms. Sharpe, so you wouldn't be caught off guard. So you wouldn't bad-mouth the company when you didn't get the promotion you wanted."

Promotion? Who was worried about that? She was about to be fired. Danielle frowned, suddenly struck by something troubling.

"How did you get that footage?" she wanted to know.

Did Chip have a spy in her midst? Was it Henry? Another employee? Edna Gresham? She had retired suddenly after years of reluctance to do so. Maybe Chip had bribed her to spy for him.

Or, Danielle thought dismally, it might have been Jason who'd gotten that footage. He'd been at the store without her, "working" on her computer. He was the newcomer in their midst. He was the one who had a good reason to placate the board.

Maybe spying for Chip had been Jason's real mission in Kismet all along. If that was true, it was no wonder he hadn't shown any interest in apologizing for the racy photo incident with Bethany. He'd made other arrangements with Chip Larsen.

"Come now, Ms. Sharpe. You can't be this naïve," Chip said. "I have ways of getting what I need. Hamilton must have told you that about me."

"Where did you get that footage?" Danielle repeated stubbornly. "Because it's obvious you've been spying on me—"

"Spying on *you*?" Chip laughed as he put away his phone. "Did that look like you in the video? It's Gigi Marchant. She's the reason I came to this godforsaken frozen burg."

"No." Danielle fisted her hands. "It's not Gigi. It's me."

A head shake. "I know what you look like, Ms. Sharpe, even if you don't recognize me. Hell, the whole world knows what you look like." Chip attempted another woebegone look. "It's just too bad that the Internet is so damn fickle. It's a shame."

Feeling increasingly mixed up, Danielle frowned at him.

"I mean it's *me*," she specified. "It's me who's done the inventory manipulation, not me in the video. It was all my idea. Not Gigi's. She didn't even want to do it! I made her do it."

Chip didn't seem convinced about that. Or even particularly interested. He glanced fixedly over her shoulder, his attention caught by something else. Moosby's security team, maybe?

Oh, God. She didn't want to get arrested in front of her

children. If Jason was there, if Gigi was there, maybe they would take care of Zach, Aiden, and Karlie. Her hands trembled.

"You can't punish—" *Gigi*, she wanted to say. But Chip interrupted before she could defend her friend.

"You? Sure, I could." Chip transferred his gaze to her. He looked her up and down. "You think that because of your . . . *special relationship* with Hamilton I'll make allowances for you?"

"No! Of course not!" How did he know about that? "I—"

"Because you'll find, very shortly, that Jason Hamilton doesn't have any influence with the company he used to run."

Used to? Utterly confused, Danielle did what she could to salvage the situation. "If you'll let me explain, I can tell you exactly why I did it. I can tell you why it increased sales!"

Chip gave her another munificent look. "You misunderstand me. I'm not here to bust anyone for this inventory scheme."

"You're not?"

His smile beamed. "Of course not! We need out-of-the-box thinkers like you at Moosby's! I thought you were upset because Gigi Marchant was getting all the attention—"

"All the . . . attention?"

"—not to mention the promotion you've been gunning for—"

"You *read* my e-mails? My memos? My résumé?"

"—because of her innovative inventory control," Chip said, "but if that was all *your* idea, then the promotion is yours."

"Mine?" Danielle gawked at him, her heart pounding.

This was some kind of bizarro world, where rule-breaking was rewarded, cynicism was applauded . . . and chairmen of the board arrived in person to bestow riches on the worst wrongdoers.

"Yours," Chip confirmed. He reached for her hand, then gave it a shake. "Thank you for your contributions, Ms. Sharpe. We'll be in touch to give you the details about your new position."

Astounded, Danielle wobbled amid the hectic Christmas Carol Crawl hubbub. Her dream had come true. She'd won. In the most unlikely way possible, and against all reason, she'd won.

She'd won by breaking the rules. This was crazy.

Chip was . . . *happy* because he believed she was *scheming*?

"You had me going there for a minute," Chip said with a final grin and a shake of his head. "The look on your face when I told you about the inventory stuff! You seemed completely freaked out." He cozied up uncomfortably close to her. "I'm glad I wasn't wrong about you, Ms. Sharpe. Don't worry—with me, you don't have to worry about toeing the line or pretending to be nice. Next time you think someone else is getting the job you want—like Gigi Marchant might have today, for instance—you feel free to go for the throat. I won't stop you. I like a fighter."

Then Chip chuckled again, shook her hand again, and left.

Danielle was still staring after him, feeling dumbfounded and perplexed, when Jason came into view. Just at the edge of the town square, he hunkered down in front of Zach—who, on Danielle's orders, had taken his white peppermint drinking chocolate to a bench in front of the enormous Christmas tree while she spoke with Chip. While she watched, Jason explained something to her son. Zach nodded. Jason smiled. A few seconds later, Zach cooperatively got up, tossed Danielle a grin, then went to join Aiden and Karlie . . . with Gigi and Henry? What the . . . ?

That was weird. They hadn't planned any babysitting today.

On the other hand, seeing Jason round up her kids and place them in Gigi and Henry's care wasn't half as weird as what had just happened during her encounter with Chip. Knowing that only one person in Kismet could shed any light on the situation, Danielle tossed away her unwanted latte and headed toward Jason.

Having gotten Zach securely settled with Gigi and Henry, Jason finally turned to his next and most urgent task: Danielle.

He glanced up, saw her coming straight toward him, and stopped short. To his surprise, Danielle looked . . . cautiously cheerful. But completely confused. And undeniably shamefaced, too. All at the same time.

What the hell had Chip told her?

Whatever it was, it couldn't possibly have reflected well on him, Jason knew. Even so, he kept going toward her. Partway there, he nodded toward a semiprivate spot near a credit union that wasn't open for the Christmas Carol Crawl. Danielle caught his lead and met him there under a municipal Christmas banner.

Maybe he'd been wrong about Chip, Jason mused as he looked more closely at Danielle. Maybe his chairman of the board wasn't gunning to have Jason replaced anymore. Maybe Chip hadn't even recognized Danielle, Jason pondered, and they'd been having some sort of casual, stranger-to-stranger conversation. After all, *he* hadn't known she was the Moosby's manager when he'd arrived.

"You'll *never* believe what Chip just told me," she said.

Okay. There went that hope.

But at least Danielle didn't seem mad. That was good.

Knowing that the best defense was a good offense, Jason jumped right in. "Whatever it was, it was probably a lie."

She looked puzzled. "He promised me a promotion."

"He did?"

"Try not to sound so surprised. I'm qualified."

"I know you are. It's just that—" Jason stopped. He tried to regroup. "I thought Chip was here for something else."

I thought he was here to ruin my future with you.

Danielle glanced away. "Well, he *was* here for something else. Sort of. He was here to give my promotion to Gigi."

"To Gigi?" Perplexed, Jason studied her. "But she doesn't want to be promoted. She likes it here with Henry."

The same way he wanted Danielle to like it there with him.

"I know. But it turns out the qualities Chip is looking for in his executives aren't exactly what I thought they were."

She seemed downcast about that. Also a little . . . guilty?

"He doesn't like brilliance, innovativeness, and hotness?"

"I'm not joking about this." Her gaze skirted away from his, then back again. "Haven't you talked to him? Didn't he"—Danielle shifted uncomfortably—"*show* you anything?"

This was it. Briefly, Jason was tempted to pretend that *#sleighride* and *#truelove* were breaking news to him, too.

But he was a better man than that. So he squared his shoulders, looked straight at Danielle, and said, "He didn't have to show me anything. I already knew." He paused. "It was me," he confessed. "I'm the one who sent that footage to Chip."

Danielle narrowed her eyes. "*You* sent it?"

"Only as a way to show him how much I'd changed!" Jason swore, wishing he'd never sent Chip that sleigh-ride footage from the B&B. He stepped closer, needing to make her understand. "I did it partly because *you* thought it would be a good idea."

"How could I? I didn't even know you had it!"

"You told me again and again to make peace with the board," Jason reminded her. "You told me to 'feel free' to 'use' you!"

Danielle's expression told him that she remembered their conversation on the way to the Galaxy Diner, all those days ago.

"Not that way," she said. "Not by betraying me!"

"I never meant to betray you," Jason promised. "All I wanted, when I sent that sleigh-ride footage to Chip, was to buy us more time together. That's it! I thought if he saw how much I'd changed, how much I enjoyed being with you and the kids—"

Danielle went absolutely still. "Sleigh-ride footage?"

Jason paused. Something wasn't right here.

"With me *and the kids*?" Danielle specified.

What had she just been talking about, if not the sleigh-ride footage? "Isn't that what Chip showed you?" he asked.

Danielle seemed reluctant to explain what Chip had showed her. Instead, she crossed her arms. "I want to hear about the sleigh-ride footage. Because *we* went sleigh riding together. You, me, and the kids. So if Chip has footage of that, too—"

"Of that *too*?" Jason couldn't help asking. "Did Chip show you footage of something else?" he persisted.

"Nice try. You sound very convincingly confused."

"I *am* convincingly confused."

"I'm not. If you think I'm not smart enough to figure out what's been going on without Chip filling in every last detail for me, you're wrong," Danielle said heatedly. "Tell me what the sleigh-ride footage was. Then we'll get to the . . . other footage."

Her unaccountably piercing look confused him.

"I'm not the one who sent the most recent footage," Jason hurried to assure her, assuming that's what she meant by "other footage." "All I sent to Chip was the first batch."

Danielle's jaw tightened. "There were *multiple batches*?"

She had to know that. They appeared to be talking about at least two of them. "I know it seems bad," Jason began, "but I—"

"You're damn right, it seems bad!" Danielle paced a few

feet away and then back again, obviously too irate to listen to him explain the specifics. "I don't care how many 'batches' you *claim* you're personally responsible for—"

"Wait a minute." He didn't like her tone. "*Claim?* I'm telling you the truth." Belatedly, sure. But even though he'd made a few mistakes, his integrity was still rock solid.

He still hated to be doubted. Especially by her.

"—one batch is too many!" Danielle persisted, not listening to him. "You know me well enough to know that I wouldn't want my kids photographed without permission." She paced again, shaking her head. "I can't believe you'd think I was fine with Chip creepily poring over images of Aiden, Karlie, and Zach!"

Oh hell. Jason's self-righteousness faded. Slowly, he said, "Chip wasn't the only one who saw that sleigh-ride footage."

"Who else, then?" Danielle demanded to know, wheeling around. "Because I sure as hell never suggested you could use my kids to redeem yourself with Moosby's board of directors."

"I know that. I never meant for this to happen."

Danielle crossed her arms again. She stared him down.

He had no choice but to forge onward. "A lot of people saw them," Jason said in his most soothing tone. "On the Internet."

"On the Internet?"

He nodded. "The sleigh-ride footage from The Christmas House absolutely blew up on Moosby's social media channels."

Her tone turned frostier. "Social media channels?"

Evidently, Danielle's fury was the ice-cold kind. But now that Jason had begun his confession, he had to keep going.

"Stock prices soared. Sales skyrocketed. According to Chip, you and I and the kids were some kind of crazy media cross between England's royal wedding and the Kardashians."

Danielle paused while she took in the significance of that statement. Then, "We were *all* on the Internet?" she asked.

Her icy, excruciatingly exact tone concerned him. Deeply.

It occurred to Jason that Chip had done a real shit job of ratting him out, if Danielle didn't know about these details.

"It's not that bad. It's actually kind of sweet." To prove it, Jason whipped out his phone. He navigated to one of the online photos. "I tried to make it stop," he assured her. "But it was already out there. *Hashtag sleighride* was a bona fide meme."

Danielle looked at that photo. Rapidly, she thumbed through several more. She gritted her teeth. "Sort of like *hashtag truelove*?"

Belatedly, he remembered what Mark and Crystal had said at The Big Foot Bar. Danielle was smart. Of course she'd connect the dots quickly. "I guess the 'social media monkeys' had to concoct a variety of hashtags to keep up interest. They wove together videos and photos into a 'true love' storyline."

"A storyline?"

Jason didn't like the glacial sound of that. Rapidly, he pocketed his phone. Out of sight, out of mind? Now that he'd come clean, he dared to hope that everything would be all right.

"That's what they called it," Jason admitted. "But it was *real* for me." He tipped up her chin, trying to make Danielle look at him. "I hope it was real for you, too."

Damningly, she fell completely silent.

"If you'll just let me explain," Jason began, "I—"

"I think you've said enough. More than enough."

No. She *had* to let him explain. He'd been counting on that.

Especially *now*, when it really, truly mattered.

"I can tell you how it all happened. It's not that bad."

"It's pretty bad." Danielle broke away from him. She paced a foot away and then back again, her reindeer headband bobbing, offering an incongruously whimsical counterpoint to the situation. "You went behind my back. You used me and my kids for your own gain with the board. You betrayed me—"

"It wasn't like that." Jason shook his head.

"—and you made me look like a fool!" Danielle threw up her hand, then shot him an infuriated look. "I told everyone how I felt about you. *Everyone!* That night at The Big Foot Bar—"

"It doesn't matter what other people think." Jason ignored the people nearby, the carols drifting in the air, the stupid Santa hat on his head. He couldn't believe she refused to listen to him. "It never did. You're you. I'm me. Together, we—"

"There is no 'together.' Not for us. Not anymore."

"Not online, you mean." He couldn't bring himself to believe that Danielle meant anything else. "I know how you feel. Believe me, I do. I'll try harder to make Moosby's stop," Jason promised. "I'll talk to the social media people. I'll shut down the damn channels!" But first . . . "I just need you to know—"

Danielle cut him off. "*Don't* try to explain. Not now. Not about this. Not when you're not even sorry."

"I *am* sorry! I swear." Hadn't he already said that? In his turmoil, he couldn't remember. Desperately, he reached for her. "You listened to me before, about Bethany. Please listen now."

At that, Danielle gave a wry chuckle. "I've heard too much already." Her bleak gaze met his. "I'm not as gullible as you think I am, Jason."

"No. I meant everything I said to you." He couldn't believe this was all going so wrong. With a lump in his throat, Jason reached for her hand. "When I said I loved you—"

"It barely rang true." Awkwardly, Danielle wrenched her gloved hand from his. She lifted her chin. "Given your pathetic performance at the bar when you told me that, I can't believe *anybody* bought into that *hashtag truelove* meme. Least of all me."

"I bought into it," Jason told her one last time. "*I* did."

"Well," Danielle told him, "you're the only one." She drew in a breath, glanced around the square, then straightened her shoulders. In an impressive display of either fortitude or good acting, she looked unfeelingly at him. "Please have your things out of my house by the end of the Christmas Carol Crawl. We'll all be out for a while yet. It ought to be easy for you to—"

"*Easy?*" A harsh laugh escaped him. "Nothing about this is easy."

"If you expect me to feel sorry for you after all you've done—" Danielle broke off. He could have sworn tears glimmered in her eyes. "Nobody's perfect. But you—you *had* to know how I'd feel about you going behind my back. First Mark, now you—"

That was the last straw. Jason didn't want to hear about her lousy ex-husband. He knew Danielle had trouble trusting people. But it was all supposed to have been different with *him*.

With *them*, together.

But it wasn't. Now it never would be.

"You'll tell the kids good-bye for me?" His throat ached as he said it. "I don't want them to think I just disappeared."

"Maybe it would be better for them if you did." Danielle closed her eyes. "Just . . . go, all right? Go back to California and forget about Kismet. It's better that way. For everyone."

Except him, Jason knew. Because he really did love it there. Because of Danielle. Because of Aiden and Zach and even Karlie. He knew he could have brought her around eventually.

Now he'd never get the chance.

"Hey, I'm already gone," Jason said. There was no point staying where he wasn't wanted. If all he had left was his pride, he knew he might as well preserve it. So he held up his hand in a stoic good-bye, turned around, and walked away.

* * *

As Jason left her, Danielle managed to hold her tears in check. At least for a few crucial seconds, she did. As Jason was swallowed up into the crowd, a sob finally burst free.

Quickly, she stifled it. She swabbed her cheek with her gloved hand, then sucked in a steadying breath.

She couldn't just *cry* in the middle of the town square.

At least, she consoled herself, she'd managed not to be the pathetic dumpee this time. Unlike with Mark, she'd managed to be tough with Jason. She'd acted as if she didn't mind having her heart torn in two. Then stomped on. Then steamrollered and left to wither like a cast-off Christmas tree on New Year's Day.

Truthfully, she did mind. She minded everything. She minded that Jason had betrayed her, and she minded that she'd let him do it. She minded that she'd stupidly trusted him, and she minded that she'd allowed her children to become close to him.

She minded that she still wanted him, in spite of it all.

For someone who prided herself on being smart, Danielle knew, she could be pretty damn dense when it came to love. Just as with Mark and her broken-up marriage, she'd been too slow to see the signs, even when they were right under her nose. Thanks to her own idiocy, she'd gotten burned. Again. Probably forever.

Maybe she'd done a few less-than-aboveboard things too, Danielle knew as she wrenched a tissue from her purse. But next to Jason's treachery, her own promotion-related maneuverings, divorce-payback goofiness, and sexual shenanigans were small potatoes. Compared with Jason's willingness to sell her out to the Moosby's board—along with her children!—so he could make a good impression, everything she'd done was laughably trivial.

Well, everything *except* her inventory manipulation, of

course. But weirdly enough, she'd dodged a bullet there. Thanks to Chip's ruthless approach to toy retailing, she'd actually been rewarded for the most dishonest thing she'd ever done.

Well . . . maybe the *second* most dishonest thing, Danielle admitted to herself reluctantly. Because if she was truthful, the *most* dishonest thing she'd ever done was to claim she'd never believed Jason cared about her . . . followed closely by saying it would be better for all of them if he went back to L.A.

Neither of those things were true.

She couldn't have borne it if he'd known it, though.

She didn't want *anyone* to know it. That's why Danielle knew she couldn't stand around moping. She had children to take care of, Christmas carols to sing . . . a public façade to protect. After all that had happened—so publicly—during her divorce, she'd be damned if she'd play the victim again now. So Danielle squared her shoulders, adjusted her reindeer antler headband, and headed to the other side of the square where Gigi and Henry were entertaining her children—in between tossing her curious looks.

Eventually, she'd get over this. Somehow.

She had to. Because without hope, all she had was her pride. And even though pride couldn't snuggle with her at night, wake her with kisses in the morning, and make her laugh during the day the way Jason had, it could damn well keep her neighbors from looking at her with pitying eyes . . . all over again.

If that same sense of pride could have somehow kept her from wishing things were different with Jason . . . well, it would have been all she needed. Almost.

Jason nearly walked right past Chip Larsen. He was too bereft, too confused, too heartbroken to pay much attention to the crowds of people he pushed past on his way to Danielle's house to pack up his things. But then he heard . . .

"Wow, Hamilton. Small-town life must not agree with you." Chip leaned away from the window of an antiques shop and came toward him. He had the gall to grin. "You look like shit."

"Yeah. Seeing you has that effect on me." Jason delivered him a crushing look. "You just had to tell her, didn't you?"

"Tell Ms. Sharpe? About the social media stuff?" Chip pretended innocence. "*I* didn't tell her. *You* did that, buddy."

"I'm not your buddy. Plus, screw you, Chip. I know you told her, because—" Suddenly reconsidering things, Jason broke off.

Haven't you talked to him? Danielle had asked earlier, referring to Chip. Didn't he . . . show you anything?

He didn't have to show me anything. I already knew, Jason had volunteered. It was me. I'm the one who sent that footage.

But he and Danielle hadn't been talking about the same footage. There was other footage somewhere—something Chip had shown Danielle that had had nothing to do with *#sleighride*.

Jason was the one who'd whipped out his damn phone and, in an effort to make her feel better, shown her the photos himself.

"Because?" Chip wheedled in a leading tone.

"You bastard." Jason shook his head. "You knew I'd think you and Danielle were talking about *hashtag sleighride*. That's why you looked straight at *me* while you were talking with Danielle earlier." He'd seen Chip watching him while he'd been making arrangements for Henry and Gigi to babysit Karlie and Aiden. "You wanted to make sure I saw you. So I'd have to tell her."

"It's more believable that way. Coming from you."

He didn't understand. "But why? Why here? Why now?

You loved all that *hashtag sleighride* bullshit. Why kill the golden goose?"

"Social media trends have short shelf lives," Chip told him with a shrug. "People on the Internet are fickle. You and Danielle started trending downward."

"So you came here and deliberately broke us up?"

Chip chuckled. "I didn't have to. That would have happened anyway, once you found out that Ms. Sharpe lied to you about all the B&Bs being booked. Everyone knows what a stickler for integrity you are, Hamilton." He gave Jason a pitying tsk-tsk. "It's too bad. You must have really liked her to swallow that line *and* slum it for weeks in her little shack across town."

"It's not a shack." God, Chip was a snob. Jason tightened his jaw. "And Danielle couldn't have done that to me."

"Because you're too smart?" Chip rolled his eyes. "Or because you don't believe her townie influence extends to calling in favors with all her hometown hotelier buddies?"

Reluctantly, Jason remembered the strings Danielle had pulled to arrange their private sleigh ride at The Christmas House. It was possible, he knew, she'd done more than that.

"You don't know what you're talking about. You wouldn't recognize decency if it smacked you in the face." Jason stared Chip down. "Danielle Sharpe is decent. She's kind and good—"

Annoyingly, Chip smirked. "Decent, huh? Interesting take, given the inventory manipulation that's been going on at the Kismet Moosby's. That's why I came here. To expose it." He gave Jason a long look. "I know you're going to pretend you didn't know it was happening, but by the time I'm done explaining it to the board—and showing them the videos I have to prove it—"

Didn't he . . . show you anything?

Those were the videos Danielle had been talking about.

No wonder she'd seemed confused. Shamefaced. Concerned.

Chip or his spy must have caught Danielle manipulating inventory at Moosby's. Could that really be true? It was conceivable, Jason knew, given the irregularities he'd seen.

All the same, he would have bet his life that Danielle had a good reason for whatever she'd been doing. He trusted her.

Even after all they'd been through and how hurt he was in that moment, he trusted her. He didn't want to . . . but he did.

"—they'll all agree it has to be dealt with," Chip was saying. "It's a long game I've been playing, and a clever one, too. I've known about Ms. Sharpe's inventory stunts for a while now. She was good, but not that good. People who aren't used to deceit never are. All I needed was to get *you* close enough to her to make sure you looked guilty as hell by association."

"But you just gave Danielle a promotion."

An indifferent shrug. "It's possible she misunderstood me."

Under his breath, Jason swore. Chip wanted to destroy him. That was no secret. Danielle had accidentally provided the means for Chip to do so—and gotten herself in his crosshairs in the process. But there was one thing that Chip hadn't counted on.

"Nobody will believe you. It'll be just like Bethany—"

"Ah. That's where you're wrong. You see, those harmless nudie photos were personal. But this is business. This is fraud." Chip pursed his lips, looking at Jason with mock dismay. "There's plentiful proof of this wrongdoing. *Plentiful*."

Jason knew how comprehensive Chip's spy had been while getting footage of him and Danielle and the kids for Moosby's social media channels. Surely that spy would have been equally thorough while documenting Danielle's potential missteps.

"So the way I see it," Chip was saying now, "your partner

in crime, Ms. Sharpe, is going down for this. Because Moosby's will prosecute, of course."

Full of disbelief and enmity, Jason stared at him.

"Not if I say *I* did it," he heard himself say. "Alone."

Apparently, he was still a gullible idiot. For her.

"Not if I say it was *my* idea," Jason went on. "Just mine."

Chip actually laughed. He shrugged. "If that's the way you want it . . . who am I to stand in the way of your resignation?" His grin broadened. "In that case, we could forget the fraud."

Hell. Chip had done it, Jason realized. He'd forced him out. He'd made him do it to himself. And he'd never even seen it coming. Jesus, he'd underestimated this bastard.

Jason tightened his jaw. "Then let's. It's done. I'm gone."

He turned away without a backward glance and strode back toward Danielle's house.

She'd never know he'd saved her. But he would.

That would just have to be enough for him.

Chapter Nineteen

Six blocks into the Kismet Christmas Carol Crawl, Danielle began to feel that she might actually survive her heartache.

Yeah. This was working. She was moving on, lickety-split.

Already she'd successfully sung three and a half holiday songs with her kids—even if she had forgotten some lyrics and sounded a little robotic. She'd choked down a bite of Aiden's favorite Christmas sugar cookie with only minor stomach cramps to show for her efforts. She'd chitchatted stiltedly with her caroling neighbors. She'd done her best to ooh and ah over the ornaments in a shop window, the "sick" guitars displayed in another store window with ribbons all over them, and the fat, frolicking puppies at the local shelter's Adopt A Pet event.

There, Aiden gazed up at her with shining eyes. He sat in the middle of a litter of Labrador puppies, being climbed on and slobbered over, looking happier than she could remember.

"Can we get them, Mom? Can we? Please? Puh-leeze?"

Danielle looked at the puppies, with their wagging tails, big brown eyes, roly-poly bellies, and stumpy, clumsy legs.

"Those puppies will only break your heart, Aiden."

Silence fell. At Gigi's puzzled look, Danielle regrouped. "I mean, we don't have room for five puppies. Let's go."

"But I want them! I can take care of Rudolph now." Her son gulped in a huge breath. His chin wobbled. "I can! Ask Jason!"

"Hey, where is your stupid new boyfriend, anyway?" Karlie peered around the shop in which the shelter had set up its adoption event. "Shouldn't he have caught up to us by now?"

"Oh, so *now* you want to see him? *Now* you like him?" Exasperated, Danielle flung up her hands. Where had this reciprocal interest been when Jason was trying so hard with Karlie? She rounded on her daughter. "*Now?* After everything?"

"After . . . what everything?" Karlie looked confused. "I just thought it might be funny to hear his big, dumb voice singing, that's all. So far, I've been gypped of that, so . . . *I* think we need five puppies, too." She crossed her wiry arms. "Like, today."

"Yeah." Zach matched Karlie's obstinate look. "Me too."

Inwardly, Danielle groaned. She knew darn well Zach wasn't that into the idea of getting a puppy (or five). He liked cats. But when the three of them ganged up on her, it was so much more difficult to stand her ground. Especially when she didn't have another parent or authority figure on hand to back her up.

With a glimmer of hope, she glanced at Gigi and Henry.

"Do not look at me, g-friend. French people love *les chiens*."

"Those puppies aren't what you're mad about, boss."

All right then. There'd be no help from that quarter.

Oddly enough, in that moment, as Danielle looked at Karlie's defiant little face, she realized that her daughter *did* like Jason. She'd been hazing him all this time—testing him to make sure he was good enough for her, her brothers, and her mom.

Unfortunately, he'd failed.

But Danielle hadn't wanted to admit that when she'd rejoined everyone for the carol crawl. She still didn't.

"So, where is J?" Zach persisted, looking around without budging. "You said he'd probably catch up to us after a while."

"'Probably.' *Probably* is what I said." She'd said it because when she'd started to explain that Jason had gone back to California—*forever*—she'd almost bawled. She'd settled on a tiny fib to stop the waterworks. "We should just keep going with the Christmas Carol Crawl. There are lots of stops left." She attempted a smile. "Isn't this fun? Come on!"

Determinedly, Danielle started walking. Her fuzzy orange jacket fluffed along dramatically with her movements. She envisioned herself being tough. Being strong. Being alone.

Gah. Her shoulders crumpled. She almost tripped.

"Mommy, you're going the wrong way. And you almost ran into that big pile of dog food, too." Aiden laughed. "Silly."

He hadn't budged from the puppy zone. In fact, other interested potential pet adopters were starting to sling her son dirty looks. Danielle hurried back to him. She swallowed hard.

It was time to go big or go home.

She turned to the shelter volunteer. "We'll take all five."

Gigi's mouth dropped. Henry looked troubled.

Aiden whooped with joy. Zach had fashioned a hat out of his Christmas carol songbook and was balancing it on his head.

Karlie lowered her arms-akimbo pose. She frowned. "Jason is gone, isn't he?" she said. "He isn't ever coming back."

Nope. He isn't. At the thought, Danielle swallowed past a lump in her throat. In the midst of accepting some clipboarded puppy-adoption paperwork from the shelter volunteer, she felt her hands quiver. But, bravely, she said, "This has nothing to do with him. This is about us." *Here we go.* "And my new job."

Gigi eyed her. "That toad you were talking to earlier was Chip Larsen?" She shuddered with distaste. "I hope you washed the hand he shook. There is not enough soap in the universe."

Henry agreed. "That guy's a creeper." He gave a dismal headshake. "I hope you won't have to work closely with him."

Privately, Danielle did, too. She still had doubts about accepting the executive position Chip had offered her. What if Moosby's HQ expected bigger, nastier rules-defying from her? What if they wanted her to compromise constantly? Lie regularly?

On the other hand, she was doing a bang-up job of fibbing right now by pretending she was all right with Jason's leaving.

Maybe, as Chip thought, she was a natural at this stuff.

That idea was almost as disheartening as the day she'd had so far. She didn't want to live down to Chip's expectations.

"New job?" Finally, her promotion news penetrated Zach's consciousness. He scowled from beneath his homemade hat. "The job in L.A.? The job we all hated? That job?"

"This isn't about any job," Karlie butted in knowingly. She nodded at the paperwork in Danielle's hands. "It's about Jason. She's trying to bribe us to make us forget he was ever here."

"Hey!" Danielle protested. "Everybody loves puppies!"

"Not bribery puppies." With clear concern, Gigi laid her hand on Danielle's arm. "Is this true, what Karlie says?"

"Of course not!" Danielle lied, lied, *lied*. Why wouldn't they all just leave her alone to forget her heartbreak?

She was *trying* to appear A-OK with all this. Couldn't anyone see how hard it was to be betrayed? Twice? Publicly?

"My mom did this last time, too. With Dad," Karlie

informed everyone. "We scored big on toys and treats after Dad left."

Appalled to hear her daughter's take on her parents' broken marriage, Danielle turned to Karlie. "That's not . . . entirely . . . true."

"She *really* liked big, goofy Jason, too," Karlie announced in a nonchalant tone. "I could probably get a pony this time."

Aiden's eyes brightened even more. "Puppies? *And* a pony? Yippee!" He grinned. "*I* like your new job already, Mommy."

Oh God. She *was* trying to bribe them.

Worse, she was a little bit glad it was working.

"We *really* don't have room for a pony," Danielle told her children, just to keep their payola expectations reasonable.

"J has room for a pony," Zach piped up. "He has a *huge* house in California. In L.A. I think it's near the beach. Plus another place in New York, and I think one in London, too."

Unhappily reminded of her *ex* fake boyfriend's status as a megamillionaire, Danielle frowned. Wasn't that just like her, to stick a big lump of coal into her own stocking this year?

If she'd been a little less wounded by Jason's betrayal—a little less heartbroken by the way he'd used her and her kids—she was the one who could have scored big. Who didn't want a handsome, wealthy, brilliant, famous, generous boyfriend?

Jason was so down-to-earth most of the time, she'd forgotten all those adjectives applied to him. To her, he'd just been Jason. The man who made her giddy with a single smile.

Humph. No wonder she'd been so damn gullible.

Although she couldn't help wondering . . . What *would* Jason have said if she'd let him explain? What would he have done if she'd given him the benefit of the doubt? She'd been so shocked, so caught off guard, so (admittedly) defensive about the secrets she'd been keeping (hello, inventory shenanigans) that she'd been 100 percent ready to believe the worst about Jason.

Maybe that hadn't been entirely fair.

But who needed fair when you could have puppies?

Determinedly, Danielle picked up a pen. Attentively, she started writing. "There are six of us, so we can each think up a name—if you and Henry will collaborate, that is, Gigi."

The name-choosing clamor she expected didn't kick off.

She glanced up to find everyone staring at her dubiously—and, in the case of her three children—worriedly.

"Aren't you going to warn us not to overfeed them first?"

"Aren't you going to assign a poop-scooping schedule?"

"Aren't you going to make sure they don't have rabies or something?" Karlie looked baffled. "Mom, you've cracked."

They were right. Ordinarily, Danielle realized belatedly, she would have carefully weighed the decision to get a quintet of puppies at Christmastime, when her house was full of gifts, poinsettias, and shiny things that attracted teething puppies.

"Don't crush my groove," she complained. "This is *fun*."

They still looked apprehensive. All five of them.

"I have a bottle of good wine *chez moi*," Gigi said in a carefully nonchalant tone. "We could drink it and talk? Now?"

"Nope." Manfully, Henry stepped up. "It's gone beyond that now, Gigi." He tossed her a heartfelt look. "I'll handle this."

Gigi gave him an admiring smile. "Ah, *bon. Merci beaucoup*."

Danielle guffawed. "You? Be serious, Henry."

"I'm dead serious, boss." Mano-a-mano style, he pointed from himself to her. "You and me—let's take this outside."

* * *

The hellish thing about the Riverside Hotel in downtown Kismet was that it was so damn friendly.

The last thing in the world that Jason felt like doing after lugging his belongings there from Danielle's cozy house was being friendly. To anyone. But the die had been cast. He'd been doing so many meet-and-greets and other appearances (in person *and* online, Jason cringed to recall), that there wasn't a soul in town who didn't know him . . . or feel they ought to.

The bellman who opened the front door talked to him in gregarious tones about the Lions' latest Thanksgiving Day game. The desk clerk who cheerfully handed him his key card—thereby inadvertently confirming Chip's allegation that Danielle had lied about all the local rooms being full—filled up the check-in process with chitchat about the Christmas Carol Crawl. The bartender offered up free beers from the adjacent bar. The housekeepers made excuses to visit the lobby and flirt with him.

Finally, Jason had almost made his getaway—or at least made it to the gleaming, old-fashioned elevator bank—when the concierge left his holly-wreathed and lighted lectern to shake Jason's hand and inquire about how the toy business was.

Before Jason could formulate an answer that didn't involve his own voluntary (but unintentional) resignation, someone else strode over from the hotel's bar, moving at a pace clearly designed to catch up to Jason. He must have been spotted while the bartender was waggling those free beers in his direction.

"The toy business is just as cutthroat as it ever was," a man said, striding closer. "That's how the toy business is!"

Upon hearing that unmistakably jocular voice, Jason started. He turned. It couldn't be . . . "*Mr. Moosby*?"

"In the flesh." His white-haired mentor grinned broadly at him. His eyes twinkled, just as blue as they'd ever been.

Alfred Moosby had become, in his golden years, a dead ringer for Santa Claus, it occurred to Jason. "Or, you know, in the jeans, long underwear, three pairs of socks, T-shirt, sweatshirt, boots, coat, earmuffs, scarf, gloves—"

"Don't be such a baby, Golden State." At the sight of his longtime friend and partner—who really *was* kitted out in all the cold-weather gear he'd just mentioned—Jason nearly bawled like a baby himself. "It's barely below freezing out."

The words were already out before he realized he'd repeated what Danielle had teasingly said to him some time ago.

Damn it. When was she going to get out of his head?

"Hey, it's your fault I'm here making like Nanook of the North." Mr. Moosby raised his duffel bag. "Guess what I've got in here? Those prototypes you asked for. All ready to go."

"Oh. New toys?" the concierge asked interestedly.

"New hope!" Mr. Moosby told him. "That's what I've got."

His delighted laughter made Jason's heart sink. It was apparent that when he'd asked for Mr. Moosby's help with having those prototypes made—*without* involving anyone from Moosby's corporate—his mentor had gotten the idea they were kicking off a new venture together. All Jason had been trying to do was make those few toys. As one-offs. He'd expected to be starting a new future with Danielle, not rewinding his life to the days when he'd created new toys and Mr. Moosby had produced them.

"Those soulless suits at HQ will be sorry they pissed you off. On the trip here, I had four separate offers to buy the contents of this duffel bag sight unseen." Mr. Moosby winked at the concierge. He nodded at Jason. "My boy's got magic in him."

His tone was proud, his bearing dignified, his manner full of love and camaraderie. Just being near him made Jason choke up all over again. *Hell.* He was a real crybaby today.

"Thanks, Mr. Moosby." Sucking back the sobs that threatened to unman him right there in the lobby of the

Riverside Hotel, Jason extended his hand. "Thanks for coming. I appreciate it."

Appallingly, his voice broke on the words.

Inwardly, Jason swore. The *last* last thing he needed today was to start going soft. But there was something about seeing his familiar, cheerful, frankly beloved mentor that untied all his damn defenses. With a single look, Mr. Moosby had hurtled him backward into his clueless, vulnerable, desperate-for-validation, gangly fifteen-year-old's body. The same kid who had strived so hard to be tough strived now to be even tougher.

"A handshake?" Mr. Moosby guffawed. "Keep that pansy-ass fancy stuff for those chumps on the board! C'mere, son!"

With a roar of welcome, Mr. Moosby drew Jason into a huge, backslapping hug—the kind of hug that men gave each other after going into battle. In response, Jason's eyeballs burned.

He would not *cry*. He wouldn't. He hugged back, then quit.

As he withdrew, Mr. Moosby gave him a concerned frown—an astute one. "Hey, why the long face? Did something happen?"

Everything happened. He'd lost his job. He'd lost control of Moosby's. He'd lost Danielle. He'd lost hope.

But Jason couldn't admit any of that. Not yet. Not until he'd had a chance to refocus and figure out a fix for all of it.

Well . . . at least a fix for all of it that pertained to Moosby's. Because he'd be damned if he'd disappoint his mentor.

"Nah. I just realized I refused a free beer, that's all," Jason cracked as he angled his head toward the decorated bar just off the hotel's lobby. Inside, multicolored Christmas lights twinkled. "Let me buy you a free beer, too."

"Sounds good to me." Mr. Moosby hefted his duffel bag in one hand. He slapped Jason on the back with the other, then led the way to the bar. "Don't wait up for us, Dante!"

The concierge tipped his hat. "Have a good time, sir!"

Evidently, the two of them had already met—and become fast friends. Jason wasn't the only one, he remembered, who had a knack for charming people. Mr. Moosby did, too. Even if he—like Jason—didn't much care for employing that particular skill with the "chumps" on the board.

Loping to catch up with his energetic seventyish mentor, Jason dropped his gaze to that duffel bag. The items inside were the first new toys he'd created in years. It sounded as though Mr. Moosby had done his share of talking them up with people, too. That was just like his mentor. He liked to brag about Jason—about the excellent partnership they'd always shared.

These days, in an era of superstar CEOs, fast-flying tech rumors, and rampant boom-and-bust speculation fueled by those very same rumors, Mr. Moosby's idle conversations could spark bidding wars, ignite IPOs, and generate invaluable publicity.

After all, if news had leaked about Steve Jobs developing a new tech invention or Mark Zuckerberg creating a new online venture, the business world would have gone crazy. Similarly, gossip about a new project between Jason Hamilton and Alfred Moosby could leave a lot of people wanting a piece of the action. Maybe that, Jason considered, was the edge he needed.

Maybe the way to avoid letting down Mr. Moosby wasn't to focus on fixing Moosby's HQ. Maybe it was to let go altogether.

"Come on, slowpoke!" Mr. Moosby waved. "We've got a lot to talk about." He raised two fingers to the bartender. "Your best two free beers, Genevieve," he said, "for me and my partner."

Jason couldn't help noticing the way heads turned, even in rustic Kismet, at Mr. Moosby's use of the word "partner."

There were probably several things he could do to make sure Mr. Moosby was all right, Jason realized—starting with making their "new venture" a *real* fresh start . . . now that he was free to do so. Unfortunately, Danielle was a thornier problem.

He couldn't dazzle her with creativity or wow her with wealth. He couldn't impress her with his resilience or amaze her with his business acumen. He couldn't win her back.

All he could do was do his utmost to forget her.

There wasn't enough beer in the world to accomplish that feat. But, just then, Jason decided to try drowning his sorrows anyway. His hopes had been dashed. His future had been irrevocably altered. He was on his own for Christmas, too.

Because, just then, he didn't much care about jetting to Antigua to have a beachside Christmas. His family would only push and pry and fuss over him the way they did, wanting to know all the details and then help him over his heartache. He didn't want to rehash all of it. It was just too raw. Too painful.

At the end of the bar, Mr. Moosby ignored the pint glass that Genevieve had offered. Instead, he raised his beer bottle in a toast. "To you!" he told Jason. "To new beginnings."

"To you," Jason returned, sliding onto a barstool and then lifting his own bottle of beer. "To making those jerks who took over your company regret forcing you out."

Mr. Moosby stopped with the bottle halfway to his lips. He lowered it a fraction. His eyebrows rose. "Ah. This ought to be interesting. They finally pushed you to the breaking point, eh?"

Jason only grunted, then swallowed some beer. "Let's do this." He clinked his bottle with Mr. Moosby's. "You in?"

"I was in from the moment you called." Mr. Moosby drank.

Then, offering Jason an excited grin, he got down to work.

"What's this all about, Henry?" Danielle rounded on her longtime employee the moment they reached the sidewalk outside. "I don't know why you think we need to talk, because—"

"Because I've been where you are," Henry interrupted, not wasting any time getting down to the heart of things. "Because I know what it's like to be scared, like you. Because even though I'm a dude, I had my heart broken, and it took a long time to get over it. But now I am over it, and you can be, too."

Argh. His considerate, well-meaning tone touched her. His valor in confronting her this way impressed her. All the same . . .

"You know, I could just fire you and end this conversation right now," she said. "It's within my purview. There's an insubordination clause in the Moosby's handbook that would—"

Henry actually laughed. "Wow. Chip Larsen really got to you, didn't he?" An incisive look. "This isn't you."

He was right. Danielle sagged. Wearing her jacket, reindeer antlers, tinsel boa, and striped gloves, she leaned against a nearby building as the Kismet Christmas Carol Crawl continued.

She really didn't like the idea of working for Chip. When it came right down to it, Danielle wondered, did she truly want to work for a company whose policies she disagreed with so strongly? For a company where she'd felt compelled to break the rules? That wasn't like her. Not at heart, it wasn't.

Maybe, in addition to being brokenhearted, she was about to be unemployed, too. Because Chip probably wouldn't allow her to turn down a promotion—one he'd personally come to Kismet to award—and then let her remain employed in her current position.

No wonder Jason had gotten burned out working at Moosby's HQ. It probably *did* suck as much as he'd told her it did.

She wouldn't have wanted to apologize to Chip, either.

"Everything is all messed up, Henry," she admitted.

"Nah. That's just what you're telling yourself."

This time, it was her turn to laugh. It was better than crying. Marginally. "Right. So I'm just imagining it all?"

"No. That's not what I mean." Companionably, Henry leaned on the building beside her. "I mean, everybody tells themselves stories about what's happening to them. They do it all the time. Every day, without noticing." He grinned. "For instance, right now, you're probably telling yourself some variation of 'Henry is an interfering asshole who won't leave me alone to wallow in misery, the way I want him to, that jerk.'"

Danielle grinned. "Well, that's just the truth."

"Is it?" He gazed out at the town square, watching a few costumed carolers pass by. "What if I told you I had crucial information—information you don't have—that changes everything?"

Dubiously, Danielle raised her brows. "Such as?"

"Such as, I'm a time-traveler whose return to his real timeline depends on making you and Jason reconcile. Today."

"Nice try. No go."

"Such as," Henry tried again, "Gigi promised me sexual favors if I could cheer you up within fourteen minutes."

"Weirdly specific. Also, boundaries!"

"As if Gigi doesn't tell you about our sex life." Henry's eyes sparkled at her. He rubbed his hands together and tried again. "Such as . . . Chip Larsen is holding Mr. Moosby hostage, and the only way Jason can free him is to do . . . whatever made you mad."

Unwillingly, Danielle admitted, "That *might* change things."

Henry nodded. "See? Told you so. Your story might be

wrong. That's all I'm saying. Maybe you don't have all the facts."

"But that's *not* what's going on," she pointed out. "I can't wish away what happened with kooky stories! Jason did—"

"It doesn't matter what the details are," Henry cut in before she could specify all the ways Jason had taken advantage of her, let her down, and disappointed her. "What if," he went on musingly, "the *best possible* explanation was correct?"

Danielle scoffed. "The *best possible* explanation? That's probably correct about one in a million times. If that."

"Maybe this is that one time," Henry insisted. "For instance, I thought Gigi kept flirting with me as a joke. I kept her at arm's length because I didn't want to fall for it. Also, because her accent is pretty intense, and I can't always understand what she's saying. Right there, just by having a conversation, I'm potentially going to look super stupid."

"Gigi really likes you!" Danielle said. "She always has."

"I know that *now*. I know that Gigi *really* liking me is the *best possible* explanation for her flirting with me. But I didn't know that a month ago, and I almost screwed myself out of a good thing. Because I was scared. Because I wanted to protect myself. Because I didn't know the *real* story behind her flirting. I wanted to be safe, and it was keeping me from being happy."

Danielle toed her boot in the snow. Holiday carols drifted on the air all around them. Christmas lights flashed nearby.

She'd never felt *less* merry than she did in that moment.

"I'm glad you're happy now, Henry. I really am."

"You could be happy, too," he insisted. "Just try it."

"I *did* try! Don't you see?" She shook her head. "That's why I'm so upset right now. I tried, and I got stomped on."

"Did you?" Henry paused. "Or maybe you just told yourself that story. Is there really *no* other way to interpret what happened between you and Jason? Is *your* story the only story?"

"It's the best story. I know that much."

"I'm serious. This technique can help you."

Well . . . "I didn't *precisely* let Jason explain," Danielle confessed halfheartedly. "I was *really* mad. With good reason!"

Henry nodded. "Well, you feel what you feel. But maybe—"

Before he could tell her *again* to reconsider things, Danielle frowned at him. "You're ruining my perfectly good sulk," she grumbled. "Logic has no place in heartache."

But Henry only remained, silently and convivially, near her, obviously waiting for her to do what he'd suggested.

"Fine!" Danielle exhaled, ready for a hasty return to the conversation she'd had with Jason. Reluctantly, she reconsidered the things he'd said to her. "He didn't mean for it to come to this," she remembered. "He told me . . ." *It was real for me. I hope it was real for you, too.* Overcome with regret, she shook her head. "He told me a lot of things—most of which I can't believe."

"Why not?"

"Because it will make me look like a fool!"

"So? Maybe you already look like a fool."

"Henry!"

"Maybe Jason looks like a fool, too," Henry pointed out. "He'd probably like to avoid that as much as you would."

"Jason *never* looks like a fool." *Damn him.*

Even while revealing his underhanded dealings, he'd looked handsome. Confident. In control and unreservedly charismatic.

Although, it occurred to her, Jason *had* been preoccupied with what one person thought of him: *her*. She was the reason, if she could believe him, that he'd sent that footage to Chip.

You told me again and again to make peace with the board, he'd said earlier. *You told me to "feel free" to "use" you!*

Hmm. Maybe Jason *had* misunderstood her. Maybe he'd been motivated by a misunderstanding—caught up in something he'd never intended. After all, she'd mistakenly trusted Chip, too.

She'd trusted him not to be a total creep. But he was.

He had to be, to make her, über-responsible person that she was, consider unemployment as a viable alternative to working with him.

Unaware of her contemplations, Henry burrowed his hands in his pockets. "All I'm saying is, if you *do* look stupid, it's already happened. You can't undo it now. What else?"

Even more grudgingly, Danielle closed her eyes. She remembered Jason . . . his face, his hands, his miserable expression.

"He was sorry," she said. Then, "He should have been!"

Henry held up his hand. "Finding the best possible explanation isn't about assigning blame. It's about being open to the possibilities."

"But it's his own fault this happened!" Danielle blurted. "He's the one who *confessed.* He's the one who—"

"If he confessed, he must have thought you would forgive him," Henry said. "Until that moment, he must have been getting away with it. So he didn't *have* to confess at all, did he?"

Well, *no*, Danielle realized unhappily. Jason *had* been getting away with it. She hadn't suspected that she and her kids had been splashed all over the Internet. Not for one second.

Not until Jason had volunteered that awful truth.

"He thought I would forgive him," she said. "I didn't."

"Hey, it's never too late."

Danielle burst out laughing. "Of course it's too late!"

"Why?"

"Because—" She pinwheeled her arm, trying to come up with a sensible sounding reason. "Because we broke up, that's why."

"That's only the end if you let it be."

She shook her head. "He's leaving town. I told him to."

"Maybe he won't leave."

"Of course he'll leave!" Danielle shook her head, unwilling to hope for a second chance. "That's what makes sense."

"So, the best possible explanation here," Henry summed up, "is that Jason did something he didn't mean to do, he was sorry for it, and he tried to explain, believing you'd listen to him."

"Humph. Your 'technique' makes *me* out to be the bad guy."

"No, you have a best possible explanation, too. You were surprised, you were hurt, and you were too upset to give Jason what he needed at the moment he needed it most. Maybe," Henry added, "Jason was upset in exactly the same way."

And couldn't give you what you needed, either, Danielle thought . . . *like an hour to calm down so they could really talk.*

Instead, Jason had deliberately stalked away from her.

Maybe he'd been just as stuck in the moment as she'd been—just as unable to see his own weak spots and get past them.

"I'm *not* feeling better about things," Danielle groused.

"You're only human. So is he." Henry looked straight at her. Gently, he said, "I don't know much, but I know one thing. You can't ever be safe, but you can definitely be happy."

"I want to be *both*," Danielle insisted obdurately. Wasn't that what love promised? "If I try hard enough, if I wait long enough, if the right man comes along, *then* I'll be—"

"Safe?" Henry shook his head. "Never ever. The scariest thing in the whole world is falling in love. Because in order for it to work, you have to be totally real with each other."

Uncomfortably, Danielle laughed. "You had it wrong

before. You're not from the future—you're from my worst nightmares."

She didn't want to bare herself to anyone. That felt too risky. Too untethered. Too vulnerable. No way, no how.

Unbothered by her complaining, Henry shrugged. "If you're not going to take a chance now," he said, "then . . . when?"

That stopped her cold. When *would* things be right?

"I can't do it," Danielle said. "I'm not strong enough."

And that's when she realized the worst part of all.

It wasn't just that she was afraid someone would hurt her (although she was, and would have been crazy not to be). It was that she was afraid she couldn't survive it if they did.

"You'll never know what you can do if you don't try," Henry said. "And you'll definitely miss out in the meantime. When you think about it," he added, "it's a lot like ice-skating."

"This is *nothing* like ice-skating."

"Some people are cautious." Henry stuck out his arms and mimed someone tiptoeing along on skates. "They inch onto the ice bit by bit. Some people cling to the wall the whole way." He squeezed shut his eyes and clutched the building behind them. "Some people are too excited to care that there's any risk, and they blunder right onto the ice first thing." He simulated jolly marching, arms swinging like a kooky marionette. "However they do it, though, sooner or later, everyone is skating."

Skeptically, Danielle frowned at him. "I know you want to help, Henry, but honestly, I don't see what this has to do with—"

"Everyone," he continued, "except the people who stay on the sidelines. They never get to skate. And that's sad."

That did it. "I don't want to be a sideline person."

Henry nodded. "Then you'd better start skating."

Chapter Twenty

In the end, Jason cracked. Full of beer and sorrow, he poured out the whole sad story of Danielle, *#sleighride*, and all the rest to his kindly mentor. It felt . . . *horrible* to get it out.

Inwardly, Jason swore. Wasn't this kind of mushy stuff supposed to be cathartic? What the hell was the matter with him?

"The way I see it," Mr. Moosby said as he thumbed the label on his beer bottle, "you have to try again to explain."

"No." Vehemently, Jason shook his head. "No way. I tried that already, remember? I tried multiple times to tell Danielle why I did what I did."

"Did those 'multiple times' happen during the same conversation? Say, within fifteen minutes of each other?"

Grumpily, Jason looked away. "Yeah. So?"

"So they only count as once. That's just the way it is, especially with women." Mr. Moosby gave him a sympathetic smile. "Also, if you tried to fix the problem at the same time—"

"Of course I tried to fix the problem." Remembering his desperate promises to yank the *#sleighride* footage, to shut down Moosby's social media channels, to *fix* it all, Jason gave him an exasperated look. "What else was I supposed to do?"

"Listen to her. That's it, at first. Just listen."

"Listening doesn't fix a damn thing. Besides, *she* didn't listen to me," Jason complained, "so I don't see any reason—"

"Ah. You wanted to be heard, did you? Huh. Imagine that."

At Mr. Moosby's smug expression, Jason broke off.

He frowned. Grumbled. "I see what you did there."

They *both* had to listen. That was the whole point. Leave it to his longtime friend and sometime co-creator to make him see the obvious, when he'd been too stubborn to see it himself.

Fortunately, Mr. Moosby wasn't the type to gloat. "Look, son. The missus and I have been married a long time. We've worked out a few things. One of them is, don't screw around with leaving up the toilet seat, because a wife *will* end you."

"I shouldn't even have brought this up. I don't know—"

"And another one," his mentor continued doggedly, "is that the more you're meant for each other, the likelier it is your sore spots are going to rub up against each other. It's like a law of nature or something. You've gotta learn to work with that—to stick with it when things get hard."

"Sounds kinky." Jason swilled his beer. Signaled for more.

"Show some damn respect," Mr. Moosby barked. "It's not kinky, it's the truth, and I'm not just shooting the shit over here. So sit up straight, clean out your ears, and take notes!"

Grudgingly but respectfully, Jason straightened on his barstool. He couldn't resist striking a blasé expression, poking a finger in his ear, and waggling it, smart-ass style, though.

"I'm about to impart some wisdom on you," Mr. Moosby went on, "starting with this: whenever you think you're absolutely right, that's when you're probably the most wrong.

Whenever you refuse flat-out to give an inch, that's when you ought to dole out a mile. And whenever you want to bail out more than anything else in the whole world," he finished, "*that's* when you stay."

That sounded like a bunch of old-man platitudes to him, Jason told himself. Things that were far easier said than done.

"Is that what you do with Mrs. Moosby? You give in?"

"Giving in doesn't mean giving up, wiseass. Smarten up."

"Do you?" Jason persisted, ignoring that cheery jab.

"You mean if I'm having one of those screw-you, set-fire-to-the-world, just-leave-me-the-hell-alone kinds of days?"

Jason nodded. That summed up *his* mood today, for sure.

"Yep. I do," his mentor confirmed with a nod. "It's not easy. It's *definitely* not easy. But it's worth it."

Jason gave a doubtful snort. "Like hell you do."

"Like hell I *do*!" Mr. Moosby eyed him like the wise old Santa clone he was. "What else am I gonna do? Start over?"

His tsk-tsk made that answer plain. Jason drank more.

"After all these years with Bessie, I'll be damned if I'll break in a new model," Mr. Moosby informed him with a grin. "She understands me. She accepts me. And I accept her."

"Yeah. It's tough to get to that point when someone won't even listen to you." Jason pulled out his wallet, intending to put an end to this sentimental, much too personal conversation. He and Mr. Moosby had already put together a plan for dealing with Chip and the board of directors. They didn't need to keep talking anymore. Not today. "Danielle won't even let me explain what happened and why. You know how much I hate that."

"Oh, waaah. Stop acting like such a crybaby."

Shocked, Jason stared at him. Evidently, touchy-feely time was over with. Even more grumpily, he tossed down a big tip.

"What makes *you* so special," Mr. Moosby persevered,

"that the world is supposed to stop everything and listen to you?"

"I have a right to explain myself! To be heard."

Mr. Moosby shrugged. "She had a right not to listen."

"Whose side are you on, anyway?"

"Your side." Mr. Moosby gave him a fond look. "That doesn't mean I don't think you're being a shortsighted horse's ass right now. I do." Ignoring the money Jason had put down, Mr. Moosby signaled Genevieve for more beers. His clear-eyed gaze swerved back to Jason. "Has it ever occurred to you that maybe what happened to you wasn't personal? Would that make a difference?"

"Of course it was personal. We were the only ones there."

"That doesn't mean it was about you. Maybe it was about her. Maybe she just couldn't listen right then. Maybe you won't ever know why, either." Mr. Moosby picked up his second beer. He could nurse them like the unlikely championship penny-pincher he'd always been. "That doesn't mean she never will."

"She never will," Jason said morosely. He didn't dare hope.

"She never will if you never try again. Shirker."

"What did you just call me?"

"You heard me." Blithely, Mr. Moosby adjusted his earmuffs. Then he added, "Do you know why our partnership worked?"

"Because you're so damn nurturing? Like today?"

Mr. Moosby ignored his sarcasm. "Nope."

More seriously, Jason guessed, "Because you needed me for my toy-making. And my ability to schmooze. And my incredible—"

"Hold on, Big Head." Mr. Moosby held up his hand. "Geez, have you've been hanging around with a bunch of suck-ups, or what?" Incredulously, he shook his head. "I needed you for those things, sure," he agreed heartily. "But

I also needed you because you had something I didn't. Something that kept me from expanding my toy store for all those years before your petty thievery made me think about taking on a new broom jockey."

Jason harrumphed. "Broom jockey. That's what that asshole should call that unauthorized biography of me."

At his mention of that, Mr. Moosby . . . *smirked*? What the . . . ?

"Hmm. Okay, we'll get to that in a minute," he promised enigmatically. Then, "What you had—and I didn't—was the ability to roll the dice. To take chances. To wipe out big, if it came to that." Mr. Moosby pantomimed what Jason could only assume was an epic surfing wipeout. "Back then, you had nothing to lose. But I did. While everyone else was protecting what they already had, you were just grabbing for more with both hands."

Jason frowned. "Hey, something beats nothing any day."

"*Exactly*." Mr. Moosby looked pleased. "It sure does. And against all common sense, you made me a believer back then." He spread his sweater-covered arms. "Look at us now."

Oh hell. Belatedly, Jason recognized the moral to this story. "If you think Danielle will forgive me because she's impressed by my insane naïveté, it's long gone now. For good."

"Is it?" Mr. Moosby pushed. "Because as far as I can tell, you're still a damn rookie when it comes to being in love."

He was right. Ridiculously and embarrassingly . . . he was right.

Jason bit back a swearword. "This is making me feel worse."

"It's making my hemorrhoids act up. These bar stools . . . ugh."

"Sorry." Stifling a grin at Mr. Moosby's aggrieved tone, Jason made a move to get up. "There's no point going on about this anymore anyway. It's over. She told me to leave town."

Mr. Moosby snorted. "You could already have driven to Grand Rapids and hopped a plane back home by now, and we both know it. You could have hired a private jet, called in a helicopter, or hired a car to take you. You didn't do that, though, did you?"

No. He hadn't been able to bear the thought of quitting.

Especially of quitting on Danielle.

But Jason was finished baring his soul. And Mr. Moosby was going to need medical intervention if they kept on gabbing. So he—firmly—changed the subject. "That biography—do you know something about that?" he asked. "I shut it down once, but—"

"Yeah, you did, you punk. I had to do some pretty fast talking to get the deal in the works again." Mr. Moosby grinned, then took a mouse-sized sip of beer. "Can't even let me enjoy my damn retirement, can you? You just had to get a hand in."

"Huh?" Totally confused, Jason stared at him. "I what?"

His mentor sighed. "That 'unauthorized biography,'" Mr. Moosby informed him while making air quotes like one of his grandkids, "is about *me*, you moron." He rolled his eyes. "When my publisher leaked to the press that it was about Moosby's 'infamous' cofounder, everyone assumed it was about you."

"It *was* about me." Jason shook his head. "Wasn't it?"

He'd been threatened with the specter of that book so often by the board that it seemed inconceivable it wasn't about him.

"The hell it was! It's about me!" Mr. Moosby pounded his chest. "Me! Do you think nothing interesting ever happened to me, just because I'm old? I have stories that'll set your hair on fire! I happen to be a pretty good writer, too."

Flabbergasted, Jason stared at him. "But it's an *unauthorized* biography," he reminded Mr. Moosby. "That means it's not approved by the subject. Or written *by* the subject, for that matter. So if *you're* the subject . . ."

"I'm a savvy marketer, that's what I am." Mr. Moosby nodded at another passing hotel staffer. Had he met *everyone*? "It's common knowledge that unauthorized biographies sell better."

"So you pretended that's what yours was. Unauthorized. You old dog." Jason laughed, shaking his head. "That move alone makes me wonder if you're right about those hair-raising stories of yours."

"I am right. I wasn't born white-haired and doddering, you know. I had a life before you came along, and I'll have a life after you're gone, too." Mr. Moosby gave Jason a straight look. "I had to do something. Retirement was making me nuts. Bessie was worried. She's the one who got me a laptop to write on."

Jason frowned. "I'm sorry you had to leave Moosby's."

Mr. Moosby waved off his concern. "I'm not. I don't mind being rich, that's for sure! That's because of you. I knew the deal going in—trade off some control for a big payday. I know the stores have my name on them, but they're not *me*. They're just a part of me. A big part. But not the whole enchilada."

Suddenly, Jason couldn't help wondering what Mr. Moosby's "whole enchilada" would entail. He'd thought he knew his mentor inside and out. It turned out he didn't. Not entirely.

"They're not *you*, either," Mr. Moosby informed him.

"Not anymore, they're not. I quit, remember?"

"Yeah. About that . . ." Mr. Moosby's gaze sharpened. "You don't seem too broken up about not going back to Moosby's corporate."

"If I could," Jason admitted, "I'd work in one of the local toy stores someplace. I'd forgotten how much I liked it—talking with people, demoing toys for kids . . . getting ideas for new toys."

Mr. Moosby patted his duffel bag. "*These* are winners."

Jason slumped his shoulders. "Nobody'll ever know that. Not now. Anyway, they weren't supposed to be winners. Just gifts."

Gifts for Karlie, Aiden, and Zach, to be precise.

"You know," Jason mused as he lifted his beer bottle again, "I'd actually begun thinking I could make a difference in this town. There's a factory that's closing here. Lots of workers got laid off." He gave a rueful headshake. "I'd actually started thinking *I* could buy that factory. *I* could hire those workers."

"If you did, Chip and the board would shit a brick."

At that typically blunt remark, Jason grinned.

"If they thought you were buying a *factory*?" Mr. Moosby pressed. "A factory for our mysterious new venture?"

Their combined gazes fell on his duffel bag.

"Nah." Jason shook his head. "You're the production guy."

"And you're the creative guy. This could work."

"I don't care about work anymore. What we talked about before, getting even with the board of directors, it's—"

"Petty? Small-minded?" Mr. Moosby chortled. "Mean?"

"—just talk," Jason acknowledged. He took another swig of beer. "I'm mad, yeah. But I don't want to be that guy. That guy who can't move on. That guy who lives on revenge." He gazed across the bar, considering it. "If I do that, they win."

"From what you've told me," Mr. Moosby mused, "that guy would definitely never get a smarty-pants hottie like Danielle."

And that was the crux of it, Jason realized. Wasn't it?

He wasn't trying to get Danielle to listen to him. Or let him explain. Or do any of the rest of the bullshit he'd been telling himself all this time. What he wanted her to do—what he wanted everyone to do, but especially her—was respect him.

Appreciate him. Admire him. Assure him that, despite his tough beginnings and his willingness to bend the rules, he wasn't the same scrawny, defiant, vulnerable kid he'd once been.

Wasn't that what he'd been afraid of, all along? That he didn't deserve his success? That he might lose it at any second?

Now he had lost part of it. And he was still standing.

In fact, losing Danielle had hurt him far more.

"Or would he?" Mr. Moosby went on. "I mean, you said Chip has proof of Danielle's inventory manipulation. You thought it was damaging enough to make you quit to keep it from being exposed. So . . ." His mentor raised his eyebrows. "Maybe you're making this woman out to be a lot nicer than she really is."

"She's *nice*," Jason insisted heatedly, "and more."

"All right, all right." Mr. Moosby held up his hands—and offered a brash grin, too. "Don't get your Jockeys in a bunch."

But his friend did have a point, Jason realized reluctantly. He was the one who'd thought Danielle was judging him. He was the one who'd bristled at her suggestions that he kowtow to the board, apologize to the public, and make nice with his critics.

Maybe, Jason thought in retrospect, Danielle hadn't been judging him. Maybe she'd simply been applying the only principles she had: her own. *She* would have worked harder to satisfy Chip and the board. *She* would have said she was sorry, as many times as necessary. *She* would have defused every criticism by working harder, faster, better, and longer.

She was the one, he realized too late, who'd thought her promotion was hanging on Jason taking all those same steps. She was the one who'd wanted, so desperately, to give her kids what she thought would be a better life in L.A.

Knowing Danielle as he did now, Jason couldn't fault her for that.

She would have done anything for Aiden, Karlie, and Zach.

Even pretend all the B&Bs were full to keep her famous CEO boss nearby while she schmoozed him . . . right into falling for her.

That part, he figured, had probably been an accident. And once Danielle had realized things were turning real between them . . . well, she could have explained what she'd done. But she hadn't. Just as *he* hadn't explained about *#sleighride*.

"If Danielle is so nice," Mr. Moosby said, "you probably shouldn't be wasting time getting drunk with an old man."

"You're not so old."

"And you're not so smart, if you can't figure out by now that you shouldn't be sitting on your ass right now."

Jason took offense at that. "What am I supposed to do?"

Mr. Moosby gave him a long look. "Trust her," he said.

Trust her. That was it?

That *was* it, he realized an instant later. He'd trusted Danielle *not* to have committed the inventory fraud Chip had accused her of—at least not without good reason. Would it really be so impossible for him to trust that she might stick by him?

Even if she *hadn't* done that the first chance she'd had?

"If you want Danielle to give you the benefit of the doubt," Mr. Moosby said as he studied his beer, "you're going to have to do the same for her. You might even have to go first."

Everything in Jason rebelled at that. "That's not fair."

"You want fair? Or you want love?"

Jason looked away. Crabbily, he grumbled.

"You want another chance? Or you want regrets?"

Even less articulately, Jason grumbled some more.

"You want to man up?" Mr. Moosby persisted. "Or you want—"

"*I want her*," Jason said, as clearly and as loudly as he could. Maybe that would shut up his mentor. "Okay? I want her."

"Then go get her, champ. I know you can do it."

Mr. Moosby's warmhearted look assured him it was true.

Jason had always believed in Mr. Moosby. He did in that moment, too. A weird sense of relief engulfed him. "You know," he said gruffly, "you were supposed to mail those prototypes."

But Mr. Moosby could read him. As always. "You're welcome."

"You were supposed to enjoy your golden years."

"Watching you fall ass over teakettle in love with a small-town mom is pretty damn entertaining." Mr. Moosby saluted him with his beer. "I knew this would happen eventually."

"You knew I'd fall in love with a small-town mom?"

"I'm not going to admit otherwise, if that's what you're suggesting." Mr. Moosby drew himself up, exuding his usual air of joie de vivre. "How many kids are there?"

"Three. Two boys and a girl. Six, eight, and ten."

Mr. Moosby chortled again. "Ha! Are *you* ever in for it."

But, all at once, Jason felt ready for that.

If he had Danielle by his side, he felt ready for anything.

"I'll know where to go to get good advice," he said.

A headshake. "To Bessie, that's where," Mr. Moosby guessed.

"To you," Jason assured him. "You can count on it."

For a moment, they were both silent amid the bar's twinkling Christmas lights and low-playing holiday music. Then . . .

"You know," Mr. Moosby mused, ignoring the sentimentality in Jason's assurance, "you can't 'go get her' when you've been drinking this heavily. You might do something stupid."

"I've already done something stupid." *I walked away.*

"Something stupider."

"That would be a stretch."

"All the same," Mr. Moosby advised, "you'd better sober up first. A plan of action wouldn't go awry, either, hotshot."

"I'm already on it," Jason assured Mr. Moosby—who, as usual, was undeniably right about everything.

Then Jason set aside his beer, got busy making a plan that would make up for all he'd done, and then got busy making sure that Danielle—the woman of his dreams and the keeper of his heart—couldn't possibly resist him when he implemented it.

Chapter Twenty-One

The day after her breakup with Jason, Danielle called in sick at work. Most of her employees boggled at her absence—because she'd never taken a sick day for herself, only to take care of her children—but Gigi and Henry understood.

"Take all the time you need, g-friend," Gigi said.

"We'll handle everything here," Henry promised.

Chip Larsen, on the other hand, was notably *less* understanding about not being able to reach Danielle. He had called six times and left an equal number of (probably irate) voice mails. Danielle hadn't listened to a single one.

"Whatcha doing, Mommy?" Aiden wandered into the living room where she'd been curled up on the sofa beneath a knitted throw with a notepad and pen in hand. "It's kinda late to write a letter to Santa. I don't think he's going to get it in time."

If he had gotten it, Danielle knew, her letter would have included only one item: *please give me Jason for Christmas.*

Okay, and maybe one more: *and a new job. Thanks a million.*

But Christmas was only days away. Miracles took longer than that, she knew. Even if Santa was in charge of them.

"I'm writing a letter of resignation." She'd decided not to accept the executive position Chip had offered. She wanted to be able to look at herself in the mirror every day. Doing whatever devious, "ambitious" things Chip would ask her to do would make that impossible. "I decided not to take that job in L.A. I told you about."

"Oh. Okay." Blithely, her son nodded. She glanced up as he held out his hands to her. "Will you help me with my mittens?"

At a glance, Danielle deciphered the problem. As usual, Aiden had gotten his mittens—which were on strings to avoid losing them—mushed up inside his coat sleeves. Smiling, she gestured for him to come closer. She wiggled out one mitten.

"It's pretty nice out." Danielle double-checked his snow pants and boots. She gave his knit hat a yank to position it more securely on his head, then flipped up his hood and tied it in place, too. "Are you and Zach going outside to play?"

"Not Zach. Just me." Her little boy held out his arms, letting her pull down his coat, too. Aiden held still while she arranged his scarf, muffler-style, over his nose and mouth.

"All right. There you go." Danielle glanced at the clock. It was early afternoon. There were a few hours of daylight left. "Stay in the yard, okay? I'll check on you in a bit."

"Okay! Later, Mommy!" Aiden put out his arms, starting zooming, then sped to the front door like an airplane.

An instant later, the door slammed. He was outside.

Shivering at the blast of frigid air her son's departure had let inside, Danielle snuggled more deeply beneath her throw.

If Jason had been there, she couldn't help thinking, she would have been as warm as toast. She would have been laughing. She would have been flirting. She would have been apologizing, too. She was sorry they'd ended things the way they had.

But when she'd returned home yesterday, there'd been no sign of Jason—no sign he'd ever been there, in fact. He'd cleared out his belongings so thoroughly it was as if she'd dreamed him. Except, Danielle imagined, she could still catch a whiff of him, now and then, on the knitted throw she'd chosen.

Remembering that, she resisted an urge to inhale. Deeply.

She could have tried to track down Jason. She could have swallowed her pride and asked around town. Because someone would have seen Jason leave. Someone would have given him directions, sold him a ticket, or noticed him driving away.

But Danielle hadn't done that. She hadn't been able to.

She was still embarrassed. Still heartsick. Still stuck.

She wanted to step off the sidelines and skate. But without any assurances of success—without a plan or to-do list or rule book—Danielle wasn't sure how to begin. Her life wasn't a movie. She couldn't race dramatically to the airport to stop her beloved from leaving town. For one thing, the TSA wouldn't have let her inside the terminal gates without a valid ticket—which she couldn't afford. For another, she had children to care for. She couldn't just pick up and start making sweeping romantic gestures with three elementary-school-age youngsters in tow.

For another thing . . .

"I'm going outside, Mom." Zach stopped at the foot of the sofa, near the glittering family Christmas tree. He was outfitted in his puffer coat, hat, and snowboarding goggles. They were, at the moment, perched on his head atop his hat.

"Keep an eye on your brother while you're out there," Danielle told him automatically as he put on his goggles. "If his lips start turning blue, bring him inside, okay?"

Aiden was notoriously reluctant to quit taking part in any activity he enjoyed. Once he started, he wanted to continue. In the summer, he swam until he was wrinkled and sunburnt. In the fall, he rode his bike until his legs wouldn't pump the pedals anymore. In the spring, he splashed in puddles until soaking wet and shivering. He had every ounce of impulsivity she lacked.

"I will." Zach glanced outside. "Don't you want to come?"

"Aw, that's nice of you to invite me, sweetie, but I've got a little more to do here." She glanced up from her resignation letter. "I'm not taking that job in L.A. after all."

"Cool. That means I win ten bucks from Karlie."

With that, her son sauntered to the door and went outside.

Left alone beside the twinkling Christmas tree lights, Danielle gazed at her letter, not really seeing it. She'd genuinely thought this Christmas would be different. She'd thought it would involve Jason. But he'd gone. He wasn't coming back. Right now, he was probably drinking mai tais on the beach while enjoying the warm sunshine in Antigua with his family.

"Bah humbug," she groused. "*That's* not Christmas."

Christmas in Kismet was where it was at. Even now.

Somebody ought to tell Jason that.

Somebody like *her*.

Galvanized by the thought, she sat up straighter.

Yes. She could do it! That was a perfectly rational excuse—er, *reason*—to see Jason again. As a lifetime Kismet resident, Danielle told herself, she owed it to her community not to let an outsider leave with a bad impression. She'd be a bad townie to do anything else! In fact, she should start immediately.

Feeling enlivened for the first time in two days, Danielle got up. She put down her resignation letter, then paced across her living room. From outside came boyish whoops of delight and occasional shouts of "Over here!" or "Like this!" but she knew that was typically rambunctious behavior from her little boys.

From the corner of her eye, as she passed her living room's picture window, Danielle glimpsed one of her neighbors standing across the street. She'd been walking her beagle and had stopped on the sidewalk, probably to admire the strings of holiday lights that Jason had helped Danielle hang on the eaves.

They were certainly nice lights. As proof of that, another of her neighbors slowed his own walk, then stopped to view them, too. A passing car even putted along, its driver gawking.

It was too bad she didn't live in the Glenrosen neighborhood, Danielle told herself. She probably could have won the holiday lights competition—if she'd had Jason's help.

"You're quitting your job?" Karlie blurted from behind her.

Startled, Danielle turned to face her daughter. Like Aiden and Zach, Karlie was equipped with cold-weather gear. Her snow boots dwarfed her skinny legs; her scarf trailed the floor.

As she buttoned her coat, her troubled gaze lifted to Danielle's. "Does this mean we're going to L.A. after all?"

"No," Danielle assured her. "It means I'm going to start looking for a new job. A better job. Right here in Kismet."

"Great. I owe Zach ten bucks now." But although Karlie's tone was typically sarcastic, her expression was undeniably relieved. She hurried over and hugged Danielle. "Thanks, Mom."

With her daughter engulfed in her arms, Danielle blinked back a sudden onslaught of tears herself. "I didn't know you were that dedicated to being a townie. You should have told me."

"You're a townie! You should have known already."

Karlie pulled away. She gave a sentimental sniff.

They both smiled at one another. Danielle felt awash in relief. Because of her own shortsightedness, she'd almost done something that would have been disastrous for all of them.

What did she know about sunshine and surfing, anyway?

Her plans to move away had been well intentioned, but her family was better off in Kismet. She'd find a way, somehow, to give her kids enriching experiences. Maybe they'd travel more.

Karlie hooked her mittened thumb toward the door. "I'm going outside for a while," she said. "Do you want to come too?"

"Thanks, sweetie. But I've got a few things to do in here."

Like call Jason. After all, she couldn't just hop a jet to the Caribbean. Although she wasn't sure what time it was in Antigua, she did know she didn't have any more time to waste.

On the verge of dialing his number, Danielle hesitated.

"What's so fascinating outside today, anyway?" she asked.

Ordinarily, it occurred to her, all three of her children didn't volunteer to head outside in the snow. Simultaneously.

"Oh, nothing." Karlie waved. "See you later!"

With a nod, Danielle dialed. There was a moment of silence as the connection was made, during which she considered . . .

Had her daughter just *crinkled her nose* at her?

That was Karlie's surefire tell. She was up to something. There was no doubt about it.

Frowning, Danielle strode to the armchair where she'd left her jacket. She picked it up, intending to follow Karlie outside.

"Just a minute, Karlie!" she called, hastily pulling on her boots, hunching her shoulder to hold her cell phone to her ear.

Her phone slipped. Ringing now from her living room floor, it lit up with Jason's photo.

The sound of a "Jingle Bells" ringtone came from outside.

Confused, Danielle listened. It happened again.

Her kids didn't have cell phones. Not yet. And Karlie . . .

. . . had almost made it to the source of that jolly sound.

Jason.

He stood, Danielle saw as she opened her front door, in the middle of her snowy yard, surrounded by various-size balls of snow and the curvy, indented snow tracks made by forming them. He was wearing a heavy-duty parka, along with a dapper scarf and knit hat, and he was frowning intently at the cell phone he'd just taken from his pocket. It was playing "Jingle Bells."

Dazedly, Danielle stared at her ringing cell phone.

Then she stared at Jason. He was here. *He'd come back.*

As she watched in befuddlement, Karlie marched over to Jason. She sized him up. She examined what he'd done to their yard. She shook her head. Then she flung her arms around him.

Their hug lasted a good fifteen seconds. Karlie appeared to be squeezing for all her might. Jason appeared to be astounded.

If there'd ever been a good reason for ignoring a phone call, that was it, Danielle thought with burgeoning hopefulness. Because it was obvious that Karlie had finally decided to invite Jason into their family. Now all he had to do was accept.

"So, how good are you at building snowmen?" Jason asked Karlie as their hug ended, his voice drifting on the wintry air. "Because right now, we have a ton of different sized snowballs, but no real plan to put them all together. We need help."

"Don't worry." Karlie figuratively rolled up her sleeves. "I've got this." Then she tossed him a vivid, openhearted smile.

Danielle nearly wept right there. Maybe, she dared to hope, everything would be okay. Because if Jason was there, and she was there, and he was . . . putting away his phone? How *dare* he?

"Hey!" Danielle shouted, waggling her phone. "It's *me*!"

Jason angled his head at her in confusion, and she realized the idiocy of her response. He didn't have to pick up the phone. Not when she was standing in her doorway thirty feet from him.

As she watched Jason intently, waiting for one of them to make a move, Danielle felt her heart start to race. What if he hadn't come back for her? What if he'd just missed the kids?

What if he'd simply wanted to build a few snowmen?

Uncertain but hopeful, she lingered in her doorway with her jacket half on and her heart in her eyes. She *so* wanted him.

An instant later, Jason smiled at her.

His heart, she realized, was in his eyes, too. Danielle knew it because she could feel the connectedness still stretching between them, fragile but unbroken.

He'd come back. For her. Just for her.

Well, for Karlie, Aiden, and Zach, too, but still . . .

Before Danielle even knew what she was doing, she was striding across the snowy yard, heading straight toward him.

"You called me," Jason said as Danielle reached him.

He couldn't believe how beautiful she looked, how sweet and hopeful and full of everything he'd ever needed. Even with her fuzzy orange jacket half on and half off, with her scarf crooked around her neck and her hat on inside out, she looked . . . *perfect.*

"That means I don't get to go first," he said.

He could tell she was confused by that. But he didn't have time to explain about Mr. Moosby's philosophy of someone having to go first when it came to giving each other the benefit of the doubt. Just then, all Jason had time for was her.

As Karlie busily took charge of her new snowman project, bossily directing her brothers in rolling and assembling their new snowy friends, Jason stepped closer to Danielle.

He marveled at her, shaking his head. He couldn't believe he'd let himself lose her, even for a little while.

If it took everything he had, he would win her back.

"You came back." Danielle shook her head too, appearing to marvel at him, as well. "I thought you were gone forever."

"Gone forever?" His throat closed up. Gruffly, Jason swallowed the less-than-macho tears threatening to ambush him. "No way. Why would I leave? Especially forever?"

Danielle laughed, but she sounded choked up, too.

"Because that's what makes sense," she said. "You

know—temp guy falls for townie girl. They have a whirlwind romance. Things fall apart. Guy leaves to go home. End of story."

"Not our story." Jason stepped even nearer. From across the street, the neighbors who'd stopped to watch his snowman progress—and the progress of his other project—lingered still. "Our story can go on from here, if we want it to."

"I want it to!" Danielle searched his face as though hoping he did, too. "I'm *sorry* I didn't let you explain. I'm sorry I didn't handle things better. I'm sorry I ended things the way I did! I was shocked and confused, and Chip had just finished congratulating me for being a horrible person—"

"His mistake." Jason tightened his jaw. "He'll regret it."

"—and I was afraid that was true, at least a little bit, and afraid that the whole town was going to feel sorry for me all over again, because I let someone make a fool of me again—"

"I'm sorry. I *never* meant to hurt you." Jason felt desperate to make her feel better. But he knew he couldn't. Not yet. He tried to content himself with reaching for her hand.

It almost worked. Especially when she squeezed him back.

"—and I didn't know if I'd survive it if we broke up," Danielle continued in a shaky but determined voice. Her gaze swerved to meet his. "But you know what? I did. I'm okay."

Oh. Maybe he'd been the only one, Jason realized too late, who'd been devastated by their split. Was she . . . *consoling* him?

No, he remembered. She wanted things to go on with them.

She'd said so about twelve seconds ago.

In the silence that fell while Jason contemplated all that, Karlie's voice burst out from across the yard, sure and steady.

"Make those snowballs bigger!" she directed her brothers. She paused long enough to cast a fond, delighted look at Jason. "We're going to need a whole boatload of carrots. And lots and *lots* of buttons. Maybe some charcoal briquettes for eyes?"

As Zach and Aiden diligently went on working, Karlie nodded.

"Well?" Danielle prompted, giving Jason a nudge to his parka-covered chest. "Aren't you going to say anything?"

Solemnly, Jason said, "I'm listening to you first."

"Oh." Her eyes sparkled at him. "Well . . . I'm done."

"Are you sure?" Maybe this was a trick.

"This isn't a trick. I'm sure."

Thrilled and startled by their synchronicity, Jason smiled. He gestured to the front of the yard. "Did you see my project?"

Danielle squinted. "No. Are those . . . *letters* in my yard?"

"They're wires. Bent into letter shapes. Wrapped in Christmas lights. Staked into the ground," Jason explained.

He was, after all, famously creative and innovative.

Also, he'd had to do *something* while sobering up.

Danielle puzzled over them. "They're backward."

"They're facing the street. Because *that* message is for your neighbors, friends, and everyone in town you're worried about having made a fool of yourself in front of." He breathed in, hoping she liked it. "It's to tell them you *didn't*."

Squinting harder, Danielle turned her head. She studied the lights, which were just beginning to come into prominence, now that the wintry sun was falling lower in the sky. "E. L. L . . ."

Patiently, Jason waited. He really should have escorted her across the street with the amused onlookers. Mr. Moosby had been right about all of this. Jason *was* a rookie at true love.

Gradually, she deciphered . . . "Jason. Loves. Danielle."

"Now everyone knows it," he announced. "*Everyone*."

She turned her shocked face to his. *"Jason loves Danielle?"*

If she felt *that* surprised, Jason realized with dawning concern, then he hadn't done his job properly. Not yet.

"I do, you know," he said. "I love you so much that I think someone is going to have to come up with a new word for the way I feel about you. Because it's that big. That awe-inspiring."

"Awe-inspiring?" She looked impressed. "Really?"

"Really." Nodding, Jason put his hands to her cold-pinkened cheeks, then turned her face to his. He gazed into her eyes, wishing he could lose himself in them forever. "I love you more than sunshine. More than warmth. More than beer and fast cars and whoopie pies. When I met you, I knew my life had changed. In a single instant, you looked at me and you made me feel—"

"Annoyed? Bossed around? Overcharged for gas?"

"—*whole*," Jason told her. "Because with you, I feel like more than myself. I feel like more than I've ever been. I think something, and you say it. I want something, and you give it."

"Unless it's time to explain," Danielle said, "then I'm—"

Before she could apologize again, Jason stopped her.

Intently, he said, "I'm sorry. I'm sorry I hurt you. I'm sorry I didn't listen to you. I'm sorry I gave you a reason to doubt me! I swear, I never meant to do that." Somberly, he went on gazing into her eyes, even as the crowd of neighborly onlookers slowly grew in the distance. "You have to know—because you know *me*—that I would *never* hurt you on purpose."

Valiantly, Danielle sniffled. She nodded. "I do know that. I was just so scared! I guess I wasn't thinking straight."

"I wasn't, either," Jason admitted roughly. "Not when I saw how hurt you were—not when I knew that *I'd* done that to you!" He stroked his thumb over her cheek, savoring the warmth of her beside him. He wanted it to go on and on. Preferably forever. "I want to make it up to you, if you'll let me," he swore. "I want to show you that I can do better. I want to devote all my time to making you happy."

"*All* your time?" Danielle gave him a teary-eyed grin, then a wink. "That could lead to some pretty . . . *complete* happiness."

Her saucy look gave him renewed hope. If she wanted him for sex, she could want him for more, right? But just to make sure . . .

"I don't mean just *that* way." Mindful of the kids still building snowmen nearby, Jason shook his head. "I mean in *every* way. When you wake up in the morning, I want you to smile, just because you're happy. When you go to work, I want you to do it with a grin on your face, just because you're happy."

"That last one is . . . going to be tricky," Danielle began.

But Jason was on a roll. He didn't want to stop to deal with practicalities and details. He knew they could sort out those. "When you drink eggnog, when you wrap presents, when you breathe . . . I want you to be happy. If you're not, I'll fix it."

No, wait. Fixing it was bad, Jason remembered. Uh-oh.

"Unless you only want me to listen!" he assured her, feeling himself growing giddy with the joy of being near her again. "Then I'll do that, and I'll be *awesome* at it. I promise. Whatever you want, Danielle, I want to give it to you. Whatever you need, I want to bring it to you. What's mine is yours. I'll share it all. Everything I have and everything to come."

"Do you happen to have a puppy butler?" Danielle inquired. "Because if such a thing exists, we're going to need one."

Quizzically, he frowned. "A . . . puppy butler?"

"You know, someone fancy who helps take care of puppies. If they have housebreaking experience, that would be a big plus."

"But you don't have any puppies."

Danielle breathed in. "A lot has changed since you left."

"I never left!" Jason reminded her. "Not really." Then, "Anyway, I'm back now. So if you want a puppy butler, it's yours. If you want half a dozen puppy butlers, they're yours."

"One is probably sufficient," Danielle said with a teasing grin. "I hope one can multitask. There are five puppies—"

"*Five* puppies?"

"—at the vet right now, being spayed and neutered," Danielle confirmed, "but once they come home, it will be perfect. Because there are five of them, and five of us!"

Jason counted, not sure if she meant what he hoped. "There are five if you count *me*," he said, heart pounding.

Danielle smiled. "Of course I'm counting you! I'm counting *on* you." She brought her hands to his chest. "I'm counting on your big heart and your massive intellect and your supersize—"

"Careful now. There are children nearby."

"—generosity and your extra-large sense of fun." She shook her head, giving him another lovably mischievous look. "You didn't think I only wanted you for one thing, did you?"

If she meant sex . . . "No. But it's pretty fantastic."

Danielle agreed. "I didn't want to give my heart to anyone," she said in a more somber tone. "I didn't want to try again. I thought I wasn't ready. But then you came along, and you smiled at me, and you respected me, and you made me laugh."

"Sometimes even on purpose," Jason cracked with a grin.

"And before I even knew what was happening . . . that was it. I was falling for you," Danielle said. "I mean, how could I resist? You had everything I needed—even when I didn't know I needed it." She inhaled, gazing wonderingly into his eyes. "I didn't know I needed a shoulder to lean on, but I did. I didn't know I needed a defender against the big meanies of the world, but I did. I didn't know I needed a partner to help me take on work, and this town, and even Christmastime, but I did."

"You were doing perfectly well on your own," Jason reminded her, still awestruck by her proficiency. "And you know it."

"I know. I was. But it's all *better* with you." Danielle straightened his scarf, then looped her hands companionably in its luxurious, warming folds. "You get something out of this arrangement too, you know," she went on. "Because any—"

"Is it a discount on gas money? Because I could really use that."

"—man who's brave enough to take me on deserves some major spoils for persevering," Danielle promised him. "It's not been easy up till now, and it probably won't be *too* much easier later, given how crazy things sometimes get around here."

"It'll be a little easier." Teasingly, Jason held his fingers a few inches apart. "With both of us together."

Danielle nodded. "But in return," she said, "you get a family. A home. A puppy and a partner and a Christmas stocking with your name on it. You get hugs and hellos, bedtime stories and snowball fights." Here, Danielle glanced at her happy, snowman-building brood. "You get *me*, loving you, as much as you can possibly stand. And then some. Because I'm afraid now that I've started, I can't ever stop loving you. No matter what."

"I'd have to be nuts to want you to."

"Because you're a good man, Jason," Danielle told him. "You're generous, strong, and kind. You're smart, creative, and full of more handsomeness and sex appeal than ought to be legal. And I'm so glad you chose me—"

"We chose each other. End of story."

"—because that means you can see the same thing I do."

Danielle swept her gaze to his. Held it. "We belong together. No matter what comes, I promise I'll stick by you. I'll trust you."

Humbled and overwhelmed by her admiration and devotion, Jason nodded. He'd *needed* those things from her, he realized, more than he'd known. Manfully, he cleared his throat.

"Will you trust me to fill your yard with snowmen?"

"Absolutely." Curiously, she looked around at the messy works in progress. "The kids saw you doing this out the window earlier, didn't they?"

Jason nodded. "It may have helped that I rolled the same enormous snowball"—he pointed to it—"past the window about six hundred times. I thought *you* would look eventually, but you didn't. Then all three kids saw me, but only Aiden came out."

"Then Zach," Danielle remembered. "Not long afterward."

"And finally Karlie." Jason aimed a warmhearted look at her. "She was a tough one," he agreed, "but she's pretty great."

"No no no!" Karlie yelled on cue. "The snowmen will tip over if you do it like that," she informed her brothers. "Do it like—" She broke off with a frustrated sound. "Here. Let *me*."

Together, Jason and Danielle smiled. "Pretty great."

"I didn't even have to bribe her with gifts," Jason said.

Danielle widened her eyes. "You brought gifts?"

"What kind of Kismet Christmastime newcomer would I be if I didn't bring gifts?" He nodded at his rented SUV. Inside it was Mr. Moosby's duffel bag of prototypes. "Speaking of which . . . is there some way to gain honorary townie status? Because I'm interested in making this place my home base from now on, and—"

"But what about Moosby's?" Danielle interrupted, looking aghast. "What about selling toys?" She aimed a perceptive look at him. "You love working with customers. You know it's true."

"It is. That's why I've worked out a way to do even more of that in the future." Jason put his arm around her, then turned them both to face the snowmen. Cheerfully, he waved at the neighbors. "I'll tell you all about it over dinner. My treat."

"If you think we're having anything except a frivolous dinner composed entirely of pies-in-a-jar from Kristen Miller's diner . . ." Danielle grinned. "Well, you'd better think again, pal. Because our reunion calls for a big-time celebration!"

"I couldn't agree more." Jason peered at the snowmen. There were now two largish three-tiered lumps close by them. Also, three smaller two-tiered lumps next to those, all wearing hats. Followed by . . . "Are they making five little snowmen puppies?"

He and Danielle looked at Zach, Aiden, and Karlie, each of them now crawling around in the snow, rolling snowballs of various sizes, then arranging them in a crooked row.

"Looks like one big, happy family to me," Danielle said.

"Those are *definitely* snowmen puppies. Five of them." Examining their growing size, Jason pursed his lips. He turned to Danielle. "Exactly how big are those puppies you got?"

"You know . . . puppy size." Her eyes sparkled at him. "I'm not sure how big Labrador puppies grow up to be. Do you know?"

"You brought home *five* of them without researching first?"

"I was backed into a corner." Danielle waved to her neighbors too. "It seemed like a good idea at the time."

"Hmm. Maybe my freewheeling nature is rubbing off on you," Jason said. "Before you know it, you'll be abandoning to-do lists and clipboards forever."

"Not likely. Somebody has to be in charge of things."

"Somebody has to get a bigger house for those puppies."

Jason glanced behind him at Danielle's modest abode. "I know the kids didn't want to move to L.A., but do you think they'd mind if we built a bigger place here in Kismet? Maybe on the lake?"

Danielle looked at him as though he'd just asked her if grass was green, water was wet, and Christmas was fantastic.

"First, you're not sure if it's okay to buy a round of drinks for a bunch of recently laid-off workers down at The Big Foot," Danielle said. "Now you don't know if the single mother you just started dating would like a custom-built mansion?"

"I never said *mansion*, per se—"

"It was implied, moneybags." She grinned. "You don't fool me."

"—and the dating will only last until you agree to marry me."

Openmouthed, Danielle stared at him. *"Marry you?"*

Jason laughed. Dutifully, he tried to look abashed.

"Whoops. That was supposed to be your Christmas surprise."

"Let's," Danielle said, "have Christmas right now."

"Nope." Smiling, Jason drew her into his arms. Feeling full of love, contentment, and more Christmastime good cheer than anyone honestly had a right to, he kissed her. "I'm afraid you're just going to have to wait for that big diamond ring."

"Big diamond ring?"

This time, he doubted he looked abashed at all.

"Uh-oh. I guess the cat's really out of the bag now."

Danielle gave him a playful swat. "I can't *believe* you're going to make me wait for such momentous presents."

"I waited for you," Jason reminded her. "You were worth it."

"You were, too." Danielle smiled at him. "You big tease."

Knowing he was guilty as charged, Jason changed the subject. "Anyway, all that waiting time will give you a chance to show me how to build a snowman. The proper way."

She arched her brows. "*You* think there's a proper way?"

"Nah," Jason admitted, "but I bet *you* do."

Danielle laughed. "You know what? You *are* perfect for me."

Then she took his hand, led him to the first of the snowmen, and got down to the important business . . . of loving him.

Chapter Twenty-Two

Growing up in Kismet, Danielle had experienced a lot of varied Christmastime traditions. She'd caroled and spritzed, wassailed and mistletoed. She'd constructed gingerbread houses, made homemade ornaments, and pinned the tail on Rudolph. She'd strung lights. She'd gone sleigh-riding and tree-shopping, gift-buying and charity-giving. She'd even left out oats and carrots for the mythical reindeer along with milk and cookies for Santa.

But in all her years as a verifiable Kismet townie Christmas expert, Danielle had never had a holiday like the one she did the year she met—and fell for—the man of her dreams.

Even if he *did*, she'd learned, have an irksome habit of doling out Christmas gifts laboriously one at a time . . . when her family had always enjoyed a frenzied free-for-all opening spree.

"Come *on*," Danielle grumped on Christmas morning beneath the sparkling tree, with her children and Jason surrounding her and a cup of much-needed coffee at her elbow. "At this rate, opening presents is going to take us all day!"

"That's the idea." On the sofa beside her, Jason kissed her. He cradled, very protectively, one particular gift on his lap. "I've never had a Christmas like this one before. I want to make it last. I want to savor it. I want to—"

"Is it my turn yet?" Aiden asked. "Can I go?"

At her son's eager expression, Danielle gave in.

She nodded. "Sure, Aiden. Karlie, would you please help your brother find one of his gifts?"

Just as eagerly, Karlie nodded. Along with her brothers, she'd assumed her usual place at the foot of the Christmas tree, near all the booty. She crawled around amid the presents.

"I can *read* my own name!" With a hilariously exasperated look, Aiden pulled out a wrapped package. He frowned at the tag. "But not who this is from. It doesn't say 'Santa' or 'Mommy.'"

Zach glanced at it. "It says 'Jason.' 'Love, Jason.'"

"Yay!" Aiden tore into it. A few seconds later, he pulled out a huge empty fishbowl, a big packet of fish food, and . . . "A robo fish food feeder!" he shrieked, casting an overjoyed look at Jason. "You really made it! Just like we talked about."

Jason smiled back at him. "It's our collaboration. I'll show you how to use it after breakfast, if you want me to."

But, with a child's lack of inhibition about trying something new, Aiden was already expertly operating the gadget. He looked at the fishbowl, then the piece of cardstock inside it. He pulled it out, then handed it to Karlie to decipher.

"This is a certificate for all the rest of your fish," his sister told him, reading. "Dasher, Dancer, Donner, Cupid . . ." She hesitated, then added brightly, "Nemo and Justin!"

"*All* the reindeer fish!" Aiden confirmed. "Hooray!"

Zach was next. He pulled out a gift. Looked at the tag. "From Jason." Primly, he glanced up. "Thanks very much, Jason."

Then he ripped into the package like an untamed wolf.

"A custom Lego set!" He turned the box. "It's got a motor, like Mindstorms, but without so many pieces." Zach looked up. "This looks *sick*. I'm going to build the whole thing myself."

"If you want help," Jason promised, "I'm right here. I happen to have a few connections in Denmark, so when I called . . ."

He went on to explain the special arrangements he'd made with his friends in Billund, where the Lego Group was headquartered.

But Karlie was already reaching for her gift. With decorum, she peeled off the tape, folded back the giftwrap, then . . .

"*Fashion Makeover EXTREME?*" In polite bafflement, Karlie examined the video game box. "But I've already got this game."

"Not . . . quite." Jason's eyes shined with hopefulness and care. "If you look a little more closely, I think you'll find—"

"*Fashion Executive EXTREME!*" Karlie amended, hastily reading the description. "In this version, the stars are the designers, not the models. In this version, you play as the boss, not the human clothes hangers in bikinis. *And* you earn points by *doing* things, not by standing around looking pretty and being judged on your makeup." She glanced up. "Awesome! It's just what I wanted!" she gushed. "But this game doesn't even exist, so . . ."

"I made it," Jason explained. "I got on your mom's computer at work, remotely accessed some tools I keep on my home system in California, and developed a modified version of the game."

"You can *program*, too?" Danielle asked. So *that's* what he'd been doing in her office all those times he'd slipped away.

"Of course I can. It's not all race cars made of napkins and paperclips," Jason said with a grin. "It's not the nineteenth century. I'm not whittling all the toys with a penknife."

Duly impressed, Danielle congratulated him. "Your skills are even more far-reaching than I'd realized. I guess that bodes well for your new venture with Mr. Moosby."

"*Our* new venture," he reminded her with a loving look.

They'd discussed this already. "The 'Original Moosby's' toy stores we've taken over here in Michigan will be ours to run."

"While Mr. Moosby handles the logistics of production and shipment at the new factory in Kismet," Karlie recited.

Evidently, she'd been eavesdropping on their conversation about Jason selling some of his Moosby's shares in exchange for separation and ownership of the regional Midwest toy stores.

"That's right, brainiac." Jason tugged her long braid. "I'm not sure I made that game challenging enough for you. I might need to take another run at it—do another mod that's tougher."

"Nah. I'll try this one first." With a contented look, Karlie nodded at Danielle. "How about you, Mom? You open one!"

Danielle could hardly wait. She fidgeted, glancing at the beribboned, tellingly petite, jewelry-size box on Jason's lap.

At that moment, though, Jason's phone rang.

He ignored it. But Danielle recognized the ringtone.

"'Darth Vader's Theme'?" she asked. "From *Star Wars*?"

Jason only shrugged, then silenced his phone. "That means it's Chip. I forgot to take him out of my phonebook."

With a quick swipe, Jason did so. Then he put away his phone. But Danielle couldn't let things go so easily. Not after all the havoc Chip Larsen had tried to wreak on both of them.

"What do you think he wants?" she asked.

Jason offered an indifferent look. "Probably to get in on the ground floor of an exciting new investment opportunity."

"New investment?"

"The business world has been all abuzz with news of a rumored new collaboration between two star toy entrepreneurs."

Karlie perked up. "You mean you and Mr. Moosby?"

All the kids—and Danielle—had met that kindly, energetic man before he'd left Kismet to spend the holidays with his wife, Bessie. They'd all liked one another immediately. Having Alfred Moosby around had been like having another grandfather there.

"This one's a keeper, rookie," Mr. Moosby had told Jason, giving Danielle a spontaneous hug. "You be sure to treat her right, you hear?"

Naturally, Jason had agreed. Now, he nodded at Karlie.

"Yes, like me and Mr. Moosby. Before we'd even officially agreed to work together again, rumors of our 'new' partnership wound up on Twitter and some other social media sites. I think Chip probably wants to get in on the ground floor," Jason went on, "but this is one venture that won't have public investors. This time, Mr. Moosby and I are going to retain control."

Danielle nodded. "Poor Chip," she said, pretending to be sorry. "Just because he can't be involved doesn't mean he won't hear about how successful it is. All the time, probably." In a wry tone, she added, "You know how it is with social media—once something is out there, you can't just take it back."

The kids nodded sagely. They were more informed about social media these days, now that Danielle had shared Moosby's photos and online videos with her kids shortly after Jason had returned. She'd carefully explained the situation to them so they wouldn't be too worried or freaked out. But Zach, Karlie, and Aiden had been thrilled with their fifteen minutes of fame.

"My teacher gave me a better table at lunch," Zach said.

"My friends wanted my autograph," Karlie confided.

"My friends aren't on the Internet," Aiden told her with a shrug, "so they don't care. But I like the pictures."

Danielle's friends, it turned out, had all believed that Danielle had accepted the online media hullabaloo with Jason as an inevitable part of dating a world-famous superstar CEO . . . and that she just hadn't wanted to brag about her part in it.

"I had no idea people thought I was so modest," Danielle had said to Jason. "Secretly, I'm the world's biggest egomaniac."

"Everyone is," he'd replied with a grin. "On the inside."

In the end, all the chaos had died down pretty quickly. Now that it was over, Danielle found she didn't think about it too much. She'd forgiven Jason for his accidental part in it—but not for his deliberate withholding of that gift he'd hinted about.

"So it's your turn now, right, Danielle?" Wearing a purposely innocent look, Jason peered at the pile of gifts under the Christmas tree. "I think there's a big one over there."

"I want the one on your lap," she specified. "Gimme."

"Mom!" her children chorused in unison. "That's rude!"

Darn it. Why had she taught them manners in the first place? Sighing as she glanced at Jason's rugged, handsome, amused face, Danielle tried again with a more conciliatory tone.

"Gimme *please*." She wiggled her fingers. "Okay?"

Jason lifted his gift to her. And his eyebrows. "Oh. You mean *this* gift? This one right here? But that one is bigger."

"Jason!"

His answering grin made her melt. "All right," he acquiesced. "But this one has to be delivered in a special way."

"By Santa! By Santa!" Aiden guessed at a shriek.

"Not by Santa. By me." Wordlessly, Jason slid off the sofa. He knelt in front of Danielle. He took a deep breath. Then, with the Christmas lights dancing off his face and the carols playing in the background, he took her hand. He opened her palm. He placed his gift in her grasp, then nodded. "If you take this," he said, "I'll be the happiest man you've ever met."

At his motion, all the puppies awakened. They started scampering around his feet and legs, alerted to the presence of one of their favorite playmates. Danielle loved that everyone loved Jason so much—kids, puppies . . . and her included, of course.

Reverently, with a proper sense of the importance of this moment, Danielle undid the gift's bow. She took off the paper.

She glimpsed Jason's agonized expression and stopped in the midst of unwrapping her gift. "Is something wrong?"

He gave a frustrated growl. "Are you unwrapping that so slowly *on purpose*?"

Danielle laughed. "You're the one who wanted to savor Christmas, one gift at a time. Remember?"

"Just keep going." He gestured. "Open the box!"

Smiling—and moving excruciatingly slowly—Danielle did.

The diamond engagement ring inside took away her breath.

Heart pounding, she transferred her gaze from its brilliance to the face of the man she loved. Slowly, she nodded.

"I will," Danielle said. "Now, forever, and always."

Jason smiled at her. "I was right," he said. "This *is* worth savoring." He broadened his smile. "Maybe you can do it again?"

"Mooommy!" Aiden wiggled amid the puppies. "Come *on*!"

"Maybe later," Danielle promised Jason with a kiss. "I'll stage a full reenactment for you, as many times as you want me to." She looked at him, then at her children, her heart full. "Right now, we have a real Kismet Christmas to get on with."

"Yeah, about that . . ." Jason tipped his head to the side, plainly reconsidering his stance. "I might have been wrong about the whole take-it-slowly method. Kids, what do you think?"

Zach, Karlie, and Aiden looked at each other.

"Free-for-all!" they yelled jubilantly. "Woo-hoo!"

Happily, Danielle gave her permission. The mêlée that

happened next wasn't dignified or painstaking . . . but it was loving.

So was the unabashed look that Jason gave Danielle as he got up from his kneeling position. He pulled her into his arms.

He kissed her. "Next year, we're inviting the puppy butler. My feet are all slobbered on. My toes have doggie breath."

"I love you anyway," Danielle told him with a grin.

Then she kissed him back with all her heart, put on her ring, and got busy showing Jason exactly how much she loved him—on Christmas, on New Year's Day, and on every day of the year.

All while reveling in how very much he loved her back.

It could not, at any time of year, have gotten any better than that.

Dear Reader,

Thank you for reading *All He Wants for Christmas*!

Christmas is one of my very favorite holidays, and I suspect it's one of yours, too! I'm so happy that you decided to spend some time with me in Kismet this year. My little town is getting pretty crowded these days, but I just couldn't wait to share Karlie, Aiden, Zach, Gigi, Henry, and Mr. Moosby with you—along with Jason and Danielle, of course! I hope you had just as much fun reading about their holiday romance as I did writing about it.

If you did (and you're curious about my other books, including the rest of the Kismet Christmas series!), please visit my website at www.lisaplumley.com. While you're there, you can check out first-chapter excerpts from all my contemporary, historical, and paranormal romances, sign up for my free new-book reminder service, catch sneak previews of my upcoming books, request special reader freebies, and more.

By the time you read this, I'll be hard at work on my next contemporary romance. I hope you'll be on the lookout for it. In the meantime, I love connecting with readers, so I'd be thrilled if you would follow me @LisaPlumley on Twitter, like my page on Facebook at www.facebook.com/lisaplumleybooks, or circle me on Google Plus at www.google.com/+LisaPlumley. See you there!

Best wishes,
Lisa Plumley

P.S. Turn the page for some delicious Kismet whoopie pie recipes!

Jason can't stop eating whoopie pies from the bakery next door to Moosby's toy store in Kismet! His favorite is these gingerbread spice whoopie pies with creamy filling.

This easy recipe makes nine big whoopie pies, so you'll have plenty to share.

Gingerbread Spice Whoopie Pies
with vanilla cream cheese filling

COOKIES

3¾ cups all-purpose flour
1 teaspoon baking soda
1 teaspoon salt
1 teaspoon ground cinnamon
1½ teaspoons ground ginger
½ teaspoon freshly grated nutmeg
¼ teaspoon ground cloves
¾ cup softened butter
¾ cup packed brown sugar
1 large egg
¾ cup molasses
¾ cup buttermilk

Get ready: Preheat oven to 375 degrees. Lightly grease 3 baking sheets or line with parchment paper; set aside.

Prepare dry ingredients: In a medium bowl, whisk together flour, baking soda, salt, and spices; set aside.

Prepare wet ingredients: In a large bowl, cream together butter and brown sugar with an electric mixer until mixture is light and fluffy. Add the egg; beat until incorporated.

Mix: Add half the dry ingredients to large bowl; mix just until combined. Add molasses and buttermilk; mix to combine. Scrape bowl if necessary, then add remaining dry ingredients. Mix just until batter is smooth.

Shape and bake: Use an ice-cream scoop, spoon, or ⅓-cup measuring cup to scoop batter onto prepared baking sheet, making 6 evenly spaced rounds per sheet (for a total of 18). Bake for 15 minutes, until a toothpick inserted in the center of each cookie comes out clean. Remove baking sheet from the oven and place on a rack to cool completely before removing cookies from the baking sheet.

FILLING

8 ounces softened cream cheese or Neufchâtel cheese
3½ cups confectioner's sugar
2 teaspoons vanilla extract
1 to 2 Tablespoons milk (as needed)

Make filling: Place the cream cheese or Neufchâtel cheese and confectioner's sugar in a medium mixing bowl. Mix at low speed until the mixture begins to come together. Scrape the bowl, then add vanilla. Mix again. Add milk, if necessary, then beat until filling is creamy and smooth.

Assemble: When cookies are completely cool, it's time to turn them into whoopie pies! Spread a generous spoonful of filling onto the bottom of one cookie. Top with another cookie, then press together gently to make a whoopie pie. Repeat with remaining cookies and filling. Enjoy!

After a Christmastime trip to the Kismet ice-skating rink, Karlie's favorite treat is a pumpkin chocolate chip whoopie pie. Even non-townies can enjoy these!

This easy recipe makes 8 soft, traditional size whoopie pies.

Pumpkin Chocolate Chip Whoopie Pies
with creamy vanilla filling

COOKIES

1½ cups all-purpose flour
½ teaspoon baking soda
½ teaspoon baking powder
½ teaspoon salt
2 teaspoons pumpkin pie spice
1 (15-ounce) can pure pumpkin (not pie filling)
1 cup packed brown sugar
½ cup vegetable oil
1 large egg
2 teaspoons pure vanilla extract
1 (12-ounce) package mini chocolate chips

Get ready: Preheat oven to 375 degrees. Lightly grease 2 baking sheets or line with parchment paper; set aside.

Prepare dry ingredients: In a medium bowl, whisk together flour, baking soda, baking powder, salt, and pumpkin pie spice; set aside.

Prepare wet ingredients: In a large bowl, stir together pumpkin, brown sugar, vegetable oil, egg, and vanilla until thoroughly combined.

Mix: Add the dry ingredients to large bowl; mix just until combined. Scrape bowl if necessary, then add mini chocolate chips; mix until batter is smooth.

Shape and bake: Use a small ice-cream scoop, spoon, or ¼-cup measuring cup to scoop batter onto prepared baking sheet, making 8 evenly spaced rounds per sheet (for a total of 16). Bake for 12 minutes, until a toothpick inserted in the center of each cookie comes out clean. Remove baking sheet from the oven and place on a rack to cool completely before removing cookies from the baking sheet.

FILLING

6 ounces softened cream cheese or Neufchâtel cheese
6 Tablespoons (¾ stick) softened butter
2 cups confectioner's sugar
2 teaspoons vanilla extract
1 to 2 Tablespoons milk (as needed)

Make filling: Place the cream cheese or Neufchâtel cheese, softened butter, and confectioner's sugar in a medium mixing bowl. Mix at low speed until the mixture begins to come together. Scrape the bowl, then add vanilla. Mix again. Add milk, if necessary, then beat until filling is creamy and smooth.

Assemble: When cookies are completely cool, it's time to turn them into whoopie pies! Spread a generous spoonful of filling onto the bottom of one cookie. Top with another cookie, then press together gently to make a whoopie pie. Repeat with remaining cookies and filling. Enjoy!

Zach and Aiden love these flavorful cranberry pecan whoopie pies. The secret ingredient is fresh orange zest in the filling, which makes for a zingy, energizing treat!

This easy recipe makes 9 whoopie pies . . . but don't eat them all at once!

Cranberry Pecan Whoopie Pies
with creamy orange filling

COOKIES

3 cups all-purpose flour
1 teaspoon salt
2 teaspoons baking powder
¾ cup butter
1 cup sugar
2 large eggs
1 Tablespoon vanilla extract
⅔ cup milk
½ cup chopped dried cranberries
½ cup finely chopped toasted pecans

Get ready: Preheat oven to 375 degrees. Lightly grease 3 baking sheets or line with parchment paper; set aside.

Prepare dry ingredients: In a medium bowl, whisk together flour, salt, and baking powder; set aside.

Prepare wet ingredients: In a large bowl, cream together butter and sugar with an electric mixer until mixture is light and fluffy. Add the eggs one at a time, beating well and scraping the bowl after each egg. Add the vanilla; mix thoroughly.

Mix: Add the flour mixture and milk alternately, beginning with about 1 cup of the flour and ⅓ cup of the milk. Beat well after each addition. The final batter should be fairly thick and fluffy. Lightly mix in dried cranberries and toasted pecans, stirring just until combined.

Shape and bake: Use an ice-cream scoop, spoon, or ⅓-cup measuring cup to scoop batter onto prepared baking sheet, making 6 evenly spaced rounds per sheet (for a total of 18). Bake for 15 minutes, until a toothpick inserted in the center of each cookie comes out clean. Remove baking sheet from the oven and place on a rack to cool completely before removing cookies from the baking sheet.

FILLING

6 ounces softened cream cheese or Neufchâtel cheese
¼ cup softened butter
2½ cups confectioner's sugar
freshly grated zest of one orange
1 to 2 Tablespoons orange juice (as needed)

Make filling: Place the cream cheese or Neufchâtel cheese, softened butter, and confectioner's sugar in a medium mixing bowl. Mix at low speed until the mixture begins to come together. Scrape the bowl, then add orange zest. Mix again. Add orange juice, if necessary, then beat until filling is creamy and smooth.

Assemble: When cookies are completely cool, it's time to turn them into whoopie pies! Spread a generous spoonful of filling onto the bottom of one cookie. Top with another cookie, then press together gently to make a whoopie pie. Repeat with remaining cookies and filling. Enjoy!

Although Danielle's favorite holiday treat is a delicious Peppermint Chocolate Mousse Pie-in-a-Jar with Candy Cane Sprinkles from Kristen Miller's Galaxy Diner in Kismet, she still has a soft spot for these similarly flavored chocolate-peppermint whoopie pies.

This easy recipe makes 8 classic-size whoopie pies.

Classic Chocolate Whoopie Pies
with marshallow peppermint crunch filling

COOKIES

2 cups all-purpose flour
1¼ teaspoons baking soda
1 teaspoon salt
⅔ cup cocoa powder (preferably Dutch process)
½ cup softened butter
½ cup granulated sugar
½ cup packed brown sugar
1 large egg
1 teaspoon vanilla
1 cup buttermilk

Get ready: Preheat oven to 375 degrees. Lightly grease 2 baking sheets or line with parchment paper; set aside.

Prepare dry ingredients: In a medium bowl, whisk together flour, baking soda, salt, and cocoa powder; set aside.

Prepare wet ingredients: In a large bowl, cream together butter, sugar, and brown sugar with an electric mixer until mixture is light and fluffy. Add the egg; beat until incorporated. Add the vanilla; mix thoroughly.

Mix: Carefully add the flour mixture and buttermilk alternately, beginning with about 1 cup of the flour and ⅓ cup of the buttermilk. Beat well after each addition.

Shape and bake: Use an ice-cream scoop, spoon, or ¼-cup measuring cup to scoop batter onto prepared baking sheet, making 8 evenly spaced rounds per sheet (for a total of 16). Bake for 12 minutes, until a toothpick inserted in the center of each cookie comes out clean. Remove baking sheet from the oven and place on a rack to cool completely before removing cookies from the baking sheet.

FILLING

½ cup softened butter
1¼ cups confectioner's sugar
2 cups marshmallow cream (such as Marshmallow Fluff)
1 teaspoon vanilla
¼ teaspoon peppermint extract (optional)
4 candy canes, crushed (see note, below)

Make filling: Place the softened butter and confectioner's sugar in a medium mixing bowl. Mix at low speed until the mixture begins to come together. Scrape the bowl, then add marshmallow cream, vanilla, and peppermint extract (if using). Mix again. Add crushed candy canes, then beat until filling is creamy and smooth.

Assemble: When cookies are completely cool, it's time to turn them into whoopie pies! Spread a generous spoonful of filling onto the bottom of one cookie. Top with another cookie, then press together gently to make a whoopie pie. Repeat with remaining cookies and filling. Enjoy!

Note: To crush candy canes, place in a large zipper-top bag, then use a rolling pin or bottom of heavy saucepan to crush candy canes into irregular pieces.